FREE
FALL

FREE FALL

KYLE MILLS

HarperCollins*Publishers*

FREE FALL. Copyright © 2000 by Kyle Mills. All rights reserved. Printed in the United States of America. No part of this book may be used or reproduced in any manner whatsoever without written permission except in the case of brief quotations embodied in critical articles and reviews. For information address HarperCollins Publishers Inc., 10 East 53rd Street, New York, NY 10022-5299.

HarperCollins books may be purchased for educational, business, or sales promotional use. For information please write: Special Markets Department, HarperCollins Publishers Inc., 10 East 53rd Street, New York, NY 10022.

This book was printed on acid-free paper.

FIRST EDITION

Designed by Phil Mazzone

Library of Congress Cataloging-in-Publication Data
Mills, Kyle, 1966–
    Free fall / Kyle Mills.—1st ed.
        p. cm.
    0-06-019333-6
    PS3563.I42322 F74 2000
813'.54—dc21   99-43528

00 01 02 03 04 ❖/RRD 10 9 8 7 6 5 4 3 2 1

ACKNOWLEDGMENTS

In no particular order, I'd like to thank Darrell and Elaine Mills for their support on so many fronts. My wife Kim, who didn't have to suffer quite as badly with this book, but whose pain was no doubt still significant.

Armando Menocal, Jeff Scully, and Mike Fischer for their help with those horrible cold weather activities. Special thanks to Sam Lightner for the geography lessons, proofreading, and all the belays.

Pete Groseclose for helping me cover up my embarrassing lack of knowledge where firearms are concerned. Jeannie Barrell for yet another geography lesson.

Mike Kahoe for some unfortunate inspiration.

And finally, my friends in New York: Robert Gottlieb, Matt Bialer, John Silbersack, Caitlin Blasdell, and the rest of the gang at Harper and William Morris.

May your trails be crooked, winding, lonesome, dangerous, leading to the most amazing view. May your mountains rise into and above the clouds.

—*Edward Abbey*

PROLOGUE

"**W**ould you back off?"

The voice was desperate, frustrated. An exaggerated whisper that was a little louder than a conversational tone but hadn't quite reached the resonance of a shout. Fred Clausen pinched his lips between his teeth and was forced to bite down fairly hard to keep from laughing. He took a step to the side and watched the concentration return to his partner's face as the young man tried again to shove the key in the lock.

The dented and only partially attached doorknob didn't seem to be in any danger of giving in, so Clausen leaned his back against the cinderblock wall and took some of the weight off his arthritic knees. The faint light from the large neon sign at the other end of the parking lot flashed white then red, over and over again, giving an alternately angelic and devilish quality to his partner's expression as he continued to complete what should have been the simple task of opening Room Fourteen.

The architecture of the Pagoda Motel took a shot at Oriental but didn't quite make it—unless, of course, they had trailer parks in Peking. Six detached buildings had been carefully lined up on a treeless expanse of asphalt at the edge of the city, separated from the street by nothing more than a barely noticeable seam where the blacktop of the parking lot met the blacktop of the road.

Clausen brought his wrist up close to his nose and had to wait a few seconds for a car to drive by and reflect enough headlight to defeat the gloom. His watch read eleven thirty-two. He should have been into bed listening to the pleasant rhythm of his wife's snoring a half-hour ago.

1

The light from the passing car had also been sufficient for his overly enthusiastic young ward to unlock the door and dive through. He reappeared a moment later, his face a mask of anger and purposefulness.

Clausen reluctantly bounced his back off the wall and shuffled past him into the stale-smelling belly of the room, his feet causing quiet crunching sounds as they found old food and God knew what else hidden in the thick red shag. He headed straight for the TV and flipped it on, then picked up the phone by the bed and used it to jab at a particularly dark and utterly unidentifiable stain on the bedspread. It didn't appear to be tacky, so Clausen dropped onto the bed while his partner jerked the curtains fully shut and put the stout leather bag he'd been carrying on the table under the window.

"What the hell are you doing? Are you ready?"

"Ready for what?" Clausen grunted out, scooting to the bottom of the bed and using his toe to jab at the television's volume button. Soon the housewife on the screen was pitching her dish detergent at a decibel level that vibrated the ashtray on top of the set.

"I don't mean to bother you, *Fred*, but do I have to remind you that we have a job to do? Maybe you could find the strength to pitch in a little."

Clausen let his head loll over and he watched with feigned interest as his new partner cleared the predrilled holes in the wall that separated the room they were in from the one next door. The kid was hopeless. He had the look: close-cropped hair, a body that was thin and ramrod straight, a grave, dignified expression that seemed to hang on at the corners of his eyes even on those rare occasions when he laughed.

And then there was the wardrobe. They were there to take dirty pictures of a guy in a hotel that rented rooms by the hour—a casual dress affair if there ever was one. So what did he do to blend in? He took off his suit jacket and put on a blue windbreaker that looked suspiciously like it had been pressed.

Clausen had tried to teach the kid how to get by in today's FBI. How to swipe police collars and pad arrest numbers, how to suck up to the supervisors and ASACs—everything he'd learned in his pleasantly uneventful twenty-five years in the Bureau. And what did he get for all that effort and goodwill? A cold stare. No future, this one. No future at all.

"Anything worth looking at?" Clausen said, struggling out of the pit in the center of the mattress and trying to ignore the pain in his lower extremities as he knelt down on the floor.

They'd been shadowing this high-society prick for three mind-numbing weeks now. Their orders had been explicit as to the high level of surveillance required, but had been cautiously vague when it came to things like what it was they were after. Now it looked like a light was about to dawn.

Clausen reached for the reel-to-reel tape recorder under the bed and slipped the headphones over his ears, effectively blocking out the sound of the television behind him.

His young partner was completely engrossed in his effort to assemble the tiny box of a camera he'd pulled from his bag, so Clausen crawled over to the section of compromised wall beside the bed's Formica headboard. The reel-to-reel was still recording silence as he pressed his eye up to one of the small holes and took in what seemed to be a mirror image of the room they were in.

Their subject—or perhaps more accurately, victim—had done only a marginally better job of blending into this part of town than Clausen's partner: old, dirty polyester slacks, a black T-shirt with an obnoxious slogan peeling off in large flakes, tennis shoes with one sole flapping. The effort had been wasted, though. Even calculatedly uncombed, it was obvious that his thick brown hair had been expertly trimmed. His fine, pale skin was equally well cared for and the quiet air of superiority that made him look older than his thirty-two years was too perfect to have been learned; it had to have been bred into him.

The black woman he was slowly circling was less interesting. One of the countless street-walking hookers who could be seen gathering in small flocks on almost every corner in this part of town. Clausen concentrated on her for a moment, trying to calculate why their victim had chosen her over all the others.

She seemed pretty much generic. Taller than average maybe, and a bit more stocky. Not really fat, it was just that she didn't have that angular thinness many of her peers carried as badges of their addictions. She was also no spring chicken—probably nearing the end of her useful life in this kind of work. Of course, her clothes were typically impressive, constructed of boldly colored fabric designed to shimmer in dim streetlight and accent the outline of skimpy underwear beneath. Makeup was equally heavy and haphazardly applied. An unnaturally colored wig covered her head.

Clausen pulled away from the wall and flipped the headphone off his left ear. "Is it me or were we taking pictures at that boy's wedding less than two weeks ago? I mean, I know those blue blood chicks probably aren't what you'd call wild in the sack, but damn, I—"

"Could you just *be quiet*?" Another harsh, scolding whisper. Clausen ignored it.

"I'm telling you, son, I know about these things. I see rocky times ahead for this guy's marriage." He affected a sad shake of his head. "I don't know about you, but I think I'm going to wait the full year Emily Post allows before I send a gift."

That was the comment that finally did it. His young partner pulled his face away from the camera in front of him and whipped his head in Clausen's direction. His eyes seemed to have sunk a little in his head, probably due to the extreme tension in his facial muscles. "Are you having a good time, Fred? Are you?"

Clausen smirked.

"We have a job to do!" the young agent continued earnestly. "An important job."

"An important job, huh?" Clausen leaned back into the peephole and watched the hooker next door begin a seductive dance to the music in her head.

"Son," Clausen said, sitting back on the carpet and leaning against the bed. "This is nothing but institutional par-a-noia. I think you could safely say that we're violating that boy's civil rights for no good goddamn reason."

His partner was concentrating on his camerawork again and except for the barely perceptible ripple in the muscles of his jaw, he didn't react to Clausen's analysis.

"You just gonna stand there, or are you going to come over here and get some of this?" The woman's voice barely rose above the interference coming through the headphones. Clausen sighed quietly and rose to the small peephole again. He watched her reach out and saw the young man jerk backward out of range. "Don't touch me!"

The woman didn't seem at all surprised by what Clausen thought was kind of a strange request to make of a paid-for hooker. He watched the young man take another step back and nod toward a corner of the room hidden from the FBI agents' view.

The sound of muffled footsteps was closely followed by a second girl coming into view. She crossed behind the woman standing in the middle of the room and came to a stop between her and the young man, who seemed to have temporarily stopped breathing. Clausen felt a brief burst of adrenaline shock his nerve endings as he carefully examined the new player in their little drama.

She was so tiny. Her thin body was devoid of curves and wouldn't have reached five feet if she'd stood on her tiptoes. Her complexion seemed a little darker than that of the other woman in the room, but it could simply have been her lack of makeup or the frame of dark curls shadowing her face. Her clothes were less professional, too—a simple one-piece blue dress with buttons down the front. One thing was certain, though. This girl was still looking forward to being a teenager.

The older woman took a tentative step toward her client again, and again he moved back. Her expression of confusion melted into a sly smile when the man jerked his head toward the young girl standing silent between them.

"Why don't you come on up here with me, honey," the woman said. Clausen could see the self-consciousness and hesitation in the little girl's face as the woman took her hand and helped her up on the bed. The girl scooted back and laid her head on a dirty pillow, her dress sliding up her legs far enough for Clausen to see what looked like a pair of white-and-orange polka-dot panties. The slightly nauseous feeling in his stomach started to grow when he realized that they weren't polka dots at all. They were fucking cartoon characters.

Jerking away from the peephole, he fell backward onto the grimy carpet. "No way," he mumbled, meeting his equally horrified partner's gaze. "There's just no fucking way." Clausen rose slowly to his feet, slid his .38 from its holster, and started purposefully for the door.

"What the hell are you doing?" his partner said in a loud whisper, then jumped up and blocked the door. Clausen grabbed the lapels of the young man's windbreaker and tried unsuccessfully to shove him out of the way. "What the hell are you doing?" he repeated, eyes trained on Clausen's right hand that, in addition to the nylon lapel of his windbreaker, was holding a loaded pistol.

"What the fuck do you think I'm doing?"

"We aren't authorized to interfere, Fred. You know that. We're just here to record events. Now come on. Let's do our job."

"Our job?" He released one of his partner's lapels and pointed to the wall they had been looking through. "Our job is in that room right now." He tried to push past again, but his young partner shoved him roughly back. "Yeah, Fred, our job is in that room. We are going to gather the evidence that we were ordered to gather. You think I like this? I have a daughter not much younger than that girl. I'd like to go in there and hold that son of a bitch down while you put a bullet in the back of his head. But I can't. There are bigger things at stake here—"

"Pull your head out of your ass! There's *nothing* at stake here."

"It doesn't matter what you think, Fred. It doesn't matter what I think. We have clear orders."

Clausen slowly lifted his gun hand until it was aimed at his partner's chest and looked into his eyes. They were clear and unafraid, glowing with the light of a man young enough to think he could make a difference. A kid who had been stroked into thinking he could save the world.

But Clausen was too old to use that excuse. Old enough to know that this assignment was bullshit. And what was even more bullshit was that he was going to let this go. He could already feel his righteous indignation fading as thoughts of his pension and a retirement full of warm beaches and umbrella drinks crowded into his mind. He let his gun fall to his side and watched his partner return to his camera as though nothing had happened. He stood motionless in the middle of the room for what seemed like a long time. Finally, not sure what else to do, he took a few hesitant steps toward the wall and put his eye back up to the hole, intentionally focused only on the man who was the subject of their assignment. By the look on his face, the show playing out on the bed was the center of his universe. Clausen forced himself to follow the man's gaze and watch as the older woman used her teeth to slide the girl's panties over the sneakers still tied to her feet. The little blue dress was completely unbuttoned now, revealing the uniform brown of the girl's barely pubescent body. Clausen felt the breath catch in his throat as the woman began running her tongue in slow circles up the girl's thin legs. He had to look away when she buried her face between them.

Their subject was standing now and had managed to tear his attention away from the show in front of him long enough to slip on a pair of rubber surgical gloves. Clausen closed his eyes hard and backed away from the wall. When he opened them again, his partner was looking at him with a mix of sympathy, uncertainty, and pain on his face. It was more emotion than he'd thought the little bastard capable of.

"You do what you gotta do," Clausen said, starting for the door again. "But I'm not part of this. You can write it up any way you want to, but I'm not staying here to find out what he does to that little girl with those gloves."

1

Tristan Newberry glanced up at the seemingly endless rows of gray metal shelves surrounding him and immediately spotted the ancient black man as he came around a mountain of file boxes.

"You ready for another one?" the man said as he continued to shuffle, slightly stooped, in Tristan's direction.

"Guess so." Tristan wedged a toe under the box at his feet and lifted it a few inches off the floor. Still a little heavy. The old security guard, as the only other human being inhabiting this forgotten warehouse, insisted on helping lug files around. But at seventy-two, his back wasn't what it once was. Tristan crouched down, pulled out a few of the heavier looking bundles, and laid them on the floor.

"Watcha doin'?" Carl said, continuing to deliberately close the distance between them. Same question every day.

"The bottom of this box looks like it's about to fall through." Same answer every day.

Carl nodded sagely and accepted the white lie with a grateful smile.

Tristan hefted the box with an exaggerated grunt and presented the light end to the old man who got a firm hold of it and began shuffling slowly backward. "Probably ought to cut down here," he said, adjusting his trajectory a bit. "Looks like we got another leak the other way."

Tristan looked up at the tangle of pipes running across the ceiling and tried to spot the particular one that Carl was talking about. The insulation surrounding most of the lines had started to rot years ago and now the condensation was beginning to slowly drip on the mindless government drivel contained on the shelves below. After the first few weeks of being trapped there, Tristan began to notice that the distinctive smell of mold was still clinging to him on his drive home. Now it hung on even after his evening shower.

This wasn't how things were supposed to have worked out.

He'd been a year into his law degree at Georgetown University when the economy had gone into a tailspin. By that time, he'd already sold damn near everything he owned to pay for tuition and was up to his eyeballs in credit card debt and student loans. But who cared? In less than two years, he'd graduate and sign on with some prestigious law firm for a hundred grand a year, right?

Wrong. Last year's law school graduating class probably had more lawyers in it than there were practicing. And they were all going after the same ten jobs. He'd recently run into a friend who had passed the bar six months ago, working in a video store.

So he'd no choice but to drop out and take a shot at landing a job in one of the few growth industries left in America: the government. Or more specifically, declassifying documents through the newly fortified Freedom of Information Act.

He showed up for the open interview and was directed toward a waiting room so full of other potential applicants that some of them had been forced to stake out small areas of industrial green tile and sit on the floor. After a few seconds of milling through the crowd and discovering just how jealously those tiles were being guarded, he'd headed for the door. What chance did he have? He was just a penniless law school dropout from a poor farming family with no connections and no background in government work.

He'd been halfway down the hall, and nearly to freedom, when a young woman in thick, black-framed glasses jogged up behind him and took him by the arm. He could still hear her voice: "Mr. Newberry. I'm sorry. You were directed to the wrong interview."

He'd followed obediently through the maze of hallways, stairs, and elevators, long enough for his normally infallible sense of direction to start to spin, then was deposited in a small, windowless office somewhere deep in the building.

It was there that he had met some bald guy with marginal dental work and heard the rather cryptic legend of the Misplaced Documents. The guy had gone on to tell Tristan how his résumé was most impressive—

which it wasn't—and how he seemed to be imminently qualified to help in the search—which he wasn't. Blah, blah, blah.

At first he hadn't been that interested in the man's story. He just wanted a secure job that would pay enough to keep him living at a reasonable standard until the economy turned around. But the more the guy talked—in circles, mostly—the more captivated he became. Bald Guy—he honestly couldn't remember his name—had told him that the person they were looking to hire would be kind of the Indiana Jones of the National Archive. Now, how could anybody resist a pitch like that?

"On three," Carl said.

Tristan followed Carl's lead and gently swung the box as the old man counted. On three they dropped it on the card table Tristan had been using as a workspace since his first day.

"I'll go grab the stuff you took out," Carl said, already moving off in the direction they'd come from. Tristan nodded absently and peeked into the box. What would it be today? Farm subsidy budgets from the 1940s? An in-depth statistical analysis of the height of wheat versus inches of rainfall? Whatever.

As was so often the case, the reality of the job hadn't quite lived up to the initial hype. The real story was that, a while back, some government moron had deposited a hand-truck full of apparently sensitive FBI documents in the middle of an Agriculture Department storage facility. And now they needed to be found before the warehouse could be emptied into the public domain.

It hadn't seemed like a particularly monumental task until Bald Guy had started slapping down thick stacks of bound paper.

"Revision of the filing system," he'd said. Slap.

"Original warehouse closed down, documents moved." Slap.

"Broken water line, documents moved again." Slap.

"Construction." Slap. It had gone on like that until there was a paper trail nearly eight inches in height teetering on the desk.

Strangely, though, the job was right up Tristan's alley. Since grade school whenever he'd taken those tests where you had to find patterns in streams of numbers or geometric shapes, he'd always scored off the scale. He'd told Bald Guy as much during his interview and gotten a disinterested smile that seemed to say "lucky for us."

Tristan sighed heavily and rubbed his temples as he dropped into the worn canvas chair. Day in and day out, it was the same. Endless hours cross-referencing old government records he could care less about, trying to follow the murky trail of a few pointless FBI needles in the Ag Department's haystack.

When he'd finally pulled his nose out of the endless procession of boxes and files to look around him, though, it had finally struck him how strange his situation was. Why was he here alone, with only an ancient security guard to watch over him? Or more accurately, a security guard and a battery of video cameras. Tristan looked up at the sleek, ultra-compact camera bolted to the dilapidated wall in front of him and wondered again who was watching. Not Carl—as near as Tristan could tell the cameras didn't output anywhere in the building. It had started him wondering. When he'd told Bald Guy about his childhood test scores, had that smile really said "lucky for us"? Or had it said "we know"?

It was little things like that that had kept him interested. He'd always been burdened with an overactive sense of curiosity. Why wasn't anybody checking up on him? He hadn't talked to Bald Guy, or anyone else in a position of authority, since he'd started. Why did some of the file records seem almost intentionally cryptic and obtuse?

It looked like he might be getting closer to finding out. A hell of a lot of detail work and two back-to-back strokes of blind luck had led him to the section of the warehouse from which he was now pulling boxes. Four months, six days, four hours and thirty-three minutes of mind-numbing torture and he was finally starting to get somewhere.

Tristan leaned forward and turned up the small television resting on the edge of the table, but his attention was instantly diverted to his portable computer when it picked up the vibration and the screensaver came on. A million pixels glowed out the picture of a man struggling up a snow-covered mountain surrounded by sky. Tristan reached out longingly and touched the screen, but withdrew his hand when Carl came around the corner and dropped a portion of the remaining files on the table.

"Who you votin' for, Tristan?"

"Huh?"

Carl nodded toward the TV screen where the highlights of last night's presidential debates were being rerun for the hundredth time.

"Oh. I don't vote."

"What do you mean you don't vote? You're a college boy. If anybody should, it ought to be you. You understand it all." Carl pointed at the screen. "I'm starting to like that Hallorin guy. I mean, he always seemed like he had something to say, but he was such a hard-ass. Now, though, he seems . . . I don't know, less . . . "

"Glasses," Tristan said absently as he centered a dusty file in front of him.

"What?"

"It's the glasses. In the last election, when the economy was riding high, everyone wanted to be associated with the government—take credit for the boom. Now, with the Dow at forty-five hundred, it's a whole new ballgame. No one wants to look like a politician. Senator Hallorin, our previously obnoxious third-party candidate, has gone with eyeglasses. And as you pointed out, they have the added benefit of softening his image." Tristan motioned to the screen with the binder-clipped stack of paper in his hand. "Now our clever Democratic candidate has completely bucked the conventional wisdom of facial hair being the political kiss-of-death and gone with the beard for the same reason. Senator Taylor, our flat-footed Republican front-runner, missed the boat again. His only recourse now is to shave his head. But since he's leading by thirteen points, don't hold your breath. Packaging, Carl. It's all about smoke and mirrors."

The old man shifted uncomfortably and shoved his gnarled hands in his pockets. "I really don't think it's what they look like that's important, it's what they say—"

"What they say?" Tristan interrupted, feeling his mood darken as it always did when the subject of politics came up. "They aren't saying anything." He pointed to the television again. "Our Democratic hopeful's gotten used to all the limos and butt-kissing he gets as vice president and doesn't want to be pounding the street looking for a job. So he'll tell you that he's dedicated to supporting the poor and out of work. But then he'll get real vague when it comes time to tell us exactly how he plans to pay for it."

Carl tried to say something, but Tristan cut him off.

"Then there's ol' Bob Taylor. He'll try to blame the sad condition of the country and the world economy on the current Democratic administration, and try to make you forget that the Republicans have controlled Congress through all this and that he's been a major power in that party since the dawn of time. Notice how, when he talks about his history of leadership, he never mentions Congress? No, he always talks about the past—his days as head of the CIA, the Cold War, the Carter years.

"And last, but not least—except in poll numbers—we have your newly bespectacled Independent candidate, David Hallorin. He'll try to convince the public that the country's current condition is the result of years of mismanagement by both established parties, which is essentially true. What he'll leave out, though, is that the parties have pretty much just followed the public's mandate to not rock the boat—boat rockers don't get elected. And while he's dancing around the fact that the American people got exactly what and who they asked for, he'll offer up all kinds of ridiculously oversimplified solutions to America's complex problems, that, even if they would work, he'd never be able to get passed. If he wins—and he won't even come close—the established parties will combine forces to ensure that he never gets anything done so they'll never again have to worry about a third-party candidate becoming a serious threat."

Carl began to shuffle off toward his miniscule office near the front door of the warehouse, his shoulders a little more stooped than usual. "Wait! You haven't told me who *you're* voting for Carl," Tristan called after him.

"Guess it'd be stupid for me to even bother," the old man said as he disappeared around one of the myriad box-stuffed shelves.

Tristan leaned out around the table and tried to catch a last glimpse of the old man. "Don't be that way, Carl." He leaned out a little further, but still couldn't see around the shelf. "Come on, man. Don't take me so seriously. I'll buy you a beer after work and tell you why I'm full of shit."

There was no answer, but Tristan knew that by five o'clock the old man would have forgotten everything but the beer offer.

He quietly admonished himself as he started through the pile of papers in front of him. Not everyone wanted or needed to hear his brilliantly cynical analysis of the American political system. He didn't even know if *he* wanted to hear it anymore. Time to just deal with the fact that his carefully laid plan of being a millionaire at thirty-six was as dead as any dream could be. A bunch of useless politicians had seen to that.

Tristan started into the stack of paper in front of him, flipping quickly from page to page, taking in the gist of each document or binder of documents. When he was satisfied they were of no interest, he placed them in a neat pile to the right of his chair.

Within a few hours, it was starting to look more and more like another dead end. This box was no different from any of the others. Luck or no luck, he knew it would take only a minor error on his part or on the part of the documents he was relying on to completely throw him off.

Tristan swung a fist at the box in frustration, knocking it to the floor. He was about to start refilling it when he noticed a creased piece of paper caught under one of the flaps at the bottom.

He gave it a cursory glance and then dropped a stack of documents on top of it before his mind had a chance to fully process what he'd seen. A moment later, he was on the floor overturning the box and sweeping the loose files out of his way. Snatching up the single sheet of paper still trapped in the flap, he stared at the letterhead. The mundane Department of Agriculture seal he'd seen fifty thousand times in the last four months, six days, seven hours and twenty-two minutes had been replaced by the seal of the Federal Bureau of Investigation.

Tristan realized that the silent camera above was recording the fact that he was kneeling on the floor with his mouth hanging open. As the initial shock of actually finding something started to wear off, he was left a little deflated. He stood as casually as he could, tossed the memo back into the open box, and started randomly reshuffling the stuff on his desk as he tried to think through his situation.

If it was a false alarm, a lone piece of misfiled paper, it didn't mean much. But what if it wasn't? What if he was right and he was closing in on the documents he'd been hired to find? This was the government—he wasn't being paid for results, just for showing up. There would be no bonus for a job well done, no big promotion. What if he'd just worked himself out of a job?

Tristan hefted the box and started struggling back toward the shelves where he'd found it. He concentrated on staying relaxed, knowing that there was a camera at the other end of the path cut through the metal storage units and that it was monitoring his progress. He turned right into the row of shelves where he'd found the box in his hands and slid it back into the empty space it had left. He stretched his back in an exaggerated motion, using the opportunity to scan the walls and shelves around him and confirm that he was no longer in a camera's line of sight.

When he had completely satisfied himself that he wasn't being watched, he began quietly pulling down the boxes that surrounded the one he'd just replaced. He dumped the first three out on the floor and began pawing through the contents as quickly and efficiently as he could. Five minutes of less than methodical rummaging produced a few more loose FBI documents where they shouldn't have been, but nothing anyone would care about. Maybe the strange circumstance of his hiring and job description was nothing more than typical government inefficiency.

He glanced at his watch and guessed that he had about another five minutes before his disappearance from the camera-covered areas of the building started to look unusually long. He refilled the boxes at his feet and put them back where he'd found them, then pulled down three more, dumping their contents onto the floor.

Six was the magic number.

Down near the bottom, beneath a six-inch thick document on foreign lettuce production, he found a brown accordion folder tied together with a nylon strap and sealed with a large sticker depicting a faded FBI seal. The label at the top right carried a single word: PRODIGY.

He placed the folder on the floor behind him and repeated his search pattern, dumping another three boxes on the floor. Ten minutes beyond the five he'd given himself, it seemed clear that this sealed folder was unique. Had the rest of the Misplaced Documents been broken up and disbursed over the years? Did they even exist?

He knew what he was supposed to do now. Call the number on the card he'd been given—Baldy's number, he guessed—and hand it all over. It had been made quite clear to him that when he found the probable location of the documents, he was to do nothing but get on the phone.

Tristan pressed his back against the shelf behind him and slid to the floor. He dragged the folder onto his lap and felt his heart begin to pick up its pace as he fondled the nylon strap.

The right thing to do was to make that call and hand all this stuff over to the powers that be. But what would happen then? There had been no promises made. While this wasn't a great job, it paid pretty well and he was more or less his own boss.

Tristan began thumping his fingers rhythmically on the file in his lap. What if he just forgot to mention that he found the stuff? He could come in every day and go through the motions for the cameras. Long lunches, good paycheck, no pressure. Then, when the economy started to show signs of recovery, he'd take the money he'd socked away straight down to the Georgetown front office and jump-start his education.

But what about the file in his lap? He looked down at it. If he was right and the story he'd been fed was a load of crap, then the government was looking for something specific. There might be something in it worth reading. Hell, it was his duty to read it, right? What if it contained a cure for cancer or something?

He ran his index finger over the seal affixed to it, aware that he'd been hidden away in this corner of the warehouse for far too long now.

The months of speculation and suspicion quickly overcame his nervousness, though, and he worked the knot out of the nylon string holding the file together. Why he didn't cut it he wasn't sure, since he was going to have to tear through the seal anyway. It just seemed wrong.

He held his breath for a moment, making a final, irreversible decision, and gave the flap on the folder a tug. The seal ripped halfway. Its tenacious grip on the brown cardboard made him even more uneasy. He suddenly wasn't sure that he wanted to do this. He wanted to stand, to put it back, but his curiosity wouldn't let him.

He gave it one last tug and dug out the individual folders inside. The first contained various FBI documents, all in customarily small type and dense language. He gave up on the first paragraph of the first memo when the edge of a photo slipped from between the pages.

The quality was poor and had a strange fishbowl quality. He'd never seen a surveillance photo, but he imagined this was what one looked like. It must have been taken through a two-way mirror or a hole in the wall. The picture depicted a group of well-dressed young men and women, none probably older than thirty. The mens' jackets were off and the top buttons of their shirts were undone. They were all sitting in a circle on the floor of a well-appointed office, surrounded by beer bottles and passing around a flat tray that looked empty. Tristan pulled the rest of the photos from the folder and found that the shots became more interesting. The tray was actually a mirror and the people were snorting something through it with a rolled-up piece of paper, or more likely dollar bill—the picture was too grainy to see clearly. The composition of the photographs was definitely centered on the young man on the right, with numerous 8x10 glossies of him with the mirror in his face and the alleged dollar bill partway up his nose. Tristan couldn't place him, but he did look vaguely familiar. No doubt the accompanying documents would clear up any confusion.

Not quite ready to wade through a hundred pages of FBI droning to ferret out a pertinent piece of information, he moved on to the next folder and found pictures of a similar indiscretion by a similarly clean-cut young man.

He continued to flip quickly through each folder, finding a stack of photos in each. Some—mostly drug related—were obvious crimes. Some just looked like chance meetings between two people, though one was always a young, relatively clean-cut male. Those would probably benefit even more from the accompanying narrative.

Tristan opened the last file, this time finding that the photos were not loose in the folder, but had been sealed in a manila envelope. He hesitated for a moment, but then reminded himself that it was already too late to turn back and tore into it.

His breath caught as he slid the first picture from the envelope. It was an extremely graphic depiction of two naked black women lying on a bed in the throes of passion. Or at least the throes of lesbian sex. As he moved his face closer to the photo, he could read the expression on one of the women's faces—it was more intimidation and confusion than passion. He could also see that she wasn't a woman at all. She was just a little girl.

Tristan flipped through a few more of the pictures, finally stopping to examine one focused on a naked young man at the edge of the bed. He was sitting in a folding chair, eyes locked on the show playing out in front of him. Judging from the condition of his penis, he was enjoying himself immensely.

Tristan dropped the photos onto the floor and pulled another handful from the envelope. There were probably fifty or so in all, ten times the number in any of the other folders. The ones he'd originally pulled seemed to be from the middle of the stack. They were more or less in chronological order, starting with everyone clothed, then to the woman doing things to the little girl, and finally to the young man's enthusiastic participation.

Tristan stopped on a close-up of the young man's face. Despite the sexual release etched across it, the features looked familiar—in the same vague way three or four of the others had.

He shoved the pictures back in the envelope and flipped to the stack surveillance records riveted to the inside of the folder. A few more minutes. He'd milk a few more minutes away from the camera.

2

One of the Inquisitors glanced in his direction for the first time since they'd filed in, forcing Mark Beamon to make a half-hearted effort to sit up straight in his chair. The attention was short lived, though, and before he could completely correct his slouch, the woman had turned away and was, once again, deeply engrossed in whispering with her co-conspirators. In theory, Beamon was to be the star of this show, the reason they had gathered there, but right now he felt more like an ornament. And the longer he was ignored, the more he could feel it in the pit of his stomach.

Beamon turned to look behind him at the empty benches lined up between him and the distant double doors he'd entered through. There were no cameras and spectators were nonexistent. Other than himself and the five members of Congress towering over him at their enormous desk/podium, the room contained only a few young aides who seemed to have perfected the art of melting into whatever wall they stood against.

If it weren't so goddamn dangerous, the whole thing would have been funny. Nothing he said here today was going to make any difference. His future, or lack thereof, was preordained. This was all just an elaborate play, staged solely for the benefit of its actors.

Beamon reached for a pewter pitcher at the edge of the table but found that it was as empty as the glass tumblers surrounding it. He looked up at Congresswoman Candice Gregory, the chairperson of the panel, and confirmed that she and her cohorts were still debating amongst themselves. Probably as to what version of the truth would be most politically convenient to the group as a whole.

Satisfied that his services were not yet necessary, he attempted to clear his mind and relax. The setting of this hearing had obviously been carefully devised to make him sweat. He wasn't going to let it work.

"Mr. Beamon . . . *Mr. Beamon!*"

Beamon snapped back into the present and smiled politely. "I'm sorry, ma'am. Are you ready for me?"

"If it wouldn't be too much trouble," she said coldly.

Beamon kept the calculatedly idiotic smile painted across his face as a number of unspoken and pointedly unflattering responses went through his mind, knowing that things were only going to get uglier. Lately, the political arena had become a very small lifeboat on a very rough sea. And worse, the men and women desperately clawing for a dry spot in that lifeboat saw him as the guy swimming around the hull with a drill.

"Please state your name and occupation for the record."

"Mark Beamon. I'm the Special Agent in Charge of the FBI's Flagstaff office."

He'd have guessed it impossible, but the expression of the man to Congresswoman Gregory's right became even more smug as he leaned into his microphone. "It is my understanding that you have been suspended from the FBI, sir."

He was from one of those redneck states, though Beamon honestly couldn't remember which. One of those assholes whose ridiculous good ol' boy drawl got thicker every time he came up for election.

"Call me a professional hearing attendee, then," Beamon said, and then instantly regretted it.

There was a quiet tittering from the previously silent young people pressed against the walls of the room. All except two, who looked on gravely. It wasn't hard to guess who they worked for.

Congresswoman Gregory chose to ignore Beamon's jibe, as it wasn't directed at her, and moved on. She began flipping loudly through a thick bound document in front of her, effectively cutting off her colleague before he could protest Beamon's "lack of respect for these proceedings" or "flippant attitude toward their important task" or whatever stock political phrase the situation called for.

"Mr. Beamon, I know we've all carefully read your report on this matter, but I think we'd appreciate a brief overview in your own words."

Beamon couldn't help frowning slightly—the report *was* in his own words. He'd spent months writing it. "I was investigating the Church of the Evolution—"

The Southern congressman leaned into his microphone again, provoking mildly annoyed expressions from his colleagues. "To clarify, sir. You had been directly ordered, on a number of occasions, not to pursue this investigation. Isn't that right?"

Beamon sighed a little too loud. His microphone picked it up and bounced it off the walls. "I was investigating the death of two people and the subsequent disappearance of a young girl. A decision was made by FBI management, based on the significant financial resources and political clout of the church, that the investigation would be . . . problematic. Unfortunately, since the church actually *had* the girl and intended to kill her, I felt compelled to focus on them as suspects."

As seemed to be the custom of the political elite, the man seemed completely oblivious to the fact that Beamon had been proven right in the end and, judging by his body language, felt he'd won the exchange. ". . . and that, in part, resulted in your suspension."

Beamon let his mind go blank for a moment and stopped his growing anger before it could screw him. What could he say? "Uh, yes. It was certainly one of the factors."

"Please continue," Congresswoman Gregory cut in.

"During the investigation it came to my attention that the church had set up an extensive and highly sophisticated phone-tapping system. They'd incorporated a small long-distance carrier called Vericomm that connected calls through the Internet. In essence, all calls had to go through the church's mainframes before being dispersed to available bandwidth over the Net. They used that as an opportunity to record and listen to calls. Long-distance rates on this carrier were very cheap—five cents a minute all the time. They simply offered the service to anyone they were interested in."

"And when you became aware of this system, did you notify your superiors at the FBI?"

"No. At that time, you could say that me and the Bureau weren't speaking."

"So you took action unilaterally."

Beamon eyed the empty pitcher nervously, coughed, and then nodded. "Yes. I was able to get into the database where their more interesting tapes were stored and download a number of the recorded conversations. Many, as you know, involved political figures. When I completed my investigation and found the girl who had gone missing, I turned those tapes over to the FBI."

She looked at him suspiciously. "And I suppose you are now going to tell me that you have no idea how those tapes were leaked to the press."

"If you ask me, yes I will."

The group stared down at him and he just stared back. Finally, one of the men Beamon hadn't yet heard from spoke up. "I think we're asking, Mr. Beamon."

"As your colleague pointed out, I'm on suspension," Beamon started again, satisfied with his minor triumph. "I was on suspension prior to turning over those tapes and I am still on suspension. I would have no way of knowing what happened after the FBI took possession of the wiretaps."

"Illegal wiretaps," Congresswoman Gregory interjected.

Beamon leaned back in his chair in silence. There it was. The direction all this nonsense was headed.

The tapes he'd delivered, and that had subsequently been leaked by parties unknown to him, consisted of activities by the political elite so heinous that they wouldn't have been overlooked even at the peak of America's prosperity and the voter apathy that an economy flush with cash could buy. Now, though, with unemployment hovering in the low- to mid-teens, the public was out for blood. And it seemed that the men and women in front of him were going to do everything they could to see that it was Beamon, and not they, who bled.

If they could convince the American people that Beamon himself was morally bankrupt—if they could make him out to be a rogue agent, using the power the government had entrusted to him to look through public keyholes—that might be enough to divert the public's attention. Powerful politicians today, they would say to the American people, but tomorrow it might be you.

"The taps were illegal," Beamon said, leaning forward again. "But certainly not perpetrated by me or the FBI."

Congresswoman Gregory nodded and let silence once again fall over the large room. She was obviously trying to get him to say more, but years of dealing with the press had clued him in to that little trick.

Finally, she reached out and pulled a few loose sheets of paper from a folder in front of her. "These are memos and performance reviews relating to you." Her tone had changed to that of a disappointed mother. "They span a number of years." She perched a pair of reading glasses dramatically on her nose. "Allow me to quote from them. 'Disregard for chain of command.'" She flipped a page. "'Possible illegal activity.'"

Another page. "'Excessive drinking.'" She held up a form of some kind. "This is a physical you failed bringing into question your ability to do your job."

Beamon once again wasn't sure how to respond. Frankly, his admittedly questionable ability to run two miles without having a heart attack and his unfortunate history with alcohol seemed to have very little to do with the tapes he had uncovered.

He was working out a way to say that in as respectful a way as possible when the young congressman on the far left cleared his throat. Beamon had never met him, but recognized him as a member of David Hallorin's Reconstruction Party. "I'd like to say something, if I may," the man said to a uniform rolling of eyes on the panel. "I've read the same documents you have and they made me uncomfortable. I asked myself why it was that Mr. Beamon had been called in to consult on so many high-profile cases if he's the disaster he looks like on paper." He shot Beamon a conspiratorial glance and continued. "I personally know a number of FBI officials and last night I called them. I gave them the following scenario: Your child has been kidnapped and the kidnappers are threatening to kill her. Who in the FBI do you call? I talked to eight men and one woman. Seven of the nine named Mr. Beamon here. I think that's pretty remarkable. What's even more remarkable is that six of those seven had an obvious and violent dislike for Mr. Beamon." He leaned back and pointed to the rest of the panel with his pencil as he continued. "Interesting? Yes. Important? Not in the least. The tapes exist and, unfortunately, they're public. The question isn't how they were obtained, it's how the men and women we heard on those tapes managed to attain the positions of responsibility they did."

"There are no cameras in here, Jacob," the Southern congressman sneered into his microphone. "I think you can take the day off from campaigning."

It seemed that the Reconstruction Party wasn't interested in seeing this witch-hunt carried through, though Beamon doubted it was because of their deep respect for his life's work as much as the fact that none of their ranks had been implicated in the Vericomm scandal. But in this business you had to take your friends where you found them.

He watched the shouting match that ensued with morbid fascination, too absorbed to notice the young woman who had quietly padded up behind him until her mouth was only inches from his ear.

"Mr. Beamon. David Hallorin would like a few moments of your time after the hearing."

Beamon jerked his head around and looked at her with an expression that in retrospect must have been somewhere between that of a startled deer and a condemned man. She was polite enough to ignore it. "If you'll just see me when you're finished here, sir, I'll have a car brought around for you."

The argument on the podium started to die down as the young woman walked silently to the back of the auditorium and faded into a wall. Congresswoman Gregory was somewhat red faced, but managed to regain her composure and center the thick folder in front of her again. "Mr. Beamon I'd like to go through your report with you. If you could turn to page two-seventeen of your copy, I have some serious concerns about your timeline."

3

Tristan Newberry held the front door to his apartment building open with his foot and grabbed the plastic grocery bag that contained his work clothes off the sidewalk. They smelled like nervous perspiration, as did the sweatshirt and cotton pants he was now wearing. It seemed like the tickle of sweat running down his sides hadn't stopped since he'd left work the day before.

He stepped into the empty foyer and looked up the stairs in front of him. Another bulb had burned out while he was gone, throwing deep shadows across the relatively clean but not so well-maintained stairwell. He'd hoped that getting home would calm him down, but it seemed like his arrival was having the opposite effect. He suddenly wanted to be back on that plane, with thousands of tons of steel and thousands of feet of air protecting him.

Tristan glanced at his watch. Eight P.M. Mrs. Dunn would have just gone to bed and he just didn't think he could handle one of her screaming fits about noise right now. He pulled his shoes off and stuffed them in the bag with his clothes, then started up the stairs in his stocking feet. With a little luck, he'd avoid a confrontation and soon be suffering from his newfound insomnia in his very own bed.

He was almost to the top of the flight of stairs when he heard a quiet rustling in the hall to the right. He stopped short and, remembering that his approach had been nearly silent, remained motionless and listened with an almost athletic intensity. A few moments later he heard something sliding on the floor. He didn't know if it was the effect of his nerves and an overstimulated imagination or if it was real, but whatever it was, he would swear it sounded like it was coming from right in front of the door to his apartment.

His mouth went suddenly dry and he could hear his heartbeat in his ears. They'd found out. Somehow they'd found out. He looked down the semidark stairs behind him, wanting to run, but knowing it would be pointless. They'd know he was there. They would have been watching.

It had only been twenty-eight hours since he'd discovered the file, but he'd replayed tearing that seal in his head at least a hundred times. He wanted to take it back—to have shoved it, unopened, back into that box and walked away under the watchful eye of those silent cameras. But it was too late for that now.

What was he going to do? He looked back down the stairwell for a moment, then faced forward again. What could he do? Holding the bag of dress clothes in front of him like some kind of pathetic shield, he sucked in a deep breath and ran up the last few steps. It seemed like every muscle fiber in his body had tensed to the point of imploding by the time he jerked himself into the center of the hall to face the source of the noises he'd heard.

The woman lying on the floor next to the door to his apartment didn't seem to notice his arrival. She was flat on her back; head propped on a dusty backpack, eyes closed. Her chest rose and fell in an even rhythm.

He took a few cautious steps forward and looked down at her. She was wearing a purple sweatshirt and green cotton shorts. Other than that, nothing but a pair of black sandals that were partly held together with duct tape.

Tristan let out the breath that he hadn't realized he was holding and dropped the bag of clothes on the floor next to her. "Darby. Jesus Christ."

The young woman opened her eyes and a slow smile spread across her face. "Tristan!" she said, holding both arms out in front of her. He grabbed her right hand and with his help, she sprang up into his arms and gave him a hug that lifted him off his feet. When she dropped him back to the floor, she took a step back and ran her fingers through his hair. "My God, what did they do to you?" Her voice was just the way he remembered it, a little slower than most people spoke, but with the words slightly slurred together so she still got sentences out in roughly regulation time. A few years back, *Cosmopolitan* had done a brief article on her in a series entitled *Extreme Women*. In it they'd described Darby Moore's voice as "having a smile in it." He'd laughed for a good ten minutes at the sheer corniness of the statement, but had never actually been able to come up with a better description.

Tristan managed a grin and covered his closely cropped hair with his hands. "The government doesn't go for the long hair thing. I kept the ponytail, though. If you're nice to me I'll let you see it."

"Got a shrine, huh," she said, throwing her pack over her shoulder.

Other than her nose, she'd hardly changed in the two years since he'd seen her last. Her already broad shoulders were maybe a little broader, making her look shorter than the five-six he knew her to be. The definition in the muscles in her forearms seemed a bit more pronounced, but that might have been an illusion brought about by the deep tan that uniformly covered all her visible skin. Her light brown hair was tied back in its ever present ponytail, though it had worked its way halfway down her back—a good six inches farther than he'd ever seen it before.

Tristan reached out and grabbed her chin, turning her head back and forth to examine spiders-web scars crisscrossing the sides of her nose, which now sat slightly crooked on her delicately featured face. "It's got character. I like it. But I thought they said they were going to make it good as new."

"They told me better than new," she said. "What they didn't tell me was it was going to take, like, three surgeries in all." She shrugged. "I figured having a perfect nose would be like having a new car. You'd always be worried about bumping it into something or leaving it out in the sun too long, you know?"

Tristan pulled a key from his pocket and slid it into the door. "Darby, you're one weird chick."

"Yeah, but I'm so much fun," she said, pushing past him into his apartment. "Man, look at this place! It's huge!"

"It's a dump, Darb." Tristan stepped through and pulled the door closed behind him. For some reason, he felt some of the tension that had been slowly sucking the life out of him for the past twenty-eight hours fade as he watched her run the fifteen feet into the kitchen and look through the door at the back.

"What? You have *another* room back here, too?"

Tristan laughed quietly as Darby eyed his dishwasher and then stuck her head in his refrigerator. If you wanted to impress a woman with your run-down six hundred and ten square foot apartment, it was key to pick one who had spent her entire adult life living in a van. "How long have you been waiting out there, Darb?"

When she peeked back around the refrigerator door, she had a foot of celery hanging from her mouth. "You mind if I eat this?" She didn't wait for an answer but vanished behind the door again. "Since this morning. I was headed south and I thought I'd stop by."

"Shit, Darby why didn't you call? I could have had someone let you in."

He heard the clinking of jars as she continued her exploration of the fridge. "You know how expensive long distance is, Tristan." Her hand suddenly appeared over the door and pointed in the general direction of her backpack. "If I'd called, I couldn't have afforded to buy that." He looked down at her pack. As unarguably the finest woman mountain climber in the world, he knew that Darby had never bought a piece of equipment in her life. Manufacturers fell over themselves to give her stuff for free. He alone had over three thousand dollars worth of her cast-offs. "Uh, the pack?"

"No. Look inside."

He unclipped the top and pulled out the bottle of wine wedged between a pair of sweatpants and six cans of tuna.

"Who says you can't get a decent bottle of wine for under five dollars," Darby said, kicking the door of the refrigerator closed and dropping a handful of food on the counter.

"Mmmm. Chateau de Ghetto."

"Sandwich?"

"Sure."

Tristan walked into the kitchen and reached around her for a corkscrew before noticing the screw top. "I think I'll save this one, Darby. Why don't we open one of mine?"

"Whatever."

"So where have you been?" he asked, working a corkscrew into a thirty-dollar bottle. He'd suffer this shit apartment, he'd drive a beat-up car, he'd even eat meat loaf three times a week, but life was too short to drink cheap wine. "Last I heard you were in Borneo. That was, like, six months ago or something."

"Yeah, Borneo. I went in with the idea of checking out these huge, really steep limestone cliffs they've got over there." She held up her mustard-covered knife and used it to illustrate the severely overhanging nature of the rock. "Anyway, I was there for only like two weeks when I got dengue fever. Ended up staying with this tribe of reformed headhunters till I got better. Spent my twenty-seventh birthday sitting in a river to keep my temperature down and watching for snakes."

Tristan nodded knowingly. "Best birthday you ever had, I'll bet."

She grinned, but didn't let her concentration waiver from the sandwich she was creating. "Yeah, it was pretty cool."

"Well, you didn't have dengue for six months."

She shook her head. "Nah. I started feeling better after a few weeks. Finally got to go check out those cliffs. They're epic—I've *got* to climb one. I was on my way out drinking a beer in Miri—that's Malaysia—when I ran into some people from *National Geographic* who were heading into the jungle to try to study one of those Borneo rhinos."

Tristan walked into the living room and dropped into a chair, strangely exhausted by the conversation. Sometimes he felt like he'd aged twenty years since he'd quit climbing and returned to the real world.

"You all right, Tristan? You look kind of tired."

"I'm fine. Borneo has rhinos?"

"Yeah, they're really amazing. Smaller than an African one, but really hairy. I don't think any nonnative had ever seen one."

"I assume they have now."

Her face lit up. "Oh, we got some amazing pictures. I'll have to show you my slides."

She poked at the sandwiches until all the vegetables fit inside the edges of the bread, then brought them over. After accepting a glass of wine from him, she sat down on the floor with her sandwich in her lap. "So what about you? Still in school? Weren't you getting a masters in taking over the world or something?"

"It was a law degree," Tristan said.

"Whatever."

"I dropped out. Got a job."

She rolled her eyes and let out a loud lung full of air. "No wonder you look like hell. You've got to get your life together, man."

"Get my life together?"

"I know you. You're gonna fall into this work thing and one day you'll wake up and you'll be sixty. And you know what you'll have done?"

"I'm sure you're going to tell me."

"You'll have spent your life pursuing enough money to buy a bunch of crap you didn't need."

He nodded slowly and took a bite of his sandwich, trying to force down the image of the file that had suddenly crashed back into his mind. "Somebody's got to work, Darby. You know, keep the streets safe, build piece-of-shit vans for climbers to drive, fly airplanes to Borneo."

She shook her head slowly, making a slice of carrot wave back and forth until she sucked it all the way into her mouth. "Yeah, but it doesn't have to be us. Look at you, man. It's killing you. I can tell. I'm going to France next month. Francois just bought a house within biking distance to the cliffs at Buoux. He says I can set up a tent in his backyard and stay as long as I want. Why don't you just quit and come with me? We'll get a couple of cheap courier tickets over there, then we can pretty much live for free."

"I can't just quit, Darby. Life's a little more complicated than that—"

"Is not." She finished off the rest of the sandwich in one Herculean bite and chewed furiously. "Tell you what." Chew. "Why don't you blow off work for a couple of days and come to the New River Gorge with me?" Chew. "We'll do a few routes, drink some beer by a nice campfire." Chew. "Give me a chance to break you of this herd mentality you've developed since I've been gone."

4

"I can appreciate that suspended FBI agents don't rate limos, but I figured I'd do better than a golf cart," Beamon said, half to himself and half to the back of the driver's head. He took one more shot at adjusting himself into a comfortable position in the cramped backseat and then just gave up.

"No one rates a limo, Mr. Beamon." The driver glanced in his rearview mirror for a moment and then returned his attention to the congested Georgetown street. "You've probably heard that Senator Hallorin is kind of a stickler for saving gas. This car not only gets great mileage, but it actually runs on natural gas."

Beamon knew all that, of course—Hallorin had made damn sure everyone in America did. He had turned the image of his six and a half foot, two-hundred-and-fifty-pound frame unfolding from the back of these underpowered, propane-propelled vehicles into a cornerstone of his presidential campaign, softening the impact of his one dollar per gallon gas tax proposal with surprising effectiveness.

"It's amazing, really," the driver continued in a monotone that suggested he had been forced to memorize this little speech. "Cheap, environmentally safe, and all you lose is a tiny bit of acceleration. You don't even notice it after a couple of weeks."

"Uh, huh." Beamon reached for the one amenity that was included with the car: a small phone set into the armrest between the front seats. He had his own cell phone in his pocket, but what the hell. Hallorin could afford it.

He gazed lazily out the window as they drove along M Street. It was only about eight o'clock, but the sidewalks were nearly deserted. Many of the bars and shops he remembered from his tenure in D.C. were gone, victims of the hot air finally exploding from America's economy. The large picture windows that before had framed expensive clothes and yuppie revelers were now dark and dominated by tasteful "for rent" signs.

"Hello?"

The woman's voice at the other end of the line instantly relieved some of the tension he was feeling about being called to a mysterious meeting with one of the country's most powerful men. Strangely, though, that sense of relief worried him a little bit.

"Hello?" the voice repeated.

"Hey, Carrie."

"Mark! I've been trying to reach you at the hotel. Another hour and I was going to start calling the bars." She paused for a moment. "I was starting to worry when I didn't hear from you. Was I right to have?"

Beamon smiled and straightened his legs halfway out across the backseat. "I don't know yet."

"I'm sure what you meant to say was, 'I was in and out in five minutes, I'll be on my way back as soon as Congress is done slapping me on the back and giving me cigars.'"

"I was in and out in six and a half hours, no cigars, and it wasn't my back they were slapping."

"But were they happy with your respectful and concise answers?"

"No. But I'm starting to think that might be a good thing." Beamon looked up at the driver for a moment, wondering how much he should say in front of the man. He decided it didn't matter. Hallorin probably already had a transcript of the hearing sitting in his fax machine.

"We've had months of media frenzy over those tapes, two high-level resignations and God knows how many indictments in the works. It was a fishing expedition—they were looking for something they could use to divert the attention of the press."

"And you didn't give it to them, right? You didn't let them make you mad and bait you into saying something stupid."

"Your lack of confidence in me is startling, Doctor."

"Answer the question, Mark."

"The answer is no, I didn't. But I doubt it mattered. The only reason I was there was because they would have looked silly having a hearing without a witness. They'd already made their minds up about this before

I'd ever opened my mouth. It's gone way beyond me."

Beamon pitched forward as his driver slammed on the brakes and laid on the horn.

"Are you in the car, Mark? What time will you be back?"

"Well, I am in a car, but it's not mine."

"Whose car are you in?"

"David Hallorin's."

Another pause. This one much longer.

"Carrie? You still there?"

"*The* David Hallorin?"

"Uh huh."

"Why, Mark? *Why* are you in his car?" There was a tired frustration in her voice that didn't really surprise him. He'd been in a hell of a bind when they'd started their relationship and it seemed to have gotten worse every day since. If she was smart, she'd have moved to Alaska and changed her name by now.

The driver swung the car right and slowed, starting up a steep, winding road. Beamon looked down at the lights of the city and the dark streak cut through them by the Potomac. "I don't know, Carrie, but I guess I'm about to find out. Try not to worry, okay?"

"You make it hard."

A large iron gate that seemed to have been built in the middle of the street began swinging open in front of the car. "Look, I've got to go. I'll tell you all about it when I get back."

"I don't know what's going on, Mark, but take my advice and run away."

"I'm going to do my best, believe me. See you in a few hours."

Beamon replaced the phone and surveyed the floodlit landscape around him as the car moved slowly through the gate. Hallorin's house wasn't yet visible, but Beamon could see a powerful glow escaping a group of trees more than a half-mile in the distance. He tried to roughly calculate the cost of this kind of acreage so close to Georgetown, but more than twenty years on a government paycheck wouldn't allow him to count that high.

"What's that?" Beamon said, pointing to something that looked like a primitive machine that had been turned into a piece of lawn art. He leaned in close to the window, but the glare reflecting off the metal sculpture made it impossible to read the plaque on the pedestal.

"It's an original piece of Henry Ford's assembly line," the driver said.

"I don't know exactly what it did—helped put the body on the chassis or something like that."

Beamon nodded and sank back into the narrow seat. It made sense. According to one of the countless daytime TV programs Beamon had watched since his suspension, David Hallorin had quit his job as a D.C. prosecutor while he was still in his twenties, borrowed against everything he owned, and purchased a failing tractor parts manufacturing plant in Maine. Over the following two decades, Hallorin had clawed his way to the top of the industrial heap with an aggressive program of embracing and often creating new technology in the field.

Hallorin had explained his transition from manufacturing to politics as a need to give back to the country that had given so much to him. He'd won one of Maine's Senate seats in his first go-round, promising to bring the efficiency and can-do attitude of American business to the government, and begun a policy of outspoken criticism of the political elite.

The media had always given him a little more than his due time-wise, but it had been mostly for his entertainment value on slow news days. It was usually Hallorin decrying the moral bankruptcy of the country's leaders, Hallorin predicting doom for the then booming economy, Hallorin proposing a long-term plan that included a substantial amount of short-term pain for an electorate with a low threshold for such things.

Like most of America, Beamon had given Senator David Hallorin a hard second look when Asia's economy had stumbled, recovered slightly, and then crashed violently almost exactly as he had predicted. When the rest of the world's economies followed Asia into the toilet and the former Soviet Union had briefly turned dangerously nationalistic, Americans had begun to ask why Hallorin had been the only person watching the store over the last decade. This change in attitude had not been lost on the astute senator, and six months ago, he had announced his bid for the presidency.

It had been an unorthodox campaign from the start, beginning with introductory television spots that spun the yarn of Hallorin's rise in the world of manufacturing and entry into politics.

His opponents had seen blood in those early spots, laughing behind closed doors at their colleague's surprising ineptitude at campaigning on a national level. They'd instantly mounted a counteroffensive, pointing out the fact that Hallorin had replaced people with machines at every opportunity. The strategy had seemed sound until Hallorin had shown the American people the jobs that he'd created—building the machines, operating them, repairing them, exporting them. And it had then turned into a disaster for Hallorin's opponents when he pointed out that not one of his companies used any foreign labor and that many of the companies supporting his political competition manufactured in such exotic locations as Vietnam, Mexico, and Korea.

Pundits everywhere took notice, asking themselves if Hallorin was a lucky amateur or a brutal player who had drawn his opponents in for the kill. As far as Beamon knew, the jury was still out on that.

"You wouldn't have any idea why Senator Hallorin wants to see me, would you?" Beamon said over the quiet hum of the mahogany-lined elevator as it took them to the second floor of Hallorin's twenty-thousand-square-foot home. His escort, an efficient-looking woman who's name he'd already forgotten, looked horrified. "I'm sure I wouldn't."

Of course not.

They finished the ride out in silence. When the doors finally opened it was into a room so large that Beamon literally wasn't sure where the other end of it was. Pausing after he'd stepped out of the elevator, he looked up at the ceiling at least thirty feet above him and examined the elaborate frescoes that covered it. His escort must have been used to the reaction, because she seemed to automatically pause as his eyes wandered to the heavy gold-leaf molding running along the top of the walls and then to the pandemonium in front of them.

Despite the fact that it was closing in on nine o'clock, the room was packed with people of all ages, sizes, and races charging back and forth carrying boxes, computer printouts, cell phones, portable computers, whatever. No one seemed to notice Beamon and his escort as they threaded their way through the room.

"He runs his campaign out of his house?" Beamon had to raise his voice to be heard over the background noise.

"Wait here, please," the woman said, ignoring his question and melting into the riot. Beamon turned his attention to the bank of televisions secured to the wall, each silently playing various news programs from across the nation. Next to them was a colorful poster at least five feet high. In large black letters it read: "R: 33, D: 26, U: 16." Beamon assumed that those were the latest poll numbers for the Republican candidate, Democratic candidate and Undecideds. Beneath that was "28 days to go!" And beneath that, in bold green letters was: "Us: 19."

Beamon reached for the pack of cigarettes in his jacket, thought better of it, and went back to examining the numbers on the poster again. Hallorin had fought a valiant and insanely expensive campaign, sprinkled lightly with flashes of brilliance, or perhaps dumb luck, depending on who you asked. But despite everything that had happened, it looked like America wasn't ready for a man like him. Less than a month to go and he was still in the cellar.

"Mark!"

A small knot of young people scurried away like frightened animals, creating a clear path for David Hallorin to rush up and completely envelop Beamon's hand. "Thanks so much for coming. I know you're anxious as hell to get out of D.C. Come on back to my office."

Beamon followed without a word, watching Hallorin ignore the people rushing to get out of his way. Even Beamon had to admit that he cut an incredibly imposing figure. Usually politicians used the tricks of television to make themselves seem more powerful and presidential, but if anything, Hallorin had been forced to use the medium to tone himself down. What Beamon was seeing now was the uncensored David Hallorin. The mildly stylish glasses and the thin lenses that had given a more cheerful glitter to his cold gray eyes were missing now, as was the warm brown-and-tan color scheme that had replaced the blacks and charcoals that he'd favored before his presidential bid. What was even more noticeable, though, was the way he walked. It wasn't something you saw that much of on television, but it was quite remarkable. It seemed that every motion was punctuated by a strange sense of physical power, a barely contained whirlwind.

Hallorin stopped at an unobtrusive door in the back wall, threw it open, and stepped aside to allow his guest to go first. Beamon paused for a moment, stifled a sigh and stepped through. No good could come of this. Of that he was sure.

The office was much smaller than Beamon had expected, but other than that was fairly typical. The obligatory antique desk favored by men of power dominated and was surrounded by uncomfortable-looking chairs. Strangely, the two bookcases along the wall were full of books and not the reaffirming knickknacks and souvenirs that were the staple of most politicians.

"Nice place you have here," Beamon said, and instantly felt stupid for opening his mouth.

Hallorin fell into the chair behind his desk and motioned to the one in front of it. "You think so?" He looked around him at nothing in particular. "Kind of a vulgar display of wealth, actually. I built it when I was much younger and much more impressed with myself."

Beamon thought the answer had a slightly practiced ring to it, like his driver's speech about the car—but couldn't be sure. His normally acute perceptions were unreliable around politicians—meeting with one always made him want to take a shower. Admittedly, the sensation was less urgent with this one than with most.

Hallorin looked like he was about to continue when the phone on his desk rang. He sighed and held up a finger as he picked it up.

Beamon only partially listened to Hallorin's half of the conversation— he was answering the person on the other end with one-word sentences, obviously wary of giving too much away to his guest.

Beamon leaned forward and took a framed photograph from the desk before realizing that he probably shouldn't be grabbing at David Hallorin's personal effects. Too late now.

The woman in it was quite beautiful, with medium length blond hair and the tall, thin body of a model. Next to her stood a much younger David Hallorin. His jet black hair was a little more severely cut and the crow's-feet around his eyes were a little shallower, but other than that he looked pretty much the same. The picture, Beamon knew, was at least ten years old—that's how long Hallorin's wife had been dead.

"She was killed by a drunk driver," Hallorin said as he replaced the handset.

Beamon felt he should say something consolatory, but couldn't come up with anything that wouldn't sound stock. "I remember the legislation you tried to have passed after her death."

Hallorin leaned back in his chair. "Before she died, I didn't really know anything about the problem. The thousands killed every year."

Despite being something of a drunk himself at the time, Beamon had supported Hallorin's stand: Drunk drivers would have their licenses revoked for the rest of their lives on the first offense. He couldn't remember the proposed penalty for the second offense, but it probably involved pliers and thumbnails. More power to him.

"I'm sorry you never got it passed," Beamon said sincerely. "I believed in what you were trying to do."

Hallorin looked him straight in the eye. "That's because you and I are rare birds in the government, Mark. We put results above politics. The American people are just now coming around. I think they'd sleep better knowing their children's stomachs were full than knowing that there—"

Beamon finished the sentence in his head. "—are a bunch of generals at the Pentagon sitting on $700 toilet seats." It was one of Hallorin's favorite lines.

"I'm sorry," Hallorin said. "I'm making a speech."

Beamon studied the man. Had the senator seen through his normally infallible poker face and read his disinterest? He'd have to be more careful in the future. "I have to wonder why we're meeting, Senator."

"Why do you think?"

"I assume that it relates to the Vericomm tapes. But I'm not sure what I can tell you that wasn't in my report or won't be on the transcript of today's hearing."

"The last tape just cuts off," Hallorin said bluntly. "Why?"

"It's in my report, Senator. I was downloading those wiretaps from a central mainframe where they were stored. I lost the feed."

Hallorin laced his hands in front of his chest. "You're sure?"

Beamon got the impression that they were negotiating but wasn't sure for what. Hallorin seemed to be searching for something in his expression. Whether or not he was telling the truth? Whether or not he had a price?

"I'm sure, Senator."

Hallorin didn't respond, but continued examining Beamon's face for whatever it was he was looking for. After another thirty seconds or so, he must have found it.

"I know what you're thinking, Mark. That my credibility has benefited greatly from the discomfort of some of my colleagues."

Beamon looked on impassively. He *really* didn't want to be here. His life was already too complicated for him to comfortably manage, and frankly, he truly, deeply, didn't give a shit who the next president was.

"I've been critical in the past, it's true," Hallorin continued. "But I think things are starting to get out of hand."

"I thought your campaign was about clearing the air," Beamon said, paraphrasing one of Hallorin's ads as respectfully as he could and concentrating on not letting his skepticism show.

"The air's getting a little too goddamn clear," Hallorin said, raising his voice a bit.

He stood, rising to his full height for a moment and then leaned forward against his desk. "The people of the world are looking to be led out of the hole they've dug for themselves. If we don't do it, the Europeans or Japanese will. We've just started a new millennium and we're at a crossroads. Will we regain our power or will we fall from grace?"

Beamon tried unsuccessfully to count the number of metaphors and clichés in that little speech as Hallorin walked around his desk and put a hand on his shoulder. "Americans are losing confidence in their country, Mark. Yes, some of that's benefited me, but it's gone too far now."

Beamon shifted uncomfortably. Despite the sincere resonance of Hallorin's voice, he just couldn't buy it. Men who attained what Hallorin had in the world of politics were men who never got tired of being proven right—it just wasn't possible for their egos to be overfed. "There are no more tapes that I'm aware of, Senator."

"I have your word on this?"

"You have my word."

Hallorin stood in the doorway of his office watching Mark Beamon wander slowly through his campaign headquarters and didn't immediately turn when he heard the voice behind him.

"Do you believe him, David?"

Hallorin finally closed the door turned to face Roland Peck. "I do."

Peck nodded and walked quickly to a straight-backed chair against the wall that seemed to fit his small, thin frame better than the heavily padded one centered in front of Hallorin's desk. "Yes, yes. I'm afraid I do, too," Peck said, wiping away a thin coating of perspiration that made his pale, almost translucent, skin seem to glow from some internal power source. His hand caressed the side of his sharp nose and then moved down to smooth the meticulously trimmed red mustache growing from his upper lip. The motion was nothing more than one of his many elaborate ticks, an obsessive-compulsive ritual that told Hallorin the young man was concentrating on other facets of the problem at hand.

"There's nothing in Mr. Beamon's profile or history that would suggest he would lie," Peck said, abruptly clipping each word and phrase as he always did. "Nothing that would suggest he wouldn't turn all of the tapes over to the FBI. No, nothing."

"He might have held back some information to help him in his suspension hearing," Hallorin offered, slipping back into the chair behind his desk.

"No. No. He's not a game player, that one. And my sources say his suspension is based completely on hearsay evidence. Most of it relates to a newspaper article about his alleged drinking problem that came out in the *Flagstaff Chronicle*. The article was retracted though, so—"

"Then the alcohol problem was a fabrication?"

"Oh, no, no, no. It was very real. The question was whether it *impaired* his ability to do his job. An impossible question to answer, but it's clear that he has one of the best conviction records in the Bureau. In short, Mr. Beamon was a drunk, but not at work. One could use the rather dramatic phrase, 'He gets the job done.' Yes, absolutely."

Hallorin took a deep breath. "*Was* a drunk."

"Mark's got a girlfriend," Peck half said, half sang. "A psychiatrist, no less. I understand that she's henpecked him down from bourbon to beer. Light beer, I think."

Hallorin laced his hands on top of his head and leaned back in his chair. "If he's that talented, should we be making a place for him in this organization?"

Peck barked out a short laugh that shook the air for a moment. "Your Mr. Beamon is uncontrollable—no, no, that's the wrong word. Unstable. And worse, completely apolitical. He has a juvenile arrest record that, if you put it into a notebook as I have, leaves considerable space between the covers—"

Hallorin cut him off. "What kind of arrests? Drugs?"

"No, no. Nothing like that." Peck paused and looked around the room, his head moving in random, birdlike motions. Another compulsive mannerism Hallorin was familiar with. Peck was thinking of an example.

"When he was seventeen, a woman who worked in the cafeteria of his high school died. Young Mark liked her, so one night, he poured a concrete monument some five feet tall in the middle of the front lawn of the school. Of course, the school had it torn out a few days later. So incensed was Mark, that he re-poured the monument. This time, he first dug down around the main to the school's electrical system and poured the base around it. Also, he mixed the concrete with .22 shells. That left a construct that could not be chipped away or pulled up. It is my understanding that it still stands today." Peck tapped his fingers together. "I tell you this generally irrelevant story because I believe it gives some insight into Mr. Beamon's psyche."

Hallorin crossed his legs and examined Peck coolly. He'd found—acquired—Peck when the man was only eighteen years old. He'd come with an advertising and business consulting firm that Hallorin had purchased sight unseen based on its inspired and wholly unconventional marketing strategies.

It had taken only a couple of weeks to realize that the genius of the organization wasn't in its management team. A few more days of investigation had turned up Roland Peck, a thin, red-haired boy toiling in a small basement office that looked like a trash dump.

Peck's tenuous grasp on sanity was obvious the moment Hallorin met him, as was his brilliance. The boy's ideas were utterly original—sometimes too much so—and showed a depth of understanding of human nature and its manipulation that Hallorin had never seen before.

On that day, he had taken the parentless boy under his wing and discarded the company Peck had worked for. Hallorin had spent years carefully cultivating a father–son relationship that would ensure Peck's undying loyalty. With the right handling, Roland Peck was the ultimate weapon.

Now, sixteen years after their first meeting, Peck controlled every aspect of the Hallorin campaign and the widespread business holdings of Hallorin Industrial. On paper, though, he was still nothing more than an assistant marketing director in one of Hallorin's insignificant real estate partnerships.

His anonymity was at times inconvenient, but absolutely necessary. Hallorin knew that Peck's sexual tastes ran well past amoral and into the bizarre. In fact, when Peck was twenty-five, Hallorin had provided him with a wife that was amenable to allowing him to act out his twisted fantasies with her—keeping the possibility of scandal to a minimum. If there were any extramarital excesses, Peck hid them with his normal brilliance.

"So where are we, then, Roland?"

"We had never counted on additional tapes, David. No, we hadn't ever counted on them. They would have been helpful, but it doesn't matter. We're still on track. It doesn't matter."

5

From his position in the back of Darby's gently rocking '76 VW van, Tristan Newberry couldn't see the ground or the trees, only the gray clouds moving through the sky. He pushed the sleeping bag off and adjusted himself into a more comfortable position on the bed as Darby turned and began maneuvering up a steep incline. The feel of the old mattress, the smell and motion of the van—it was all so familiar, so comfortable. Right now, he wished he'd never left it.

They had been inseparable—best friends. They'd traveled all over the world together: wandering from Africa's heat and claustrophobic crush of humanity, to the empty expanses of Patagonia, to the icy tundras of Tibet and the Himalaya. There had been no agenda then; nearly everything they owned and certainly everything they cared about fit in her van or on their backs. The only thing they ever had to think about was where their next adventure would take them and how they were going to finance it.

Tristan felt their progress slow and looked up at Darby as she leaned forward and squinted through the windshield. He felt the van drop as the front tire hit a rut, then a slight acceleration, and the back tires were in and out. Only the right side of Darby's face was visible, but it was enough for him to see the broad smile and exaggerated sigh of relief. No important parts had fallen off what was left of the old vehicle.

"You alive back there, Tristan?"

He stretched and kicked the sleeping bag that was Darby's only blanket into the corner of the bed. "Yeah, yeah."

"Good." The van lurched to a stop. "Because we have arrived at our final destination. How 'bout setting the emergency brake?"

Tristan smiled and slid the van's door open. A blast of cool, damp air rushed at his bare chest and face as he jumped out and began searching through the tall grass for appropriately sized rocks. Less than a minute later he was shoving the two he'd found beneath the back tires of the van. "Okay! Ease off it!"

The brake lights went out and before the tires had fully settled in against the rocks, Darby jumped from the van and ran full-speed past him toward a cathedral of a cave fifty meters away. He watched as she scrambled up a ten-foot tall boulder and stood gazing at the gray sandstone that undulated in front of her.

"This is it," she said excitedly as he climbed up the coarse boulder in his bare feet. About halfway up, he was reminded that the skin on his soles was more used to argyle and leather than to stone and dirt these days.

"This is it," she repeated as he came alongside her.

Tristan surveyed the intimidating stone wall in front of them and decided that it looked like a Dr. Seuss nightmare. Black and gray rock rose from dense undergrowth in a wave that probably averaged thirty-five degrees overhanging for about the first sixty feet, then kicked back to virtually horizontal for another forty or so. From where he stood, the cliff looked almost featureless—he couldn't make out much more than the occasional doorjamb-width edge or two-finger-wide hole. He craned his neck and looked overhead at the imposing stone roof above them. The hand- and footholds on that section were hidden, but he could see brightly colored nylon slings dangling from the roof every ten feet or so. Called quickdraws, they were the things that climbers would hook their ropes through when they were on the route. Not just any climber, though. By the looks of it, there were probably only a handful of men around the world that would even have a chance of making it to the top. And only a couple of women, one of whom was standing next to him.

"How hard?" he asked.

"In the end, I think it'll go at a fairly stiff fourteen," she said, dropping into a full split on top of the flat boulder and starting to stretch.

That confirmed it. The hardest climb in the world had a difficulty rating of easy fifteen. "Jesus, Darby . . . what're you gonna call it?" All routes up a rock face had a name—just like all routes down a ski hill had a name.

"I'm leaning toward 'Disco Girl and the Mutant Strain.'"

He laughed and shook his head. "Like I said, you're one weird chick. You warm up, I'll go grab the gear."

Tristan jogged back down to the van and began rummaging around in the various backpacks and duffels it contained. He glanced back up at Darby through the side windows just in time to see her gracefully rise from the splits to a perfect handstand. She tilted her body to one side and tentatively lifted her right hand off the rock. She stayed like that for about five seconds and then crumpled onto the boulder.

He tried not to laugh loud enough for her to hear, remembering the acrobat from the Cirque de Soleil who had developed a terminal crush on Darby a few years back during a climbing trip near Vegas. She'd been trying to duplicate the guy's one-armed handstand ever since.

"Which shoes do you want, Darb?" he yelled through an open window.

"Stingers, please.

He grabbed the pair that looked like a couple of mutant yellowjackets, stuffed the rest of the gear in a pack, and started toward the cliff. By the time he got to the base, Darby was pacing back and forth beneath the route.

He knew better than to talk to her at this point, though a comment on the quickly worsening weather was on the tip of his tongue—the wind had picked up and was kicking dust into the air in swirling clouds. He tossed the climbing shoes and a harness onto the ground in front of her and started to uncoil the rope.

Darby muttered quietly to herself as she struggled to pull on the shoes that were at least two sizes too small for her feet to prevent slipping on critical moves. She seemed to be in a world all her own as she slowly stood, slipped on her harness, and started threading the rope through it.

"You're on, Darb. Whenever you're ready," Tristan said, pushing his end of the rope through a metal device at his waist designed to lock off the rope if she fell.

Darby slid her hands into a small bag of gymnast's chalk tied around her waist to dry them and slipped two fingers into a small hole in the rock. She paused there for a moment, bouncing her forehead gently against the stone.

"Okay," she said quietly, stepping her right foot up onto a small edge no thicker than a nickel and using her fingers to pull her weight over it.

Each individual move on a climb this hard had to be performed with absolute precision. The wrong hand on a hold, moving a foot out of sequence, even a slight swivel of the hips at the wrong moment, and the climber was guaranteed a fall. Darby performed the first four moves like a ballet dancer, making them look completely effortless, though Tristan knew it would probably take him a day of effort to just get both feet off the ground on this horror show.

He moved under Darby and put his arms up. Though probably fifteen feet up, she hadn't yet reached the first piece of gear she could clip the rope through. If she fell, it would be an ankle breaker, unless he could absorb a little of the impact.

He watched nervously as she dug her toe into a small crease in the stone, tested it, then curled the middle finger of her right hand into a tiny pocket. She carefully grabbed a quickdraw from her harness and snapped it into a bolt that had been drilled directly into the cliff. Looking a little shaky, she pulled the slack rope tied to her harness up and clipped it through the 'draw. He heard her take a deep breath and expel it loudly. "That part's pretty sketchy," she said.

"Looks it," he agreed, taking up enough rope to keep her from hitting the ground in a fall, but leaving enough slack so that it wouldn't aid her effort—something taboo in this type of climbing.

She continued up, her grace fading as fatigue set in. He could hear her breathing fifty feet above him as she crouched down and made a desperate lunge, barely latching a large hold just before the rock turned horizontal. "Yeah!" he yelled. "Nice, Darby! Stay with it!"

She snapped the rope through another 'draw and hung off her right arm, shaking her left to get the blood flowing. She stayed there for over a minute, alternating arms and getting her breathing under control.

In the short ten minutes it had taken Darby to cover the first sixty feet of the climb, the weather had continued to worsen. She was partially protected by her position, but the dust was blowing around hard enough to start to sting Tristan's exposed skin. Worse, distant rolls of thunder weren't so distant anymore. Tristan looked behind him at the sky and then back at Darby, who had regained some of her composure and was dipping her right hand into her chalk bag.

This wasn't good. There was a reason people didn't hook a bunch of metal things to themselves and climb to the highest point during a storm.

"Weather, Darby!" He said simply. It wasn't bad enough to tell her to get off yet. He knew she had tried this climb more than forty times over the last year and right now she was climbing better than he'd ever seen her. If she got it, it would be the toughest ascent by a woman ever.

"You hear me, Darby?"

There was a slight jerk of her head that told him she had. She was completely focused now, too much so to speak.

She arched her back and reached out for a hold on the horizontal roof. As soon as she got the fingers of her left hand around it, her feet swung free. In one smooth motion, she grabbed her left wrist with her right hand and pulled herself up until her head almost hit the rock above her.

"Jesus," Tristan whispered to himself as she let go of her wrist. Except for her right arm reaching for the next hold, her body didn't move. She just hung there, locked into a one-arm pull up.

She didn't seem to notice the flash of blinding light that suddenly bathed them as she continued to fight her way across the roof. Tristan started counting out loud. "One Missis—"

The crash of thunder drown out his voice. "Okay, Darby! That's it! We're out of here!" he yelled when the echo had subsided. The wind had risen another notch and much of Darby's long hair had worked its way out of her ponytail. It was fluttering around in the hazy white cloud created by the chalk being blown from the bag tied to her waist. She couldn't hear him.

"Darby!"

There was probably more than fifteen feet of slack rope whipping around in the wind behind her. The next clip was only a few feet away. He saw her move her feet onto a small in-cut in the roof and hang there like a spider. "Come on, Darby," he said to himself. "Make the clip already."

She rocked herself back once, twice and then jumped horizontally through the air at the next hold. She missed it by a good two inches.

Tristan held the rope tight and fell to the ground as he watched Darby drop thirty feet through the dust-darkened air. When her body weight finally hit the rope, it pulled him five feet into the air. He relaxed his grip and let the rope slide quickly through the device attached to his harness, then stopped her about a foot from the ground with an enormous bounce. A moment later her feet were safely on land and she ran at him, pulling him against the cliff wall. She was laughing.

"Shit, Darby! Are you nuts?" The rain had just started and he had to yell over the dull thud of the drops hitting the loose dirt outside the cave.

She put her face in her still-shaking hands and let out a playful scream. "I was so close! Two more clips and I was at the anchors! I feel strong, man. I'm gonna get that this weekend. Guaranteed." Tristan was helping her untie the rope from her harness when she suddenly grabbed his shoulders with both hands. "Are you having fun yet!?"

"Jesus, Darby."

Tristan groaned quietly as he knelt next to the small ring of river rocks and blew at the fledgling fire it contained. Every muscle in his body was screaming, punishing him for leaving the sedentary life he'd been living and getting tricked into a climbing trip.

The storm had lost its will after he had spent about an hour out in it being dragged around the backcountry by Darby Moore. They'd crashed through bushes, waded through knee-deep mud, and forded creeks—all with Darby's excited promise that "one of the best rainy day climbs at the New is just up ahead."

He decided against trying to stand again, instead crawling to a small flexible chair he'd found in the van. Thankfully, it was within reach of the cooler and he was able to get his swollen hands around a cold beer bottle. He stared at the cap for a few moments, finally mustering the courage to grab hold of the serrated edge with what was left of his skin and give it a hard twist. The pain was just like he remembered it.

The sun was about halfway set and the reddish light was fighting its way around the clouds still lingering from the afternoon thundershowers. At the edge of the clearing they were camped in, the world seemed to fall away as the tree-covered slope turned steep and dropped a thousand feet to the New River.

Tristan took a deep breath of air that smelled strongly of decaying leaves and campfire smoke and then turned his attention to Darby. She was about twenty-five yards away, standing naked in a trickle of a waterfall coming off one of the cliffs that surrounded their campsite. The flattening light heightened the contrast between the white skin of her breasts and hips and the deep brown of the rest of her. He watched her as she flipped her long hair over in front of her face and let the water run off it in a long stream.

Even after a couple of years to reflect, he still wasn't sure if he'd figured out their relationship. They'd slept together, of course, but had always been careful to not let it evolve into lovemaking. By silent agreement, they'd limited it to being just another fun activity they could do together.

There had been no shortage of women since they'd parted—a fortunate trick of genetics had made Tristan's face and body conform to what the media currently considered ideal for a male. So now he sat around smoky bars with women who made plans. Lots of them. Children, mortgages, a membership to the country club. Perhaps, if they were particularly adventurous, they would consider a fully guided trip to London. No set date, mind you. Someday when the economy was better.

Tristan took another long pull from his beer and focused on Darby again. The sun had finally disappeared over the mountains and she was more or less just a gray outline turning slowly beneath the dully-shimmering flow of water. She spoke four languages fluently, had been everywhere, had done everything. She was at the top of a sport that tolerated no weakness, fear, or lapses of concentration in its participants. In short, the most amazing woman he had ever known.

And he'd let her go. In the end, there'd been no choice. Despite the Zen way she liked to picture herself, Darby Moore was the most focused and driven person he had ever known. If it had come down to a choice between him and the rock, he'd have lost.

But it was unfair to blame it all on her. He would have never been satisfied living a life where tomato soup consisted of free hot water from 7-Eleven mixed with ketchup packets purloined from McDonalds. And when he tried to picture her at a law firm cocktail party, all he could see was her filling her pockets with peeled shrimp and cold cuts. But now things looked like they might be changing, that he might have finally tripped over a little bit of luck. If it held, maybe things could work out for them after all.

The flames sputtered, then sunk into the red embers in front of him. He winced and cursed himself for stacking the wood so far from the chair and cooler that he had hoped to not move from until it was time to climb into the van and pass out. He struggled to his feet and selected from the small pile a few pieces of wood that didn't need to be broken. The hiss of the fire as he tossed the half-green branches onto the coals was loud enough to cover the sound of Darby's approach. He was a little startled when two brown arms wrapped around him from behind and he felt the initial cold of mountain water soaking his back, followed closely by the warmth of her naked body.

"Missed you, Twist."

He smiled at the sound of his old nickname. He hadn't heard it in years. "That's because you just spent six months living in a grass hut with a bunch of headhunters."

"Oh, come on," she said, rubbing his shoulder with her chin. "You were the best climbing partner I ever had."

"You're just saying that because you want to get lucky."

She was silent for a moment. "Maybe. But you weren't a *bad* climbing partner."

6

Carrie Johnstone looked down at her daughter and smiled. Emory had one tiny hand around a vertical slat in the deck's fence and the other held a small cup that a few moments ago had been full of orange juice. She looked like a little prisoner.

Carrie squinted against the glare of the sun and followed her daughter's gaze to the meadow below them or, more precisely, to the black and brown horses contrasted against the fading green of the grass. "Pretty, isn't it, honey?"

Emory nodded, but maintained her unbroken concentration.

Carrie walked up next to her daughter and leaned against the rail, running her fingers through the little girl's curly brown hair. Except for the small log-and-cedar home behind them, the modern world didn't seem to exist there. It was as if it had been swallowed up by an endless expanse of trees, rolling hills, and flat meadows. It really *was* beautiful.

She turned when she heard footsteps behind her. Tom Sherman emerged from around the corner of the house first, with Mark Beamon not far behind.

Carrie reached out when Beamon came into range and slung a playful arm around his waist. "This is amazing, Tom. If I'd have known how gracefully FBI agents retired, I'd have hitched my wagon to an older one."

Sherman smiled in acknowledgment, but his face seemed to hold onto a hint of sadness until he crouched down next to Emory. "You know what one of those horses told me?"

Emory looked over at him with as stern an expression as the five-year-old could muster. "Horses can't talk!"

"Can't talk? Are you kidding? Some of them are practically blabbermouths! One of them told me that she was hoping a little girl would come and ride her tomorrow." He pointed out into the meadow. "It's that black one with the white face." Emory pressed her own face as far as it would go through the slats.

This was only the second time that Carrie had met Tom Sherman, despite the fact that he and Mark had been best friends for more than a decade. She had met him for the first time a little less than a year ago, but that had been before his daughter died and his wife left him. Before he had retired. At their first meeting it had been difficult to picture the quiet, gray-haired man with the soft eyes as the man who had risen at warp speed through the ranks of the FBI to become the youngest associate director in the history of the organization. Now, it was completely impossible. His introspective nature had grown into introversion and he seemed to have trouble tracking on long conversations.

"So have you been able to get anything out of him?" Carrie said as Sherman stood and left Emory to dream about tomorrow. Her boyfriend had been characteristically tight-lipped about the hearings he'd been involved in.

"Not yet," Sherman said. "Being a psychiatrist, I'm sure you understand that you have to tread lightly around Mark's delicate psyche."

"Tell me about it."

Sherman turned to his friend. "Well?"

Beamon leaned against the table behind him and frowned, obviously not happy to be talked about like he wasn't there. "They were completely won over by my effusive charm."

Sherman pulled his glasses down on his nose and glared at Beamon. For a brief moment, Carrie saw a glimmer of the man that had taken control of the FBI at the age of forty-six.

"What?" Beamon said. "Shit, Tommy, you're still probably one of the most connected guys in Washington. *You* tell me how it went."

Sherman swirled the ice in his glass and drew it slowly to his lips. "Okay, I will. You didn't give them what they wanted, Mark."

"What was it they *did* want?" Carrie said to neither of them in particular. They looked like they were in one of those staring contests little boys favored so much.

Sherman spoke first. "They were looking to trip Mark up. To cast enough doubt over the legality of how the tapes were obtained, or the man who obtained them, that they could fabricate doubt as to their validity. Or at least divert the attention of the public. That's what they wanted, and that's what Mark didn't give them."

"That's good, though, right?"

Sherman softened when he looked over at her. "I don't know, Carrie. I just don't know anymore. When the Vericomm tapes were leaked it was like a bomb going off in the Capitol building. The public's apathy toward their elected officials' behavior had already started to turn to rage and this just amplified it. The politicians are getting desperate. And when people like that get desperate . . . " He let his voice trail off and Carrie looked over at Beamon. He was slowly running his finger up the side of his can of Miller Lite, trying to gauge how much was left by the temperature changes in the aluminum. "I don't know what's going to happen, Carrie," he said finally. "There's nothing I can do now."

"You could ride off into the sunset," Sherman said. Carrie silently thanked him for broaching a subject she'd been skirting for months.

"Excuse me?"

"You heard what I said."

"Come on, Tommy, you know that everything relating to my suspension was a bullsh—" He cut himself off as he looked down at Emory. "They've got nothing, and next week they're going to bring me back to full duty. The whole thing's already got the director's rubber stamp across it."

Sherman didn't reply right away. He seemed to be trying to decide something. How much to say.

"If they do bring you back, Mark, it won't have anything to do with justice." He spoke slowly, now. Deliberately. "You make it a little too obvious how important your job is to you."

Beamon tried to interrupt, but his friend held up his hand and silenced him. Carrie fought off a moment of confusion. She'd never seen anyone with the power to make Mark Beamon shut up before.

"You've put yourself in harm's way here, Mark, and now you're going to make it worse. You think they'll send you back to Flagstaff?" Sherman shook his head. "No way. They'll find a reason to transfer you back to D.C., where it's easier to keep an eye on you. They'll dole out the jobs and cases to keep you pacified, and then they'll find a way to hang you."

Beamon slid up on the stone table behind him and took a sip of his beer, the muscles in his jaw tightening perceptibly. He needed to hear this no matter how much it hurt him, Carrie told herself. And he needed to hear it from the only person who had even a remote chance of getting through to him.

"Mark," Sherman continued, "you're bigger than life at the Bureau. A hundred years from now, people are still going to be telling stories about the moronic stunts you pulled and the rabbits you managed to pull out of your hat. But it's time to walk away now. It'll only add to your legend." Sherman motioned around him. "I'm telling you, retirement isn't half bad. You do a little consulting work when you feel like it and play golf when you don't. No more politics, no more crap. Once you have a little time for yourself, you won't know how you lived without it."

The silence lasted a long time. Carrie could see that Beamon was building something up inside and moved back to her former position along the rail to let Sherman take the brunt of whatever it was. Cowardly? Sure. But sometimes cowardice was the better part of valor.

"Screw you, Tommy," Beamon said, not looking up from his beer. "How old were you when you retired? Fifty-six? Well, I'm nowhere near that. You walked out the—" He lowered his voice. "Associate fucking director. I crawl out a disgraced SAC." Beamon waved his arm around him. "Your family owns half of Chicago, so you retire to your Dupont Circle brownstones, your ranches, your villas, and your horses. What do I get? A one-bedroom apartment and a job as a night watchman somewhere?"

"Mark!" Carrie scolded. "Tom's just trying to—"

Beamon jumped off the table and brushed passed them, picking up Emory as he went by. "You want to go see the horses close up, honey?"

Carrie watched for a long time as Beamon and her daughter trudged down the muddy hill toward a distant buck-and-rail fence.

"I did my best, Carrie," Sherman said in a customarily melancholy tone. "I'm sorry."

"You did more than anyone else could have."

"It wasn't enough."

"It's an impossible situation, Tom. The FBI's been such a big part of his life for so long, he isn't sure who he is without it. He won't let himself see all the other things he has in his life." Carrie surprised him by suddenly smiling and clinking her glass against his. "You may have failed at saving him from himself, and I imagine that Emory will be demanding a pony for Christmas, but the trip won't be a complete loss if you can show me how to do that trick."

"Trick?"

"The one where you make Mark shut his mouth."

Sherman nodded slowly. "I'm getting old, Carrie, and my powers are waning. I can only do it once per visit these days."

7

Tristan Newberry opened his eyes, but it was like being blind. The clouds had rolled in again, obliterating the stars and sliver of a moon that had glowed over them as they ate by the campfire. He propped himself up on his elbows and turned his head slowly back and forth, trying to make out the lines of the interior of the van with no success. Two lousy years in the city and he'd already forgotten what real darkness and silence felt like.

He settled back into the makeshift foam mattress, slipping his arm under the covers and running a hand down Darby's side. Her back was pressed up against him, the warmth of her overpowering the cold damp of the fall night. Just like old times.

He closed his eyes again and let his exhaustion overcome the dull pain in his joints and muscles. He was almost out when he felt Darby drive her rear end into his hip.

"Darby? Shit, man, I'm trying to sleep," he said, putting a knee against her back and giving her a halfhearted shove. "What?"

He heard her shift her position in the darkness and then what sounded like her head rising from the pillow. "Did you leave food outside?" Her voice was groggy.

"Huh?" The hypnotic sense of half-sleep had slipped away enough that another few seconds of this and it would take half-an-hour trying to get his thrashed body comfortable enough to drop off again.

"I heard something outside." Darby yawned. "You left food where animals could get to it, didn't you?"

"No," he whined, throwing the covers up over his head.

He heard her head sink to the pillow again, and he let his eyes close and conjured the memory of their last trip to Europe. The blackness and quiet hum of the wind outside became a sun-bleached seashore and the crashing of waves against bone-white cliffs as he finally dropped off thinking of her and French limestone.

The next time it was an elbow.

He groaned quietly and tried to read his watch. The clouds had parted enough to see the vague outline of the cluttered van and to give the windows a mirrorlike glow, but not enough for him to be able to figure out what time it was.

"There's something outside," he heard Darby mumble into her pillow. "You left food out." It was a statement now, not a question.

"Didn't," he protested.

He moved away from her, pressing himself against the back wall of the van. He'd been in similar situations with Darby in the past: freeloading varmints, tent air vents clogged with snow, early morning weather checks. He knew that if he was stubborn enough long enough, she would eventually get frustrated and face the cold world outside of the sleeping bag herself.

Fortunately, she hadn't changed. No more than two minutes had gone by when he felt a cold draft as she wiggled out from under the covers. A groggy smile formed on his lips when he heard her start to fish around for a pair of shorts.

"With my luck, it's probably a bear," he heard her say over the swish of fabric as she dressed and started strapping a pair of Tevas to her feet.

He closed his eyes again and pulled the sleeping bag over his face before the overhead light—one of the few things he remembered still working on the old VW—flickered on.

"Jesus, Darb. Close the door," he said as she jumped out into the tall grass and the outside air started to circulate in the van. She didn't respond and there was no sound of the door sliding shut. In fact, there was no sound at all.

Tristan slowly pushed the sleeping bag from his face and squinted against the light that, for some reason, seemed wrong. He pushed himself up on his elbows and looked out the open side door. The dome light overhead *wasn't* working. What illumination there was, was leaking around Darby's silhouette as she stood motionless in the powerful beam of a flashlight.

Tristan raised his hand to partially block out the light, letting his eyes adjust and shaking off the grogginess still clinging to him.

"Hello?" he heard Darby say.

No answer.

"Hello?"

Her voice was slow and steady like always. The hint of uncertainty beneath it would have been undetectable to anyone who didn't know her well. He saw her take a step forward and had to adjust his hand as the glow around her became brighter.

"Stop right there."

It was a man's voice. Tristan took a deep breath and let it out, trying to muster the will to overcome a sudden sense of weakness and fear. "Who are you?" he said, swinging his feet over the edge of the bed and standing. He'd wanted to sound angry, forceful, but it hadn't worked—his voice shook perceptibly. Calm down, he told himself. Just people looking for a campsite. Worse case, a couple of drunk rednecks. This was West Virginia, after all—the progeny of the hillbillies from *Deliverance* and their sisters probably lived down the road.

Some of his confidence returned as he slowly convinced himself that he and Darby were faced with nothing more than some locals who had been out spotlighting deer.

"Get that goddamn flashlight out of our faces!" There, that had sounded better.

He jumped out of the van and stood next to Darby, aware that the harsh light illuminating them would bring out the definition that still existed in the muscles across his bare chest and arms. Hopefully that would be worth a little intimidation value.

"I said—" he started again, but went silent when Darby tapped him on his bare leg. "It's okay, Tristan." She pulled him gently to the side, exposing the open door to the van. As they moved, the flashlight followed them and briefly illuminated a pistol in what seemed to be a disembodied hand. Tristan started to step back involuntarily, but Darby put a hand on his back. She had seen the gun but gave the illusion of being completely unaffected.

"We don't have much," she said, "but if you need it, you're welcome to it."

"Are we?" the man holding the flashlight—and the gun—said. At the word "we" Tristan heard a loud rustling coming from the darkness at the edges of the flashlight's beam. In reality it must have been almost inaudible, but to him it sounded like an explosion. These weren't locals. Darby didn't understand—they had to get out of here.

He grabbed her arm and, in one swift motion, pulled her hard to the left. The sharp stones that littered the ground tore at his bare feet as he tried to drag her out of the light and toward the trees at the edge of the clearing. He'd made it no more than ten feet when Darby's arm slipped away and he fell over what was left of the pile of wood they'd gathered to keep the fire going.

By the time he'd untangled himself from the branches, it was too late. The beam of light arced toward him and he felt a powerful hand grab the back of his neck. He rolled over onto his back, hearing more than feeling the sharp branches breaking beneath him. He was about to take a wild swing at the man holding him when the cold metal of a gun barrel pressed into his throat.

"Tristan! Calm down!"

It was Darby's voice, but he couldn't process it. He looked around him as best he could as the man with the flashlight walked slowly toward him. The path of illumination as the flashlight swung loosely from the man's hand alternately lit the brown rust on the side of the van, the red and yellow of the fall leaves on the trees, Darby being held from behind, but never the man's face. When he finally stopped a few feet away, all Tristan could see was a thin layer of dust clinging to a pair of expensive black dress shoes.

He continued to watch helplessly as the well-dressed legs turned and walked back toward Darby. As the man moved away, the rest of him slowly became visible: the perfectly pressed wool slacks, the blinding white of his shirt, the red tie loose at the neck. He could see the quiet confusion on Darby's face as she examined the man approaching her. Obviously, not the flannel-clad West Virginia native she had expected.

"You didn't really think this one through, did you?" The man was looking at Darby, but his words clearly weren't directed at her. One of his gloved hands suddenly moved up and grabbed hold of Darby's face as he spoke. In one explosive motion he threw his weight forward and drove the back of her head into the passenger side window of the van.

She didn't make a sound. Tristan heard only the dull crack of the safety glass and saw her slide down the door, struggling to get her arms to work well enough to use them to cushion her landing.

He felt the bile rising into his throat as he watched Darby try to remain in a sitting position. She didn't seem to want to fall completely to the ground but didn't look like she knew why.

"No!" he shouted.

He'd seen Darby being blown wildly into a rock face at the end of hundreds of feet of rope, he'd seen her fall into a deep crevasse on a remote Himalayan peak, but watching someone purposefully hurt her ignited something in him that he'd never felt before.

The man holding him must have seen or felt it, because he moved the barrel of the gun to Tristan's mouth. The pressure of the metal against his teeth created shooting pains that went through his gums and into his head. There was nothing he could do. He opened his mouth and tasted the metal as it slid against his tongue.

"Take a look, boy," the man on top of him said, pushing the end of the barrel against the inside of his cheek and forcing him to turn his head back toward Darby.

He did as he was told when his cheek was pinched painfully between the gun barrel and the hard dirt beneath him. The man with the flashlight crouched down in front of Darby and took hold of her face again. She reached up and closed a hand around his wrist, but her normally uncanny strength was gone.

"No, you didn't think this through at all."

This time his words were punctuated by the sound of Darby's skull denting the metal door of the van.

8

Darby had felt this way many times before. Clinging to some nearly nonexistent handhold or standing on a dangerously unstable cornice of snow and ice. The feeling that the slightest move, the tiniest muscle twitch would send her hurtling into space. But those situations had a certain familiarity, an almost comforting simplicity. Right now, she felt lost—like the world she found herself in was no longer her own.

Darby let her eyes move slowly across the small room, taking care to keep her head completely motionless. The walls were covered with yellowed and peeling paper that had once depicted blue horses ridden by red soldiers. The furniture seemed too well cared for to belong: a small bed with a delicately worked quilt bedspread, a child's writing desk of expensive and exhaustively polished hardwood, a richly painted dresser, and a deep chest that she imagined was full of a little boy's toys.

She had no idea where they were or how long it had taken to get there. She'd woken up in the back of a windowless van with a splitting headache that had continued to grow in intensity as she was pulled from the vehicle and marched into this old farmhouse.

The medical-looking white straps that had bound her wrists during the trip had been removed, leaving her free . . . to do what? Stand helpless and confused in the middle of the floor?

Darby let her gaze wander to the only door in the room, afraid to focus directly on the man standing next to it. He didn't look much older than she was, despite the fact that his hair was turning prematurely gray at the temples. He was thin, athletic, and clearly, extremely uncomfortable. His weight shifted from one foot to the other every five seconds or so and his eyes darted back and forth to the heavy closed door next to him, the bed in the corner, the window—but never at her or the other people in the room.

Darby strained her eyes left until she could see Tristan. He looked so scared and angry; naked except for a pair of boxer shorts. There was blood running from the corner of his lip, a bright streak of color set off against the dull brownish-red splatter patterns drying across his face. He was struggling uselessly as the man who had knocked her senseless at their campsite looped a rope through his canvas handcuffs and secured him to the chair he was sitting in. She hadn't actually seen the man clearly until now, and her strained examination of him just confused her more. He had a solid, stocky build and a strangely square face, topped by close-cropped dark hair that made him look kind of military.

Tristan stopped thrashing and let his chin drop toward his chest in defeat as the man gave the rope binding him one last tug. The desperation and pain etched across his face made her turn her eyes away.

They'd spent two years together—maybe her two favorite years so far. He had been so fired up about everything—all energy and no judgment. But his kindness and enthusiasm had been infectious and she had always been there to keep him from doing something stupid and getting himself killed. Until now. In the end, it looked like she was going to be the death of him after all.

It had taken a while to learn to think around the razor-sharp pounding that was tearing at the back of her skull, but after some effort, she had managed to string together a few coherent thoughts.

There was only one possible reason this was happening to them. It had to be something she'd seen, somewhere she'd been. These men, conservatively dressed and disciplined, had government written all over them. Could it have been the old plane she'd come across in the Laotian jungle? The thick plastic packaging of its cargo had mostly been reclaimed by the indigenous vegetation, but where it hadn't, the heroin was still very much in evidence. The plane had been an old Dehaviland, and judging by what was left of their clothing and other personal belongings, the two skeletons in the cockpit had been American. She had taken photographs and delivered them to the U.S. Embassy along with the general location of the plane.

Then she'd never thought it about it again. Beyond hoping to ease the pain of the dead men's families, the plane meant nothing to her. A decaying relic from a time in history to which she felt no connection. A forgotten monument to a world she chose to live at the very edges of.

Tristan shouted something at the man standing behind him, the rage in his voice registering with her though the actual words didn't. She moved her eyes slowly to the opposite corner of the room and the man standing in it. As far as she could tell, he hadn't moved an inch in the last five minutes. His eyes were glassy and unblinking, and seemed to be aimed directly at her right hip. She decided to take a chance and tilted her head down slightly so that she could try to see what he was seeing. That nearly imperceptible move, as she somehow had known it would, broke the man from his trance. His head came level and he pushed himself from the wall he was leaning against, starting toward her. She could hear Tristan shouting again. Something about her.

"Hello, young lady," the man said. He stepped close, breathed in deeply and held it. His head nodded forward and he raised it slowly, carefully inspecting the black sandals on her feet, the deep brown of her legs, her green cotton shorts, her white T-shirt. Only then did he exhale. His breath didn't smell like anything.

"We have some questions we want to ask," he said, tilting his head forward again and focusing on her crotch. "They won't be hard. No, not hard at all." The thin red mustache under his nose barely held onto the tiny droplets of clear fluid forming on it as he spoke. Darby wasn't sure whether they were spit, sweat, or both. All she knew was how this thin, twitchy man made her feel. She had to fight to resist the urge to step back away from him and tug at her shorts to cover more of her bare legs.

"I think we can get to the bottom of things, don't you?" he said, stepping in even closer and brushing his chest against hers. For some reason, he tried to make the contact look accidental, a product of his careful examination of the scars that ran along the edges of her nose. She'd noticed him crouch slightly before they'd touched, though, so that their nipples would make contact. His were hard.

He turned briefly toward the man standing behind Tristan, careful to stay as close as possible to her. "Gag him."

The stocky man didn't immediately follow the order. "Sir, don't we want him to ta—"

"Gag him!" His shout was almost as high pitched as a scream. Darby heard Tristan start to struggle again, but kept a watchful eye on the man in front of her as he refocused on her crotch. "How close are those other houses?"

His voice was quieter now but thick with excitement. For a moment, she wasn't sure if he was talking to her or the man she could see out of the corner of her eye, yanking Tristan's head back and forcing his mouth open.

"I don't know," was the answer. "A half a mile, maybe."

"Are they occupied?"

"I don't know, probably."

"You don't know much, do you?" the man in front of her said coldly. A sad look crossed his face. "I'm afraid we aren't going to be able to listen to that beautiful voice of yours either. And it is beautiful, isn't it? Say something. Go ahead. Do it. Say something."

She hesitated for a moment. "Why don't you let him go? He doesn't have anything to do with this."

The man looked delighted. His thin mustache curved along his upper lip as he smiled, revealing tiny little teeth and finally dislodging a few of those unidentifiable droplets. "He doesn't? What makes you say that?" There was a playful lilt in his voice that was infinitely more frightening than his angry scream a moment before.

"He doesn't know anything about the plane," Darby said, hoping to get things out into the open.

"The plane," he repeated, and turned to the man who was busy securing whatever he had stuffed in Tristan's mouth. "Isn't she precious?" He looked over at the old bed in the corner. "Tie her down on that—no, wait. Wait. We need something to cover it. I have a blanket in my car. That will do. Yes, that will do."

Darby was too focused on his face as he stepped back to notice his hand coming up between her legs. He pinched her there—hard—and she yelped at the sudden pain and jumped back. The man who had finished gagging Tristan ran forward and got between them as Darby closed her right hand into a fist and started pulling it back.

"Yes, we'll need that blanket. We'll need it," he said, hiding behind his much larger associate and walking backward toward the door. Darby made a move to get around the bigger man but he held an arm out and stopped her. She watched through her anger as the red-haired man continued backward toward the door, registering that her fury just seemed to excite him further. It was clear through his slacks that it wasn't only his nipples that were hard.

"Can I get anyone anything?" he said as he reached behind him and opened the door. "A glass of water, perhaps? I believe we may be here for a while."

As he disappeared though the door and closed it behind him, Darby saw the horror on the face of the young man standing guard near the wall. For the first time, their eyes connected. She couldn't find any cruelty or hardness there in the brief moment before he turned away. In fact, he looked closer to panic than she was.

The door clicked shut and the man in front of her closed his thick fingers around her shoulder, shoving her hard in the direction of the bed.

What was happening? Suddenly the theory that had brought some small bit of reality to this situation started to slip away. Why would anybody care this much about an old Air America plane? Could it have been something else she'd seen but hadn't registered? In the former Soviet Union? Cambodia? Afghanistan? Was it all a mistake?

The man pushed her again, and she looked behind her at the bed. The bright colors of the quilt seemed to burn through the thoughts clogging her mind, leaving the image of her tied helplessly to the head- and footboards, and that odorless little man free to do whatever he wanted to her. That wasn't the way she was supposed to die.

She allowed herself to be pushed back another foot or so, feigning a loss of balance and adding a short whimper of fear. She looked over at Tristan for a moment—he was fighting so hard against the ropes that the chair was coming fully off the floor. Then she shot her hands out and wrapped them around the thick neck of the man in front of her.

Darby had the unusual ability to support her entire body weight with any one of her fingers. When all ten suddenly dug into the skin and muscle of the man's neck, he gagged with enough force to cause spit to fly from his mouth. They both froze for a split second, him from surprise and the sudden interruption of blood flow to his brain, and her because she had never hurt anyone before in her life.

Out of sheer necessity, she was able to defeat her uncertainty first and drop backward, pulling him toward her and simultaneously kicking at one of his legs.

When her back hit the floor, she instantly started to roll left to avoid having the man come down on top of her. She was about halfway clear when she heard the sound of shattering glass and felt the man's body arrested in midair.

She didn't know what had happened and didn't look back as she jumped to her feet and sprinted at the young man guarding the door.

She could see that his hand was already inside his jacket, and by the time she had covered half the room, his gun was leveled at her face. She launched herself forward, trying to cover that last ten feet before he could move his index finger a quarter of an inch. It was hopeless. She already knew that.

He sidestepped her easily and she hit the wall, landing hard on the wood floor. The gun was aimed at her chest now and she could see the man's finger tightening on the trigger.

A deep calm washed over her as, for the fourth time in her life, she found herself seriously considering what death would be like. She let her eyes close and waited for the crack of the gun and the pain of the bullet hitting her chest.

There was nothing, though. No gunshot, no sound of the man she'd knocked down getting to his feet and running across the room at her. Nothing.

When she opened her eyes again, probably less than a second later, the younger man was still hovering over her. His finger was still tight across the trigger, but he wasn't moving.

"The door!"

It was Tristan's voice. He'd managed to spit out most of the gag in his mouth and was shouting around it.

She shook her head, trying to clear it. She was still alive.

"Darby!"

She could hear it now. Footsteps pounding up the stairs on the other side of the wooden door. She shot the man hovering over her a quick glance, then rolled over and threw herself at the door. Her hand slammed against the knob and pressed the lock button just as the weight of a human body hit the other side. The violent rattling of the knob and door-frame mixed with muffled shouts and the pounding of fists against wood.

Darby flipped around and was about to run to Tristan when she saw the man she had fought with lying on the floor by the bed. His hands were wrapped around his neck and blood was spurting between his fingers with the rhythm of his heartbeat. Around him, the old curtains billowed in the cool breeze coming through the window his head had gone through. They were edged with red and made a sickening slapping sound every time they hit the wall.

"Darby! DARBY! For God's sake!"

She looked over at Tristan, who was still thrashing wildly in his chair, and then back at the man on the floor. Could the bleeding be stopped? She hadn't meant . . .

"DARBY!"

No. His life was gone. She'd killed him.

Darby forced that thought from her mind as she ran to Tristan and unbuckled the canvas shackles around his wrists. He jumped out of the chair the moment he was free but didn't seem to know what to do next. They both looked up at the young man standing against the wall. His gun was hanging loosely from his hand.

"I'm not a killer," he said over the desperate pounding and shouting coming from the other side of the door. He seemed reasonably convinced but not entirely certain.

"We've got to go, Tristan," Darby said, grabbing him by the arm and dragging him toward the window before the young man could rethink his value system. She tried to ignore the feeling of warm blood splashing over her open sandals as she pushed the remaining glass from the broken pane and followed Tristan out onto the roof. They stood on the edge of it for a moment, looking down at the ten-foot drop into a gravel side yard. Darby looked at Tristan's bare feet and then behind her through the window. The man who had let them go was moving toward them and his gun was no longer hanging limp from his hand. It was aimed directly at them.

She grabbed hold of Tristan and pulled him off the roof with her just as the first shot sounded. She heard him grunt in pain as they hit the ground, but she ignored it, rolling to her feet and dragging him up with her. "No time to complain, Twist! Come on!"

She heard the second shot ring out as they ran desperately toward a densely wooded butte two hundred yards away. She looked back at the window just before the third shot and realized that the man wasn't aiming anywhere near them. It was a show for the benefit of his colleagues.

"Come ON!" she said again. Her fingers dug deep into his bicep as she pulled him along behind.

She heard shouts that sounded as if they were coming from outside the house, but didn't look back again. All they had to do was make the trees, then they could take the steepest line up the butte. No son of a bitch in a suit was going to be able to keep up with her there—even if she had to carry Tristan on her back.

9

Mark Beamon looked around him at the familiar blankness of the conference room and then out the windows across from him at the silent procession of agents and support staff as they moved through the halls.

It seemed like he'd spent a good half of the last six months of his life trapped in these barren cubes, waiting to be questioned, poked, and prodded about his role in the Vericomm fiasco. He looked up at the clock and confirmed that he'd been sitting there for exactly twenty-nine minutes. The lack of creativity and spontaneity in government service was no more evident than when his persecutors were trying to gain a psychological advantage. They would leave him to stew for a half an hour. No more. No less.

The delay actually did have an effect—but not the one they were looking for. In these empty rooms, forcibly shielded from the external stimulation he was always careful to surround himself with, he surrendered to his newfound urge to look inward. It was something Carrie would undoubtedly encourage but was turning out to be a kind of dangerous skill to be developing this late in life.

What was he feeling right now? Nervousness? Not really. The outcome of this meeting had been preordained. The Office of Professional Responsibility—the FBI's answer to Internal Affairs—had found a great deal of smoke, but had been unable to find any actual flames still burning in the embers of his ill-fated investigation of the Church of the Evolution.

Regret? No, he'd do the same thing again.

Disappointment? There it was, the current front-runner.

Tom Sherman had been right—as that son of a bitch almost always was. The FBI, and its big brother, the U.S. government, was only interested in Mark Beamon as far as they could use him. He knew that but couldn't find the strength to use the knowledge. As much as he wanted to tell them to shove the job they were about to give back to him, he couldn't. Even with Carrie and Emory there to help, he didn't know if he could fill the void it would leave in him. And that was just downright pathetic.

Beamon watched through the windows as Gerald Reys, his FBI-appointed inquisitor du jour, came around the corner and stopped at a water fountain. He was obviously aware that he still had thirty seconds to kill before the half-hour was up.

As near as Beamon could tell, they didn't get much worse than Reys. He was a humorless, lifeless, company man, completely devoid of imagination and personality. His only qualification for his job seemed to be a naturally mean spirit and an inexhaustible fervor for poring over mundane government documents. He had a peculiar talent for taking anything anyone had accomplished in life, processing it, and finding some obscure reason to attribute that success to luck, nepotism, or cheating. Not surprisingly, his investigation into Beamon had quickly degenerated into an inexplicable vendetta, though they had never met before this inquiry and hopefully never would again.

Beamon didn't recognize the two rather serious-looking men flanking Reys as he came through the door. Normally, he would have at least stood and introduced himself, but he just couldn't summon the will to care who they were. He just wanted to get his job back and leave with his tail between his legs. In situations like this, brevity sometimes could be mistaken for dignity. Hopefully, this would be one of those times.

"Mr. Beamon."

Reys looked dangerously confident as he laid a manila folder down on the table. He looked at it, and not Beamon, as he spoke. "I've come across a document that's generated a great deal of interest in my office."

Beamon put his elbows on the table and rested his head in his hands. "This is a rubber-stamp meeting, Gerald. You don't have anything. There's nothing for you *to* have—there never was. Come on, I promised my girlfriend I'd take her out for dinner."

"I have to apologize for the last-minute nature of this line of inquiry, but this document just came to my attention." He always talked like that. Like he was reading from a government study.

Reys pulled a thin stack of papers from the folder in front of him and slid them across the table. "I have to ask you if you recognize this report."

Beamon sighed and calmly pulled a pair of reading glasses from his pocket. Just a minor delay, he told himself. He'd still get out of here, employed and in time to make his dinner reservation. He flipped through the papers, reading every fifth word or so. Three pages into it, he honestly didn't remember having ever seen it. Toward the end, though, there was a faint glimmer.

"I think it may be a report someone in my office wrote on the church investigation. I wouldn't swear to it, though."

"I'm sure you wouldn't," Reys said, letting a condescending smile pass his lips. "In fact, it *is* a report written about your investigation. A somewhat negative report."

Beamon had made it to the end of the document by this time and the faint glimmer was getting brighter. He looked behind Reys at the two men standing against the wall, wondering again what their place in all this was. He was ninety-percent sure that he'd never seen either one of them in his life.

"I don't mean to seem like an asshole here, Gerald, but so what?"

"You were asked to sign off on this document. Do you recall what you did?"

Beamon searched his memory again. As an SAC he was asked to sign off on what seemed like a thousand pieces of paper a day. "Unless I'm confusing this with something else—which is very possible—I vaguely remember it being inaccurate and leaving out almost two weeks of the investigation—a generally shoddy piece of work. I think I told the guy that wrote it to go back and do it again."

"And then what?" Reys probed.

Beamon felt his frustration growing again, but pushed it back. No fireworks today. "What then? I don't know. I went to lunch?"

Reys scooped up the document and handed it to one of the men behind him as though it needed to be protected. "You destroyed it, Mr. Beamon."

Beamon stared at him for a moment, then let out a short laugh. Reys's choice of words and dramatic delivery conjured a wonderful image of Beamon huddled over a shredder in a dark office in some forgotten corner of the Pentagon. "You mean I tossed it in the garbage?" Beamon shrugged. "Yeah, probably."

Reys suddenly looked like the victorious coach of a high school football team. "So you admit that you destroyed a document relating to an ongoing investigation into your conduct?"

There was the frustration again, but this time he was less successful at pushing it away. "Give me a fucking break, Gerald! You're going to tell me you keep every draft of every report given to you?"

"And you knew that, as a matter of course, your trash is shredded."

"It's the twenty-first-fucking century, you asshole. You can't destroy documents anymore. They just sit around on disks or in memory or on backup tapes." Beamon jabbed a finger in the general direction of the folder, now in the protective custody of the man to Reys's left. "For God's sake you *have* the report you say I destroyed!"

"Yes," Reys said. "Fortunately, you weren't very thorough, were you?"

Beamon shifted wildly in his chair but couldn't find a comfortable position. This couldn't really be happening.

"Mr. Beamon, I've had exhaustive discussions with the highest echelons of the FBI, including the director—"

"I thought you said this document just came to your attention."

Reys flashed an irrelevant little smile and continued. ". . . and we've agreed to offer you a deal. Plead guilty to a felony obstruction of justice charge, and we'll recommend that your jail time be limited to six months—"

Beamon jumped up from his chair and Reys scooted back away from the table. The two men he had come in with stepped forward and blocked Beamon from crawling over the table and strangling the little prick with his ugly tie, answering the question of why they were there.

"What the fuck are you talking about?" Beamon shouted, leaning over the desk as far as he could while still keeping his feet on the carpet. "You want me to go to jail for not signing a poorly drafted document written by some kid in my office about an investigation in which you have no evidence of wrongdoing? Jesus Christ, by this time next week everyone in the Bureau is going to have a copy of the document I *destroyed*."

"Would you step back, please?" Reys said. His calm had been restored by the intervention of his two bodyguards.

"What?"

"Step back away from the table."

Beamon took a deep breath and managed to construct a façade that would pass for outward calm. When he complied, Reys matched him with a step forward.

"You didn't let me finish, Mr. Beamon. If you agree to this, you'll retire with your full pension. If not, the FBI is willing to use whatever resources necessary to prosecute you to the full extent of the law. You'll spend hundreds of thousands of dollars on a defense. I understand that you lost most of your savings in the market crash. If you lose, you're looking at bankruptcy and a potential ten-year jail term. Even if you win, you're still bankrupt, but with no pension."

Beamon felt everything come crashing down on him. Twenty plus years sleeping, eating and breathing the FBI, and this is how it was going to end for him. He wanted to say something that would express that, that would let Reys know what the political machine pulling his strings had done. How he was destroying a man's life for nothing more than the off chance it might cool the heat a bunch of amoral political hacks had brought down on themselves. But what words could do that? In the end, he just turned away and started walking toward the door.

"Three weeks, Mr. Beamon," Reys called after him. "I'll give you three weeks to make a decision. I think that's more than generous under the circumstances."

10

"**C**ome ON, Tristan!"

"I'm trying!" His voice was strained and he was breathing harder than he should have been.

"Well, try harder!"

Darby stretched her arm further around his bare waist, attempting to support a little more of his body weight. They were both sweating profusely and he was getting more slippery with every step.

The forest had closed in quickly behind them and was becoming increasingly dense as they fought their way up the butte. The good news was that the thick foliage was reasonably effective at keeping them out of sight. The bad news was that it also hid the rocks and broken sticks that were strewn across the forest floor and tearing Tristan's bare feet apart.

"It's not much further," Darby said as the slope suddenly turned into a forty-five-degree ramp of slick leaves and loose dirt. It was what she had originally hoped for—the tougher the terrain, the better the odds in her favor. It had been a miscalculation, though. Tristan was fading fast.

It didn't matter, she told herself. They were outside, away from that house, and away from the sterile-looking freak who had been so anxious to have her tied to that bed. No matter what happened next, no matter what this was all about, they were better off out here.

The positive thoughts that she had forced on herself slipped away as Tristan's legs slowed and finally stopped. He stuck a hand out in front of him and fell against the steep slope. "That's it . . . Darb. I've . . . I've got to rest."

"Now's just not a good time," she said, locking an arm under his and dragging him to the point that his knees actually made a trail in the dirt. They made it about another four feet before she fell next to him. "It's too steep and loose here, Twist. I can help, but I can't carry you." She pointed up the slope to a patch of blue sky framed by a stand of pine trees. "That's it. That's the top," she said, having no idea if it was or not. "We'll rest up there, Tristan. We'll be able to see better. Figure out what we're going to do."

He was still on his knees and sweat was running off his nose in a stream. His breathing had slowed a bit, but his recovery time wasn't what she remembered.

"You gonna throw up?"

He shook his head. "Think they broke a couple of ribs. Can't hardly breathe."

When she reached out and brushed the darkening bruise on his side, he jerked away weakly. "Doesn't look that bad," she lied. "I doubt they're broken. You'll be okay. We'll slow the pace down a little. But we've got to keep moving. We've got to."

Tristan reached out and used her shoulder as a crutch to stand. "Okay. I'm all right. Let's go."

Darby scooped up a handful of dirt to dry the sweat from her left arm and then wrapped it around Tristan's waist. He managed to ignore the pain in his side and feet, and they started forward again.

What seemed like an hour was probably no more than fifteen minutes. By the time Darby could clearly see the top of the butte, she was propelling herself by fear and force of will only. Every sound behind them—kicked off rocks, creaking trees, the flapping of wings, became a running gunman gaining on them.

When the grade eased off a bit, she stopped and released Tristan's waist, instantly feeling the blood begin to flow back into her arm. "You can make it the rest of the way, Twist," she said in a loud whisper. "Just keep going. Come on. Go!"

He grunted loudly and started crawling up the butte, trying to keep his damaged feet from contacting the ground. Unburdened, Darby backtracked by taking long jumps down the loose slope, sending a small avalanche of dirt and leaves down in front of her.

She stopped behind a rock outcropping and peered down through the trees for at least a minute. Nothing. No sounds that didn't seem to belong, no motion that couldn't be accounted for by the wind or the natural inhabitants of the forest. The entire way up the butte, she'd felt like they had barely been moving, but in the end, everything was relative. Realistically, they'd probably covered the terrain faster than ninety percent of the population could.

The brief rest had been enough to return her to near full strength and Darby was able to propel herself back up the slope at close to a full run. The patch of blue sky she had seen earlier actually did mark the top, and she came out of the trees into a small, flat, meadow. Tristan wasn't immediately visible, but the roughly foot-shaped blood trail he'd left through the brown grass was. She followed it fifty meters or so and found him lying on his back in a stand of tall weeds.

"Okay—feel better?" Darby said, grabbing his arm and pulling him up. A rush of air escaped him, but he didn't seem to have the strength to protest as they stumbled to a less exposed spot. When she let go of him, he crumpled to the ground, coughing violently. She knelt and gently scooped a hand under his right calf, lifting his foot for a closer inspection.

"Oh, Tristan," she heard herself say, and then instantly regretted her tone.

"Not . . . so . . . good, huh?" he gasped out.

It wasn't. His foot was completely covered in blood. She wiped some of it away and sat quietly as the deep gouges continued to ooze and pump.

"It's always the silly things that get you, isn't it?" Tristan said. He'd caught his breath a little and was trying to sound cheerful. "Rappelling off the end of your rope, losing your goggles . . . forgetting your shoes."

Darby began yanking at the straps of her sandals. "Maybe we can make these fit you—"

"Don't be stupid," he said, putting a hand on hers. "My feet are twice as big as yours. Besides, the damage is done."

She looked into his face. He was still so beautiful. As near as she could tell, a unique combination of perfect features, perfect skin, perfect hair, and eyes that looked so soft—no matter what the situation.

The day they'd gone their separate ways had been much harder on her than she wanted to admit, even to herself. She'd always known the day would come. Tristan wanted everything: freedom, adventure, money, love, fame. But he'd never understood that none of those things came without a cost. There was always a price to be paid.

"I'm so sorry, Tristan. This is all my fault. I . . . " Her voice trailed off.

What could she say?

"Your fault? What are you talking about?"

"There was this plane in Laos. I think that's what this must be about. An Air America plane full of heroin. I took a picture—"

To her surprise, he started to laugh.

"What are you—"

"Darby . . . " He reached out and ran a bloody finger gently down her cheek. "I stole an old FBI file from the National Archive where I worked. It has things in it you wouldn't believe. Things that could hurt—destroy—some of the most powerful people in the country."

It took her a moment to process what he was saying. "You . . . you what?"

"I stole it and stashed it in that cave near the Fisher Towers. That's where I'd been when you showed up at my apartment." He looked away and pretended to concentrate on one of the worst of the cuts on his foot. "I figured I could sell it. To the press. I'd have been set up for life. . . ." His voice got quieter as he continued to talk. "I was going to find you. We could have gone anywhere we wanted, done anything. Lived in four-star hotels instead of moldy tents. . . ."

Before she knew what she was doing, Darby punched him hard in the chest. He fell back into the grass, but not really from the impact. It hadn't surprised him.

"How could you have done something so stupid?" she said, grabbing both of his shoulders in her powerful grip and shaking him. "Don't you know what people like that are capable of? We don't even count to them. We're nothing. They'd kill us for nothing! What the hell were you thinking?"

She froze when a shout drifted up to them on the light breeze. It wasn't very close, but it would be soon.

Tristan heard the voice, too, but didn't seem to care. "Sorry, Darb. If I'd have known . . . "

She knelt and picked up one of his feet again, not listening to him. The blood flow had slowed while he was lying down, but she knew that when he stood, it would start again in earnest. He was going to get light-headed before long.

"Darby, I—" He lost his voice when she wrapped his foot in the bottom of her shirt and squeezed down a little harder than she needed to.

"Forget it," he said, pulling away and leaving a large stain on her T-shirt. He struggled to his feet and started to limp toward a short, exposed ridgeline to the north.

Darby stayed where she was, glaring at him as he moved away. He'd only made it about ten meters when she took a deep breath and pushed back her emotions. There would be time to be angry later. Hopefully. "Not that way, Tristan. We've got to go down the other side."

There was an obvious canyon running between the butte they were on and the one behind it. It looked remote, and she could see a stream running through it. They'd need to avoid roads, open areas, and other easy terrain where the men chasing them could move quickly. And they'd need water.

"You go that way," Tristan said. "I'm going this way."

She ran up to him and grabbed him by the arm. "Don't be stupid. We have to stay together."

He looked behind him at the bloody footprints he was leaving and forced a pained smile. "Don't worry, Darb. I don't care how bad my feet are—I can stay ahead of those fat-asses."

She wouldn't let him go when he tried to pull away again. "I've been in worse situations than this, Tristan, and I've never left anyone behind before."

"You've been in *different* situations than this, Darb. You've already saved my ass as many times as you're going to." He leaned forward unexpectedly and pressed his mouth against hers, then pulled away and began limping off. "I'll meet you at Summersville Lake. Near Lactic Acid Bath. Tomorrow or the next day." He paused for a moment and looked back in her direction, but wouldn't meet her eyes. "Darby. I'm sorry."

Darby leaned forward and dipped the bottom of her shirt in the quickly moving stream. The tears finally started to roll down her cheeks as Tristan's blood was flushed from the material and swirled away over the mossy rocks and rotting logs. She fell onto the bank, closing her eyes and choking off her sobs before they got out of control. Tristan was on his own now. She had to concentrate on her own problems.

Judging by the position of the setting sun, it had been a little over an hour since she'd left him. There had been no shots, no more shouts, nothing. The men who had attacked them weren't close behind her; she knew that for sure. Without Tristan's weight, she'd run down the slope at a speed made possible only by the thousands of similar descents she'd made in her lifetime.

On a less positive note, though, she had no idea where she was. How long had she been unconscious in that van? Was she five hours from the

New? Ten? Twenty? Was she still in West Virginia? How far to the nearest town?

She finally stood and started carefully downriver, picking her way through the tangle of slick boulders and fallen trees. No matter where you were in the world, if you followed running water far enough, you pretty much always ended up in civilization. Or the ocean.

She picked up her pace a little, but not so much that she couldn't keep her progress quiet. Best to make some time now; the coming dark was going to cut her speed in half. And it was starting to get cold.

11

David Hallorin leaned into the centermost microphone and looked out over the people neatly lined up on benches in front of him. "It looks like my time is running out. I think they'll let us squeeze in a couple more, though." He pointed to a woman in the back row. It was impossible to make out any more than her outline with the bright television lights bearing down on him, but that was enough. Her movements were slow, uncertain. The question would come the same way.

"Thank you, Senator."

He nodded and smiled easily. "What do you have for me?"

The imprecise, informal way of speaking was pure Roland Peck and Hallorin was still having a hard time making it work. Despite the condition of the country and the rest of the world, the American people were still too stupid and weak to focus on anything but image. Even now, they were still more easily drawn to feigned personal warmth and deliberately meaningless and endearing character flaws than to strength and leadership.

"Sir, I agree with your stand on personal responsibility and the way you want to reform the tax system . . . but I just can't agree with you on the legalization of drugs. Senator Taylor wants a more efficient government, too, but he says we can't afford to do it at the expense of our children. If the government sold drugs, everyone would be doing them." She started to sit down before she was even finished speaking his Republican opponent's words.

"Hold on there, don't take your chair just yet," Hallorin said, squinting through the lights. "I have a question for *you*."

79

She stopped halfway, and he could see the dark outline of her head move as she looked around her.

"Would you, ma'am?"

"Excuse me?" she said nervously, still not sure whether she should stand or sit.

"Would you start using drugs if they were legal?"

"No."

"Me neither." He paused, considering stopping this routine short. The rest was risky. Peck insisted that it couldn't fail—there were no less than three cameras trained on the crowd, and according to Peck, the audience's mothers and bosses would be watching. He decided to go forward.

"I want everyone out there who does not currently use narcotics, but would if they were legalized, to raise their hands." No one moved.

He scanned the audience for a few more seconds, shrugged meaningfully, and continued. "As I've said before, I like my Republican opponent. I always have. But more than that, I respect Senator Taylor's willingness to get bloodied over and over again in the war on drugs. The question is this: If you're fighting a war and you're losing badly, hopelessly, would you continue to send your sons and daughters to the front lines to be killed? Or would you change your strategy?" He leaned against the podium and made a show out of scanning the crowd before locking in on the woman who had posed the question. "Let me correct one thing you said. I believe that the U.S. government, as it's now structured, is the only organization in the world that could lose money selling drugs." There was a brief, quiet tittering from the audience that he hoped was loud enough to be picked up by the mikes.

"I propose that the right to produce and market these products be sold to pharmaceutical companies. Now, there would be no advertising and you could only buy in state-run stores. These stores wouldn't take cash or checks—no, you'd have to use a credit card specially designed for the purpose. The government could then track who was using what and how much. That would then be compared with tax returns to make sure that there were no disparities that might suggest that money was being raised by criminal activity."

"Big Brother is watching!"

The shout from the back was unamplified, but this time there was no doubt it was loud enough to have been picked up by the mikes. More Roland Peck. He'd allowed a number of staunch liberals to "sneak" into the audience. The town-hall format wouldn't look real without them, he'd said, all the while making sure that these red herrings were poorly spoken fanatics who would succumb to the carefully planned responses he'd devised.

The audience had been generally sympathetic to his positions all evening, so Hallorin chose the most forceful of the five or so retorts he had to choose from. He breathed out audibly but didn't turn toward the source of the voice. "Big Brother. The battle cry of the paranoid." More quiet titters. It had been the right choice. "Big Brother, as you say, is already watching drug users in the form of the DEA, FBI, and local law enforcement agencies. And what are they seeing? They're seeing people die. Children—in gun battles over territory, in crossfires, of AIDS, as crack babies. Remember a few years back when a group of vigilantes decided to poison the drug supply? Thousands died. You have a choice as an individual. If you don't want Big Brother to watch you, don't use drugs."

There was a smattering of applause. Positive, but respectful of the gravity of the subject matter.

"Okay, time for just one more," he said, raising his arm out over the crowd. "You, sir."

"Senator. Your rather harsh ideas on prison reform could be called ultraconservative and your ideas on drug legalization, though unique, would generally be considered far left. Time is getting short—a little more than three weeks to the election. Do you feel that your message is appealing enough to the public to move you out of third place?"

"That question sounds suspiciously professional," Hallorin said, in an easy, good-natured tone that he'd been practicing for months. "No reporters are allowed to ask questions today, you know. This forum is for the people."

"I'm an accountant. I swear!" came the unmiked reply.

Hallorin nodded and smiled engagingly. "Since I have your word . . . The problems you mention are interrelated, really. It seems to have become obvious that people are not reformed in prison—often the contrary is true. In some circles . . . " Hallorin didn't identify blacks by name, but paused slightly to let the audience fill that in for themselves. The strategic fanning of racial animosities was critical to his campaign. ". . . going to prison has become a badge of honor; a rite of passage. Let's look at the facts. Seventy percent of prisoners are nonviolent drug users. That's roughly a million and a quarter souls. Conservatively, it costs us twenty-two thousand dollars per year to keep them in jail. That's over twenty-seven *billion* dollars out of our pockets. And worse than the cost, we don't have room to keep killers, rapists, and the like on the inside. If we can free up space by releasing people who are not a threat to the safety of others, then we've made one heck of a first step to taking the streets back from the criminals."

He paused again to usher in a slight change of subject. "Perhaps it's time to say that the opportunity to live in a free society comes with certain requirements—rules. You can't kill anyone, for instance. Many of my colleagues seem to think that this is an unreasonable and unworkably complicated rule. I disagree. You know how I remember things? Sticky notes. Got 'em everywhere. So I propose that everyone could put one beside their bed so that it's the first thing they see in the morning. In big black letters it would say: 'Reminder: Don't kill anyone today.' I might even support funding to allow the government to give out packets of sticky notes, with that message preprinted on them, to every American."

He got a full laugh out of that one, as he'd expected.

"No more degrees, no more excuses. If you kill somebody and it wasn't an accident or self-defense, you go to prison for the rest of your life. Not to reform you, but to keep people who *can* follow the rules safe from you."

Out of the corner of his eye he could see one of his men jabbing desperately at his watch, and he nodded an imperceptible acknowledgment.

"I was told yesterday that the highest voter turnout in fifty years is expected for this election. That seems to surprise a lot of people. But not me. America knows that it has an opportunity to do something wonderful here. Good can come from all the pain we've suffered over these last few years. Let's make sure our children don't have to go through anything like this again."

The applause was polite but enthusiastic as he stepped away from the podium and was ushered through a door at the back by the Secret Service men who had been assigned to him. As always, they looked nervous. His utilitarian stances on the workings of the government, his outspoken criticism of popular politicians, and most of all his unwavering disrespect for the Arab world had produced quite a bit of speculation regarding the possibility of an attempt on his life. Good. That sense of danger sold tickets.

As they approached the exit, Hallorin slowed down, effectively using his solid two-hundred-and-fifty-pound frame to halt the procession. He had been told that he would meet with the press immediately after he'd finished in the auditorium. The head of his protection detail seemed to read his mind. "Sir, we've been instructed to escort you out immediately. Arrangements have been made to handle the press."

Hallorin didn't move. "What the hell are you talking about? Who gave that order?"

"Mr. Peck insisted."

Hallorin looked back down the hall toward the sound of his audience as they left the building. It had gone well. Better than expected. But the press still wasn't with him—he needed this meeting.

"Sir?"

"Goddamn it," he said between clenched teeth and then started moving again, allowing himself to be pushed toward the exit.

The interior of the natural gas–powered van had been reconfigured to be like that of a limousine: two sets of plush seats facing each other right behind a heavy glass pane that separated them from the driver. In the corner of one of those seats, with his head resting against a side window, was Roland Peck.

The van started moving the moment the side door slid shut, the motion appearing to cause Peck physical pain. Headlights from oncoming cars filtered through the tinted windows, making his skin glow stark white and coloring his bright red hair almost black.

"What the fuck, Roland?" Hallorin said angrily. "The press—"

"You did well, Senator," Peck interrupted. "Yes. I watched. Our people can handle the spin. A simple matter." Peck swallowed hard and flicked his nose with the forefinger of his right hand. It was another of the mannerisms Hallorin had come to know. There was a problem.

"The file," Hallorin said.

"We'll have it within forty-eight hours." Peck spoke without looking up and Hallorin felt a vague sense of nausea wash over him. He waited until it passed before he spoke again. "Tell me what happened, Roland."

"There was an accident."

Hallorin shot a hand out and grabbed hold of Peck's arm. His fingers went all the way around the man's thin bicep and overlapped in the back. "Tell me what happened, Roland!" Peck still didn't look up, so Hallorin increased the pressure on his arm until a wince started to spread across Peck's thin face. He almost looked like he was going to cry.

"There was an accident. An accident . . . one of our men is dead."

Hallorin released him and fell back in his seat, the words ringing in his head.

Peck still didn't make eye contact, but the story finally started to flow in frightened stops and starts. "I don't know how it happened. I left only for a moment. There were two of our men in the room and Newberry was tied up. The woman . . . wasn't."

"Stop," Hallorin said, cutting off what he knew would be an incoherent jumble of excuses, facts, and speculation. "Who's dead?"

"Anderson. He went through a window and . . ." Peck put a hand up to his throat. "It cut here."

"What did you do with him?"

"It looks like a car accident—glass from the windshield."

"You said you left them with two men—what about the other?"

"I don't know what happened—he says that the woman pushed him and he fell against the edge of the bed. He was knocked unconscious long enough for her to untie Newberry and get out through the window."

"Who is 'he'?"

"McMillan."

Hallorin knew both men. State troopers who had been with him for a number of years. He'd kept the most loyal of them around despite the increasing involvement of the Secret Service as his candidacy had evolved. The Secret Service had no allegiance. "Is there any reason not to believe him?"

Peck shook his head miserably. "No . . . I don't know."

Hallorin ran his hand through his hair and looked out over the unfamiliar landscape of Columbus, Ohio. History and fate had lined it all up in front of him: the recent scandals that had rocked the government, the onset of the economic disaster he'd foretold, the existence of the Prodigy file. The American people were like children: noisy about their need for independence when things were going their way, but ready to crawl back to their parents when that good fortune turned. This was his time in history. His time.

"Look at me, Roland."

He didn't move.

"Look at me!"

Peck slowly raised his head.

"You said forty-eight hours. That you'd have them and the file in forty-eight hours."

Peck looked like he was trying to shrink back further, but the glass behind him wouldn't allow it. "It's hard, Senator. Hard. We'll find the boy. Yes. Soon. And when we find him, we'll have the file. But the girl.

We know so little about her. And it's so hard to learn more. We can't allow anything we do to be traced back to us."

"*You* can't let anything be traced back to *you*," Hallorin corrected. "She's seen you, hasn't she?" He let that hang for a moment. Peck was valuable to him—incredibly so, but not indispensable. It would be a shame to lose him now after spending so many years learning to manipulate his many psychoses and insecurities. Yes, it would be terribly inconvenient, but if he had to, he would distance himself from the younger man and use the loyalty he had so carefully cultivated to force Peck to take any blame that could be directed at him.

"She's seen me," Peck admitted finally. "Yes, she's seen me."

"If she isn't found soon it may be necessary for you to bring in someone from the outside to help in the search. Someone not connected to us." Hallorin reached out again, this time taking Peck's face in his hands. "What will happen to all your plans without the file, Roland? Everything was so perfect. You made everything so perfect."

It had taken a great deal of time and a number of expensive psychologists, but Hallorin had finally come to understand Roland Peck. The external trappings of power didn't interest him. Only the complete dominance that was virtually impossible at this time in history meant anything. Hallorin had initially gained his loyalty, and love, by putting him in control of the marketing for his business empire. Through using his genius to create ways to tell people what to think and feel, Peck had gleaned just enough of that sense of dominance to keep him hooked.

Hallorin had put no constraints on Peck's actions with regard to the woman who had been with Tristan Newberry. While her death would have undoubtedly been rather imaginative and unpleasant, it would have been a gluttonous feeding for Peck's unusual psychological and sexual needs—another gift from Hallorin that would further bind the man to him.

"Find the file, Roland," Hallorin said. "Imagine what it could mean for you if we were in the White House."

12

Darby Moore wrapped her arms around her knees and looked down on the gray-blue mirror that was Summersville Lake. The wind was gusting gently, making the sun bouncing off the water go from a dull glow to a blinding flash every few seconds. She adjusted her position for what must have been the thousandth time, trying to get comfortable in the rocky alcove nature had carved from the dense foliage, and trying to stay calm.

She was completely invisible to anyone hiking on the trail system or climbing on the cliffs that rose above her, but the amphitheater-like rock formations bounced sound in her direction. If Tristan called to her, she'd hear.

It had taken her twelve hours from the time she'd watched Tristan limp away to when she finally came to the mouth of the canyon she had descended into—nine of those hours in the dark. The town of Conrad, Maryland, had been another few exposed miles through open fields and unprotected roads.

She'd kept out of sight as much as a dirt- and sweat-encrusted twenty-seven-year-old woman could, working her way through the quiet streets and finally slipping into an alley across from the police station. She'd watched the cops moving back and forth in the large picture window for a long time, trying to figure out what to do.

Finally, she'd decided that she had no choice. If Tristan hadn't already been caught, he would be soon—she had to go in and tell them what happened.

She had stepped from the alley and was about to start across the street when the familiar face of the man who had let her and Tristan escape appeared in the police station window. She ducked back out of sight and watched him walk out to the street, followed by a man in uniform. They spoke for a few more minutes, finally breaking off their conversation when a dark gray Ford pulled up. She didn't recognize the man driving, but she remembered the red-haired man in the backseat very clearly.

She'd taken off down the alley and in a few minutes found the only bank in town. She spent most of the next four hours in a small park with her back pressed against an oak bordered by tall bushes, waiting for what little money she had to be wired from her bank in Wyoming.

After that, she'd walked to the outskirts of town and found the old used car lot she'd passed on the way in. The little Toyota pickup truck she'd purchased there was worth about two thousand dollars. It had cost her forty-five hundred. The man who ran the lot had obviously smelled blood when she'd walked up. He'd protested at first—saying that it was impossible to sell her a car with no ID—but the protest hadn't had much emotional content. The money—nearly all she had—changed his mind.

Darby pulled what was left of her cash from the waistband of her shorts and smoothed it out on her lap, counting it for the third time that day. Four hundred and twenty-six dollars. Normally, enough to live on for months. But things weren't exactly normal.

She turned her head at the sound of a shouted obscenity floating down to her from the cliffs above. Tristan wasn't coming, she knew that. She'd probably known it the moment she'd left him. She shouldn't have let him go off on his own. She should have stayed with him no matter what.

Darby stood, careful not to bump into the branches around her and alert anyone to her presence. If someone saw her, they'd most likely recognize her. And if they recognized her, it wouldn't take long before every climber within a hundred-mile radius knew she was here. After that, it was inevitable that the news would leak out of the climbing community and reach the men who were undoubtedly after her—if they hadn't guessed she was here already.

She started back toward the clearing where the truck was parked, knowing what she had to do, and trying to convince herself that it was the smart move. In the end, though, she knew better. She was acting solely out of fear and guilt—two of the very worst emotions to base decisions on.

There was no path, and the light was failing. It was still familiar to her, though. If she kept going straight through the trees, she would end up at the top of the climb she'd been working on. From there, she'd be able to see down into the clearing where she'd parked her van.

She was vaguely aware that every step she took was a little slower than the last, but continued to force herself forward. Every few seconds she'd go perfectly still and listen for any sound that could be human. Then she'd look around her, trying to penetrate the shadows created by the trees and the thick bushes strangling them.

As she slid down a moss-covered rock into a deep puddle of muddy water and wet leaves, she noticed a dim glow gaining strength in front of her. At first she'd thought it was natural—the stronger light in the open clearing she was moving toward. But when it became obvious that it was man-made, she slammed her back against a large tree and slid down beneath it.

What the hell was she doing there? They'd be waiting for sure—armed men who wouldn't let her surprise them again. They'd probably guessed what direction she'd be coming from, too. They were probably all around her, right now, waiting for an opportunity to grab her without having to fire a shot and cause a stir in the people camped around the river.

She felt the tears start to well up again, but clenched her eyes shut and squelched them. She'd been in tough situations before, she told herself, and never resorted to crying. The tears couldn't be stopped through reason though, and soon she could feel them running down her cheeks, leaving narrow streaks that cooled quickly in the mountain air.

What was wrong with her? The answer came easily. She'd never cried before because she always known what to do. Dig in and wait out a storm or try to outrun it. Continue up a climb, back off, or bivy. She had her years of experience to rely on.

But her experience didn't extend to people purposefully trying to kill her. What was the right decision? She had no idea who was after her or who she could trust. Certainly not the police or government. The men in the file Tristan had stolen probably owned the government.

Darby looked back into the woods she'd come through, trying to penetrate the deepening shadows. She wanted to run. To get as far away from all this as she could. But she couldn't. Not yet.

She crawled now, slowly and quietly toward the dim glow in front of her. It wasn't long before she could hear the unintelligible hum of conversation over the sound of the wind and flowing water. Only a few more feet. She dropped to her belly and slid forward, inch by inch.

When she'd decided to come back here, she'd expected to find the clearing dead silent and her van transformed from her home and primary source of transportation to bait for a trap to capture her. She couldn't have been more wrong.

The clearing was bustling with activity. The glow came from the headlights of no fewer than five cars encircling her van. There were men and women everywhere—some in casual clothes, some in police uniforms, some in suits.

A camera flashed and tinged the windows of her van pink. She thought it was just a reflection at first, but when the man with the camera moved, she saw it. A single, bare foot hanging out of the open side door. From where she lay, she could see that it was covered in blood.

Darby rolled on her back and looked through the trees at the sky. The first stars were starting to burn in the east but weren't yet strong enough to close in on the just-set sun. She tried to concentrate on them and block out everything else, but it was impossible.

She'd seen dead people before. A friend of hers—a good friend—had died in her arms on K2. It had been years ago, but she could still remember the small, bright patches of blue above them as the violently gusting wind opened up cuts in the clouds and then, just as quickly, sealed them. He'd joked about having her arrange his limbs like a Roman statue—so that future climbers could enjoy a little art on their way to the summit. Then he was gone.

This felt so different, though. For Tristan to die at the hands of men who would kill for things that meant nothing—money, a job that impressed people, power—seemed so useless.

He'd been stupid getting himself involved in this. He'd always been reckless, full of plans and goals that he didn't have the focus to achieve. He had been guilty of always searching for the scam, the easy way. But he didn't deserve this.

Darby sat up slowly, feeling her head swim a little as the blood rushed from it, and from the realization that the men and women below her probably thought she'd killed Tristan. She wanted to go down there, to tell them what happened, to get them to punish the people who had done this to her friend. But that was impossible. The local cops already hated people like her and would be dying to believe that she was responsible. They would throw her in jail, then, later that day, someone in a suit would show up asking about her. The cops would hand her over and that would be it.

Darby moved to the edge of the cliff again and looked down into the clearing. The people looked like they were starting to collect near the open door of the van. Some were putting on gloves, undoubtedly in preparation for moving Tristan's body.

She buried her face in the cool leaves covering the ground and refused to cry. Instead she tried to picture him alive. To pretend for a moment that none of this had ever happened.

13

"**M**ark, wait!"

Carrie tried to keep up with him as he threw the car door open and began a half stalk, half run toward the elaborate Dupont Circle townhouse, but she was slowed by the ancient brick driveway. Her shoes were more appropriate for the quiet dinner she'd been expecting than for chasing her enraged boyfriend around D.C. When was she going to learn to be more prepared for these romantic getaways?

She managed to slip her shoes off without slowing her forward momentum much and made it through the heavy double doors before they had swung completely shut again. The entry hall was empty, but she could hear Beamon's footsteps as they continued their charge toward the back of the house. She picked up her pace a bit, but then slowed and finally stopped when she realized that chasing after him had been a reflex more than anything else. She hadn't thought about what she would do if she actually caught up. She had seen this, or something like it, coming for a long time. But he hadn't. He wouldn't.

In some ways he really was the jaded iconoclast he liked to see himself as. But beneath it all, he loved the FBI—the street agents who made it run, the life it had given him. And more, he needed it—or at least thought he did. Maybe she should have been more forceful in trying to drag him into reality, in telling him that his powerful sense of loyalty was just a little outdated and completely misguided. But then she'd be the cynic, wouldn't she?

Carrie was still standing in the entryway contemplating various plans of action when the shouts started deep in the house. It seemed almost certain that the evening would be more pleasant if she just waited in the car. Or maybe on one of the small boulders that adorned Tom Sherman's front yard. It was kind of a nice evening—cool but not cold . . .

God, she was turning into a coward. She took a deep breath and started through the old house. No matter how much she wanted to, there was really no way she could sit this one out.

When she pushed through the door to the kitchen, she saw that Tom Sherman was sitting at the dining table in a pair of slacks and an undershirt. The calm, sad expression that always seemed to grace his pleasantly lined face was still there as he watched Beamon pace back and forth, gesturing wildly and spewing an enraged diatribe, seemingly without ever pausing to take a breath. The target of his barrage was a little murky—it seemed to be aimed alternately at himself, the FBI, the wall, the floor, and Sherman.

Carrie took a seat on an interesting looking, but ultimately uncomfortable, seventeenth-century chair in the corner and watched the man she loved slowly run out of energy, falter, and finally go quiet in the middle of the room.

"You never cease to amaze me, Mark," Sherman said after a few moments of silence. He stood, walked around to the sink, and started casually loading dishes into the dishwasher. "Do you ever look outside that little bubble you keep around yourself? The economy's blown itself apart and America's looking for someone to take the blame. That caught our elected officials by surprise at first, but they eventually rallied. They orchestrated a perfect strategy of pointing fingers in irrelevant locations. They had the people completely under control. Voters blamed everyone but their guy and everyone's job was safe. Then what do you do? You release a bunch of phone taps that show America exactly what kind of people they've been putting in office and cause the fall of some of the most powerful politicians in the country. You almost single-handedly create an environment where the media is judged solely on how much dirt they can dig up, and voters place the blame for their unemployment, or bankruptcy, or whatever, firmly in the lap of men and women they have the power to vote out of office."

"I had nothing to do with the leaking of those tapes, Tommy," Beamon said angrily. "And you damn well know that."

Sherman was looking at him like he was a slow child. "No one cares, Mark. In the public's mind, you *are* the tapes—you're the one who found them. And since you and the tapes are one and the same, the powers that be figure that discrediting you is the same as discrediting them. And in the end, they might be right."

"They might be right?" Beamon seemed to have regained his energy and was shouting again. "They're fucking cassette tapes! My being in jail isn't going to erase them! There's no subjective ground here!"

"For a self-professed cynic, Mark, you live in a strangely idyllic world. Are you trying to say to me that the American people are too smart to let a bunch of politicians spin things right out of their heads?"

"Not this time! There is just no goddamn way!" Beamon yelled, turning his back to Sherman and facing the wall again. "You think the media is going to back-page evidence of major felonies by some of the most powerful people in the country because I threw away a piece of paper?"

Carrie watched Tom Sherman as he let out a humorless laugh and dried his hands on a dishtowel. She was thinking about how comfortable that rock out front had looked. This was more than she really wanted to know about the workings of the American government.

"You know what the Beltway Boys are doing right now, Mark?" Sherman said. "They're sacrificing all sorts of interesting information and people to the media—cutting off a few fingers to save their hand. And all they're asking in return is that the press focus a little attention on yet another newspaper-selling scandal. You underestimate your own celebrity, Mark. The media's going to sell a lot of newspapers and ad time when your story breaks. In the end it's all about two things: power and money. And power doesn't exist without money, so there's really only one thing."

Carrie felt an almost physical pain as she watched Mark Beamon fall into a chair, his entire body bowing in defeat. He seemed to shrink and get swallowed up by the room as he sat there with his head in his hands. Finally, he looked up at Sherman and then over at her. "Fuck it," she heard him say as he stood and started for the door that led into the hallway.

"Wait, Mark," Sherman called after him. "Come back in here and sit down. Let's talk about this."

He didn't seem to hear; he just kept walking and finally disappeared down the hall.

"I'm sorry, Carrie," Sherman said, turning in her direction. "I haven't made your life any easier, have I? I could have handled that better."

She shook her head. "It's not your fault. He should have been listening to you months ago. But now it's too late, isn't it?"

Sherman sat back down at the kitchen table. "I don't know anymore. It's gotten so big, Carrie . . ." He looked almost as deflated as Mark. "I've got calls in to no less than ten people. I should know more tomorrow."

Carrie stood and walked over to him, putting a hand on his shoulder. "You're a good friend to him, Tom. I know he doesn't tell you how much he appreciates everything you've done for him over the years, but he does. I think probably more than you can imagine."

Sherman smiled sadly and Carrie broke away, starting toward the front of the house. She paused for a moment before she left the kitchen and looked back one last time. "Do you think he could really go to jail, Tom?"

Sherman closed his eyes and nodded.

Carrie slid into the driver's seat of the car just in time to watch Beamon shove a crumpled pack of cigarettes back into the glove compartment. The image of him sitting there alone smoking a slightly bent cigarette was somehow the most depressing yet.

"Are you okay, Mark?"

"Sure."

She started the car but left it in Park. "You didn't do anything wrong."

He looked over at her, his face strangely blank. "There is no right and wrong anymore. Weren't you listening?"

"Yes, there is. You did what had to be done and you were blindsided by a bunch of people who have no sense of honor or compassion. You saved that little girl when no one else could."

Beamon took a long drag from the cigarette. "I used to think that was what set me apart, you know? That I always did what I thought was right and didn't give much thought to the consequences. But I think now it was just ego—that I'm no different than anybody else. Maybe everybody always does what they think is right and it's all just a matter of what you tell yourself the high ground is." The smile that suddenly spread across his face surprised her. "See what you've done, Carrie? You've made me introspective. I think it would have been safer for you to pass out matches at grade schools."

"A little introspection never hurt anyone, Mark." She wasn't actually dead sure that was true in this case, but it sounded good.

"Carrie . . ."

There was a depth of emotion in his voice that she wasn't sure she'd ever heard before. She held her finger up and pointed it directly at his nose. "You sound like you're about to say something deep. Some situations just call for quiet contemplation. And a lot of times, silent contemplation is even better." She reached for the steering column to put the car in Drive, but Beamon put a hand on hers and stopped her.

"I've been stupid, Carrie. Tom's right—"

"You held on too hard, Mark. You trusted some people you thought were your friends because if the situations were reversed they could have trusted you. There's nothing wrong with not seeing the entire world in shades of black."

Beamon nodded thoughtfully and leaned the back of his head against the passenger side window. "Well, it looks like my rose-colored glasses have me in a hell of a bind."

Carrie let out a short laugh that sounded a little choked, even to her. "You know one of the things I like best about you, Mark?"

"I've thought about it a lot. I have no idea."

"When all my friends at work start talking about what their significant others do for a living, it's always accountant this, lawyer that, professor this, nurse that. Then I get to say, 'Oh, Mark's the head of the FBI here.' Much more interesting, don't you think? Kind of a conversation piece."

"I guess." His voice sounded distant.

"Well, just try to imagine the rise I could get at a cocktail party with, 'He's doing time in a federal pen on an obstruction rap.'"

Beamon tried to smile but failed miserably. "Funny, Carrie. You're a funny lady. But what about Emory? She's getting just old enough to understand some of this. How are you going to explain it to her?"

"Let me worry about that."

He shook his head. "No. This isn't fair to you anymore."

"Mark, what are you doing?" she said in a cautioning tone. "You're—"

He finished her sentence for her. "Going to jail. And I'm not sure for how long. When I get out, my career will be gone and my prospects will be, well, let's say . . . limited. You're a beautiful woman with a wonderful daughter, a great career, and a terrific life back in Flagstaff."

He reached out and pulled the handle on the car door, opening it a crack.

"Mark, wait. I know you think you know what you're doing right now. But don't do this to us. And don't try to make my decisions for me."

"You know I'm right, Carrie. Don't make this any harder than it has to be," he said, opening the door the rest of the way and sliding out onto the sidewalk.

"Mark, get back in the car, right now."

"I can't. I know you too well. You'll figure out a way to talk me out of this." He leaned back through the door for a moment. "Tell Emory that I'm going to miss her."

Carrie had never seen him like this; he seemed to barely be able to get the words out.

"Don't do this, Mark."

He pushed the door closed and Carrie watched him walk stiffly down the sidewalk. When he had disappeared completely into the shadows created by the widely spaced streetlights, she leaned her forehead against the steering wheel and forced herself to take a few deep breaths. How could she have let that happen?

14

The sun had long since passed over the bright red fin of rock Darby Moore was lying on, but its heat still radiated into her chest and stomach. She couldn't bring herself to move. Somehow that fading warmth softened the image of Tristan's lifeless foot hanging from the open door of her van and drained some of the color from the pool of blood in Maryland where she'd left that man dying.

The thirty-hour drive to Utah had been agonizing. Near panic had hit her every time she passed a police car. She'd been too scared to stop anywhere familiar, thinking that someone would be waiting for her. As the little truck had turned into a self-imposed prison, she'd become more and more certain that the file Tristan told her about was the answer—the only answer. She had to get to it first, then she could use it. How, exactly, she didn't know. To expose the men who'd killed her friend? To bargain for her life? To clear her name? It didn't matter—what was important now is that she get it. Then she'd have time to think. The one thing she was certain of was that without some leverage, those men would kill her without any more thought or remorse than they'd give to swatting a fly.

Darby tried to relax and let the knots in her back loosen as she surveyed the landscape below her. From where she lay, she could see the brown/green of the canyon floor some three hundred feet below, the reddish-orange rock surrounding it, and the distant sandstone arches that leaked the sunset through them. She scooted forward a few feet and hung her head fully over the cliff, examining the way it fell away to the canyon below.

They were getting closer.

There were three of them—she was sure of that now. It was a long way down, but she could make out that two were rather heavyset, with short, dark hair and wearing bright blue jackets, jeans, and what looked like hiking boots or heavy trail shoes. Both seemed to be having a difficult time negotiating the broken rock, deep sand, and jagged plants typical in this part of Utah. They may not have been the same men who had kidnapped her and murdered Tristan, but they certainly looked like they were cut from the same generic cloth.

The third man was more of a mystery. He was wearing shorts, sandals, and a light jacket with a patch across the shoulder that reflected with the familiar color and intensity of duct tape. Unlike his more conservative companions, his hair was a colorless blond and tied back in a ponytail. More interestingly, though, his gait seemed effortless and natural as he hopped from boulder to boulder, diverting gracefully up a sandstone ramp or ledge every few minutes to get a fresh perspective on the terrain.

The small cave where Tristan had hidden the file he'd stolen was about two hundred and fifty feet below her and some fifty feet above the canyon floor. He'd obviously told them where the file was before he'd died. She tried not to think what they had done to coerce him.

Fortunately for her, the men below were discovering something she'd learned long ago—everything looked the same in this part of the world. She'd been watching them for almost two hours now as they moved methodically along the desert floor, agonizing over what she should do and hoping that they would abandon their search as the setting sun threw the canyon into shadow. No such luck.

Darby propped herself up on her elbows and looked down at herself. She'd tracked down a sweatshirt at a Goodwill store somewhere in Kansas, but now regretted the green color, which would stand out against the dusty red of the cliff face. At the same Goodwill she'd purchased, for $1.50, the threadbare pack that was strapped to her back.

The climbing shoes she so desperately needed to get down to the cave had been impossible to obtain. The chance of her walking into a climbing shop without being recognized was about zero, and that left her with nothing but her sandals.

Though better than tennis shoes, climbing in sandals was roughly the athletic equivalent of running hurdles in heels—though the penalty wasn't a twisted ankle. It was, in the colorful slang of climbing, decking. She tried not to, but couldn't help speculating as to the size and shape of the stain she'd likely leave if she cratered from this height. The image of her body spread-eagle on the desert floor in the middle of a red spiderweb pattern of her own blood was actually vivid enough to briefly supplant everything else cluttering her mind. She'd been left with no alternative that she could see, though. No use in whining about it now.

Darby looked over the edge of the cliff again and decided that the timing was as good as it was going to get. The sheer sandstone wall was shadowed enough that she wouldn't stand out too much, but not so dark that she wouldn't be able to find handholds. Unless, of course, there were none.

Darby took a deep breath, did her best to empty her mind, and swung around so that her legs hung over the precipice. After a few more unintentionally short breaths, she slowly let her body slide off the edge, leaving her dangling straight-armed from the overhanging tongue of rock she'd been lying on top of moments before.

The wind buffeted her gently as she looked down past the brown of her legs and the bloodstains still clinging to her sandals, through three hundred feet of empty air, to the green juniper trees that looked like tiny bushes on the canyon floor. She could feel the blood starting to flow into her forearms and the sweat that would soon become slick, leaking from her palms. She focused all her concentration on a six-inch ledge a few feet in front of her, trying to stay completely focused. Fear was a very real danger in climbing—it wreaked havoc on judgment and balance, and caused premature exhaustion.

She swung her legs at the ledge, feeling her hands slip slightly when she missed by a solid inch. The adrenaline that she was trying so hard to keep under control surged wildly as her forward momentum petered out and her body weight started to carry her into a backward swing that had the very real potential to pull her off and send her into space. She curled her knees to her chest to try to deaden the motion and strained with her fingers to hold the sloping edge of the cliff. Her hands started to slide back, out of control, but at the last moment found a tiny indentation in the rock. It turned out to be just enough to save her.

The blood pulsing through her forearms was starting to give her the familiar feeling of her skin being too tight. She knew from experience that she had only a few more seconds before the lactic acid started building up in her muscles and she began to lose her contact strength.

She kicked out again, harder this time, knowing that if she missed, she wouldn't be able to control the increased force of her back swing. At the last possible moment, she pulled in hard with her stomach muscles and felt the edge of her sandal catch on the ledge. She used it to pull herself in a little and let her leg take as much weight off her hands as possible—but there was no way to know if it would be enough. She closed her eyes for a moment and then let go with her left hand, bringing it slowly down in front of her as her right hand started to slip again. She managed to lodge it in a fist-sized crack at chest level just as her right hand cut loose.

It held.

She quickly swung her entire body to the right and wedged herself into a wide groove in the rock, her breath coming way too fast. Fear again, she told herself—but knew it was something more. She felt strangely at odds with nature—something she'd never experienced before. The rock was too sharp under her hands and the wind too cold against the sweat dripping down her back. She felt . . .

Darby wiggled into a slightly more secure position, reminding herself that this probably wasn't an ideal time for philosophizing. The three men below her had gathered around something that might have been a backpack, and the blond one seemed to be passing something out to the others. A moment later she saw the individual beams of light leap magically from their hands and cut through the approaching darkness. Flashlights.

Darby started down the chimney-sized groove in the rock, staying as far back in it as possible in an effort to remain invisible, but soon found that the plan had a substantial drawback. The darkness in the small fissure was deepening more each minute, making it increasingly difficult to find the small hand and footholds that were the only things keeping her from falling the remaining two hundred and fifty feet to the ground. She was being forced to rely almost completely on the friction she could generate by pressing her hands and feet on one side of the groove and her back on the other.

Her progress was painfully slow and so much harder than it should have been. If the lack of a rope and harness was eating at her concentration, the lack of the sure-footedness of climbing shoes was destroying it.

No whining, she reminded herself. The situation was what it was.

It took over an hour for her to work her way to a small alcove ten feet above the cave that contained Tristan's file. There had been two very close calls on her way down—one when she'd briefly run out of holds and friction, and the other when she'd knocked off a sizable rock that had, thanks to a soft sand landing, gone unnoticed.

The men scouring the canyon floor were close now. She couldn't see them from her position, but she could hear the crunch of their footsteps and an occasional eruption of a voice. When she finally worked herself into a position where she could spy on them, she saw that they were nearly invisible. Shadows behind the powerful beams of their flashlights, just like . . .

She waited until their search pattern had focused them in another direction and swung quickly over the lip of the cave. Her luck had finally run out, though, and she felt her hands slide from an unexpectedly polished surface on the rock and then the sudden weightlessness of falling.

It had been years since she and Tristan had stashed their gear in this cave, but she seemed to remember that its floor extended out further than its roof. In most cases she had a good memory for that kind of thing. But if this was one of those rare occasions that she'd confused one cliff with another, her fall would be broken by a pile of jagged rocks fifty feet below. And then all her problems would be solved.

She hit the floor of the cave hard. Unconsciously she had pitched her weight forward, away from the precipice, and she went face-first into the rock. Dazed, she laid there for a few moments and listened to the voices of the men outside grow loud.

They'd heard her.

She struggled into a crouch but then froze, not sure what to do. There was no time.

"What about over there?"

It was the first full sentence she'd been able to make out, no doubt thanks to the acoustics of the cave. The deep, masculine voice had a complete lack of urgency to it. She moved back to the mouth of the cave and saw the flashlights still moving in a more or less random pattern a hundred meters away. The voices hadn't turned to shouts, she realized; it was just acoustics.

She took a moment to collect herself, then crawled to the back of the cave, feeling around her in the darkness for anything that didn't belong. After a few moments the voices started to grow again in volume. This time it wasn't an audio illusion, though; the men had redirected their search and were getting closer.

When Darby reached the back wall, she turned left and started along it in a straight line, trying to conduct as methodical a search as possible under the circumstances. There were broken rocks strewn everywhere, and she could already feel the blood flowing from her bare knees and shins. But that didn't bother her as much as the realization that Tristan would have most likely buried the file with the rubble scattered around the floor of the cave. And there was no way to feel the difference between a natural and man-made formation.

"What's up there?"

She froze at the sound of the man's voice as it echoed around her.

The crack of sandstone on sandstone was unmistakable as someone started up the talus field below.

You're still okay, she told herself. *You're still okay.*

The fifty-foot climb up to the cave was difficult—solid 5.10. Anyone who would try that in this light, without the protection of a rope, was probably a friend or at least acquaintance of hers. And if they took the time to set up a rope belay, she could be long gone by the time one of them made it all the way up. But not without the file.

She pulled the backpack off her shoulders and fished around in it until she found the lighter at the bottom. The desperate shouts started below the moment she lit it and the cave came flickering to life around her.

She ran around the cave throwing rocks off any formation that looked like it might not have occurred naturally, the sound mimicking the clatter rising from below as the three men scurried to the base of the cliff.

"Fuck the shoes! Go! Go!"

Darby froze for a moment and listened.

"Move, goddamnit!"

The voice was deafening, as though it was aimed directly up at the cave. Or perhaps at someone climbing toward her. She went back to her search, frantically kicking and throwing rocks at the back of the cave until she started to hear the labored breathing and occasional grunts of a climber moving toward her. She picked up a rock and considered rolling it off the edge, but couldn't bring herself to do it. What if it was just a local guide they'd hired? Maybe someone she knew?

A gust of wind blew the lighter out as she started back the way she'd come. She flicked it again and the intensity of the flame as it exploded to life created a dull glitter beneath the sand at her feet.

She dropped to her knees and brushed it away, feeling the unmistakable cold smoothness of plastic. She shoved a large rock aside and started to dig as the sound of the mysterious climber continued to close in on her.

Whatever it was, it had been encased in at least a half-inch of shrink-wrap. She held it up for a moment, but the glare from the flame was too intermittent to see anything but its shape and deep brown color.

Darby shoved it in her backpack and slung the pack over her shoulders just as a loud grunt echoed through the cave and the blond head of the man she'd seen from the cliff top appeared at the mouth. She ran within three feet of him as he struggled to pull himself over the lip, dropping the lighter and lunging at a line of softball-sized holes gouged in the rock by a million years of water flow.

She forced herself not to look back again—there was nothing she could do but go straight up. Moving right would bring her into view of the men on the ground and left would take her back into the cave. Desperation gripped her as she threw herself recklessly at each hand- and foothold, forgetting how high she was off the ground, forgetting everything but the man behind her.

She remembered the huge hold at the base of the little alcove above the cave and launched herself at it. She felt her feet and hands leave the wall and her body arc through the night air as a gunshot sounded and a bullet skittered off the rock close enough to kick dust into her eyes. She latched the hold with her right hand and used the powerful muscles in her arm to continue her upward momentum. She rolled into the alcove and hit the back of it hard, then froze and listened for the sound of pursuit.

Nothing—only the sound of her own breathing. Then, a moment later, a quiet, heavily accented voice. "Darby?"

She leaned forward out of reflex. The voice was familiar.

"Darby, come down."

That was enough to put a nationality to the man. Slovenian. She scooted forward a few inches. "Vili?"

"Come down now, Darby."

She almost leaned her head over the edge to see if there was enough light to make out his features, but then remembered the gunshot that couldn't have come from anyone but him.

"You shot at me, Vili."

"Just to scare you." His voice was calm and even, but obviously forced. "The men I am with hired me to help them find you. To bring you to the police for what you did to Tristan."

"I didn't do anything to Tristan. You know that."

"Of course I do. Come down, we will take you to your police. You can tell them."

Whoever the people after her were, they were smart. It had only been three days since she'd escaped from the old farmhouse and they'd already found the perfect person to track her. Vili had been a professional climber for years—he knew the ins and outs of her lifestyle and probably most of her friends. But more, he hated her with a burning passion that she would never understand.

It had been three years ago on Ama Dablam in the Himalaya. She'd gone there to attempt a solo ascent of a new route on the west face of the mountain. But he'd sneaked in a week before, with a map she'd drawn, to try to steal the ascent out from under her.

She'd found him about halfway up it, his leg broken and half frozen. She'd almost died about ten times getting him down. He hadn't even tried to help; he'd just lain there and whimpered while she dragged him along the steep slopes in subzero temperatures and blinding snow. A week after he'd been evacuated by helicopter, she'd completed the route, and worse, made the cover of *Climbing* magazine.

She hadn't really been looking for gratitude and she hadn't gotten any. Apparently embarrassed by his behavior and for being saved by a woman, he'd somehow managed to convince himself that his accident had been her fault and that she'd stolen the climb from him.

"Why are you doing this, Vili?"

A shout from below floated up, but he didn't answer it. "To show the world who you really are, Darby. What you did to me."

"You would have died up there."

"You say!" His voice suddenly went from a whisper to a scream. "You forced me down. You took that climb from me!"

It occurred to her again just how pointless Tristan's death had been. He was the victim of the stunted, adolescent egos of supposedly full-grown men. Politicians searched for power, captains of industry pursued money. For climbers, it was glory. But it was all an illusion. No matter how much they amassed, they would still grow old and weak and die. Tristan should have known better.

Darby stood and looked up the pitch-black chimney cut into the rock behind her. She closed her eyes and tried to remember the most difficult sections that she had passed on her way down and project how hard they'd be in the dark and with the extra weight in her pack.

She calculated a one-in-three chance of making it to the top alive. That could be improved to fifty–fifty if she took her time, but the men below would undoubtedly take the same dirt road up the back that she had and try to be there to meet her.

"Wait!" Vili yelled when he heard Darby start up the chimney. "Darby! Wait!"

She continued on, picking up her pace when she heard him step around the edge of the cave and start the climb to the alcove. She found a spot that she could comfortably stand for a moment and looked down into the blackness. "There's a lot of loose rock up here, Vili."

She heard his progress come to a sudden halt. The meaning of her statement was clear—if he continued up behind her, she'd kick off enough debris to ensure that he took the express to the ground.

"Wait, Darby! Wait!" He switched to his native language, speaking slowly and deliberately, enunciating every word very carefully. Her Slovenian was horrible—self-taught during a six-month climbing trip there a few years back.

He repeated himself, even slower this time, and she struggled to translate. She couldn't nail every word, but the gist was that if she threw the file down he'd let her go and lead the men who had hired him away from her.

Darby reached up and tested a small flake in the rock that was just big enough for her to get her fingers behind. "Don't follow me, Vili. You won't make it," she said, pulling herself up a few more feet. He screamed something she couldn't translate and she heard the crack of another gunshot. She continued on, satisfied that there was no way he could hit her from where he was standing, and that he wouldn't follow. In the end, Vili Marcek was a coward.

15

Mark Beamon stared down at his coffee table—or more specifically, the half-eaten Big Mac resting on it. He reached out for the hamburger, but a slight cramping in his stomach redirected his hand to the cup full of Coke next to it. This was really pathetic. Not only had he grown accustomed to the no-fat, whole-grain, tree-hugger food that Carrie insisted on cooking day in and day out, he'd actually come to rely on it. His constitution had been so weakened by the endless procession of salads, bran muffins, and granola that he couldn't even drown his sorrows in a good fast food burger anymore.

Beamon pressed a button on the remote lying next to him on the sofa before he could start thinking about her again. Breaking off their relationship had been one of the hardest things he'd ever done—but he'd had no choice. As difficult as it was going to be to adjust to living without her and Emory, he knew he'd done the right thing. He had no right to drag them along behind him through this thing.

The television came to life, and the craggy yet earnest face of Robert Taylor, the Republican excuse for a presidential candidate, appeared on-screen. As always, he was talking in grand concepts: tradition, morality, ingenuity, family. The morality part seemed to be the focus tonight—or more specifically, the importance of bringing it back to a scandal-besieged political system. The confident words of a man too goddamn old and tedious to do anything that the papers would find even remotely provocative.

Beamon's eyes narrowed as Taylor started in on the meaning of integrity. Undoubtedly that old son of a bitch had spent his week shoveling the crap that Beamon was about to drown in—making deals that would save the Grand Old Party and destroy a certain hapless, former FBI agent. Nothing happened in Washington without the old man's knowledge and approval.

Beamon jabbed at the channel button and the screen flickered over to a group of well-dressed women, once again, discussing the presidential race. There didn't seem to be any escaping it. Politics was everything.

A few more jabs landed him a few more political saps. One last click and the imposing figure of David Hallorin sitting across from Larry King appeared on the screen. Beamon paused for a moment, remembering his meeting with Hallorin. He still wasn't sure exactly what had happened, or what Hallorin had hoped to accomplish.

Beamon more or less agreed with the man's politics, as much as he could agree with anyone's, and Hallorin had been reasonably pleasant in their meeting, but there was something else there; something at the edge of his perception. Maybe it was the fearful reaction of Hallorin's employees whenever Hallorin came within ten feet of them. More likely, though, it was just Beamon's all-encompassing distaste for anyone in Hallorin's line of work.

"Okay, Larry. You win," Hallorin said through the television's speakers. "Two minutes of complete, concise, honesty. That's all you can ask of a politician."

King took the challenge and said, simply, "Abortion."

Beamon laid the remote down next to him and watched Hallorin feign surprise at the directness of the question. "Starting with the tough stuff. Okay. I'm pro-choice. It's an intangible moral argument that's impossible to win by either side. In that kind of situation, a free country has to leave the decision to the individual." He looked into the camera. "Based on what we've seen lately, America's government officials can't keep their own houses in order. Do you want these men and women making choices for you about your family and health?"

"Prayer in school," King said, keeping him to his promise to be concise.

"Irrelevant!"

Beamon frowned deeply. That indignant utterance was becoming the catchphrase of Hallorin's campaign. It was showing up on bumper stickers with nearly the frequency of the "I Found It" slogan of the seventies, or the eighties' "Where's the Beef?"

Hallorin placed his large hands flat on the desk in front of him. "Children can get up early and pray at home, they can pray at lunch, they can pray after school." He shrugged. "If they want to, they can pray during class. The entire issue is ridiculous—invented by politicians to distract Americans from the problems the government has caused and is afraid to address."

Beamon watched Hallorin's eyes flash behind his—probably clear glass—spectacles. His handlers had obviously been trying to soften him, but the man still had an edge when he got riled.

"Family values."

Hallorin gave a little laugh through his nose. "I'm for them."

There was a silence too long for TV that it didn't look like Hallorin was going to fill, so King piped up. "Would you care to expand on that, Senator?"

Hallorin sighed. "As I've said before, I like and respect Robert Taylor, and I share his sense of nostalgia . . ."

Beamon went for another French fry during Hallorin's dramatic pause. He had to grudgingly admit that he respected the fact that Hallorin simply would not go negative on the Republican candidate who was kicking his ass in the polls. In fact, he seemed to be trying to make himself out to be a fan of Taylor's, only with a different spin on the world.

". . . I don't, however, share his fervor for this particular subject," Hallorin continued. "It's an issue that is simply beyond the government's control. What could I possibly do to reverse the trends of the last thirty-five years? Outlaw divorce? Legislate how much time you spend with your kids? I want a return to family values as much as anyone, but there's nothing I can do to bring it about. And no one else can either."

There was a knock at Beamon's door just as Larry King brought up the subject of capital punishment. Beamon hit the mute button but didn't get up. Other than Carrie, who was clearly giving him a wide berth, hardly anyone ever knocked on his door. Besides, he just wasn't in the mood for visitors at this particular moment.

After a few seconds it came again, with the forcefulness of a person who knew someone was home and had business more important than handing out a free copy of *The Watchtower*.

Beamon sighed quietly as he kicked his feet off the table and walked over to the door, yanking it open in one quick motion. "You're not here to serve me a subpoena are you?" he said to the man standing on his stoop. "Because if you are, I'm going to shoot you."

It wasn't that he really thought a man with a manicure and a two-thousand-dollar suit was working for that end of the court system, it was just that sometimes you felt like threatening somebody. "That's not a figure of speech, I have a gun."

The man's eyes widened and he stepped back, reaching into his silky wool jacket with comic slowness. "Are you Mark Beamon?"

Beamon didn't answer.

"I'm Christian Humbolt," he said, his hand reappearing from inside his jacket holding a business card. It identified him as a partner at Reynolds, Trent, and Layman—a law firm with New York, L.A., and D.C. addresses. "I was hoping I could have a moment of your time. I have a business proposal I'd like you to consider."

Beamon didn't move out of the doorway. He looked like he was telling the truth, but then, you could never tell with lawyers. More often than not, they themselves weren't sure. "Okay," he said finally. "You can come in. But not for long."

It occurred to Beamon that his tiny condo looked like it had been inhabited by a family of orangutans for the last month. And to add to the air of quiet dignity, he was wearing a pair of old slacks that he'd purchased when he was fifty pounds heavier and a stained Chicago Bulls T-shirt, perfectly complemented by his five o'clock shadow.

Beamon decided that he might as well complete the near perfect illusion of a paranoid schizophrenic ex-cop. "Have a seat. You can have the rest of that burger if you want it," he said as he continued into the kitchen.

At least he hoped it was only an illusion. He suddenly realized that he hadn't been outside since he'd returned from D.C.

"Uh, thanks," Humbolt said, examining the chair across from the sofa before he committed to sitting on it. "I just ate."

"How about a beer then?" Beamon opened the fridge and reached into the back as the immaculately groomed attorney considered the offer with a worried expression.

"Sure," he said, more to himself than to Beamon. "Yeah. A beer would probably be okay."

"So what is it I can do for you, Mr. Humbolt?" Beamon said, handing him an open can of Miller Lite and dropping back onto the sofa.

"I'm working for a gentleman who's interested in finding someone. I can't count how many resumes I've sent his way. . . ." Humbolt shrugged, suggesting that his client wasn't impressed with the options provided him thus far. "But when he heard that you might be available, he seemed very interested."

News of The Fall of Mark Beamon seemed to travel fast.

"Well, I'll tell you, Mr. Humbolt—"

"Christian."

"Christian. I don't have a resume. . . ."

"Your reputation speaks for itself."

Beamon wondered idly what it said and if he could sue it for slander.

"The job's yours, Mr. Beamon."

"Uh huh. Well, tell your employer that I appreciate his confidence, but I'm not really looking for side jobs."

Humbolt took a thoughtful sip of his beer and nodded. "I certainly understand. I think I might be able to change your mind, though."

"I really don't think you can."

"For a man with your background, this is a simple matter. I would think no more than a week or two."

That sounded dangerously like another deadline. Just what he didn't need.

"And it pays one hundred and fifty thousand dollars."

Beamon couldn't help but look up from his beer at that. He made some quick mental calculations. Assuming a good attorney charged three hundred dollars and hour, that bought . . . a hell of a lot of hours.

He believed it when the FBI said they'd do everything they could to see him disgraced for the greater good of the political establishment. If he decided not to take the deal they had offered him, would a hundred and fifty grand be enough to stand against that kind of a storm?

Beamon wagged a finger in the direction of the attorney. "See, there, Christian, you're making me think about things I promised myself I wouldn't think about till tomorrow. Besides, there's no such thing as an easy two-week job that pays that kind of money."

"Normally I'd agree with you, but this may be the exception." He paused for a moment. "Tell me, have you ever heard of Darby Moore?"

Beamon shook his head, still trying to calculate the cost of beating the U.S. government in its own courts.

Humbolt reached into his pocket, a little more confidently this time, and handed Beamon a photograph of a dark-haired, athletic-looking young woman somewhere in her mid-twenties. She was standing on an exotic-looking beach wearing a pair of cotton shorts and a tank top.

Beamon ran a finger along the neatly cut edge of the photograph. It seemed that there had been somebody standing next to the girl who didn't want to be identified. "I take it this is her?"

Humbolt nodded. "It hasn't gotten a great deal of press this far out, but her former boyfriend, a Tristan Newberry, was found brutally murdered in her van in West Virginia last week. They'd been on a trip together. Now, she's disappeared."

"Well, West Virginia can be a strange place. The locals—"

"No evidence of that," Humbolt cut in. "It's more likely that she killed Newberry in some kind of lover's spat and took off."

Beamon turned the photo over in his fingers. He had to admit it did sound easy. A twenty-something girl on the run. Go to her house, cut off her credit cards, then subcontract a few reasonably competent people to watch her friends and relatives.

"I'm not sure why you need me, Christian. The local cops might not be rocket scientists, but I'm betting they can turn this girl up."

"A normal girl, yes. Ms. Moore, though, is apparently a professional climber."

"A what?"

"Mountain climber."

"There's such a thing as a professional mountain climber?"

"So it would seem—though it doesn't pay very well. Ms. Moore's permanent address is a 1978 VW van. There's a fairly reliable story about her once living an entire year on less than three thousand dollars. At the time, she was residing in a tent in Yosemite National Park. Her income was generated primarily from collecting cans for their deposit value and occasionally helping the rangers rescue trapped and injured climbers. She speaks four languages fluently and she can get by in at least another four."

"I'm starting to see your problem."

"I thought you might."

Beamon was having a hard time keeping his disinterest level in the safety zone. God knew it wasn't an interesting case, but it *was* a case. Maybe the last one he'd ever look at. "Who's the kid she killed?"

Humbolt smiled and dug out a large envelope that he'd somehow been carrying around beneath his tailored jacket. He pulled another picture from it and handed it across the coffee table. Beamon's eyes lingered on Tristan Newberry for a moment—he was about the same age as the girl and spectacularly good looking, with features and a body that were almost too perfect to be natural. In this photo, Darby Moore was standing next to him, looking a little younger than in the other picture. The slight bend to her nose that had been visible in the first photograph wasn't evident in this one. Her hands were covered with heavy leather work gloves, one of which was wrapped around a brightly colored rope, the other resting on top of her head. Her face was lit up with a laugh. Beamon could almost feel the force of it through the tiny picture.

"We don't know a great deal about Newberry: He worked a low-level government job in Washington, he and Darby had a relationship that ended a few years back—"

"If I were to take this job, who would be my employer?"

"He prefers to remain anonymous."

Beamon nodded silently. People didn't part with a hundred and fifty grand easily and when they did, they generally wanted other people to know about it. Was his anonymous benefactor the one who had been cut from the first picture? A lover perhaps . . .

Beamon grimaced and forced his mind away from the problem and toward a mental image of himself eating frozen seal with a bunch of Eskimos while he chased this girl across an endless white glacier. "Mr. Humbolt. What do you think your firm would charge to defend a mid-level government employee who was being railroaded by a bunch of politicians and high-ranking bureaucrats?"

Humbolt took the shift in the conversation in stride. In fact, he looked like he expected it. "I don't really know."

Beamon just stared at him.

"I don't mean to compound the reputation of people in my line of work by not giving you a straight answer," he protested, "but I really can't. In some instances, you start rattling sabers and producing paper by the truckload and the government decides that it's just too much trouble." He snapped his fingers. "Dismissal. On the other hand, if they're motivated, they can be completely irrational in the amount of time and money they're willing to spend."

"Let's assume for a minute that they're extremely motivated."

Humbolt leaned back in his chair, but not before subtly making sure he wouldn't stick to anything. "I assume we're talking about your situation." His tone suggested that he knew more about Beamon's situation than he should have. "We'd charge a lot. And this is going to be as much a publicity matter as a legal one. You're going to need some top-notch people to spin the story right back at the government. The courageous, faithful public servant, stabbed in the back by the shadowy political brotherhood . . . that kind of thing."

Beamon sighed quietly. Not only was he looking at the cost of a legal team, but now there was a PR firm involved. He'd heard somewhere that the prison they sent the Watergate guys to had a nine-hole golf course. "I don't think I'm interested," he said, handing the pictures back to Humbolt. "Thanks again for the offer, though."

"Are you sure, Mr. Beamon? I realize you have a great deal to think about right now, but have you considered the benefit of a little diversion? Something to clear your head? Tell me, what can I do to change your mind?"

Beamon chewed on his thumbnail for a moment. As much as he hated to admit it, Humbolt was making sense. The walls of his condo were already starting to close in. It was going to be a long three weeks before he had to give the FBI his answer. And then there was the money . . .

"Three hundred thousand dollars. One hundred and fifty thousand up front. I keep that for my effort. The other one-fifty when I deliver. All expenses would be covered by you, of course."

Humbolt opened his mouth, obviously about to start negotiating, but then closed it and cocked his head. "Fine. You'll have a check tomorrow for the first one-fifty. One minor stipulation, though. Starting tomorrow, the one-fifty you get for delivery reduces by five thousand dollars per day."

Humbolt stood, leaving the envelope full of information on the table next to the remnants of Beamon's dinner. "Welcome to the private sector, Mr. Beamon, a place where results count and people don't quibble about insignificant amounts of money."

Beamon got to his feet and shook the man's hand with a touch of uncertainty. He needed the money and the diversion, that was for certain. But suddenly he was even less sure he wanted this job than when Humbolt arrived.

"What do you want me to do with her when I find her?" he said as the attorney started for the door.

"Don't contact her. Just let us know where she is. Our client wants to talk to her and convince her to turn herself in." He paused with his hand on the knob and nodded toward the envelope on the table. "It's all in there."

16

Grant Templeton paused outside the door to David Hallorin's office and put a hand on his young colleague's back. A deep silence had descended on the gothic cavern of a campaign headquarters, broken only occasionally by the rustling papers and echoing footsteps of the few remaining True Believers. It was Wednesday night, less than three weeks before the general election, and Hallorin was dead last—nine points behind Robert Taylor, the Republican front-runner, and an improved, but still pathetic, four points behind the devastatingly lackluster Democratic candidate. Templeton took a deep breath of the clean air in the hall, noting the complete lack of that seductive mix of sweat, cologne, and microwaveable food that he loved so much. Right now, this campaign smelled like it was preparing for the grave.

The young man next to him took a half step forward, but Templeton grabbed his shirt and held him back. His hand left a damp mark on the meticulously pressed back pleat.

This was the worst part of the most desperately painful job he'd ever had. The videotape in his hand contained selections from Hallorin's appearance on the *Larry King Show* the night before, and Templeton's job, as the official manager of this campaign, was to critique the senator's performance. A no-win situation, really. David Hallorin was not a man who took criticism lightly.

"Okay," Templeton said, mostly to himself. He pushed the door open and followed his eager young subordinate into the lion's den. Hallorin was on the phone, so he stopped in the middle of the floor and tried not to exist. The young man next to him continued on toward one of the chairs in front of Hallorin's desk, but Templeton stopped him, grabbing him by the back of the shirt again and increasing the size of the sweat stain on it. You didn't sit down in one of David Hallorin's chairs until he told you to. Templeton had learned that lesson quickly and painfully.

Hallorin spoke quietly into the phone for about another minute and then hung up, pointing to a chair. Templeton was aware of his boss' eyes on the young man with him as they sat. He knew that Hallorin was waiting for an explanation.

"Senator, this is Dave Jenkins. He's going to be doing our polls from now on."

Jenkins bobbed his head respectfully, but Hallorin didn't acknowledge his existence. "Where's Anthony?"

"He resigned, sir. Apparently got an offer he couldn't refuse from a—"

Hallorin wasn't listening. His face tightened and he stared out past the two men at the wall.

In all his years in the business of politics, Templeton had never run into anyone quite like Senator David Hallorin. The man seemed to think of the people who worked for him as liabilities instead of assets—leeches who had no real ability or drive themselves, so they had to attach themselves to him. And despite the fact that he didn't even bother to try to hide this attitude, he expected undying loyalty from anyone that he let bask in his glow.

Surprisingly, he often got it. The sheer force of his presence was enough to keep many of his people in line, mostly the young ones who believed in what they were doing and in the message that Hallorin had contrived. Unfortunately, though, you needed pros to run an effective presidential campaign, and most of those pros had developed a sense of cynicism to match the epic proportions of the egos they worked for.

Templeton decided to blow off the formal permission-asking phase of this meeting and walked across the office to put the tape in the VCR. Anthony, the campaign's second polltaker, had escaped first, but Templeton wouldn't be far behind. He'd put feelers out weeks ago and tentative offers were starting to filter in.

The senator said nothing as Templeton walked back to his chair and the image of Larry King appeared on-screen. The tape had been spliced together in a way that let him start with a section in which Hallorin had done well. Sneaking criticism in so Hallorin didn't notice was a delicate and subtle art.

Of course, all this was a waste of time—they were fucking *nine points* behind with the sand almost through the hourglass. Right now, Hallorin was just spending his money for the ego fix. But what the hell, it was his money.

"Tax reform seems to be the cornerstone of your campaign, Senator," Larry King said over the hidden speakers encircling the office. "But it isn't as popular as it could be because of the one dollar a gallon gas tax."

"Tax reform is where it all starts, Larry." Templeton looked over at his boss who was mouthing the words along with his television image. As always, he seemed mesmerized by his own performance.

"There's no reason that the tax system can't be so simple that you can't have your kids do your 1040s after soccer practice. As it stands, the tax code is so complex that even the IRS doesn't understand it, and I think that's unfair to the taxpayer. As far as the gas tax goes, we're not looking for anyone to pay more. The tax structure I envision will have quite a few different brackets—poorer people will pay much lower percentages to make up for the increase in the cost of gas. And if they carpool, or trade their car in for one that gets better mileage, they'll save in the end." Hallorin's face turned serious. "What we're after here is a decrease in our reliance on foreign oil to slow down the flow of U.S. dollars to the Middle East." He looked directly at the camera. "A lot of people didn't sleep well during the Cold War. I did. Members of the Politburo all had limos, beach houses, mistresses, and Sony TVs—they didn't want to die. I don't sleep so well, now, though. Make no mistake—we live in the most dangerous time in history. Technology has put great power in the hands of individuals. And religion and money have given some of those people the will and ability to use it."

Templeton hit the PAUSE button. "That was a perfect segue, Senator, we got a lot of positive feedback from that section. The Arabs are a very strong area for you—people continue to be very negative about the Middle East." He paused for a moment. "Strangely, their concern is less with the threat of violence and more the fact that they see the Arabs as the only people coming through this recession unscathed."

"Why would you be surprised by that?" Hallorin said, silencing him. "Americans are stupid and lazy. They spend all their energy worrying about what others have and none on improving their own station in life."

Templeton wasn't sure how to respond to that, or if it indeed required a response, so he pushed the PLAY button on his remote and started the tape again.

"The Democrats support an increase in corporate taxes that you are passionately against," King said.

The expression on Hallorin's on-screen face turned rock hard. It was that, right there—that pissed-off look—which was costing Hallorin a good seven points in this race. No one could help but feel intimidated by that steel-eyed glare, and people didn't want to be intimidated by their elected officials. They wanted to feel safe with them.

"The time for this kind of political double-speak is over," came Hallorin's icy response. "When are they going to figure out that this corporate tax boondoggle wore out five years ago? Look, corporations are not faceless organizations bent on raping the work force. You put food on your table working for corporations, corporations pay for your medical care, you own part of them in your retirement accounts and mutual funds, and you rely on the products produced by corporations. So who ultimately pays those increased taxes? The American people do. It's just a way the Democrats have figured out to stick you for more money without you knowing it."

"You let yourself get angry here, Senator," Templeton said, hitting Pause and wondering, once again, what he was doing. "This is the kind of thing that's killing us."

Hallorin's eyes flashed, just as they had on the television, and Templeton started a halfhearted backpedal. "What you said was right on—the message is getting through. It's just that people just aren't used to that kind of intensity from a politician."

That seemed to satiate Hallorin for the moment and he sank back into his leather chair.

There were five problem sequences on this tape. Templeton gauged that Hallorin would sit still for probably only one more. The other three got the garbage can. Hallorin would have to pick up those mistakes from the media coverage.

Templeton pressed the Play button again and they listened to King asking what piece of legislation Hallorin was most proud of being involved in.

"My declassification program," Hallorin's television image answered without hesitation. "The government was spending millions on archives and security to keep things like Civil War intelligence-gathering methods classified, and in the process, making Americans suspicious of their government. I did a simple thing. On the 'classified' stamp that people use on government documents, I put lines for the name of the person classifying it, why they did, and a date that it should be declassified. Since that piece of legislation was adopted, millions of pages of documents have been released to the public and the amount of new classified material has been cut in half. For five thousand dollars in new stamps, the taxpayer will probably save a billion dollars over the years."

Templeton stopped the tape again. "We wrote a response to that that you approved. The welfare reform you—"

"It was insignificant," Hallorin said.

Templeton heard the finality of the statement and decided not to pursue the issue. His young companion, silent until now, was less experienced with Hallorin and made the fatal decision to show off in front of his new boss.

"But it made you look sympathetic, sir. People are starting to accept your ideas—they know you're right. Our polls are showing that the gas tax isn't a major stumbling block anymore. Even drug legalization isn't the overriding problem. It's image. You chose your running mate well . . ."

Templeton winced. Strike two. Hallorin hated the man he had chosen for his vice presidential candidate—he wouldn't even lower himself to speak to him if there wasn't a camera trained on them.

"His personal numbers are excellent. Right now we're showing that there are basically two groups of undecideds at this point. Conservatives who are considering you over the Republican candidate they'd normally vote for, and Democrats who are considering voting Republican over economic issues. Many people are willing to go along with you, but they want to know you feel their pain. I believe—"

"I didn't ask you what you believe," Hallorin growled, shutting the young man up instantly.

Templeton felt for his companion. He'd made the same mistakes when he'd started on the campaign. Hallorin's utilitarian, straightforward image made you assume that he would want utilitarian, straightforward information. In the end, though, he surrounded himself almost solely with kiss-asses and yes-men. The only real exceptions were himself and that little red-haired freak, Roland Peck.

"Get out," Hallorin said to the young polltaker.

"Sir, I . . ."

"Get out! Clean out your desk and get the hell out of here!"

The phone started to ring, and Hallorin picked it up as the young man gathered his papers and started for the door, obviously unable to understand what had just happened. Templeton could feel him searching for eye contact, but didn't bother to look up. The firing was less serious than the kid thought. Since there was no one to take his place and Hallorin would continue to want numbers, Templeton would just move him to the off-site location he'd rented months earlier that housed all the people who had dared to challenge the emperor but were too critical to actually let go.

"Now?" Hallorin said quietly into the phone.

It was obvious from his tone who was on the other end: Peck. The real manager of Hallorin's campaign and, for some reason, the only person whose judgment Hallorin rarely questioned.

David Hallorin watched as Grant Templeton walked from the office and pulled the door shut behind him. It was insulting that he had to pay a man like that to "run" his campaign. Templeton was an idiot; a man who could only regurgitate what had worked before. The only thing his presence brought to the campaign was a certain credibility, and that, he told himself, was worth the exorbitant price.

"Templeton forgot something." The high-pitched voice coming from behind Hallorin was nervous, almost scared. "God. Jesus, our good friend and Savior. We agreed that you would invoke God's name at least twice an appearance."

Hallorin spun in his chair and faced Roland Peck, who had stopped a considerable distance from him. That meant bad news.

"You haven't been able to find the girl," Hallorin said.

Peck played with his mustache for a time and then shook his head.

"You promised me, Roland," Hallorin said in a fatherly voice, carefully controlling his anger. Peck responded poorly to anger and Hallorin had learned to dole it out sparingly, like a powerful drug. Too much could panic the man, and then that perfect brain of his stopped working. "What about the file?"

"We haven't found it yet," Peck blurted out.

"You haven't found it yet," Hallorin repeated. "Time is running out, Roland."

Peck walked around to the chair against the wall that he always sat in. "It all looks the same down there. Sand and rocks. Nothing but sand and rocks. We know the general location. It won't be long."

There was something that Peck wasn't telling him, he could tell by the tone of his voice and the drape of his body. He didn't pursue it, though. In the end it might be better that he didn't know. "What about the girl?"

"She's got nothing. Just the clothes on her back. It won't be long now."

"Why don't we have her, Roland?" Hallorin let the volume of his voice rise a notch, showing his displeasure at having to repeat his questions to get a full answer.

"It's hard to look. We can't have any of this traced back. None of it . . . We've hired someone independent. He's very good. He'll find her. It won't be long now. I swear."

17

Mark Beamon gunned the tiny subcompact and cursed his stupidity one more time. He could have rented the enormous four-wheel drive with the CD changer, leather trim, and back massager thing—his new employer didn't seem to be quite as coy as the government when it came to the expensing of creature comforts. Old habits really did die hard.

He heard the chassis grind against something as the front end of the car dropped into a deep rut hard enough to whip his neck. Beamon leaned out the open window into the damp, leafy-smelling air and looked at the go-cart sized front tire. The little of it that was still visible at this point seemed to be slowly sinking into the mud.

Certain that he wasn't going to be able to coax it any further forward, Beamon climbed out of the car and slammed the door. He reached in through the open window and grabbed the map off the passenger seat. It had been included in the envelope Chris Humbolt had given him and had seemed ridiculously detailed at first glance. Now, though, Beamon wasn't so sure. In this part of West Virginia, it wasn't so easy to tell a dirt road from a place where the grass didn't grow all that well.

Beamon kicked at a rock beneath his foot, mostly to hear it skitter across the dirt. The silence and stillness of the forest was kind of disconcerting—no place for a sophisticated urbanite like himself.

He switched off the car's headlights and hoped his eyes would adjust to the darkness since he hadn't had the presence of mind to bring a flashlight. Once the glare was gone, things started to look a little better. The clear sky and full moon cast a colorless glow over the dirt road and reflected black in the puddles that dotted it. He stuffed his hands in his pockets and started forward on foot, instantly breaking into a sweat despite the coolness of the night.

After about ten minutes he found himself getting used to his surroundings. He even stopped once to look down a steep slope at the moonlit New River, probably a thousand feet below. The problems that had been swirling around him lately—his imminent incarceration and likely bankruptcy, his breakup with Carrie, the fact that he was being eerily overpaid for this no-brainer—seemed to be partially swallowed up by the empty wilderness that surrounded him.

Predictably, the feeling didn't last long, fading quickly into the faint glow emerging from somewhere in front of him. He continued toward it, and by the time the trees had turned from moonlight gray to dark green, most of his problems had crept back up on him. The most urgent at the moment was just how to introduce himself to the figures he could see moving around an antiquated little van in the middle of the clearing he was heading for. He slowed, giving himself time to think before he entered into the area lit by no less than five freestanding floodlights and the headlights of two quietly purring police cars.

Mark Beamon, private dick.

Not quite the right ring.

Mark Beamon, crime scene clean up—you club 'em, we scrub 'em.

Maybe not.

Hi, I'm looking to buy a piece of shit VW van cheap.

Not quite right either.

Beamon entered the circle of light and started toward the van, but was distracted when he saw the cathedral-like cave that guarded one end of the clearing. He could see bright blue slings hanging every ten feet or so on the cliff's face and then continuing through the enormous roof. He changed his trajectory and walked toward them.

"They're called quickdraws," came a deep but unmistakably female voice behind. He didn't turn at the quiet scrunch of approaching boots, but continued to examine the eighty feet of overhanging rock in front of him. He'd read all about it. People climbed up these things, clipping their rope through the slings. If they fell, the theory was that the rope would break their fall before the ground did.

"They're called quickdraws," the woman repeated as she came up alongside him. He still didn't make eye contact, concentrating on the cliff face. In the reflected light, he could see small areas along the route that looked white. Gymnastics chalk, he knew—climbers used it to keep their hands dry. Other than that, he didn't see much. Little flaws, tiny ledges and holes. He craned his neck and looked up at the roof above him. "I understand the concept, but I sure as hell don't know how they get up there."

He heard the rustle of fabric as the woman shrugged and he glanced over at her, taking in her wide face, thick neck, and the broad hat that identified her as the sheriff. He was starting to feel a twinge of suspicion at her behavior. Shouldn't she be driving him off her crime scene with a stick by now?

The answer came to him as he continued to scan the wide stone roof for invisible handholds. After twenty-odd years of dealing with reporters, he was damn near willing to have them shot on sight. His small town counterpart, on the other hand, was probably more than happy to see her face in the papers. He turned to her and stuck his hand out. "Mark Beamon. I was with the FBI." He artfully slurred the *was,* taking advantage of the fact that the new drama surrounding his life hadn't yet hit the papers.

The sheriff leaned to one side to get a better angle on his face, then took his hand hesitantly. "Sure, I recognize you from your pictures. What are you doing here?"

Beamon smiled at her directness. Clearly a woman he could talk to. "Same thing you are. We have a passing interest in Darby Moore and Tristan Newberry."

Of course she would assume that *we* meant the FBI. But that wasn't really his problem.

The as-yet-unidentified sheriff screwed up her face as if to say that even *she* wasn't that interested in them. "Really? Why?"

Good question. He wished he knew the answer.

"It's not really something I can talk about." Again, perfectly true. He wasn't breaking any laws here. No major ones, at least. "I'd love to swap a few notes with you, though." He held up his hands in an innocent gesture. "Obviously, this isn't FBI jurisdiction—I'm not interested in the collar. If I should stumble over her first, I'll hand her over to you."

That seemed to satisfy her. She motioned for him to follow and plodded off toward the van. As they came up behind it, she grabbed a nasty-looking implement leaning against the back tire and held it up into the light. It looked like a small pickaxe about a foot and a half long. The handle was covered in rubber to improve grip and the serrated edges running along the business end of it looked razor sharp.

"Newberry was killed with one of these—the actual one is at the lab." She gripped it and gave it a short swing in Beamon's direction, causing him to jump back. She laughed and held a hand out. "I'm sorry Mr. Beamon. I didn't mean to scare you. People use these to climb up ice. They have two of them and wear these pointy things on their feet, then up they go."

"Crampons," Beamon said, deciding it was safe to step forward again.

"What?"

"The pointy things on their feet. They're called crampons."

"Oh." She looked disappointed.

"I've never actually seen one of those on the hoof," Beamon said, pointing to the ice axe in her hand. "Do you mind?" She handed it to him and he took a few practice swings. There was no doubt that you could kill the shit out of someone with the thing.

He followed obediently, still playing with the axe as she moved around to the other side of the van. When he finally looked up, he froze for a moment. "Jesus." He let the axe slide from his hand and took a hesitant step toward the open side door.

"Quite a mess, ain't it," the sheriff said. "Boy looked like Swiss cheese. She even punched holes in his feet."

"Mess" was an understatement. The van looked like someone had butchered a live cow with a chainsaw inside.

The brightness of the floodlights surrounding them amplified the gore, giving it a weird television quality. Blood was spattered over almost every surface and item inside—dried, thank God. The smell of wet blood in any quantity had a tendency to make him physically ill. Beamon let his eyes wander to the floor and saw something about the size of a quarter with what looked like dried gelatin clinging to it. A closer inspection revealed a few strands of dark hair. Part of Tristan Newberry's skull and brain.

Beamon wanted nothing more than to light a cigarette, walk to the other end of the clearing, and erase this picture from his mind. But he couldn't. The macho code of law enforcement clearly stated that he was to look unaffected and poke his head in farther.

"Of course, a lot of the stuff that was in there has been removed and cataloged—including the victim." The sheriff pointed to the bed in the back of the van. "There was a sleeping bag back there with what looked like recently dried semen on it. We're checking to see if it belonged to Newberry."

"No lack of blood samples," Beamon observed.

"Reckon not."

Beamon nodded at what looked like a full canvas sack still lying on the bed. "What's in there?"

"Rice. Probably used it as a pillow."

"She used a bag of rice as a pillow?"

The sheriff frowned deeply. "Climbers." She fairly spat out the word. "Most of 'em don't have a pot to piss in. When they first started coming here, a bunch of 'em came to the Chamber of Commerce and told us how much money it would bring into the area. What a load of crap. When it's sunny they're out here squatting on public land. When it's raining they're sitting in the local cafés all day, drinking free coffee refills and reading yesterday's newspapers." She pointed to a blood-painted box full of vegetables behind the driver's seat. Most were still covered with dirt. "Stolen from a local farmer's field would be my guess."

Beamon stepped away from the van and pulled a pack of cigarettes from his jacket. He nodded toward the vegetables as he lit one. "I've seen it before. Usually starts with turnips. Pretty soon they're on to rhubarb and Belgian endive." He waved in the general direction of the blood-spattered interior of the van. "Then this."

From her expression, he could see that she didn't appreciate the humor.

"Were there any other tracks around?" Beamon asked, letting the smoke roll satisfyingly from his mouth.

The woman didn't say anything for a moment, then shook her head. "Lots of people come up here and, you know, there's been a lot of rain."

Beamon nodded in what looked like agreement, but knew from her body language that when they'd gotten the call, every cop within a hundred miles had driven his cruiser up there and parked within ten feet of the van to have a look.

"It seems pretty cut and dried," she continued.

"How so?"

She looked at him with a touch of suspicion etched into her face. "She—Darby Moore—probably asked Newberry out here to go climbing. Near as I can tell, they'd had a long-term relationship. Newberry had sex with her and then told her he was seeing someone else." She was starting to sound a little worked up. "I'll bet it was about that scar on her nose—

have you seen pictures of her? He probably didn't find her attractive enough for him anymore. You can kind of see why she would react the way she did."

Beamon wasn't sure how to respond to that piece of conjecture, so he didn't.

"We found an article on a climbing area in Mexico in the van and a map with a route down there highlighted," the sheriff continued. "We're guessing that's where she went. Her wallet was gone and Newberry's was empty."

"Why didn't she take the map?"

"Too bloody."

"She must have been a mess, too," Beamon observed.

"Probably washed off in that waterfall."

"Did you find the clothes she was wearing when she killed him?"

She shook her head.

"Well, I doubt you could get that much blood out in a waterfall, but then, I've never showered in one. You would think, though, that somebody would have noticed a very bloody or very damp woman hitchhiking up Route 19."

"Maybe she didn't have any clothes on when she killed him. Newberry was in his underwear."

Beamon shrugged. "It's possible—worked for Lizzie Borden. But I've got to think that most people would just feel silly axe-murdering someone naked."

18

Mark Beamon looked through the windshield at the deep blue of the sky and the intricately woven foliage above him as he slowed the car to a crawl. The sun was filtering through the trees and coaxing from them a murky vapor that flowed through the open windows of the car and condensed inside.

He'd spent the better part of the morning at the local sheriff's office going through the artifacts from Darby Moore's van. He hadn't found much, beyond finally getting the sheriff's name: Bonnie Rile. And that general waste of time had left the more athletic part of the investigation for the full heat of the day.

He pulled off the quiet dirt road into a clearing, stopping his car about twenty feet from a small group of young people. There were ten or so of them, sitting in a rough circle on tattered lawn chairs and sleeping bags. A couple pulled joints from their mouths and shoved them under whatever was handy as Beamon stepped from the car.

"Howdy," Beamon said as he came up next to them. No one spoke. They just held their ground and stared at him.

It wasn't a surprising reaction. He hadn't really come to West Virginia expecting to play George of the Jungle. The most appropriate thing he'd been able to fish from his overnight bag was a pair of khakis, a leather belt, and a white button-down. His only real accommodation to the terrain was a pair of obnoxiously colored and outrageously expensive tennis shoes he'd bought in Fayetteville. Or, more precisely, that Reynolds, Trent, and Layman had bought in Fayetteville.

The young man who seemed to be in charge gave Beamon only a cursory glance and then went back to the map spread out on his lap. "Good afternoon, officer," he said as the two kids unfortunate enough to have their backs to Beamon abandoned their chairs and moved to a safer distance. He suddenly felt like he was in a spaghetti Western and it was high noon.

"I guess you'd be Jared Palermo. They told me I'd find you out here," Beamon said, watching the young man draw a large circle on the map in his lap and then cross it out. He had a strange build—not the symmetrical puffiness of the more dedicated members of the gym Carrie had insisted he join. Palermo's back and shoulders created an exaggerated V shape that looked out of balance with his scrawny legs and hard, flat chest. Most noticeable, though, were the Popeye-like forearms that looked to be larger in girth than his biceps, and the way his tan skin looked paper-thin where it stretched over his meticulously defined musculature. Beamon still didn't know all that much about this rock-climbing crap, but from where he was standing, Palermo's reputation as one of the best looked well deserved.

"Don't tell me the cops have finally decided to support our search for Darby," Palermo said with a sarcastic edge. "I know how much they'd hate to get the psycho rednecks that kidnapped her in trouble—being their cousins and all."

That wrung a few quiet snickers from the bravest of the circle, but a scowl from Beamon shut them back up.

"Don't know that much about what the cops are doing, Jared, but my advice to you would be not to hold your breath."

He finally looked up. "If you're not a cop, then who are you?"

"My name's Mark Beamon. I was wondering if you could help me out and answer a few questions."

Palermo's eyes narrowed and his bare torso tensed, causing an impressive anatomical display. "I don't know who you are, but—and I mean this in the nicest possible way—fuck you."

"I just told you who I am." Beamon pointed to one of the abandoned beach chairs at his feet. "You mind?" He flopped into the more comfortable looking of the two before Jared or any of his friends could say anything.

"I'll tell you, Jared, I figure you owe me. I've been looking for you for three hours, and that's cost me six hundred and twenty-five dollars." Beamon had calculated his five-thousand-dollar a day penalty for not turning up Darby at two hundred and eight dollars and thirty-three cents per hour. "So you can understand that I'm already in kind of a bad mood."

"This is all just a bunch of bullshit," Palermo said, his voice raising in pitch and volume. "Darby did *not* kill Tristan. No matter how much and how long you West Virginia assholes hassle me, it won't change that."

Beamon crossed his legs and locked eyes with the young climber. "Tell me, Jared. Do I look like I'm from West Virginia to you?"

Palermo tried for a few seconds to stare him down, but soon lowered his head and concentrated on his feet. "No."

"Look, I don't want to turn this into a fight. I'm getting into this thing independent of the cops and all I want is a little bit of your time. What I can offer you in exchange is a hell of a lot more of an open mind than you'll get from the sheriff's department."

That actually might have been a slight exaggeration, but it sounded good. Beamon was better than eighty percent certain that Darby had found out Tristan was sleeping with the local high school cheerleading squad or something and aerated him with her ice tool. This kind of thing happened every day and the killer's neighbors always said things like, "He/she was so quiet and polite" or "They seemed to have such a great relationship." Love could make people crazy. Hell, it was on the verge of doing it to him.

"I can *guarantee* you she didn't kill him," Jared said to a uniformly affirmative murmur from his minions. "Unless he died of sandstone poisoning."

"Of what?" Beamon hadn't heard that term before.

"Unless he decked—died in a fall, man. Think about it. Let's say Darby, for no apparent reason, decides she wants Tristan dead. What would she do? She'd wait for him to get sixty feet up on a climb and when he falls, she'd let go of the rope. No one would ever be able to prove a thing."

"Maybe it was a crime of passion. Maybe it was two o'clock in the morning and he told her she looked fat or something."

Jared put his hand out to silence the chorus of "Pleases" and "Yeah rights."

"Look, man. Darby and I have been friends for a long time—you know that or you wouldn't be here talking to me. As far as I know, she and Twist hadn't even seen each other in two years—he decided he wanted to be a lawyer and then got some fuckin' government job. She was probably passing through D.C. and needed a place to stay and convinced him to go climbing for the weekend. Where's the passion in that?"

Beamon nodded thoughtfully and leaned back in his chair. In his experience, passion could be spirited from thin air. People were just fucking nuts. And that probably went double for people who chose to dangle off cliffs and obtained half their personal possessions from a Kmart dumpster. He looked around him, lingering on the anxious young faces that made up the semicircle. Despite himself, he had to like what he saw just a little bit. They were kids who did what they wanted and ignored what society told them they had to do. After spending an unfortunate amount of time with some of the older children of his friends, he'd been wondering if any of the members of this generation could think for themselves. Apparently, some could.

"Why don't you come back to the sheriff's office with me, Jared. You could take a look at a few things for me. We could talk a little," Beamon said as he struggled out of the low-slung chair. Not surprisingly, Palermo didn't move.

"Come on, Jared. Your friends can hold down the fort on their own for an hour."

"Do I have a choice?"

Beamon shrugged. "Everyone has a choice. But I expect you'll be a lot happier in the long run if you grant me this one favor."

Palermo rose slowly to his feet, grabbed the shirt that had been hanging on the back of his chair and started toward Beamon's car. He had to push a stack of climbing books and magazines onto the floor in order to fit his thin frame into the passenger seat. When Beamon turned the key in the ignition, John Krakauer's audio book *Into Thin Air* started in the tape deck.

"Been studying up, huh," the young climber said, picking up an issue of *Rock and Ice* magazine and turning to a page marked with a paper clip.

Beamon glanced over at the glossy photograph after he had bounced safely onto a smoother section of the dirt road. It depicted Darby with her ice axe wedged into a fissure on an ice-glazed cliff face. A heavy bank of clouds had formed a thousand feet below her but thinned out enough in the distance to reveal a bright blue ocean. The only text on the page was printed in small letters along the bottom. *The North Face. Never Stop Exploring.*

"Quite a photograph," he said.

"Thanks," Palermo responded absently. "I took it."

19

Beamon waved a greeting to the cops sitting around in the sheriff's office but didn't stop. At the back of the station, he grabbed Jared's arm, pulled him into the storage room, and yanked the door closed behind them.

"Jesus," Jared breathed as he gazed down at the contents of Darby's van organized neatly on the floor and on shelves against the wall. A good half of it was encrusted with Tristan's blood.

"I'm sorry, Jared, I guess I should have prepared you for this." The truth was, he hadn't because he needed the shock value. That, combined with separating Jared from his friends and the support they provided, would hopefully throw the young climber off balance and improve Beamon's chances of getting some straight answers.

Jared's eyes crinkled up and the color that had drained from him started to slowly come back. "What the fuck, man. You can't *even* think Darby did this. What the hell happened?"

"Shotgun," Beamon lied.

Jared shook his head in disbelief. "This is so incredibly stupid. Where would Darby get a shotgun? The girl's probably never fired a gun in her life!"

Beamon gauged his reaction carefully. The details of Newberry's death had been kept extremely quiet. If Jared had heard whisperings about the ice axe, then his reaction would have gotten him an Oscar nomination.

"I don't know where she got the gun," Beamon said, looking down at the gear littering the floor. "Hopefully, I'll figure that out eventually. In the meantime, let's play a little game. You tell me what stuff in here doesn't belong to Darby."

Jared sniffed loudly and stood his ground.

"Why the attitude?" Beamon said. "We both want the same thing. We want Darby found. If you're right and Tristan's killers have her, sooner is better than later, right? And if the sheriff's right and she killed Tristan, then shouldn't she have her day in court?" Beamon leaned against a low table and motioned toward the floor again.

Jared contemplated his position and loyalties for a few more seconds and then nudged at a pile of climbing shoes with his foot, separating out a couple of pairs. "These aren't hers." Next, he hooked the toe of his sandal through a climbing harness, careful not to let his bare skin touch the blood dried on it and gracefully flipped it out onto a bare spot on the floor. "Neither is this."

"You're sure," Beamon said.

"Yeah. Darby was sponsored by Boreal, North Face, and Black Diamond. Those shoes were 5.10s and the harness was a Petzl. She'd get in trouble if she wore those."

"From her sponsors?"

He nodded. "There isn't a lot of money in climbing. It's not like you join a team and get a ten-million-dollar signing bonus—even if you're the best in the world. The only way to make a living is from guiding jobs or from sponsors—companies that pay you or give you free gear so that you'll do ads for them and such. They also pay for expeditions and travel sometimes."

"And that's how Darby supports herself?"

Jared shrugged. "I don't know if you could say Darby makes much of a living. She never wanted to be on a payroll 'cause she doesn't like being tied to a schedule. Mostly she just got gear and trip money."

Jared continued through the equipment, toeing out various articles of clothing, a rope, and some quickdraws that had all belonged to Tristan. The young climber's conclusions were no great revelation. Beamon had spent a fair amount of time pouring over recent climbing magazines and matching up the gear brands in the pictures and ads to what was strewn across the floor. He'd missed the rope, but caught pretty much everything else. It seemed that Darby bought almost nothing. Even her underwear came from some gear manufacturer or another.

"That's it, man." Jared said finally. He fell into a chair, exhausted, as though he'd just performed a grueling athletic feat. Unfortunately, he hadn't said a word about the item that Beamon was really interested in.

"You know, I've walked around the cliffs here and figured out what most of this stuff does," Beamon said, nodding at the floor. "The shoes, belay devices—all that." He pointed to the ice axe hanging on the wall. "But what the hell do you do with that thing?"

"It's an ice tool, man. You use it to climb ice. Or to protect yourself on snow."

Beamon kept his voice casual, not wanting to tip Jared off that the shotgun story was a fabrication. "What ice? It's eighty degrees outside. Could it be Tristan's?"

Jared leaned forward to get a clearer view and shook his head. "This year's carbon fiber Black Prophet. It's the one Darby uses. I do too. Looks new; she probably got it as a replacement for one she broke or something."

Beamon nodded with calculated disinterest. He'd thought it was strange that the murder weapon would be the only cold weather piece of gear in the van—his overly suspicious nature at work again. Black Diamond, the manufacturer of the axe, hadn't returned his calls yet.

"So you can use that on snow, huh? Like when you're skiing? I heard Darby's a hell of a skier."

"Fuckin' amazing, man. She's good at everything—climbing, skating, telemarking, kayaking—"

Beamon smiled. "Impressive. Where is it all?"

"What?"

Beamon reached over to the desk behind him and handed Jared a stack of ads and photos he'd torn from various magazines. The young climber shuffled through the pictures of Darby in huge parkas, on skis, in tents, astride expensive-looking bicycles.

"She's got more toys than any human being I've ever met," Beamon said. "Where you figure she keeps them? Not in her van."

Jared dropped the stack onto the chair next to him. "I dunno."

Beamon looked at his watch. Another two hundred and eight dollars and thirty-three cents were gone. That was forty-five attorney minutes.

"Bullshit, Jared. Didn't we agree that we both wanted Darby found? That that's what would be best for her?"

The young climber's face hardened. "You agreed, man."

"You say she didn't do it, Jared. You sound pretty sure. Help me find her and let's find out if you're right. What're you afraid of?"

"You want me to help you find the psycho that killed Tristan and kidnapped her, fine. You want me to help you dig into her life, no way."

"What can it hurt?"

"Darby has the best judgment of any person I've ever met. If I'm wrong and for some reason she's running—from you, maybe—I'm not going to sit here and second-guess her."

"You realize what kind of consequences that could have for you?" Beamon said, staying intentionally vague. He was on too thin ice to be making threats. The sheriff was still under the impression he was working for the FBI.

"You want to do something to me," Jared said, just as Bonnie Rile peeked her head through the door. "Then fuckin' do it."

Beamon took in a deep breath and let it out as the sheriff stepped silently into the room. "Okay, Jared, fine. Why don't you go across the street and grab a sandwich. I'll be out in a few minutes and I'll give you a ride back to your campsite—we can talk a little more in the car."

Jared didn't move from his chair, instead he sat looking around the room uncomfortably. "You know, I didn't really bring any money with me," he said finally.

Beamon rolled his eyes and pulled out his wallet. He handed the young man a ten-dollar bill.

"I could really use a beer after this," Jared said.

"Jesus." Beamon sighed, digging out another ten. He held it out, but pulled it back when Palermo reached for it. "In most of the pictures from those magazines, Darby doesn't have any scars around her nose. Where'd she get them?"

"Pakistan."

Beamon pulled the ten in a little closer to his chest. "Care to flesh that out a bit?"

"She was on Latok II when a storm hit. There were four people going for the summit that day, but she'd decided to sit it out in high camp 'cause of the weather report. So these guys call down to camp on their radio. They're freezing, exhausted, and one of them took an express down a chute and was dead. Darby geared up and walked off alone into the storm. She got two of them down to camp, but the other one couldn't walk. Even his friends told her not to go back up after him, but she did . . . " His voice trailed off and he suddenly seemed to be somewhere else.

"You've got me on the edge of my seat," Beamon prompted. "What happened?"

"The guy died, man. She tried to drag him down, but she was too spent. By the time she got back into camp, her nose was so frozen she ended up losing some of it."

Beamon picked up one of the newer photographs and looked at it. "Doesn't look that bad . . ."

"One of the guys she saved was, like, a millionaire, and he said he'd pay whatever it cost to get it fixed. So she went in and got surgery and they reconstructed it pretty well. But then they told her it was going to take two more surgeries to make it perfect, you know. So she bagged it."

"Huh?"

"She bagged it. Said the surgeries were a pain and it was good enough to keep the rain out after the first one."

"Are you finding answers, Mark?" Bonnie Rile said after Palermo had disappeared through the door with his newfound wealth.

"Finding questions." He paused for a moment. "Tell me. Were Darby's prints on the ice axe?"

The sheriff shook her head. "No, they found the pattern of her gloves."

Beamon pushed himself up on the table behind him and glanced up at a zippered nylon case in the sheriff's hand. By the way she was holding it, it was something important. She didn't seem to be immediately forthcoming though, so he didn't press.

"This is it, huh?" Beamon said, motioning around him. "This and the stuff that was still in the van when I saw it."

"All her worldly possessions," the sheriff said in a disgusted tone. "You wouldn't believe these people, Mark. Vagrants with ropes. Gypsies. That's all they are. Something like this was bound to happen sooner or later."

Beamon shrugged.

The sheriff walked past him and took a photo of Darby climbing in shorts and a halter top off the desk. "I'll bet you don't think she did it, do you? Men don't want to believe that a cute little thing like this could do something so horrible and violent. It skews their entire outlook on life. Scares them."

Beamon grinned. He just couldn't help liking this woman. She had a nutty obnoxiousness that really appealed to him. If his clock weren't ticking so loudly, he'd find out if she played golf. "Maybe it does scare us, Bonnie. But on this one, I'm inclined to agree with you. From what little I know about this girl, I expect she's capable of just about anything she puts her mind to."

He watched as she ceremoniously unzipped the bag in her hand and pulled out a thick hardback book. The jacket was painted with flowers, but there was nothing written on the front or the spine. She opened it to the first of many pages marked with sticky notes and began to read. "Men have no respect for a woman's power. They have to be shown over and over again and then still make excuses and deny it. What's wrong with them?" She flipped to another page. "Sometimes I think men never grow up but are in a perpetual stage of preadolescence. Speed on the playground and accuracy with a ball gets replaced with contests of power that they wrap everything they are up in and try to drag me into." Another page. "Just how horrible is death? There's that flash of fear when you realize it's coming, and then there's just nothing. There's the pain of a person's friends and relatives. If there's any guilt to be felt, I suppose it should be for them."

The sheriff looked up from the pages. "Believe me, I could go on. It gets worse toward the end. There's a passage about a trip she takes with a guy named Fred and how he makes her feel like she's nothing."

Beamon held out his hand and she placed the book in it.

"So we seem to have a strong woman, who, at the beginning of her diary, feels at least equal to the men in her life," Bonnie said, as Beamon flipped though the marked pages. "Then toward the end, she starts to think that it's all an illusion, that she is being dominated like the rest of us." Beamon looked up at the word "us," but it didn't slow her down. "Add to that her kind of apathetic attitude toward death, and I'd say you're right. We have a woman capable of just about anything."

Beamon closed the book and stared at the delicately painted roses on the cover, thinking about their strange contrast to the book's contents. Psych evaluations weren't his strong suit, but even he could see that the journal entries seemed to mesh with the physical evidence. Maybe the heroic stories he'd heard about Darby Moore weren't so heroic after all. What had been her motivation? To save people from death—a state she didn't seem to feel very strongly about one way or another? Or was dragging helpless men down mountains just a monstrous power trip?

It also seemed to refute Jared's theory about the method of Newberry's death. Dropping him wouldn't have been very satisfying. No, you'd want to look him in the eye before you put your ice axe in it.

"Look at the end," Bonnie prompted.

Normally he wouldn't bother. He'd send the diary off to the FBI shrinks and they'd write him a nice one-page summation of the mind of Darby Moore. But unfortunately, he wasn't in the FBI anymore.

He flipped to the back and found the pages full of short, nonsensical sentences. "Snoopy pain wants Polly Renaldo Mr. Freeze sex tick lollipop the Godzilla Tiny Tim, V9 Track," he read aloud. "What the hell does that mean?"

"Wouldn't you just love to know? Some kind of code?"

"Maybe," Beamon said, handing her back the diary and pulling his worn address book from his pocket. "Look, Bonnie, I'm going to give you a couple of addresses." He scribbled Carrie's on a pad lying on the table next to him. Under it, he jotted down a short note: "Killed her ex-boyfriend, Tristan, with an axe. Yes?"

He hesitated for a moment before tearing the paper off the pad and handing it to the sheriff. There were a number of profilers who owed him favors. Why wasn't he sending it to them? "Could you FedEx a copy to this address? It's a friend of mine who's a psychiatrist. I'll have her send you anything she comes up with." He continued to flip through his address book, finally finding the second name he was looking for and jotting it and a fax number down. Under that he wrote: "Phil, what do make of this? Mark Beamon."

He handed the paper to the sheriff. "Fax the pages with the nonsensical stuff on them to that number. It's a friend of mine at the NSA. Guy's a genius—if it *is* a code, he'll figure out a way to crack it."

"And you'll let me know, right?"

"Of course."

She seemed satisfied with his answer and left the room to carry out his instructions. After the door had swung shut behind her, Beamon looked around him at the cluttered room. He couldn't believe that he was standing in the middle of nearly all the worldly possessions of a human being and had absolutely no idea who she was.

He walked over to a small bookcase against the wall and started looking through a box of photographic slides, occasionally holding one up to the light to see more clearly. They were beautiful. Fog drenched jungle-scapes. Cliffs glowing with the setting sun. Tribal women weaving baskets. Children with deep brown skin working fields with primitive tools. Every now and then, he would come upon a poorly centered or out-of-focus picture of a smiling Darby Moore—obviously taken by one of the natives. Who the hell was this girl? That was the three-hundred-thousand-dollar question.

*   *   *

The sun temporarily blinded Beamon as he stepped from the sheriff's office, so he heard the commotion before he saw it.

"The only mistake Darby made was that she didn't just walk right by your frozen ass and go straight for the summit!" Jared Palermo shouted.

The reply was just as forceful, but Beamon couldn't quite make out the thickly accented English. He held a hand up and blocked out the glare of the sun. It seemed that Jared *had* been able to decipher the young blond man's reply, because he took a wild swing at his head. The blow glanced off harmlessly, prompting a scream from an old woman who was watching the drama unfold from only a few feet away.

Beamon trudged slowly down the steps while Jared got a hold of the back of the man's neck and started to line up a blow that couldn't miss. His opponent barely deflected the blow with his forearm, lost his balance, and they both went down into the grass. The fact that Jared landed on top seemed to delight the group of shabby but athletic-looking young spectators on the sidewalk.

Shouts of "kick his ass, Jared!" had already started in earnest by the time Beamon reached the two flailing young men. He grabbed hold of Jared's hair and pulled him off, allowing the other young man the opportunity to jump to his feet and cock a fist back. Beamon pointed at him threateningly. "Back off, asshole."

"I was only defending myself," the young blond man said, dusting himself off. Beamon couldn't place the accent more precisely than somewhere in Europe, but could at least understand what he was saying now. Whoever he was, he was another climber—skinny and rock-hard beneath utilitarian clothing and a sun-bleached ponytail.

"I should have known he would do this," the European said. "I'm sorry you had to be involved, sir. I knew Tristan and liked him very much."

Jared tried to jerk forward toward the man, but Beamon clamped down a little harder on his hair.

"And I knew Darby," the European continued when he saw that Jared was well under control. Beamon noticed a darkening in his tone at the mention of her name.

"Fuck you," Jared said.

"Because I was right, Jared?" the European said, his confidence obviously building. "Because I knew her when no one else did? Now people will see her for what she is."

This time Jared ignored Beamon's grip on his hair and launched himself forward. Beamon got his free hand around Jared's arm and used his superior weight to slow him down enough for the European to jump out of the way and start running across the street toward a large tan sedan.

"I'll see you in the mountains, you Eurotrash piece of shit!" Jared yelled to cheers from the gathered crowd. The car started moving the moment the young man jumped in, but still allowed Beamon a brief glimpse of the driver. Mid-fifties, balding, suit and tie. He had the look of an ex-cop and seemed an unusual companion for a twenty-something European climber.

"What the hell was that all about?" Beamon said as he dragged Jared back toward his car. The small crowd they passed through took the opportunity to pat Jared on the back and offer a few encouraging comments.

"Vili Marcek," Jared said as they cleared the crowd, anger still audible in his voice. "Darby saved that son of a bitch's ass a couple of years back. Ever since, he's done nothing but dis her and try to convince everybody that his fat wasn't pulled out of the fryer by a *woman*."

Beamon let Jared go and walked around to the driver's side of the car, suspecting that he'd just seen the competition for his hundred-and-fifty-thousand-dollar finder's fee. Normally he wouldn't have been worried, but the gentleman behind the wheel of that tan sedan was obviously no idiot. Beamon had never heard of Vili Marcek, and even if he had, it would have never crossed his mind to hire a climber who hated Darby to help track her down.

20

Grant Templeton put his face in his hands and sucked in a loud breath. This kind of stress couldn't be good for him in the long run. His wife was starting to complain about the shower drain not working, and he was being forced to cover up that the problem with the drain was that his hair was falling from his head by the handful.

When he finally dropped his hands, David Hallorin and his Leprechaun-like symbiant, Roland Peck, were staring at him as if he were insane. But he wasn't insane, he reminded himself. He was bulletproof.

With two good job offers on the table, he had spent the last few days quietly distancing himself from the disjointed and directionless campaign that had sprung from Peck's paranoid-schizophrenic mind. He was planning on walking out of this office for the last time at the end of the day. Hallorin didn't know it yet, but there was no fucking way Grant Templeton was going ride this ball of flame down to the ground.

Templeton looked up at the television built into the wall and the frozen image of Hallorin in the last of four new commercials Peck had nightmared up. The first three had consisted of old speeches by Hallorin juxtaposed with unfortunate and best-forgotten speeches by other politicians from roughly the same time frame.

The one they'd just finished watching—the fourth—started with Congressman Stanley Brathe preaching on family values, then cut to Hallorin describing the rampant hedonism of men in power. It concluded with a brief clip of Congressman Brathe entering a minimum-security prison in New Jersey, where he was scheduled to spend the next three to five years.

"Let me get this straight," Templeton started, aiming his comments at Peck. He'd thought he would enjoy the sense of freedom his recent job offers had given him, but in the end, he just wanted to get the hell out. "You want to run a series of ads that basically tell the American people 'I told you so'? You realize that this is crazy, right? Every poll says that the point has been conceded and that our problem is image. Any ads you run now should have Senator Hallorin frolicking with puppies and children, preferably backed up by a soothing classical piece."

Hallorin and the Freak continued to stare blankly at him but he was on a roll, so he decided to keep going. "I mean, if you have to do something this . . . bizarre, at least make Taylor the whipping boy in one of them. I mean, everything we have says that the undecideds are between us and him. If you still want to try to squeeze a little life out of this campaign, you might be able to get some mileage out of that." Templeton knew what their reaction would be. Despite the raw passion with which Hallorin hated his Republican opponent, for some reason he insisted on publicly portraying a dogged respect for the geriatric son of a bitch.

Silence descended on the room as Templeton fell, uninvited, into a chair in front of Hallorin's desk and began mentally composing his resignation for the thousandth time. He'd been rehearsing it since about two weeks into this godforsaken campaign, using it as psychological Zantec when things got ugly. Now, finally, it was for real.

"Mohamed?" Hallorin said to him finally, completely ignoring everything he'd said and moving on to the next subject. Dead man talking.

Templeton dug a crinkled piece of paper from his pocket and looked down at it. Phillippe Mohamed had recently replaced Louis Farrakhan as the leader of the Nation of Islam, and for obvious reasons, he was not a huge fan of the David Hallorin machine. Templeton knew that he should just hand over the name and phone number of Mohamed's aide and walk away, but this was just too absurd not to comment on.

"Sir," he said, then took a deep breath to calm himself. If he was ever going to succeed in getting through to Hallorin, it needed to be now. The shit was getting deep enough that some of it could potentially stick to a certain outgoing campaign manager. "Mohamed *has* agreed to a televised debate with you—" A sound somewhere between a coo and a squeal erupted from Roland Peck, throwing off Templeton's concentration for a moment.

"Of the list of venues you sent him, the only one he'll agree to is *Oprah*. As you might expect, Oprah's producers are very excited at the prospect and told me that they'll do it on twenty-four hour's notice and in a prime-time slot."

The Freak was starting to bounce up and down in his seat and looked like he was about to start spewing, but Templeton held out a hand to silence him. "I really feel like I have to say something here, Senator. While I agree that Oprah's going to be a lot less sympathetic to Mohamed than he expects, this is still going to be his crowd and an utter disaster for you. Look, we've been lucky so far. Mohamed's concentrated on attacking the Republicans and supporting the Democrats. He's pretty much stayed away from you." Templeton forced himself to clip off that sentence, deciding against telling Hallorin that Mohamed's indifference was the result of his, and everyone else's, belief that Hallorin didn't have a snowball's chance in hell of actually winning. "No matter what you do or say, he's going to label you a racist, and the media is going to take the most sensational sound bites from the show and run them out of context over and over and over. *You can't win.*"

Another long silence.

"Honestly, Grant," Roland Peck said, speaking for the first time during the meeting. "I have no idea how you've managed to rise to a position of responsibility in the world of politics. Was it just dumb luck? Yes. It must have been."

Templeton didn't move his eyes from Hallorin but it seemed that the senator was, for now, content to let his lapdog speak for him.

"It's really very simple," Peck continued, in a tone that suggested he was speaking to a slow child. "I think even you should be able to understand. You see, the stupid whites—specifically your rednecks and other Southern inbreds—will see the senator's candor during this debate as an attack on the black community and will love him for it. Now, your more educated and intelligent whites will see it as the first honest discussion on race in years and will admire the senator for his courage and vision. And finally, the niggers'll jump up and down till they're black in the face." He giggled at his attempt at a joke. "But who cares? They were going to vote Democrat anyway. You say the senator can't win? I say he can't lose."

Templeton's anger was at the edge of his control. "Look, you little son of a bitch—I've been running campaigns since you were in grade school! You have no idea what the hell you're talking about! You cannot just fly in the face of political correctness and—"

Peck started to laugh out loud, a piercing and infinitely grating sound that abruptly silenced Templeton. He'd never wanted to physically harm anyone in his life, but right now he wanted to grab that little sideshow attraction's neck and strangle the squeaky voice right out of him.

"Grant, Grant," Peck said, wiping an imaginary tear from his eye. "After all these years, you *must* have at least a rudimentary understanding of human nature. You must have picked up *something*. People need pain in their lives—they don't know they do, but they do. They spend more money than they make and get themselves in financial trouble, marry people they're incompatible with and get themselves in romantic trouble, they worried about the Soviets and the economy . . . But then what happened? The Soviet Union collapsed and one of the greatest economic booms in history started. The poor things couldn't generate enough strife in their personal lives to satisfy their habit and that forced them to dream up political correctness. Do you really think that in the world we live in today, anyone gives a shit whether the niggers are called black or African American? Or that short people are labeled vertically challenged? No. People just want their cushy jobs, fancy cars, and spiffy furniture. And they'll stab their own mothers in the back to get it."

He'd heard Peck spout this type of thing before. Apparently there was once a psychologist named Maslow who had created a list—hierarchy—of human needs. They included things such as food, shelter, companionship. Peck had bastardized that list, arguing that these basic needs were automatically fulfilled in twenty-first century America and therefore irrelevant. His version consisted of things like the need to feel superior, to cause pain, to feel guilt. Templeton had heard it all before and didn't need to hear it again. He stood and looked Hallorin directly, but still respectfully, in the eye.

"Senator, obviously you've decided to focus this campaign on a very different area than I proposed. I have a job offer that I've accepted. It's been a pleasure working with you, sir, but I think it's time for me to move on."

He walked up to the desk and offered his hand. Hallorin looked at it for a moment, then returned his concrete stare to the wall. "If you abandon this campaign now, Grant, I will do everything in my power to destroy you." His tone was matter of fact. The complete absence of emotion in his voice was somehow incredibly intimidating—the voice of a man who would kill you for a dime and never think about it again. Templeton's throat seemed to freeze up on him at the unexpected response. He hadn't rehearsed for this one and he found himself standing mute in front of Hallorin's desk.

Hallorin turned his head lazily in Templeton's direction. "And if you continue to try to distance yourself from this campaign, I will make it my life's goal to fuck you and your family so badly that none of you will ever recover." He paused for a moment. "On the other hand, if you stay where you are, there will be no place for you in my presidency, but I will say nothing negative about you—nothing at all about you—from the White House."

Templeton suddenly became aware that his hand was still hanging in the air and let it drop to his side. The White House? David Hallorin's grasp on reality had always seemed tenuous, but now Templeton was starting to question his sanity. The White House? He was a fucking distant dead last with the general election less than three weeks away. Dead goddamn last.

Hallorin looked at his watch. "I'll see you in my office tomorrow at eight A.M. to go over the new numbers."

Templeton knew he had been dismissed but didn't move. Hallorin was more than willing, and certainly capable, of carrying out his threat. He was trapped. He knew that all he could do now was turn on his heels and try to walk out of the office with as much dignity as he could.

By the time the door closed behind Templeton, Hallorin's mind had already moved on. Templeton was less than nothing. He would do what he was told to save what was left of his lackluster career.

Hallorin spun his chair to face Roland Peck, who was fidgeting violently against the wall. He watched in silence for a moment, examining Peck's nearly translucent skin, his thin, weak body, and the bizarre collage of nervous ticks that kept repeating over and over. For all his brilliance, young Roland Peck had been almost too easy. Hallorin had been able to tap into the loneliness and alienation that tormented his twisted mind and he'd quickly become dependent on Hallorin to keep the excruciating void inside him filled.

"Mark Beamon," Hallorin said finally.

Peck jumped as though he'd been jabbed with a needle. "We're all over him, David. All over him."

"It's dangerous having him involved in this. You know that."

Peck swallowed and nodded. "But he may find the girl. I think *he'll* find her. I don't know why. But it's what I think."

"Maybe. But he's hard to anticipate. There's no telling what route he'll take to her door."

"In this instance, I think I can assure you that he'll take the shortest route. We're all over him, David. All over him."

21

The heavy white flakes of early fall snow flowed into the open window on a rush of cold Wyoming air. The darkening landscape around her seemed endless: fading slowing into a monochromatic distance that never seemed quite real.

Darby Moore slowed her truck until the hum of the engine was nearly overpowered by the crunch of the tires over the snow. Not much farther, now. The familiar crooked outline of a barn appeared in front of her, a black hole in the shimmering stars breaking though the snow clouds on the horizon. She was going to make it.

Darby eased the truck to a stop and stepped out, drinking in the silence and stillness around her, letting it take hold of her and push Tristan's persistent image from her mind. Keeping her feet firmly on the ground, she bent backward, lying across the warm hood of the truck and trying to believe that she was safe there. It was a lie, though—the file tucked behind the seat made sure of that.

Two minutes was all she allowed herself before she let her head roll to the side and concentrated on the dull flicker of firelight in the windows of a small house some three hundred meters away.

The barn first.

She approached it on foot as quietly as the dusting of icy snow would allow and opened the sliding door just enough to allow her to slip through sideways. She tried not to let her mind wander, but the smell of hay brought back memories of the countless hours she'd spent in this place, laughing with friends, drinking beer, waiting for the sun to shine. It all seemed so far away now.

She stood motionless by the door for a long time, scanning the shadows and straining to hear any evidence of the men that she almost expected to be lying in wait for her. She didn't know how long she stayed like that—five minutes, a half an hour. There was nothing. Only the wind. It didn't matter—if they were there, she was dead already.

She adjusted the backpack to a more comfortable position on her shoulder and started through the semidarkness. She paused at the ladder to the hayloft, finally starting to calm down. The barn was empty. She was almost sure of that now.

She darted up the ladder and moved through the deep hay to the back wall. A large window/door to her right was wide open and the increasingly intense light generated by the moon and stars was working its way around the elaborate rope pulley system hanging in it, effectively illuminating the loft around her.

It was all where she'd left it. She lifted her mountain bike off a stack of boxes as quietly as she could and opened the untaped flaps of the one on top. First, she pulled out a down jacket and slipped it on over her sweatshirt. Then, digging down further, she found a cache of T-shirts, fleece pullovers, and sweatpants, all provided by her various sponsors and all still wrapped in the original packaging.

The second box contained a large backpack with the tags still hanging from it. She opened the drawstrings and started stuffing it with clothes, shoes, and climbing gear. In about fifteen minutes, it was completely full.

She sat back in the hay, inexplicably exhausted, and emptied the cheap pack that she had come in with of the one thing it contained. The cold plastic covering the file shimmered in the dead light, making it look even smaller than it was. It seemed impossible that it could be important enough to have caused all this. She turned it over in her hands, but couldn't see anything except the reflected moonlight. There was writing under the thick layer of plastic, she knew. But only one word had been typed large enough to be legible: PRODIGY.

She reached into the large pack she'd just filled and pulled out a knife. The blade seemed to glow as she held it against the thing that had killed Tristan and most likely would do the same to her.

No.

If she did this, it would never be over. What the file contained wasn't part of her world. If she knew, she would be forever linked to it. She would have no hope of ever getting her life back.

The guilt she felt was almost physically painful as she stuffed it back into the pack she'd pulled it from. She wanted to do it: to rip open the plastic, to make whatever it was public, to use it to hurt the men who had killed Tristan. She wanted to be blinded by anger and hate, to lash out . . .

But she'd never been blinded by anything. Her ability to detach herself from any situation, to make rational decisions, was the gift that allowed her to get away with climbing at the level she did. But sometimes it could be a curse, too. Sometimes it was hard to discern judgment from coldness and self-absorption.

She crawled back to the boxes behind her and started separating the camping gear stacked neatly in the hay when she heard an unnatural creak from the edge of the loft. Without thinking, she lunged for the shovel propped against her bike and spun around to face the ladder she had come up, but the barrel of a shotgun was already visible over the lip of the loft.

Darby threw the shovel in the direction of the ladder and started to run through the deep hay. If she could make it to the window, she could climb down the pulley system and escape. She had to make it. She had to.

"Darby! Stop!"

The voice seemed to physically grab hold of her. She slowed and turned around in time to see a woman about her age and build, but with closely cropped dark hair, drop the shotgun and pull herself into the loft.

"Oh, my God! We thought you were dead!" The woman threw her arms around Darby and held her in a powerful hug. "Jared's been sending us the articles. They say that you killed Tristan and ran! We knew that wasn't true. We thought someone had taken you and . . ."

Darby gently pushed her friend back, examining her face in the moonlight. "Have the police been here, Lori?"

The young woman looked a little confused for a moment, then shook her head. "What happened? What happened to Tristan?"

Darby took her friend's hand and pulled her down into the hay. They sat there in silence for almost a minute with Lori staring intently into her face.

What could she say that wouldn't make her sound guilty? She couldn't tell her what had really happened—that kind of knowledge would put her in harm's way. They'd been friends for a long time. She'd have to rely on the trust they'd built up over those years.

"Someone else killed Tristan, Lori. They were going to do the same thing to me, but I got away—"

"Who? Who killed him? A local?"

"I don't know," Darby said honestly.

"You have to go to the police, Darby. Tell them what happened. They think you did it!"

"I can't."

"Why not?"

"You believe that I didn't kill Tristan, don't you?"

"Of course I do, Darby. But—"

"Look, you have to trust me on this. I can't go to the police. And I can't tell you why. I'm afraid you could get hurt."

"What the hell is going on, Darby?" Lori said, frustration starting to creep into her voice.

"Are you still going to Thailand next Sunday?"

"What?"

Darby took her hand again, suddenly feeling a little dizzy. She realized that she had been so consumed with making it to Wyoming that she hadn't spent any time thinking about what would happen when she actually arrived. The plan that had seemed to completely hinge on her making it to this particular spot now felt like it was slipping into impossibility. "You . . . you told me you were going climbing in Thailand, remember?"

"I'm not going," Lori said, sounding a little confused at the change in subject.

Darby let her friend's hand slide from hers and fell back into the soft hay. When she closed her eyes it caused two small tears to run down her temples. What now? That had been her only way out. What now?

"Darby, what's wrong? Look, I talked to Sam—"

Darby was only half listening. Sam was a friend of theirs who had a house in the heart of southern Thailand's best climbing area.

". . . he said it's getting crazy there—it's been really unstable politically since the crash and it's getting more dangerous every day. There's been a travel advisory out for a while now. He said he's leaving next week and he doesn't know if he'll ever go back. . . ."

"I'm sorry, Lori," Darby said, eyes still closed. "It was a stupid idea. It would have been wrong for me to ask you anyway. I'll just have to figure something else out. No problem."

"Ask me what?"

"Nothing. Forget it."

"Ask me *what*, Darby?"

"I need to get out of here. The people who killed Tristan are still after me. I was going to ask to use your ticket."

The quiet of the Wyoming night settled over them and Darby used it to try to think. There was always more than one option. She just needed some time . . .

"I still have the tickets," Lori said, interrupting Darby's concentration. "It's a courier deal. I haven't called them yet to tell them I'm not going. I was waiting to see if things maybe would get better over there."

Darby raised her head and looked at her friend for a moment, then sunk back into the hay. "It doesn't matter."

"You'd have to use my passport," Lori said.

"Forget it," Darby said again, still trying to figure out what she was going to do next. She couldn't go to Mexico—they'd have read the maps in her van and would be expecting that. Canada maybe? Alaska? She could definitely get lost in Alaska.

She struggled to her feet, still lost in thought, and started pulling ski equipment from under a pile of climbing gear.

"Where are you going?" Lori said quietly.

"There's something I have to do."

She'd take the file up to the old forest service lookout tower. It was ten hard miles into the mountains—a place she and her friends used to stop to warm up on their way to wherever they were skiing or climbing that day. The floorboards were loose—she'd pull up a few and hide the file there. No one would ever find it. And in the time it took her to get up there, she could make some decisions about what was left of her future.

Lori watched in silence as Darby pulled on a pair of ski pants and a polypropylene undershirt, finally speaking again when Darby threw a pair of ski boots off the edge of the loft. "The snow's really messed up right now. We never got summer this year. . . ."

Darby shrugged and pulled a pair of skis off the wall.

Lori walked to the edge of the loft and picked up the shotgun she'd dropped there. "When you get back we'll cut your hair."

Darby looked down at her as she began slowly descending the ladder.

"You shouldn't have any problem passing for me; my passport picture isn't that good. Hell, the Thais think we all look the same, anyway."

22

It seemed like an impossible combination, but Beamon found himself both staring into the rising sun and having to manually work the car's wipers to keep the heavy snowflakes from freezing to his windshield. It seemed that late fall in Wyoming was even worse than in Flagstaff.

The barn became visible first, appearing out of the crystalline haze hanging over the rolling landscape. When the house next to it came into view, Beamon pressed his foot down on the accelerator a bit harder, causing a minor fishtail that almost put him in a ditch.

At his increased speed, it only took about five minutes to cover the rest of the distance and gracelessly slide the car to a stop behind a beat-up old pickup with temporary Maryland plates. More out of habit than anything, he scanned the plates of the other four trucks parked haphazardly in front of the barn. Two from Wyoming, one from Canada, and one from California. These kids got around.

Beamon stepped from the car and slammed the door. None of the five or six people inside the barn seemed to notice. They were all concentrating on something that he couldn't see through the half-open door.

"Hello!" Beamon called, leaning casually against the makeshift doorjamb. "Is—" He snapped to attention when he spotted the young woman standing at the back of the barn. "Darby Moore?" he said tentatively, stepping forward and squinting into the dim light. Instead of moving back as he expected, the woman stepped forward out of the shadows.

"Darby who?"

He could see her better now. She looked a lot like Darby: roughly the same height and weight, and the same slightly weathered complexion and general features, though her nose lacked the pleasant crookedness of Darby's and her hair was much shorter.

"You must be Lori Jaspers," Beamon said, taking another couple of steps forward and sticking out his hand. "My name's Mark Beamon."

The young woman walked right up to him and looked down at his hand as though he'd just pulled it from a bucket of nuclear waste. "What do you want?"

Beamon looked past her at the five young men standing off to her left. "Don't let me bother you," he said to them. "Go ahead and go back to whatever you were doing."

They didn't move, so Beamon just stared at them. Finally, they became uncomfortable enough to shuffle toward a large plywood and two-by-six construction near the wall. It overhung at about forty-five degrees, rising from the ground to a height of about twelve feet. The underside was peppered with small wooden handholds and the ground below it was completely covered in varying thicknesses of old mattresses. Above it, painted on the wall in large black letters was a quote: *There's a leisure class at both ends of the social spectrum.* The attribution had been obscured by a leak in the roof.

Beamon continued to watch as one of the young men hoisted himself onto a couple of holds low on the wall and proceeded up it with the grace and effortlessness of a ballerina. At the top, he dangled for a moment and then dropped into the mattresses.

"That's really amazing," Beamon said, walking past the young woman and stopping in front of the bizarre-looking construction that he knew from his research was called a "woody." As he approached, the young men moved back.

"You mind?" Beamon said, stepping up on the mattresses and grabbing onto what he figured were the two largest handholds within reach. He gave them a little pull, but it was clear that nothing short of a hydraulic lift was going to get his fat ass off the ground. He looked closer at the holds peppering the plywood overhang. Each had a word written next to it in black magic marker. The two he had his fingers curled around were Godzilla and Tiny Tim.

He smiled and shook his head. The mysterious codes in the back of Darby Moore's diary were nothing more than training routes that she didn't want to forget. His friend at the NSA wasn't going to be very happy when he found out that he'd been squandering his brain and computer power on a rock-climbing problem.

Beamon jumped up and bounced off the mattress onto the straw-covered ground, landing a few feet from Lori Jaspers. "Neat. Now where were we?"

"You were going to tell me who the hell you are," she said with almost enough anger to cover up her nervousness. "This is private property, you know."

"I told you. My name's Mark. I'm looking for Darby Moore. You two are friends, right?"

"I don't know what you're talking about," the girl said, then started chewing her lower lip like it was a tough steak.

Her companions had stopped climbing again and were watching Beamon carefully. This time, he just ignored them. "Come on, Lori. If you're going to lie, fine. But come up with something plausible. 'I haven't seen her in months,' would work. Or 'She and I had a falling out years ago.' Show a little imagination."

"I haven't seen her in months."

"That's the spirit."

"What makes you think she'd be here?"

"Well, I talked to a friend of yours, Jared Palermo, but he was less than helpful." Beamon reached into his back pocket and pulled out a crumpled page from an old issue of *Climbing Magazine*. "Ready to be impressed?" He handed it to her.

Each month, *Climbing* contained a feature about people who built their own climbing walls. This particular article featured a picture of a woody in a barn in Wyoming and named Darby Moore as one of the builders and Lori Jaspers as the owner. It occurred to Beamon that if Darby had bothered to help build the thing and had no fixed address, there was a fair chance that she used Lori's house as a base.

In fact, the possibility that she could be there right now had crossed his mind a few times, though it seemed unlikely. She had no transportation and no money—nothing but what was on her back. It was more likely that she was holed up with someone in or near West Virginia. The question that Lori Jaspers might be able to answer was where and with whom.

Darby Moore scooted forward a few inches until her eyes cleared the floor of the hayloft and she was able to see down into the barn. She felt a deep pang of guilt as she watched her friend Lori hand a crumpled piece of paper back to the man standing in front of her. She hadn't thought they'd be able to find this place. She'd been stupid. Now her friends were involved.

"So what?" she heard Lori say.

"So, I figure this is probably where Darby keeps her stuff. Maybe I could take a look," the man replied—what had he said his name was? Mark Beamon? It seemed like she'd heard the name before, but couldn't remember where. Maybe one of the men who had attacked her and Tristan had said it while she was semiconscious in the back of their van.

Darby watched Beamon make an effort to fold his arms across his chest, only to give up when the ridiculously thick red parka he was wearing wouldn't allow it. She ducked back a few inches when he turned his head in her direction and scanned the wall of the barn beneath her perch.

His face wasn't familiar, but that didn't surprise her. There had been at least three men hidden by the dark at the New River Gorge. And the men who had been with Vili Marcek in Utah had been too far away for her to see clearly. For all she knew, this Mark Beamon was the one who had killed Tristan.

She moved further back from the edge and buried her face in the straw, breathing in the comforting scent. She hadn't even been running for a week and they were already within thirty feet of her. Wasn't she clever? It would be nothing more than dumb luck if she made it out of the country.

Darby looked up when her friend spoke. "Do you have a warrant?"

"I'm not a cop," was the man's reply. "Fact is, I'm currently in the process of being fired from the FBI."

"Well, then, you're trespassing. Why don't you get the hell off my property before I go get my shotgun."

Darby felt her heart jump at her friend's tone. She hadn't told Lori or the others anything. She'd left them defenseless, with no idea what kind of people they were dealing with. This was all her fault.

The man thrust his hands deep into his pockets and turned slightly, giving her a better view of his face—the left side of it, anyway. His expression was thoughtful, not threatening. He wasn't what anyone would call a handsome man, but there was a strange humor that seemed permanently set into his face, even as a scowl spread across it. She had to remind herself again that these men had been born to lie and that what she was seeing was just a mask. The man standing two feet from her best friend would undoubtedly kill any person in this room if he thought it would get him closer to the file.

"Tell you what," Beamon said. "Why don't you call the local police— I'm sure you and your friends are real popular with them. You tell your story and I'll tell mine. Then maybe we'll call the West Virginia cops and get some of them out here. Look, we can turn this place into Grand Central Station, or you can just give me a quick tour of Darby's stuff and I'll walk out of here without another word."

There was nothing she could do. If the police came, Darby would never be able to get her truck out. She'd be trapped.

Lori started arguing again, louder this time, and Darby took the hint. She was going to have to bring this man up to the loft, but she was going to do it as slowly as possible.

Darby slid back away from the edge and began crawling silently toward the window that opened out into space at the other end. She was still ten feet away when she heard her friend tell the man that the things he wanted to look at were in the hayloft.

Darby picked up her pace, struggling to keep the dry hay from crunching beneath her knees. Behind her, she could hear the creak of the ladder as it was weighted. The window was only a few more feet.

She took a quick look behind her and then leaned out the opening and grabbed the rope hanging from the wooden pulley above. She had no idea how old the rope and the beam that held it were, but there wasn't time to worry about that. A fifteen-foot fall, unless she made too much noise hitting the ground, wouldn't be fatal.

The pulley creaked a little, but the noise just blended into the other sounds made by the old barn. She started lowering herself down the rope hand over hand, just as the man's head came up over the edge of the loft.

She'd been too slow. She was in plain view now if he should bother to look to his right. Darby took a deep breath and was about to let go and take the fall to the ground when she heard Lori yell up to the man from below.

"Her stuff's off to the left!"

His head turned away and gave Darby enough time to make a quick descent of the old rope as he clambered the rest of the way up into the loft. That was another one she owed Lori.

Darby ran through the shallow snow to the remnants of a truck half-buried in a stand of tall, dead weeds. She'd be safe there until this Mark Beamon got what he wanted. Hopefully, it wouldn't be long; the wind was already starting to cut through her light fleece jacket.

When he was gone, she'd leave. She'd drive to western Wyoming or Idaho and find an old fire road she could camp on until it was time to go to LAX and catch her flight to Thailand. Then she'd have time to think. That's all she wanted: a little time to breathe and think.

*   *   *

"This is it?" Beamon said, using his toe to nudge a pile of T-shirts that looked like they'd never been worn.

"Yes," Lori answered. He looked up into her face, wishing that he could figure out a way to get her to open up. He could see that it was hopeless, though. He wasn't going to break this case and collect his cash with the help of any of Darby's friends.

Beamon knelt down in the hay and began to dig through the boxes and stuff sacks stacked along the wall. There wasn't much of interest—mostly athletic gear, mostly unused. Everything seemed to be accounted for—the bike was there, so were the skis. Summer and winter clothing, backpacks, various sleeping bags apparently designed for different temperatures.

Very little of a personal nature, though. No pictures or address books. Nothing that would tell him if she had friends on the East Coast. The only printed materials were a bunch of maps and climbing area guidebooks—too many to give any indication of where she might have gone.

Beamon pushed away a box containing a pair of ski boots and uncovered two ice axes. He lifted them, one in each hand and looked them over closely. They looked to be exactly like the one that had killed Tristan Newberry. Both were equally chipped and gouged from what looked like a significant amount of vigorous use. The pictures he'd seen of the actual murder weapon had shown similar wear beneath the blood and hair clinging to it.

"Do you climb ice, Lori?" As far as he knew, the exact method of Newberry's untimely demise had not yet been leaked.

"Um . . . yes."

"How many of these do you have?"

"I've only got two hands," she said, still insisting on an adversarial relationship.

"So you don't have a spare that you use sometimes."

She shook her head, obviously perplexed by his line of questioning. "Spare picks?"

Beamon nodded, noting that the serrated blade at the end of the handle was removable. He'd finally gotten in touch with Black Diamond, the manufacturer that supplied Darby with her ice equipment, and confirmed that they had given her precisely two carbon fiber Black Prophet ice tools, but that if she wanted another one they'd be happy to provide it to her free of charge. Where'd the third axe come from? If he'd learned anything about Darby Moore since he'd started this thing, it was that she wasn't in the practice of buying things she could get for free.

"Fine," Beamon said finally, dropping the axes back into their box. There was nothing there that could help him. He turned and started back toward the ladder.

Two of the five men who had been in the barn when he'd come in had apparently taken his temporary absence as their cue to leave. Beamon paused in front of the woody and surveyed the three remaining brave souls as Lori Jaspers made her way down the ladder behind him. Brave souls. More likely three young men who were currently squatting there and had nowhere else to go.

"Okay, guys, here's the deal," Beamon said to them. "I need to find Darby Moore. If she killed Tristan Newberry, then she should be brought before the courts, right? He was a nice guy and didn't deserve to die. If she didn't, then running is just making her look guilty. . . ."

He surveyed the blank faces in front of him and decided that he was glad he wasn't playing poker with this crew. "Anything you could tell me, in the long run, is going to help your friend." And his legal defense fund.

Dead silence.

He really needed his job at the FBI back. This crap of not being able to haul people off and beat them with rubber hoses really put a kink in his investigative style. "Don't everybody talk at once." He waited for a few more seconds. "Okay. One more question. Absolutely no reason not to answer this one. Has anybody been out here looking for Darby since this happened? Other than me."

Nothing again. In fact, he wasn't dead sure any of the remaining men could even speak English. Not one of them had uttered a word since he'd arrived.

"Come on now. How about a guy named Vili Marcek?"

That got him a little further. There was a glimmer of a reaction from each of them, but it faded quickly.

"Come on, now. You all know damn well that he's no friend to Darby. What could it hurt to tell me if he's looking?"

"That prick called here a few days ago saying he wanted to come here and go climbing," the young man in the middle said. His accent was obviously French, though easy to understand. He looked around at Lori and the other two who, based on their expressions, had known nothing of the phone call. "What?" he said with an exaggerated shrug. "I told him that if Lori saw his face she would use a pitchfork on it."

So there it was. The competition was still running about one step ahead of him. And that was starting to piss him off. It wasn't just the money, it was the goddamn principle.

Beamon ran his finger down the Yellow Pages to the second of only two banks listed in the miniscule phone book. He dialed the number and kicked his stockinged feet up on the uncomfortable-looking bed next to him as a phone on the other end of the line started to ring. According to the guy at the gas station, this was the best hotel the town had to offer. If that was true, Beamon wasn't excited about the prospects for a nightlife. It looked like his immediate future included about ten Old Milwaukees at a place that encouraged two-stepping and was frequented by people who said things like "Howdy partner." Unfortunately, though, there were no flights out until morning.

"Hello, the Community State Bank."

"Hi. I'd like to check the balance on my account, please."

"I'll transfer you."

He looked around him at the worn-out little motel room again while he waited. Twenty-nine dollars and ninety-five cents a night. An unlimited expense account for the first time in his life and priciest room in town cost less than a decent bottle of Scotch.

The phone clicked a few times and another woman's voice came on the line. "Account number, please."

It seemed logical that if Darby Moore kept her stuff here, she'd use a local bank to hold what little money she accumulated. Of course, it was possible—likely maybe—that she just kept it in an old sock in her glove compartment. Normally his ability to get into his adversary's head was his greatest skill, but this girl was eluding him. Half vagrant, half world-class athlete, all nasty temper. He hoped that Carrie could find something useful in the girl's diary.

"I'm afraid I don't have my checkbook with me," Beamon said, trying to sound apologetic.

"Who am I speaking to, please?"

"Darby Moore." Thankfully, the name was fairly androgynous.

The sound of fingers on a keyboard.

"Mother's maiden name?"

Occasionally, the long shot came in. At this point, the other bank had told him that there was no account under that name.

"Blake," Beamon read off the synopsis of Darby Moore's life that he'd been provided.

"Thank you. The balance of your account is one dollar and no cents."

That was too small and too even to be naturally occurring. It was the balance of a person who had suddenly emptied their account and not wanted it closed.

"Yeah, see, that's not right. What do you have down as my last transaction?" Beamon said.

"Hold on." More clicking. "It was a wire transfer in the amount of $3,456.58 on October fifth."

"A wire transfer?" Beamon said, affecting a slight panic in his voice. "This is definitely not right. Where'd it go?"

This time it was the sound of pages turning. "It went to Davis National."

"Davis National? Where's that?" Beamon said.

"It's in Conrad, Maryland. Sir, did you not authorize this transfer?"

Maryland.

Beamon bolted upright in his chair and threw the phone on the bed. He could hear the woman's tinny voice muffled by the bedspread as he ran out the door.

Mark Beamon slammed on the brakes and sent the car skidding wildly into the space between Lori Jaspers' house and her barn, confirming that the piece-of-shit blue pickup with temporary Maryland plates was gone. He knew it would be. Beamon grabbed his steering wheel and slammed his head into it. Too many piss-poor assumptions and too much bullshit conventional thinking. He'd taken it for granted that Darby Moore was pretty much immobile. Sure, he'd worried that someone might lend her a car, but most of the people she hung around with wouldn't have one to spare—and probably wouldn't want to aid and abet a suspected murderer in such an obvious way. He'd had the Fayette County Sheriff's Department cut off her credit cards, so renting was out. And he'd thought it was safe to assume that a woman who collected cans to cover her major living expenses wouldn't have the money to buy a vehicle.

Beamon banged his head one more time on the wheel for good measure. What the hell was he going to do now? Normally, this wouldn't have been a problem—there were all of about three roads in the entire state of Wyoming and she hadn't been gone for more than two hours. Unfortunately, though, he no longer had the juice to call in an APB. And even if he could, his quickly dwindling bonus didn't get paid if she was picked up by some state cop.

Beamon looked through his fogged-up side window and saw Lori Jaspers and her French friend standing on the porch of her house. They looked scared—as they goddamn well should have. He threw the car door open and jumped out, stalking toward them. "She was here, wasn't she? The whole goddamn time!"

"I don't know what you're—"

"Shut up," Beamon said, taking the stairs onto the porch in one long stride and brushing past them into the house.

"Hey! You can't go in there!"

He ignored Lori's continued protests as he marched across a small, partially furnished living room into the kitchen. He opened the fridge and pulled a beer out.

"Shit!" he yelled as he twisted the top off. Lori and her friend were in the doorway of the kitchen now but were clearly too scared to enter.

This whole thing was really starting to chap his ass. Darby Moore was God-knew-where by now, and worse, she knew he was right behind her. She'd try to skip the country—he had a strong sensation about that—but he couldn't figure out how. It wasn't going to be Mexico or Canada—the cops were looking for that.

"Hey, you know you can't be in he—"

"I am in here!" Beamon shouted, then pointed at Lori with an outstretched index finger, keeping the other four tightly wrapped around the neck of the beer bottle. "Don't talk. I'm thinking."

He had a friend at the FAA watching for Darby's name on foreign flights, and when he returned to the hotel he'd add Lori's name to that. They looked a lot alike and Darby's passport had been found in her van covered with unidentifiable bits of Tristan Newberry.

Beamon had finished reading every goddamn book and magazine that even remotely mentioned Darby; he probably knew more about climbing than any other ground-dweller in the world. But after pouring over countless articles on things like keeping your rotator cuffs healthy and increasing the strength of your pinky finger, his expertise was shaping up to be pretty much useless.

So now what? The only thing he could think to do was go to Maryland—the one place he knew she wasn't—and see if he could pick up her trail there.

Beamon took a long pull from the beer bottle. At least this little side trip had cleared one thing up. Darby Moore was not being used as breeding stock by a bunch of West Virginia rednecks. She was on the run and, most likely, was still trying to pick Tristan Newberry's brains out from under her nails.

23

Mark Beamon slowed his rented Lincoln Towncar to thirty-five miles an hour and continued picking the filet mignon from his teeth. The toothpick was one of those fancy plastic jobs, supplied by an attractive and attentive first-class stewardess on his flight to Maryland. If he could milk his mysterious employer for a few more trips across the U.S. during this half-assed investigation, he'd have enough miles accumulated to skip the country when the FBI came after him. Fleeing American justice using frequent flyer miles, for some reason, appealed to his sense of style.

He tapped the brake again as he reached the city limits of Conrad, Maryland, and the Lincoln responded by floating effortlessly to under fifteen miles an hour. He gave a trailer surrounded by dilapidated cars a more than cursory glance but decided not to stop. While it was just the type of used car lot that Darby could have purchased that old truck from, he doubted that sweating the salesman would be particularly productive. Sitting around in a moldy trailer with a guy in a leisure suit trying to get an unreliable estimate of how much money Darby had left and what direction she'd driven off in seemed more like a last resort than a first stop.

"Hello," Beamon said, leaning across the counter and focusing on the oldest of the four uniformed men behind it. "I'm Mark Beamon. I—"

"You're that FBI agent," the man said, stepping forward and pumping Beamon's hand vigorously. "The guy who released the phone taps on those sons of bitches in Washington. Hell, son, what are you doing in Conrad?"

"I didn't actually leak that information," Beamon felt obligated to point out for some reason. "I just—"

"Well, hell. If you didn't you should have." The police chief turned back to his men for a moment. "This is the old boy who turned up those church tapes."

The three younger men came up to the front, each shaking his hand and a few clapping him on the shoulder. Beamon hid his discomfort, accepting the attention with practiced grace. This kind of thing happened occasionally, but he didn't seem to be able to get accustomed to his new position as folk antihero.

"All right, all right," the chief said after a few moments. His men retreated back to their desks and fax machines with appropriately respectful bobs of their heads.

"Now, what is it I can do for you, Mr. Beamon?"

"Mark. I'm looking for a girl. Her name's Darby Moore."

"That girl who axe murdered her boyfriend in Fayetteville? What're you doin' with that?"

"Well, I'm temporarily on suspension from the Bureau . . ."

The sheriff shook his head and muttered "goddamn sons of bitches." It had the ring of a sincere statement of sympathy.

"Anyway," Beamon continued. "I'm just helping out on this investigation. To keep my mind occupied, you know?"

"Sure, I understand. And I might be able to offer a little help. Davey!"

A young man sitting behind a metal desk jumped out of his chair and stood at something resembling attention.

"Didn't you talk to someone about that axe murderer girl over in West Virginia?"

"Yes, sir. About a week ago. Some cop came around looking for her. Thought she might have come through here for some reason."

"From the sheriff's office in Fayetteville?" Beamon said, a little confused. If this conversation happened a week ago, it would have been just after the murder. He knew for a fact that Bonnie Rile hadn't tracked Darby to Wyoming. Was she holding out on him? Was there something other than Darby's bank account that connected her to Conrad?

"Nah," Davey said. "He wasn't from West Virginia."

"Who was he, do you remember?" the chief said.

Davey shook his head apologetically. "You know, it was kind of a casual conversation—I barely glanced at his badge. I hadn't even heard anything about the murder when I talked to him." He paused for a moment to think. "State cop. Maybe from up north somewhere. I can't remember."

"Did you ask him why he'd be involved in a murder near Fayetteville?" Beamon said.

"Yeah. He said he was looking for her in connection with something else. That he had some circumstantial evidence that she might have come through here fleeing the murder scene . . ."

"No name, though, huh?" Beamon said.

Davey shook his head. "Sorry."

"Can you remember what he looked like?"

"Sure. Late twenties, athletic, about my height—six feet or so. Real nervous kind of guy; he looked really . . . I don't know . . . unhappy. Dark hair, but he was going kind of gray at the temples. Probably from being so nervous, huh?"

Beamon pulled a notepad from his pocket and jotted down the description. This was starting to get complicated. "You wouldn't happen to remember what day he was here?"

The young man looked down at the counter for about thirty seconds, an expression of deep concentration enveloping his face. Finally, he looked back up at Beamon. "I can't, I'm sorry. Maybe the end of the week or the beginning of the weekend."

Beamon noted the annoyed look on the face of the young man's boss and decided to do what he could to help the kid out. "Shit, I'd say that's pretty good. I can't remember what I had for breakfast." He closed his notebook and shoved it back in his pocket. "Conrad's a pretty small town, isn't it? You guys probably know just about everybody that lives here."

Davey nodded.

"Any rock climbers?"

"Rock climbers?" Davey looked behind him at the uniformed men who had been listening to the conversation. They all shrugged.

"Not that I know of. Pretty flat around here."

"Okay. One more question. This one's for all of you. Was there anything unusual going on here around the time Tristan Newberry was killed?"

"Unusual how?" the chief said.

"I don't know," Beamon admitted. "I'm fishing here."

"Well, if you don't cast a line, you can't catch anything." The chief walked back into the office and pulled a handful of files from a cabinet at the back.

"These are the dailies," he said, spreading them on the counter in front of Beamon and starting to flip through them. "Nothing," he said, closing the first file. He flipped open the second file, then quickly pushed it aside. "Nothing." Third file. "A DUI—guy from out of town hit a tree and broke his arm."

Beamon shook his head. He wasn't sure what he was looking for, but that wasn't it.

Fourth file. "Nothing." He flipped open the last file. "Some shooting out by the Bosdale place. Nothing." He closed it. "Sorry."

Beamon leaned over and looked at the cover of the last file. "What was that about the Bosdale place?"

"Sounds more interesting than it is, I expect. We got a call about gunshots out there. Probably some kids."

"What day was that?"

"Thursday."

That was the right answer. According to the coroner's report, Newberry had died on that day—though not of gunshot wounds.

"Would the Bosdales be home, you think?"

The sheriff shook his head. "Derrick Bosdale's one of those rich city guys that likes to come out on the weekends and play country gent. Haven't seen much of him lately, though. I guess with the economy the way it is, money's tight for him, too."

24

Derrick Bosdale's farmhouse looked to be a hundred and fifty years old: all rough-hewn planks and stone. It was perched on a lonely knoll overlooking the rolling western Maryland countryside and backed up to a tall, tree-covered butte. Beamon looked around himself one more time, confirming that there was nothing and no one in sight, and tried the knob on the back door again. Still locked, just like it had been ten seconds ago. He reached into the pocket of his parka and pulled out a pair of cheerfully colored fleece mittens, sighing quietly as he put them on. If he was going to start a career in the field of breaking and entering, he was going to have to find a new pair of gloves. Something in a latex, perhaps. Anything would be more dignified than the mittens Carrie had given him for Christmas.

He balled up his fist and put it through a small pane of glass in the door, flipped the deadbolt, and slipped inside. The kitchen he entered was about what he'd expected. The Bosdale family had apparently spent a great deal of money in an attempt to keep the original turn-of-the-century feel of the house and to camouflage any modern-day necessities. Useless artifacts and antiques cluttered every wall and corner, making him feel as though he was walking through a Civil War garage sale. The air smelled vaguely of mold and earth, but it didn't feel as dead as he would have expected in a house that had been closed up for months.

He had no idea what he was looking for as he walked quietly up the stairs, down the hall that ran the length of the second floor, and into the bathroom at the end. It, like the rest of the house, had a cartoonish antiquity to it and was devoid of personal effects. He turned a faucet handle and nothing came out.

Beamon started back down the hall, stopping in a small room that looked like it belonged to a young boy. What made it stand out was the unmistakable smell of paint and completely unmarked walls. If the local cops had been right and the Bosdales hadn't been around for months, it seemed kind of strange that they would bother to have a contractor come and paint a single tiny bedroom. . . .

No. He was letting his imagination run away with him. There was no evidence of Newberry having been moved postmortem. Hell, the chances that this house even figured into his case were almost nil. He was here purely out of desperation and the fact that he didn't have anything to go home to.

After a brief inspection of the two other bedrooms, Beamon took a quick turn around the ground floor. It was similarly semirenovated and pretty much empty of anything but old furniture, with the notable exception of a small office behind the living room. It alone seemed to have been spared the ravages of twentieth-century power tools and overeager decorators. The walls were cracked and discolored, and the oak floor had been worn away in the pattern of a century of foot traffic. The furniture was modern and electronics were all state of the art.

Beamon sat down in the expensive-looking leather chair behind the mahogany desk that dominated the room and started opening drawers. Once again, nothing very intriguing—general office supplies, mostly. No documents of any kind. There was a pad of stationery on the blotter with a company name on it: Deritech, Inc. Beamon pulled out his glasses and looked at the address: Lewiston, Maine.

What was Darby's connection to this town? he wondered, leaning back and putting his feet on the desk's carefully polished top. It wasn't between Fayetteville and Wyoming. And any local climbers serious enough to be friends with her would most likely be known by the cops.

Why would she detour here? Was it as simple as hitching a ride on the first car that would stop for her and going in whatever direction it took her to put miles between her and the murder scene? Somehow he doubted it. The further he got into this, the less it looked like the simple answer was going to be the correct one.

Why the out-of-state trooper? State cops didn't normally do that kind of investigation. And the story that she was wanted in another state was bullshit—the information he had suggested that she had only been arrested once in her life, for disturbing the peace.

He smiled, remembering the old police report he'd read. Darby had apparently been in the habit of picking up extra cash by getting into pull-up contests with macho types in bars. Sometimes there would be a significant number of bets—that she undoubtedly couldn't cover. She'd let her opponent go first, and then he'd have to watch that cute little thing desperately fight her way to ten or twelve repetitions, or whatever it took to win by one.

About two years ago, that little money-making scheme had backfired when she unknowingly challenged a Navy SEAL who was home on leave. He and his friends figured they'd been had when the cute little thing cranked off forty-seven to beat him. In the disturbance that ensued, Darby and a friend of hers were the only two people arrested.

Beamon turned a crystal paperweight over in his hands and went back to trying to sort out the increasingly bizarre facts of the case. Why were so many people interested in one dirt-poor girl with connections to nothing but a lover's quarrel turned ugly? He put his full mind to that question for the fiftieth time since he'd started this thing and came up with the same result: nothing.

It was time to shift gears—he was getting nowhere. There were two people involved in this crime: a killer and a victim. What if he discarded the theory that people were interested in Darby Moore? What if it was actually Tristan Newberry who had captured everyone's imagination?

25

Mark Beamon stopped in the doorway and surveyed the half-full restaurant/bar. The light was dim, but he was still able to pick Carrie out of the crowd. She seemed completely absorbed by the television bolted to the wall across from her, and Beamon followed her gaze to the glowing image of Robert Taylor. He was speaking to a small group of elderly people, wearing a tasteful sweater and no tie. The sound was off, but he was undoubtedly trying to convince them that he had the power to turn America's culture back into that of a black-and-white sitcom. It was Carrie's one quirk—she actually followed and bought into all this political bullshit. The woman dressed up to vote.

Fortunately, the circus that had been this year's presidential election was starting to die down at this point. The press was already treating Taylor like the new chief executive, and even hard-core liberals seemed to be okay with the selection, though they were trying not to be too obvious. In the end, they were just grateful that David Hallorin hadn't been able to get his campaign out of the cellar.

Beamon wandered to the bar, keeping out of Carrie's line of sight. "Light beer," he said to the bartender. "Whatever you've got."

The man dug a Budweiser out of the cooler and twisted the top off. "Do you have a table? I can have a waitress bring this over and put it on your bill."

Beamon answered by digging a five out of his pocket and slapping it on the bar. He wasn't quite ready for Carrie yet. The phone conversation he'd had with her earlier that day had been filled with unusual and

171

uncomfortable silences that he'd expected but hadn't been prepared for. It seemed as if almost overnight the casual ease of their relationship had been replaced by tension and awkwardness. He asked himself for the thousandth time if he'd done the right thing. And for the thousandth time, the answer was that he didn't know.

Beamon took a few sips of his beer and watched Taylor shake the wrinkled hands of his audience with the exaggerated warmth achieved only by the most accomplished politicians. When the scene cut to a commercial and Carrie's attention turned back to the glass of wine in front of her, Beamon started slowly weaving his way through the tightly packed tables toward her.

"Carrie," he said putting a hand on her shoulder and then quickly slipping into the chair across from her. He hoped that he had made the maneuver look effortless, but in actuality he had carefully designed it to put enough physical distance between them to solve the "to kiss or not to kiss" conundrum. "How are you?"

"Fine," Carrie said with a hesitant smile. "The question is, how are you?"

"Good. I'm good."

Another one of those silences.

"What's going on with the FBI?"

He shook his head. "I still have some time to think about it. Until I make a decision, I don't think they're very interested in talking to me."

She nodded, then they stared at each other for a while. Finally, she moved her hand across the table to a stapled stack of papers bristling with sticky notes. Darby Moore's diary.

"What did you make of it?" Beamon said, more anxious to end the excruciating lull in their conversation than to actually hear her analysis.

"I take it that this was written by the girl you're looking for?"

Beamon grabbed a menu and buried his face in it. "Darby Moore. What do you think about pizza?"

She ignored the question. "You think this girl killed her ex-boyfriend Tristan Newberry?"

The fact was, he was beginning to wonder. There were too many unlikely players and non sequiturs in this case. He was here hoping that Carrie could convince him again that this was just a simple case of love gone wrong. "You tell me."

"I'm a psychiatrist, Mark. Not a profiler. You must know twenty people who could have done a better job on this than me."

Beamon dropped the menu and spread his hands in an innocent gesture. "This is my private sector debut, Carrie. No more FBI to back me up. You have a bunch of letters after your name, so you came to mind . . ."

That, of course, was a complete lie—and there was part of him that hoped she knew it was. Besides, the profilers he knew didn't have any advantage over her in brainpower that he could see.

"Okay," Carrie said, centering the copied diary in front of her. "I've got sections marked in here if you want to read them later—they're categorized as Miscellaneous, Tristan, Power, and Death. Stuff I figured you'd be interested in."

He nodded vigorously as he tried to flag down a waitress.

"There's a very *unusual* dichotomy, here . . ." The way she dragged out the word *unusual* seemed to indicate that it was a euphemism for *bananas*. Carrie was about to tell him precisely what he wanted to still believe but couldn't: the girl was a little wacky and just snapped. Happened every day. To normal people—ones with homes, spouses, kids, jobs. People who wore watches and knew what day it was. Right?

"At times, her writing can be very lyrical," Carrie started. "She describes amazing adventures and seems very positive even in the face of hardships that would probably kill you or I. What she has to say about the places she goes and the people she meets is very insightful and sometime kind of . . . beautiful."

"I saw a bunch of her photographs from Borneo," Beamon said. "They were spectacular. People, landscapes, architecture. Really amazing."

"That doesn't surprise me." Carrie turned to one of the many marked pages in the diary and read a brief but touching passage about the sound and smell of the rain in the jungle. When she was finished, she turned the entire document around so that Beamon could see the water smudges in the blocky handwriting.

"She was actually sitting in the rain while she wrote?" Beamon said.

"No, that's the interesting part. She was looking out the window of a hut in the middle of nowhere. The smudges are from sweat—she'd been horribly ill with some kind of jungle fever. Despite that, though, she sat up and wrote this passage."

Beamon finally captured a waitress and pointed to the vegetarian pizza. Their normal compromise. "I don't know, Carrie," he said as the waitress hurried off. "You should have seen this kid, Tristan. He was killed with an ice axe—looked like he'd been run over by a rototiller. Doesn't sound like the work of a twenty-seven-year-old girl who likes to write about the sound of the rain."

"I'm going through the positive stuff first. You never let me finish."

"Sorry."

"There are a few mentions of Tristan in here, but not really that many. She writes about him only in contexts—by that I mean, she'll write about a trip that he was on or something they did together. She felt very close to him and there was a real affection between them. They definitely slept together and he was apparently quite gifted in that area, but no real passion comes through. It's like they knew that their lives would never mesh, and so they never really let themselves sink too deeply in their feelings for each other."

"Uh huh," Beamon said, and finished his beer with a final gulp.

"As far as her lifestyle goes," Carrie continued, "she seems to have only one true passion: climbing. I'll tell you, after reading everything she wrote about it, I'm dying to try it."

Beamon rolled his eyes.

"Money, a home, long-term relationships—they don't seem to be a priority for her. It's interesting, a lot of her friends are a little dishonest in the way they support themselves without working—not stealing per se, but scamming. She'll have none of it. You know why?"

Beamon shook his head.

"Because she feels sorry for us. People who work their lives away and never have a chance to really pursue the things they love. She thinks that it would be unconscionable for her to take things from a group of people who have only things."

This was all very educational, but he was more interested in the lurid details—they were his last hope. "I haven't really looked at that thing, Carrie, but the sheriff who found it read me a bunch of stuff about a weird inferiority complex she had."

Carrie flipped a few pages and read aloud. "'Sometimes I think men never grow up but are in a perpetual stage of preadolescence. Speed on the playground and accuracy with a ball gets replaced with contests of power that they wrap everything they are up in and try to drag me into.'" She looked up at him. "This is what I'm talking about with the dichotomy—it's almost schizophrenic. On one hand you have this girl who just seems to float along through life pursuing what she loves and ignoring everything else, and on the other hand, you have a woman who has this unhealthy relationship to men in general. The diary doesn't go back very far, so I don't have anything on her childhood. I'd be very interested to meet her father."

"Dead," Beamon said. "No living relatives at all to speak of."

"Well, maybe there's something there. Her ideas on death are kind of unusual. There's no mention of God or religion, more a philosophy of death being a part of the cycle of life."

Beamon shrugged. "People love writing philosophical crap about death. But we all react the same when we're faced with it."

She flipped to another page and slid the diary over to Beamon. The writing was almost illegible. The letters were large and imprecise, consisting of shaky lines and large streaks of ink. "She's in a tent here, Mark. Somewhere in Asia. Her friend is dead, and it's her expectation that she's not far behind. I'd say that she was being faced with it."

Beamon read what he could in the dim light. Carrie was right. It was a farewell. The overall theme was simple. No regrets. He wondered how many people could say that same thing sitting alone in the frozen darkness waiting for the Grim Reaper to ski up to them.

"So what we're seeing here," Carrie said, "is the part of Darby Moore that *could* have committed this crime. There may even be a clue as to what drove her over the edge."

"Really?" Beamon said, a little too enthusiastically. "That'd be great."

Carrie looked at him strangely for a moment, then flipped to a page toward the end. "She goes on a trip with two men and suffers from a horrible feeling of powerlessness. It's here that the earlier passages come together in a picture of a woman who is obsessed with dominance."

Beamon skimmed the section of the page that had been highlighted. Carrie was right—Darby seemed to write about her feelings in a casual, good-natured tone, but they were clearly there and definitely strong. He flipped back a page and skimmed it.

Chris and Fred have completely dominated me this entire trip and there's just nothing I can do about it.

Chris and Fred. Beamon scrunched up his face and slid the diary back onto the table. Chris and Fred . . .

"Is something wrong, Mark?"

"No. I'm okay, go on."

"The indifference—no, that's the wrong word—acceptance of death I don't think is important in and of itself. Just because you've faced death before doesn't mean you'd find it easier to kill someone. But when you combine it with her deep-seated feelings of inadequacy and powerlessness, you may have someone capable of something like this . . ."

Beamon closed his eyes and let out a low moan. When he opened them again, he said, "What if none of that powerlessness stuff was there? What then?"

"I don't think you can just ignore the entire side of her personality that would—"

"Humor me."

She was silent for a moment. "Okay. I would say it was very unlikely that she could do something like this. She loves life, has no violent fantasies that she expresses in writing, and most importantly, had never allowed her feelings for Tristan Newberry to progress. If anything, I think she'd have been happy for him if he found another woman."

Beamon's beer bottle was empty, so he reached across the table and started in on her glass of wine. "I was reading about this climbing route that just got done. It overhangs like fifty degrees. The crux—the hardest move—is one where you have half of the first digit of two fingers in a tiny hole, your feet are on two things the size of nickels stuck to the rock and you have to jump for a hole that will only fit one finger."

"Really? That doesn't sound possible, does it?" Carrie said slowly, obviously wondering where this sudden change in subject was going.

"Darby's friends Chris and Fred were the ones who finally did it. They're considered two of the most powerful climbers in the world. Either one of them could do multiple pull-ups off a single pinky."

Carrie stared at him for a moment. "Physical power. Are you saying that Darby is writing about physical power?"

Beamon put his head in his hands and stared down at the table. "There are entire books written on it. Magazine articles. Studies. Climbers are obsessed with it. Getting strong enough to make it to the next level."

Carrie flipped through some of the marked pages in the diary, quickly scanning each one and finally stopping at the last sticky note. "Men have no respect for a woman's power. They have to be shown over and over again and then still make excuses and deny it. What's wrong with them?" She read and then dropped the copied diary on the table. "I feel really stupid."

"You feel stupid? I've been thinking about this thing twenty-four hours a day for the last week. Shit."

"If she didn't do it, then who did? And where is she? Do you think someone might have her?"

"I know for a fact no one does," Beamon said. "Or at least no one did as of a few days ago."

"Then what?"

"I don't know," he said through a mouthful of thumbnail. "Maybe she and Tristan were attacked and she got away. Then she found out she was a suspect and just kept on running." That theory didn't work on an impressive number of levels. "Or maybe the person I'm working for killed him and he's got to get to her to keep her quiet."

"What would make you say that?"

"I'm being paid too goddamn well. Good guys are notoriously cheap. Shit." He leaned back and forced a smile, despite the growing feeling that this situation was going to get his ass shot off. "Never a dull moment, huh? How's Emory?"

26

Mark Beamon climbed the stairs as quietly as he could without actually looking suspicious. The building was silent around him, as he'd expected. It was one o'clock in the afternoon and the apartment complex he was in screamed low-income working class. Anyone who was making enough for mom to stay home with the kids was living a few blocks north, and the temporarily or terminally unemployed were spread out to the south.

At the top of the stairs, Beamon turned right and quickly found the door to Tristan Newberry's apartment. There was no police tape—again, as he'd expected. Bonnie Rile in Fayetteville had warned Tristan's parents and the landlord about entering the apartment, but had taken the perfectly reasonable position that there was no reason to rush out and search it.

Beamon looked around him at the empty hall and reached into his trench coat for the half-sized crowbar propped under his arm. He shoved one end between the door and jamb and leaned his body weight into it. The old wood gave easily but not without a protest that echoed through the hallway. He slipped through the half-open door and forced it closed behind him, cursing his lack of skill with locks. If he was going to keep doing this kind of thing, he was going to have to find someone to teach him a little finesse. Perhaps that was the bright side to his impending imprisonment—a chance to learn from the pros.

The apartment was pleasantly messy and just a bit dirty, with worn, mismatched furniture strategically placed to make the most of the limited space. The living room and kitchen were more or less combined into one open area with only two doors in it, the one he'd just come through and one at the back through which he could see the edge of an unmade bed.

The question now was what the hell was he here to find?

He'd started this case calculating an eighty percent chance that Darby had just gotten plain pissed off and killed her boyfriend. God knew that statistics supported the fact that if you were going to be hacked to pieces, it was going to be done by someone who loved you.

He'd given half of the remaining twenty percent to the possibility that Darby was currently the love slave of two guys named Clem and was residing in a shack somewhere deep in the woods of West Virginia. Her visit to Wyoming seemed to debunk that theory.

The last ten percent, as it always was, had been reserved for the "something else" category: papal conspiracy, spontaneous combustion, or whatever.

But now where was he? There were at least two private investigations into this incident that he knew of, he had mysterious out-of-state cops sniffing around for Darby, he had a diary that suggested Darby's relationship with Tristan Newberry was more warm than hot, and a murder weapon that may or may not have been hers. His "something else" category had ballooned to a healthy seventy percent.

The shaky theory that this was about Tristan and not Darby was about all he had left. As it turned out, finding a girl with tentative human relationships and the ability to live for six months on thirty-eight cents and a couple of fruit roll-ups wasn't as easy as he'd hoped.

Beamon decided to start his search with the refrigerator. As he'd suspected, it contained the remnants of a six-pack. He doubted Tristan would miss one little beer, so he took one and tried unsuccessfully to unscrew the top.

Setting the beer down on the counter next to two breadcrumb-covered dishes, Beamon slipped on a pair of brand-new latex gloves. It took less than a minute to find a combination corkscrew/bottle opener in the bottom of one of the kitchen drawers. He carefully wiped off any prints he might have left on the bottle and opened it. The beer smelled bitter—one of those goddamn microbrews—but it was better than nothing.

He noted the empty wine bottles next to the two plates and the similarly crumb-covered cutting board, and tried to reconstruct Darby and Tristan's second-to-last evening together.

Darby had probably just popped in unannounced. That fit with what little he knew of her personality. Besides, an anticipated visit from an old girlfriend would have rated a better dinner and at least a partial tidying of the apartment. So she'd showed up and they'd cracked open a couple of bottles and gotten fairly drunk, based on the fact that they were both as skinny as rails.

As near as he could tell from talking to various climbers in West Virginia, the two hadn't arrived at the New River Gorge till around three the next day, so they probably spent the night in this apartment and slept off the alcohol before driving off in Darby's van.

Beamon walked into the even messier bedroom and found long dark hairs on one of the pillows on the bed. He reached for one, but then stopped himself. He had no access to a lab anymore. He'd just have to assume they were Darby's. He grabbed hold of the blanket and was going to pull it back, but decided that looking for sex stains on sheets was a little lower than he was willing to stoop at this point. Wouldn't prove anything—based on the pictures he'd seen, there would have been any number of women willing to generate stains with Tristan Newberry.

Beamon stepped over two bath towels lying on the floor and stopped in front of a collection of framed pictures on Tristan's dresser. The theme seemed to be outdoor adventure: him with groups of similarly athletic-looking people standing on top of mountains, in forests, alongside kayaks, on skis. Darby was in three of the seven, but in only one was she even standing next to Tristan.

On the edge of the dresser was a pile of cards that looked like they'd been recently emptied from Newberry's wallet. A library card, a social security card, a Blockbuster Video card, a punch card from the Sub Czar promising a free sandwich, a national park pass. All things he wouldn't have needed on a long weekend excursion to West Virginia and wouldn't want to lose. Beamon did the same thing himself when he went on trips.

He opened the drawers of the dresser and pawed through them, but found nothing more interesting than an unusually thick stack of postcards held together with a rubber band. Most were from foreign countries, depicting spectacular vistas and partially covered with brightly colored stamps. Beamon read through them quickly, finding that most concisely related an adventure the writer was embarking on or had just completed. He separated out the four from Darby. The messages were short and not particularly personal—generally reports on the quality of climbing where she was. *Gasherbrum sucked. Lost some of my nose but still have all my fingers. Could have been worse* was about as sappy as she got, supporting Carrie's theory that the relationship between them wasn't exactly what one would call frenzied.

Beamon wandered back out into the living room and sat down at a computer set up in front of the only window in the apartment. He pulled up the answering machine software and found no messages. It took a few minutes, but he managed to find the message-recording screen and hit Test.

"This is Tristan," a young, cheerful voice said from the two speakers set up alongside the monitor. It was kind of startling. The only contact with Newberry that Beamon had was looking at pictures—most of them depicting not Tristan Newberry but what was left of him.

"I've got the ringer off because I'm not feeling well. I'll get back to you as soon as I can." An obvious plant, in case the office called while he was off climbing.

Beamon minimized the answering machine and clicked on the address book icon, discovering that Tristan had had a lot of friends but that most of them were spread throughout the country and the world—not a single local number. The only D.C. exchange was under the heading "Business." No address had been recorded.

Beamon dialed the number. Maybe a talk with Tristan's coworkers would shed some light. One thing he'd learned in his years as an FBI agent was that the acquaintances of murder victims just loved to theorize.

A machine picked up on the second ring. "Please leave a message after the tone," was all it said. The information he had suggested that Newberry had worked for the government, but that seemed a bit concise for a federal organization. He considered leaving his name and number, but something told him it would be a mistake.

After an unproductive search of the rest of the files contained on the computer, Beamon stood and started in on the tiny living space. Another twenty minutes ended with more questions than answers. Most of the dust that uniformly covered the apartment had been scraped from the overfilled bookshelves along the wall, suggesting that most, if not all, the books had been recently removed. Of course, there could be a number of mundane explanations for that. Beamon dropped to his hands and knees and crawled around on the cheap carpet for a few minutes. The indentions made by the legs of the furniture were mostly dead on. But a few were off a good half an inch.

He retrieved his beer from the kitchen and lay down in the soft cushions of the sofa, trying to let the kinks fall out of his back muscles. Even in first class, this constant plane travel was taking its toll.

He hadn't thought much about the fact that the apartment's only corkscrew seemed to be at the bottom of a drawer and that there were two uncorked wine bottles on the counter, thinking that Darby had probably opened it with a Swiss Army knife or something. But combined with the bookcase and furniture, it seemed to suggest that the place had been recently searched. Not by the West Virginia cops, though—he was sure they hadn't been there yet, and cops were never this neat anyway. Who, then? Beamon's own enigmatic employer? Vili Marcek and his to-be-named-later companion? The out-of-state cop who had been sniffing around Conrad, Maryland? There was no lack of options.

Beamon picked up his beer and brought it with him into the bedroom, where he stuffed the sandwich shop punch card on Newberry's dresser in his pocket. It was time to quit screwing around. He needed to find this girl and figure out what the fuck what was going on before one of them got themselves in trouble.

27

"**Y**eah, I'll take one of those turkey ones but no sprouts, okay? I hate those things."

The young black girl behind the counter went to work on his sandwich without a word. It was late in the afternoon and the Sub Czar was empty except for the two of them. Beamon watched her assemble his sandwich with quick, deft motions, then followed her along the counter to a cash register. "I'll take a bag of chips and a Coke with that, too, please," he said, fondling Tristan Newberry's sandwich punch card in his pocket. He considered pulling it out and getting the last punch needed for a free sub. After some thought, though, eating a dead man's sub for dinner didn't seem right. He'd already tested the gods by drinking the kid's beer.

"Eight seventy-three," the woman said.

Based on the punch card, Beamon was assuming that Newberry often ate at this broken-down deli in the middle of an equally broken-down D.C. industrial park. It seemed likely, then, that he worked somewhere close. Unless these sandwiches were a hell of a lot better than they looked, the Sub Czar just wasn't a destination restaurant.

"You know, I was supposed to meet a friend of mine here for lunch," Beamon said digging a ten out of his wallet. "Obviously, I'm a little late."

The young woman's mouth hung open, effectively displaying her utter disinterest in his dining arrangements.

"I think he comes here a lot," Beamon continued, holding up his wallet so that she could see a picture of Newberry that he had cut down and nestled in one of the plastic flaps next to a photo of Emory. "He didn't tell me which building he worked in, though. You wouldn't know him

185

would you? His name's Tristan." He had to maneuver the wallet in front of her face as she painstakingly ignored it.

Finally, she gave the photo an annoyed glance. "Yeah, I see him in here. But I don't know where he work."

"Could you maybe tell me which way he goes when he leaves? I could probably find him."

"What way he goes? Hell, I don't know."

Beamon glanced down at the picture and then behind him at the large glass window that looked out on the street. "If I were a woman, I think I'd definitely want to watch him walk away from me."

She snorted loudly and a smile spread slowly across her face. "Yeah, he ain't bad for a white boy. Real sweet, too." She pointed out the window. "He go that way."

"Mark Beamon. I was with the FBI," Beamon said quietly to himself as he wandered up the broken sidewalk, munching on the last of his potato chips. He'd almost perfected the slurring of the word *was* in the sentence and tried it a few more times as he approached yet another rusting metal warehouse.

So far, nearly every building he'd been to was empty and locked up tight, a testament to the less than wonderful economy. Of the two occupied spaces he'd come across, one housed a company that rented port-a-potties and the other a group of men who had damn near started projectile sweating when he'd spoken the letters FBI. Some kind of stolen merchandise storage facility, he guessed. Two utterly recession-proof businesses.

Beamon tossed the potato chip bag into a loose pile of garbage along the curb and pushed at a heavy door in the side of Warehouse 4-G. While there was no sign identifying the occupant, the door wasn't locked, so he stepped inside.

The office/reception area he found himself in was a tiny, faded green room with a low counter along the back and an ancient-looking security guard standing behind it. This was looking a little better. The government had apparently gotten a deal on this particular shade of green paint sometime back in the seventies and covered nearly every wall they owned with it.

"Hey, you're that FBI agent I saw on TV," the guard said as he approached.

Beamon smiled engagingly, happy not to have to test his artful slurring again. He held out a hand to the old guard, who took it excitedly.

"Name's Mark Beamon."

"Sure. Beamon. That's it. Damn. Carl Whitlock."

"Nice to meet you, Carl." Beamon looked around him. "Maybe you can help me with something. I'm looking for the place a guy named Newberry worked."

Whitlock's deeply lined face seemed to suddenly take on a few more years. "This is it. This is where he worked."

"I guess you heard what happened, then."

"Yeah. They came and picked up his personal stuff a few days ago. Guess they're gonna close this place down now. Probably as early as this week. Just as well."

"What did Tristan do here?"

"Here?" the old man said, as though there was no way Beamon could be interested. "It's just a warehouse. Government keeps a bunch of old files here. Tristan worked on them."

"Worked on them?"

Whitlock shrugged his bony shoulders. "It's part of that new declassification thing."

Beamon nodded. It was possibly the only piece of legislation David Hallorin had ever been able to ram through Congress, and a good one at that. It had been too easy to classify documents and keep them classified without thinking. Beamon himself had been guilty of that—no one had ever gotten a kick in the ass for being too careful.

"Listen, Carl. I'm looking into Tristan's death—"

"Really?"

"Yeah, really. Maybe you could help me. Is there anyone here that Tristan knew well? That he talked to a lot?"

"Well, I'm the only one here, but we talked all the time. We were good friends."

Beamon thought he had misunderstood the man. "Good. Then I'll need to get some information from you too. But what about the people Tristan worked with directly? The people—"

"There are no other people. Just us."

Beamon scrunched up his brow and leaned forward across the counter, which allowed him to see through the open door that led to the warehouse section of the building. Not much was visible, but from what he *could* see of the file-stacked shelves, it would be a hell of a job for one person to go through them all and sign off on declassification.

"Okay, fine," Beamon said, still a bit perplexed. "Did he ever talk about a girl named Darby Moore?"

The old man's eyes narrowed perceptibly. "That's the girl who murdered him."

"Allegedly murdered him, Carl. Allegedly."

The old man seemed already convinced of her guilt, as was everyone who didn't know her. "I've been trying to think since I heard," he said. "My memory's not as good as it used to be. I don't know. He might have."

"So it's possible that in your entire relationship with Tristan . . . how long?"

"About four months."

"Four months. It's possible that Tristan never once mentioned her in all that time?"

Whitlock looked uncomfortable. "It's possible, I suppose. I don't know. He used to talk about all the places he'd been and things he'd done with lots of different people. She could have been one of them. In fact, she probably was."

More corroboration for Tristan and Darby's lack of a relationship. "And he didn't mention that he was going climbing for a few days." It seemed unlikely that he would, since it had been obvious from his answering machine that he was playing hooky.

The old man shook his head. "Called in sick Tuesday. He *was* in a hurry to get out of here on Monday, though. We were supposed to have a beer after work."

That was interesting. Accounts seemed to agree that Tristan and Darby didn't arrive at the New River Gorge until Wednesday. Of course, it was possible that he was actually sick, but Beamon doubted it.

"Okay, Carl," Beamon said, shoving his hands in his pockets and nodding toward the entrance to the warehouse. "You mind if I take a quick look at where he worked?"

Whitlock flipped up a section of countertop and let him through. The warehouse that opened up behind the office/reception area was even more expansive than Beamon had expected. "It would take one person three lifetimes to get through all this stuff," he said, looking down the seemingly endless rows of overflowing shelves.

"More than that for Tristan."

Beamon glanced over at the old man. "What makes you say that?"

Whitlock suddenly looked a little guilty. He lowered his voice to a volume more suitable for speaking ill of the dead. "I've worked in other places, too, you know. There were more people on staff, for sure, but well, each one went through box after box, you know? Sometimes I wondered if they really even read any of it. Not Tristan; he went through everything real careful. Every day, I'd help him pull a couple of boxes from here or there, and he'd stick his head in them for hours. He was real thorough."

Beamon walked over to an empty table and glanced up at a video camera that looked too new and high-tech to belong in this dump. "Is this where he sat?"

The old man nodded.

"So you say he didn't go through the stuff in order?"

"Nope. He's been all over this place. Just takes them from wherever he feels like."

Beamon ran his palms across the table and tried to picture Tristan sitting behind it. None of it seemed right. Beamon had worked for the government his entire adult life, and he could say with some certainty that this wasn't the way things were done. "Tell me, Carl. Do you remember where the last box Tristan was working on came from?"

The old man nodded and pointed toward the back of the building. "He'd been working on some stuff from back there for a while, and then went back to where we got it from and pulled a bunch of the boxes off the shelf. I heard the racket and went back to check on him. He was sitting on the floor throwin' stuff around. Didn't even notice I was there."

"Did he normally do stuff like that?"

"Not that I ever saw."

"Could you show me where?" Beamon said.

Whitlock seemed anxious to cooperate as they walked down the narrow aisle, but started to look uncomfortable when Beamon began peeking in the tops of the boxes that Tristan had been so interested in before he died. When he pulled one of the boxes onto the floor, the old man finally spoke up. "I don't know if you should be doing that, Mr. Beamon. I mean, I know you're an FBI agent and all, but, well, maybe I should call for authorization. . ." His voice trailed off. He was obviously waiting to be talked out of that particular action, either because he wanted Tristan's killer brought to justice, or because it would cause more work for him. Beamon was about to oblige when he realized that Whitlock might be his ticket to meeting the man in charge of this rather odd little government backwater.

"I wouldn't want you to get in any trouble, Carl. Why don't you do that."

Beamon dug a handful of files and loose papers from the box at his feet as the old man started dejectedly back to his office.

About ten minutes, and forty or so tedious government documents later, Carl came rushing back holding his hand over the receiving end of a cordless phone.

"Mr. Beamon!" he said breathlessly. "They say you have to leave here immediately!"

Not an entirely unexpected reaction. Beamon reached up and pulled another box off the shelf. He grabbed a piece of paper from it and wrote on the back in bold letters.

TELL THEM I'M ARMED.

Whitlock stared at the message and seemed to still be staring after Beamon had dropped it on the floor and started digging through the new box.

"Uh, sir?" he heard the old man say into the phone. His voice was hesitant. "He says he's armed." The shouting over the other end was clearly audible, though indecipherable from where Beamon sat.

Whitlock held out the phone. "He wants to talk to you."

Beamon waved his hand dismissively, not bothering to look up from the documents he had spread across the floor.

"He won't talk," Whitlock said into the phone. The click as the person on the other end slammed the handset down seemed to echo through the building.

"They're coming."

"Thanks, Carl," Beamon said absently, concentrating on the problem taking shape before him. "You wouldn't happen to have any hot coffee back in your office, would you?"

Thirty minutes later, Beamon was leaning his cramping back against an empty shelf with six boxes and countless pages of government documents piled up around him. Newberry had obviously been through those particular six and had apparently been excited. Papers and files had been stuffed haphazardly back into them, in stark contrast to the neatly packed boxes surrounding them.

Despite Newberry's interest, though, the only thing Beamon had found that wouldn't put a speed freak to sleep was some old FBI stuff. Even that, though, was only noteworthy because it was misfiled in a bunch of Ag Department droning. It consisted mostly of old Hoover-era stuff—endless memos on petty crimes and even pettier criminals, budgets, internal pissing contests, commies hiding under the sofa cushions, and what have you. Beamon flipped over an original memo signed by the Hoov himself, and started scribbling on it what he knew about this case from a Newberry-centric point of view.

Tristan had been working alone in a warehouse full of classified documents for four months. He was working slowly, seemingly randomly. On his last day in the office, he breaks out of his pattern—finds something interesting enough in one of the boxes to come back here and rifle through the ones around it, not even bothering to take them back to his desk. Based on what Beamon knew about the epic dullness of everything and everyone involved with Agriculture, it seemed reasonable to assume that the misfiled FBI documents were what got him so fired up. Had he been looking for them? His work pattern and the fact that he was alone might suggest a search. Or was all this just a bunch of far-fetched mental masturbation? Beamon decided to assume that it wasn't and resumed working on his timeline.

Next, Newberry rushes out of there, standing the security guard up for a beer, calls in sick, does something unknown for a day, then goes on a climbing trip with Darby Moore. Then he turns up dead—tirelessly perforated with an ice axe. Darby takes off, detouring through Conrad, Maryland, then to get her stuff in Wyoming, then disappears again, obviously running. Who was she running from? The cops? Why didn't she go straight to them if someone else killed Newberry? It would have been the natural reaction for anyone in her position.

Then—and this was his favorite part—an impeccably dressed attorney comes to his house and offers him three hundred thousand dollars to find the girl on behalf of an anonymous client. And by the looks of things, Beamon wasn't the only one who had been hired for this particular job.

There was a loud crash as the front door to the building was thrown open, breaking his concentration. Beamon carefully folded up the piece of paper he'd been doodling on and shoved it under the shelf behind him as two D.C. cops started closing quickly on his position.

"Come out from there!" one of them shouted. "And, boy, I better be able to see your hands!"

Beamon stood slowly and shuffled out into the open with his hands on his head. The larger of the two cops kept an automatic trained on his chest as the other rushed forward and pushed him roughly to his knees and then to his face.

Beamon was read his rights and searched, wincing slightly when his arms were yanked behind his back and handcuffed. When he was safely bound, the cop covering him holstered his weapon and helped drag him to his feet. As soon as Beamon was standing under his own power, an imposing man in a gray business suit appeared through the door at the other side of the building and walked purposefully toward them. While he hadn't taken part in the fireworks, his grave, supervisory expression said clearly that he was in charge.

"I guess you're the man I've been looking for," Beamon said, being less than cooperative as the two cops tried to drag him from the warehouse. "Did Tristan Newberry work for you?" He craned his neck to keep the man in view as he was pulled past. "Where did all these files come from? Why aren't they in the National Archives? Why is this place being closed down? And who the hell *are* you?"

Carl flashed an apologetic smile just before the two cops used Beamon's face to push the door open and marched him to the cruiser parked on the sidewalk. One of the cops opened the back door of the car and the other shoved him through it in a coordinated effort that suggested a significant amount of practice. Beamon struggled into a sitting position and leaned out the open door so they couldn't close it. The man in the gray suit was just then walking though the door that Beamon's head had been so instrumental in opening.

"No answers for me today?" Beamon said as one of the cops lined up to slam the door on his leg.

"Wait," the man said, stopping and cocking his head slightly to the right. "All right, Mr. Beamon. Fine. My name is Price. This is one of many satellite warehouses used for overflow while we go through document declassification. Tristan Newberry worked here before he was killed. This facility is being closed down because we've cleared enough space in the central warehouses to consolidate these documents. I believe that was all your questions?"

The cop holding the door wound up to slam it and Beamon pulled his leg back just in time to avoid a cracked shin. He immediately hooked a toe under the driver's seat and pulled himself up to the metal screen separating the backseat from the front. "Hey, Price! How many government workers does it take to screw in a lightbulb?"

If the man knew the answer, he wasn't saying.

The truth was, there was no punch line that Beamon was aware of. All he knew was that the answer wasn't one. The U.S. government did not send a twenty-six-year-old kid alone into a warehouse full of classified government documents and tell him to knock himself out. Hell, there was probably a chain of command fifty people deep just to schedule the cleaning of the Pentagon's toilets.

Beamon leaned back into the seat and tried to move his hands into a more comfortable position as the two cops slid into the front and eased the cruiser back out onto the quiet street.

"Come on, guys," Beamon said. "I haven't been arrested in years. How 'bout a little siren?"

28

David Hallorin was focused almost completely on his peripheral vision. At the edge of it, he could see the studio audience lined up in rows that ascended into the darkness and Oprah Winfrey standing on the stairs near the stage.

To the cameras and the millions watching the images they recorded, though, he was concentrating on Phillippe Mohamed, nodding thoughtfully as the bow-tied leader of the Nation of Islam spoke in precise, clipped sentences.

The last fifty minutes had been the most difficult of Hallorin's career. It was critical that he show enough respect for Mohamed to keep his message from being degraded by obvious personal animosity, but not so much that Mohamed's many powerful white detractors would see Hallorin as weak. It was a nearly impossible balancing act that he had pulled off brilliantly. He already knew before seeing the tape that he had created one of the most riveting pieces of television ever broadcast.

Hallorin was still only half listening as Mohamed continued the diatribe he'd started some three minutes before. They were all the same—the evil of white America, the clandestine conspiracies to keep blacks down, the popular fantasy of African-American history.

". . . pattern of slavery and degradation."

Mohamed folded his hands in his lap and let his final words hang, staring at Hallorin with the polite smile that seemed permanently etched into his face. Hallorin didn't reply right away, making it look like he was giving the man's words the deep thought that a very vocal minority of Americans thought they deserved.

"*I* believe," Hallorin started slowly, "that it's critical for the African-American community to look forward to its future and not backward to its past. The slavery issue is always there, lurking in the background and creating an atmosphere of guilt and distrust. So let's talk about that for a moment." He took a sip from the glass of water next to him, mostly for the drama of the pause, but also because the television lights were close to making him break into a sweat—something no politician could afford.

"Less than five percent of white Americans ever owned slaves—the rest of them were just working their fields and trying to raise their kids. Anyone from that small group who actually participated in the slave trade died generations ago—it's unlikely that anyone in America has ever even met a person who owned a slave. On the other side of this story are the hundreds of thousands of white Americans who died freeing the slaves. But again, this is irrelevant—the people who participated at that time in American history have been dead for a century."

Hallorin crossed his legs and let an ironic smile cross his face. "Look at my situation. Right now, my opponents are glued to their TV sets waiting for me to say something they can use against me. Likewise the press." He looked over at Oprah. "Present company excepted." The light on the camera covering him flashed off for a moment so that another could pick up Oprah's nodded acknowledgment.

"Are they doing this because they hate me? Because they have some kind of prejudice against me? No, it's because if I'm president they can't be. And, if to gain the presidency, they have to climb over my carcass, they will." He looked straight into the camera. "That's not meant to be a slight against my opponents. Frankly, within certain bounds, I'd do the same to them." He readjusted his gaze back to Mohamed, who had a wonderful tendency not to interrupt. "In a free society—and this is a free society, or Ms. Winfrey wouldn't be one of the wealthiest entertainment moguls in the world—the person who gets the prize is the one who wants it the most. My sense is that many African Americans lack a clear focus as to exactly what it is they want."

"But, Mr. Hallorin," Mohamed said, taking advantage of a brief pause. "If I am not mistaken, you are last in this presidential race."

Hallorin smiled. Roland Peck was a true wonder. After watching probably five hundred hours of Mohamed on tape, Peck had anticipated nearly every statement Mohamed had made. He'd called that last one almost verbatim.

"You prove my point, Reverend," Hallorin responded smoothly. "I want the presidency, sure, but I want it on my terms. I promised myself that I would be completely honest with the American people—that I would say exactly what I believe—and that I would not personally attack my opponents. In the end, if that philosophy hurts me I have no one to blame but myself."

Mohamed's frustration continued to build as Hallorin used Peck's carefully crafted responses to subvert everything the man said. "Yes, Senator," Mohamed said, the anger starting to show around the edges of his well-practiced serenity. "Your ideas on personal responsibility and social Darwinism are well documented. Anyone who does not fall into step with white society will be selected out. Victims of your horrifying ideas on welfare reform and your Eugenics Machine."

He'd actually given Mohamed too much credit. The Reverend was apparently going to continue walking into Peck's right crosses until the network felt sorry enough for him to turn the cameras off.

Hallorin raised his eyebrows just the way he'd practiced and affected a little uncomfortable squirming in his chair. "I didn't think it would be my responsibility to defend the African-American community tonight, but I feel obligated to point out that there are more whites on welfare than blacks."

Mohamed just glared back at him. Checkmate. What was he going to do? Tell the millions of people watching that there was a much higher percentage of blacks on welfare? Not exactly beneficial to his cause.

"Hold on there, Senator," Oprah said. He turned toward her with a calm that he didn't feel. Peck had been less efficient with their host's reactions. His philosophy and strategies centered on the weakness in people, which worked ninety percent of the time. Unfortunately, Peck was completely baffled by those rare individuals whose lives were not ruled by fear and jealousy. Oprah Winfrey seemed to be one of those people: perilously intelligent, dangerously popular, and with no identifiable agenda.

"This Eugenics Machine that the Reverend mentioned," Oprah continued. "I think we'd all like to hear a little more about that. I know I would." The audience murmured their agreement.

Hallorin looked down at his feet for a moment and then back at his host. "If you went to the worst elementary school in America, you would probably find a child in a classroom playing with a computer that is more sophisticated than any you'd find on the desk of your government officials. People are *demanding* a smaller, more efficient government. People are *demanding* lower taxes. And in order to give them that, we are going to have to actually *use* the technology that's out there. The machine we're talking about—and that's been the subject of so many half-truths and sensational sound bites—relates to welfare reform. It actually exists. In fact, I personally used it in a recent test. It looks like an automatic teller machine. You put in your welfare card—works like a credit card—and then depress your finger on a pad. A laser gives it a tiny prick—can't even feel it—and in less than two minutes, this new technology analyzes your blood, confirming your identity and health status and screening for drug use. If all is clear, your card is funded with your welfare stipend. If not, you're referred to the appropriate counselor—"

"Let's tell the truth, Senator," Mohamed said, cutting him off for the first time. It was a shame the program was nearing an end. A few more jabs and he'd completely lose that plastic composure of his.

"By health screening you mean pregnancy and AIDS tests. And as for the narcotics test, well, wouldn't you just be screening for the drugs that your administration would be providing these people through your legalization program? Isn't that right?"

Hallorin looked into the crowd. "I know that Reverend Mohamed believes that this is all very sinister, and he's good at making it sound that way, but it really isn't all that interesting. I won't apologize for wanting to provide free counseling and clean needles to people with drug problems. If you have AIDS, it is critical that you get to someone who can help. If you're pregnant, it's also critical that—"

Mohamed cut him off again, finishing his sentence for him. "—you give up your baby to the white government so that it can be given to white couples to have its uniqueness and identity stripped from it. And there would be no choice under your administration, would there? Your government would provide no help to support that baby as long as it stays in the hands of the parent. The children will just starve. A problem that solves itself, yes, Senator?"

"I do not support additional money for welfare dependents who have additional children, if that's what you're referring to. I don't know any working Americans who get a raise if they have a child, and I'm not sure that welfare recipients should be given benefits that other American families don't have. They, like everyone else, need to carefully consider the demands that a child will place on them, both financially and emotionally. Welfare is a temporary helping hand, not a lifestyle."

"And if we don't quietly surrender our children? Is that when the tanks roll in?" Mohamed's voice was nearly at a shout now. Wonderful television.

"I've heard you talk about this tank issue before, Reverend, and I have to say I'm a bit confused. I had my best research person look into it, and the only reference she could find related to a former mayor of Washington, D.C., asking for the National Guard to help patrol the streets. I believe she was black, though, and that her request was rejected by Congress."

That pretty much finished it. The broadcast wound down into its final minutes with Oprah giving each man time for a short summation that couldn't hope to even scratch the surface of what had been said there that day.

Mohamed's was uncharacteristically disjointed and ineffective—the product of the endless blows he'd taken during the show. People would be talking about this for years, Hallorin knew.

The Secret Service came out immediately after the cameras cut off, but Hallorin brushed them off and walked over to Mohamed. "I appreciate you meeting with me, Reverend," he said, offering his hand. "I think we gave people something to think about, don't you?"

"PERFECT!" Hallorin shouted, leaning forward and slamming his fists against the Plexiglas that separated him from the men driving the van. The barrier flexed dangerously and the state trooper and Secret Service agent up front jumped in their seats and turned to look at him. He drank in the intimidation in their eyes for a moment and then turned to Roland Peck, who was in his usual position crammed into the corner. "Fucking PERFECT, Roland."

"We'll get heavy media time for at least four days," Peck said. "I think some positives even from the liberals for opening up an honest dialogue on race. The focus groups we had watching the program were eating it up. Even the group made up of poor niggers was much less negative than we expected. Yes, much less. Our people will be working with all of them tonight and we'll be ready with spin tomorrow—though I don't think we'll need much. We'll see how far out of context the clips the media uses are." He turned and looked out the window, which was fogged from an early freeze. "According to this morning's numbers, you're up—a twenty-two now. The Democrats are holding at twenty-six and Taylor is down one at thirty-three. I predict you'll get two points out of tonight. The undecideds are slower than molasses this year, but they're going to have to start coming out of the woodwork soon. Another plus is that the forward movement is going to do a lot for morale. Very much so. People have been drifting away from the campaign. . . ."

Hallorin felt his elation darken. He'd remember them. Every fuck who had walked out on him. He'd remember.

"What about Mark Beamon?"

Peck tried to squeeze himself further into the corner. "It's what we feared. What we feared. He isn't staying on track. Looking hard into Newberry all of the sudden and not at all for the girl, it seems."

"You said you could control him, Roland. Is it possible that Beamon's beyond you? That a disgraced alcoholic could—"

"No," Peck said, his voice too loud and too high pitched for the confines of the van. Hallorin shrugged noncommittally. Peck, he knew, was insanely jealous. Even the slightest hint that Hallorin might think someone else his intellectual equal sent the man into a complete frenzy.

"He *is* under control! He's nothing more than a stupid redneck from Texas. His investigative abilities are the math tricks of an idiot savant. He can't *see* anything but what's caught in his tunnel vision."

"Prove it to me, Roland. Get him back on track or stop him, I don't care. There must be something we can use against him."

Peck shook his head. "There's plenty to be had, but he's never been smart enough to keep any of it secret. He doesn't seem to care. And now with him facing a possible prison term . . ."

"What are you suggesting, Roland? Are you suggesting we do something overt to stop him?"

"I'll take care of it," Peck said simply. Hallorin could hear in his voice that he was testing. He wanted Hallorin to end the conversation there, to prove that he still had confidence in the man he had treated like a son. Hallorin reached a hand out and gently stroked Peck's cheek. "This is becoming a comedy of errors, Roland." Peck tried to pull away, but Hallorin grabbed him by the back of the neck. "There's no room for that, is there? The election is in two weeks and you've given me nothing. I *will* be the president of the United States. I won't let anything get in the way of that." Peck tried to pull away again and Hallorin closed his hand tighter, holding him immobile. "Do you understand?"

29

Tom Sherman dodged yet another dazed hooker and fell back into step behind the D.C. cop who was escorting him toward the station's holding pen. "Let's pick it up," Sherman said, letting the irritation creep into his voice. The man looked back at him, about to say something smart-assed, but then wisely thought better of it and upped his pace a bit.

Sherman's anger and frustration at this situation was the first thing he'd felt in a long time—the first thing that had broken through the fog that descended on him after his daughter's death. He found himself having to struggle to maintain outward calm as they continued through the broken hallways and past the grimy people inhabiting them. If any harm had come to his friend, the cop responsible for putting a former FBI agent into the general population was going to take a serious fall.

They stopped at a steel door with a small grate set into it, and Sherman watched impatiently as the cop in front of him fumbled with his keys. It was dead silent on the other side of the door. Sherman leaned around his escort and tried to look through the window grate.

"Easy, now . . ."

The voice was Beamon's, hesitant, cutting through the eerie silence. Sherman looked down at the cop, who seemed to have finally turned up the correct key. "Get me through this goddamn door, now!" The lock clicked and Sherman pushed the man aside, rushing through the door and running down the corridor, hoping that there was still something left of his friend to bail out.

". . . I'm not saying that there aren't some fine automatic weapons on the market, I'm just saying that they're never going to be as reliable as a wheel gun."

Sherman slowed his pace to a walk as the cell Beamon was occupying came into view. He was sitting cross-legged on the narrow bench along the back wall, casually dressed in a pair of jeans and a T-shirt. No less than ten dangerous-looking young black men took up the rest of the cramped space, with the bigger ones sitting next to Beamon on the bench and the weaker-looking ones on the floor. They seemed to be hanging on Beamon's every word.

"But I got motherfuckin' fourteen in my clip," a young man with a teardrop tattooed next to his eye said.

Beamon looked at him and took a calm drag from his cigarette. "Son, if you need more than two to get the job done, you shouldn't be playing with guns."

Everyone in the cell erupted into laughter.

"Looks like my ride's here," Beamon said, standing and tossing what was left of his pack of cigarettes to the young man who had been the target of his joke. "Good luck to you gentlemen. Hopefully, I won't see you in prison."

Beamon stopped as he and Sherman approached the glass double doors that led to the street. "I, uh, think I probably have some papers to sign, Tommy."

Sherman grabbed hold of his arm and pulled him along behind. "No, you don't."

"What about my stuff?" Beamon protested. "They've still got my—"

"It's being delivered to my house." He gave Beamon's arm another tug. "Do you mind? Let's get the hell out of here before they change their minds."

Sherman's Cadillac was illegally parked directly in front of the station, though no one had mustered the will to ticket it. By the time Beamon slipped into the soft leather passenger seat, Sherman had already started the engine and was pulling away from the curb. Beamon barely managed to get the door closed before it clipped a parked cruiser.

"What the hell are you doing, Mark? Practicing?" Sherman said, turning and staring at him over his glasses in that patented expression that had struck fear into the hearts of at least half of the FBI's workforce at one time or another.

"Don't do that, Tommy," Beamon said, pointing at his face. "I hate that."

Sherman turned back and concentrated on the road. "Do you have any idea how many markers I had to call in so you could just walk out of there?"

"Yeah, I do. And I appreciate it."

His friend didn't seem to hear. "What do you think is going to happen if this little episode gets back to the Bureau? You don't think they're going to use it? Pull your head out of your ass, Mark."

"Look, it's—"

"Shut up. Just shut up for once. Look, Mark, whatever happens, the next few years are going to be tough for you. There's probably nothing you can do about that now. But when that's all over, you're still going to have half your life ahead of you. What are you going to do with it?"

Beamon sunk a little further into the leather seat. "It's not something I've spent a lot of time thinking about."

"Well, maybe you should start, because you're really screwing up here. What is this I hear about you and Carrie?"

"Come on, Tommy. She didn't need to be dragged into this."

"What right do you have to make a decision like that for her? Take it from me, Mark. None of this other crap matters in the end. She's the best thing in your life. Walking away from her is as big a mistake as you've ever made."

"Maybe. But it was mine to make." Beamon leaned his head against the window as Sherman maneuvered through the heavy D.C. traffic. They were out of the city and onto a lightly traveled rural highway before either of them spoke again.

"What do you know about David Hallorin's declassification program, Tom?" Beamon said, hoping that his friend would allow himself to be drawn into a less volatile subject matter.

Sherman didn't answer for a full thirty seconds. "What does that have to do with a girl who killed her boyfriend in West Virginia?"

Beamon realigned his gaze from the rolling countryside speeding by to the side of his friend's face. When they'd worked together, Beamon had found Sherman's near omnipotence somewhat disconcerting. He still did. "Maybe nothing. I don't know."

Another long silence. "You probably know more about it than I do, Mark. I was long gone from government service before that piece of legislation. A good program that was long overdue, from what I heard."

Beamon nodded. "I thought so too . . ."

"But?"

"I don't know. Tristan Newberry worked alone in an old warehouse full of government documents—apparently part of the declassification program. As near as I can tell, the last thing he looked at was a box full of misfiled FBI stuff from the seventies."

"What do you mean he worked alone?"

"I mean he worked alone. He and a security guard were it."

Sherman's brow furrowed noticeably as he considered that. "And you think he might have stumbled across something in those old FBI files that got him killed?"

"You tell me. You were there."

Sherman shrugged. "You've heard the stories, Mark. Most of them are true. Hoover *did* keep his eye on important people. But after he died and Rehnquist took over, that pretty much ended. Frankly, anybody powerful enough to have been targeted by Hoover would be either well into their eighties or dead by now. With the political witch-hunt that's going on and the leaking of the Vericomm tapes, I can't imagine that the press would be very interested in the indiscretions of a bunch of men who, if they're lucky, are in a nursing home."

Beamon sighed loudly. "Yeah, I'm reaching here. If I was eighty-five years old and someone came up with a thirty-year-old tale of illegal conduct, I'd take the respirator out of my mouth and laugh in their face. And if it was sexual misconduct—hell, at that age, I'd be proud."

Beamon reached for the cell phone anchored between the seats and dialed the number of the law firm that had hired him. "Chris Humbolt, please. This is Mark Beamon." He was put right through.

"Mark. How are things going? It's been a week since we've talked."

Subtle, but what he meant was "it's been thirty-five thousand dollars since we've talked."

"It's going well," Beamon lied. "I'm closing in, but I need some help— someone to do a little research for me. I assume that you have a Harvard-educated whiz kid around there who knows everything about everything?"

"Princeton, actually, and her name's Cindy. Tell her what you want and it will be magically produced. Hang on, I'm putting you through to her."

There were a few clicks followed by a cheerful voice. "Hello? Mr. Beamon, are you there?"

"Cindy, hi. I hear you're the resident research queen."

"Never heard it put that way, but I guess I am."

"Here's what I need. Information regarding the speculation that J. Edgar Hoover used the FBI to conduct illegal investigations and surveillance."

"Whew," she breathed into the phone. "You're talking about a fair amount of data, there, Mr. Beamon."

"Mark."

"Mark. Could you narrow it down?"

"'Fraid not. I don't exactly know what I'm looking for. Give me a good cross section and make it fit in one box I can lift—keeping in mind that I'm not very athletic. If I need more detail on anything I'll call you."

"Not a problem. ASAP, I assume."

"What else? I'll let you know where to send it."

"I'm on it. Bye."

Beamon hung up the phone and leaned back into the seat.

"What are you doing, Mark?"

"What do you mean?"

"Run away." Sherman paused briefly, the concentration etched on his face. "Marry that beautiful woman who loves you and take a shot at the good life."

Beamon ignored his friend's comment. Marriage and stepfatherhood just wasn't something he needed to be thinking about right now. "I can't quit now, Tommy. You know that."

"Too much like losing?"

"I want to see how it turns out."

"There's not going to be a happy ending for you in this, Mark. Jesus, I just had to get you out of a goddamn D.C. holding pen."

"Look, Tommy. I'm not sure this girl did what everybody thinks she did, okay? I feel a little sorry for her. I also think I'm being played. I have a pretty strong feeling that somebody's setting me up and I'm getting pretty fucking tired of it."

"Let the police handle this, Mark. That's their job."

"Okay, how about this, Tom? I need the two hundred and sixty-five grand to get a lawyer because I didn't like the D.C. holding pen and don't want to spend the next two years in a place just like it. Incidentally, weren't you supposed to be looking into that for me?"

Sherman nodded. "I have looked into it for you and you know what I found? That you are a profoundly unpopular man. Did you really put a bra in Jerry Tracker's suitcase before he left the National Academy conference?"

"It was a joke, for Christ's sake! How the hell was I supposed to know he was actually having an affair with a woman who wore a double D?" Beamon's voice lowered to a mumble. "And who would have thought that brain-dead kiss ass would ever get promoted to an assistant director slot."

"Look, Mark, I don't have any details yet. What I do know is that there are some very powerful people in the government intent on using you as a diversion and some very powerful people in the Bureau who are more than happy to just stand by and laugh."

"Honestly, Tom. I was hoping for a little more dazzling insight."

Sherman seemed uncertain as to what to say for a moment, then he slowed the car and pulled over to the side of the road.

"What are you doing, Tom?"

"Look," he said, turning fully to face him. "You know how people at the Bureau used to like to speculate behind my back on how much I'm worth?"

"Sure," Beamon said. He himself had joined in on some spirited and often drunken debates on that very subject.

"What's the popular theory these days?"

"I think you're up to about fifty mil."

Sherman nodded thoughtfully. "Truth is, I lost more than that when the market crashed and I barely noticed."

Beamon laughed. "You're kidding."

"No, I'm not actually. Look, my point is this—"

"I know what your point, is, Tommy. And I thank you. But I can't take your money—"

"How about a job then? I can—"

"Tommy—enough. You can't keep running to my rescue every time I shoot myself in the foot. I'm a grown-up, remember?"

30

Darby could barely see the outline of her arm and the deep cut across the back of it. She pushed the wound closed and spread a liberal amount of Krazy Glue across it, then let the breeze blow it dry. The combination of stress and hunger-induced light-headedness was making her clumsy and she'd walked right into the open cap on her truck. Tomorrow, she would make the drive to town and find some food. It would have to be at a free happy hour buffet or a grocery store that gave samples. Despite the added risk of being recognized in one of those places, she had no choice—she wasn't sure she had enough gas to make it to the L.A. airport as it was.

She pulled her sleeping bag up a little higher around her neck and propped herself against the tire of her truck. The tiny clearing she was camped in was almost pitch black—dark enough now that she wasn't sure if she was seeing the outline of the tall pines that surrounded her or if her mind was filling them in from memory. She'd been there for a few days now, thirty miles from the nearest town and ten from the nearest paved road. She didn't dare build a fire, so there was little more than the cold and her hunger to keep her company. Normally that wouldn't have been as much of a problem, but the mental games she'd perfected while trapped for endless hours in tents and storms didn't work when she jumped at every twig snap and wind gust.

On the way there, she'd stopped at a library with Internet access and spent as long as she had dared searching for information on herself and Tristan. She'd found that most was on climbing-related sites and consisted of wild speculation in her favor. Jared Palermo had apparently organized an exhaustive search of the mountains surrounding the New River Gorge, pulling in climbers from all over the country. She hoped she'd get a chance to thank him someday. There weren't many people lucky enough to have friends like that.

The national media hadn't taken much interest in her, thank God. With the election coming up and the condition of the economy, they had bigger fish to fry. What she *had* learned was that the police were looking for her, convinced that she was responsible for Tristan's death. She'd also learned how he died—hacked apart by an ice tool. The image of Tristan's bare foot hanging from the door of her van had haunted her since the night she'd seen it. With that new piece of information, though, her imagination had connected the rest of his body to it. The vision came to her every night: Tristan, brutally slashed, staring blindly through the blood-splattered windows of her van.

She told herself over and over that he had known what he was getting himself into when he stole the file. That she was not responsible. That revenge was the reaction of the stupid and violent. But then she remembered watching Tristan run along that ridge, leaving bloody footprints in the dead grass. She remembered lying to herself that he'd be okay on his own—that splitting up was the right thing to do.

She'd seriously considered going to the FBI, but the men who had kidnapped them looked as much like FBI as anything else. If Tristan was telling the truth about the file contents, there was no way she could trust anyone involved with the government.

Taking it to the press had crossed her mind. But wouldn't they be looking for that? Wouldn't they be waiting for her? Besides, what kind of credibility would an itinerant climber accused of murder have?

There was too much swirling around her now. The police, Vili, Mark Beamon, Tristan—they were all too close. She couldn't think. In three days, though, she'd be on a plane to somewhere the U.S. government couldn't find her. A place where she could breathe. Then she'd be able to work this all out. There was no such thing as a hopeless situation, she told herself. Bad decisions were what got people killed.

Darby lay down on the rocky ground and closed her eyes, feeling the cold of the ground work its way through her sleeping bag. She'd tried sleeping in the back of her truck, but it had quickly closed in on her. She felt safer out in the open. If she had to, she could run up into the snow-capped mountains that towered over the little clearing where she was camped. At least there she'd have a chance.

31

Mark Beamon forced himself to run up the steps of the D.C. townhouse Tom Sherman had loaned him, hoping that the physical motion would somehow clear his head—or at least improve his mood.

By the time he'd reached the landing, it still hadn't worked, so he kept up the pace across the narrow walkway to the front door. There was a medium-sized box sitting in front of it, and he nudged it with his shoe as he pulled his keys from his pocket. Whatever it was, it was heavy. Leaning over, he blew a thin layer of dust from the top. The return address read: "Reynolds, Trent and Layman."

It took considerable effort, but after a couple of tries, he managed to lift the box and work it through the door into the large, empty living room. When he let it drop, the impact caused a faint jingling in the empty beer bottles lined up on the hardwood floor. Sherman had just added this place to his collection and it didn't have a stick of furniture in it yet. He made daily offers to let Beamon stay with him at his place—all of which Beamon had politely declined.

He tossed his jacket on the floor and attacked the tape on the box with one of his keys. It took some doing, but eventually the flaps popped open and he was faced with what looked like a week's worth of neatly stacked folders, books, and copied newspaper articles. He dug around in them at random for a few seconds, turning up a couple of errant video tapes and an eight-by-ten color photograph of J. Edgar Hoover's head superimposed on the body of a woman wearing a bright yellow prom dress. There was a sticky note on the picture that simply read "HA!" in a neat, feminine hand.

Beamon tossed the picture aside and grabbed a single sheet of legal notepaper covered in the same handwriting.

Mark:

Enclosed (obviously) is the information you requested. Since the parameters were pretty broad, and information pretty voluminous, I just hit the highlights. Almost everything here has a considerable amount of supporting data that I didn't send. If you see something that piques your interest, call me and I'll dig into it for you.

Cindy

Beamon dialed his home number on his cell phone and entered the code to retrieve his messages as he sat down on the floor next to the box. The machine beeped on and a high-pitched male voice that was unfamiliar to him came over the phone.

"Mr. Beamon? I'm sorry I missed you. My name is Roland Peck and I work for David Hallorin. I was hoping to get together with you as soon as possible at my office in D.C. Please give my secretary a call at 202–555–2600 when you get this. I look forward to meeting you."

Beamon found himself staring across the barren room at the wall as the machine on the other end of the line shut itself off. Who the hell was Roland Peck and why the hell was David Hallorin still sniffing around? Was he still after the additional Vericomm tapes that didn't exist? A little political blackmail to help his flagging campaign? This was getting ridiculous—the last thing Beamon needed right now was to be targeted by a desperate political candidate as his campaign went down in flames.

Beamon set the phone down and looked over at the box lying on the floor next to him. There was a time that work had been an escape for him, something that he could completely immerse himself in and drown out the noise in his life—relationships, politics, financial problems, whatever. The longer he looked at that particular box, though, the less it looked like an escape and the more it felt like a trap. He couldn't put his finger on why this supposedly straightforward case was eating a hole in his stomach—but it was. He smiled to himself. It was a feeling he had started to miss.

Beamon made it through the bulk of the data in just under three hours. The incredibly gifted Cindy Whoever had separated everything into discrete packages, based on date and subject matter, and had included a concise but well thought-out index. Most of the articles/chapters/files didn't deserve more than a glance, consisting of little more than the poorly supported ramblings of the press—mostly dated well after J. Edgar Hoover's death. Beamon was able to combine the information in the box with his own knowledge of FBI lore and do a fair job of separating fact from fiction.

So far, the box seemed to hold nothing new. He already knew that Hoover had kept a watchful eye on the political store. But that was decades ago—who the hell would care now? The families of long-dead politicians? Unlikely. Even if there were a huge government conspiracy to uncover, the world Hoover lived in didn't exist anymore. People were focused on the here and now.

There was something, though. Something in the back of Beamon's mind telling him he was on the right track. He dropped his hand into the box again and grabbed another stack of documents.

It took an hour to get through the rest of the loose paper. He pulled out one of the last copied newspaper articles before he hit the dog-eared Hoover biographies that lined the bottom of the box and smoothed it out in his lap. It was one of the most current things he'd seen, dated April 1998.

Washington—Recently released FBI documents show that the Bureau kept tabs on former President John Kennedy as far back as World War II, when, as a young naval officer, he had an affair with suspected Nazi spy Inga Fejos.

Kennedy's involvement with Fejos, recorded on FBI surveillance tapes in 1942, was the first in a series of rumored flings that caught the attention of FBI director J. Edgar Hoover. The files were among seventeen thousand pages of documents made public Wednesday by the National Archives.

The information on Kennedy's relationship with Fejos, stamped "Personal and Confidential," was held in Hoover's private files.

Despite the fact that the FBI found no evidence that either Kennedy or Fejos passed state secrets to Germany, the release of this information could have been devastating to Kennedy's political ambitions.

Beamon took a quick sip from the warm beer he'd found hiding in his collection of empties, wondering idly what Kennedy had done for Hoover to keep that little tidbit quiet.

It was this kind of renegade snooping that had prompted Congress to change the rules on how long an FBI director could serve. Instead of simply cleaning up their act so that a man like Hoover couldn't go into the blackmail business, they'd limited the tenure of FBI directors to ten years. The theory was that the new director would be on his way out before he'd completely figured out the organization he controlled and therefore would never gain enough power and know-how to go on any political fishing expeditions. An interesting example of the surprisingly common practice of hamstringing government agencies that were just a little too efficient.

In this case, though, maybe it hadn't been such a bad idea. As much as had been written on the subject of Hoover, Beamon sometimes wondered if it even scratched the surface. Just how much control over the government had that crotchety old screw been able to exercise? Frightening.

He was about to toss the article on the teetering pile of castaways when something he couldn't identify stopped him. He laid the article back in his lap and stared at it for almost a minute, trying to figure out what it was that was suddenly bothering him. He lifted it closer to his face and reread the first paragraph.

> . . . the Bureau kept tabs on former President John Kennedy as far back as World War II, when, as a young naval officer . . .

What if . . .

Beamon leaned back against the wall behind him and turned his now empty beer bottle over and over in his hand.

What if Kennedy wasn't the only one? It would make sense—why would he have been? If you were interested in tracking politicians' personal foibles, why wouldn't you start early—keep tabs on young up-and-comers before they became older, more powerful, and more guarded. Hoover had almost unlimited manpower. So what if only one out of every ten of his subjects ever made it to a position high enough for the information to be useful? Nothing ventured, nothing gained.

Beamon did some quick mental calculations. If such a program had existed toward the end of Hoover's lifetime, the subjects would probably be between sixty and seventy. Plenty young to still be concerned about the release of any graphic information on their youthful indiscretions—particularly now with the economy-driven shift in the public's attitude from apathy to lynch mob. And, of course, in the midst of the most important presidential election in fifty years.

Beamon grabbed the note that Cindy had written her number on and dialed it.

"Hello, Cindy Abrahms."

"Cindy? Mark Beamon. What are you doing there? It's eleven o'clock."

"Eight. This is L.A. Did you get the box I sent?"

"I did. An amazing job. If you ever decide you make too much money and want to take on a frustrating, thankless job, let me know. I'll put in a good word for you at the Bureau."

"I'll keep that in mind, thanks. Did you find any of it helpful?"

"Maybe. There's a newspaper article on Kennedy and the fact that Hoover was watching him when he was a kid—"

"In the corner of it, there should be a handwritten number," she interrupted. "Could you read it to me?"

Beamon looked down at the article in his hand: 103-6B.

He heard some shuffling on the other end, and then, "Okay. Here it is . . . yeah. Sure. Did you want some more stuff on this?"

"The article says that a bunch of documents were released on the subject. Any chance you could get a hold of them?"

"Sure. I've got to deal with the government on this, though, so I hope you're not in a hurry."

"As soon as you can will be fine."

"I'm on it. Anything else?"

"That's it, thanks. And go home. It's late."

He hung up the phone and leaned his back against the wall. Where the hell was this thing going? He had a young kid working alone in a warehouse going through government documents in a pattern that suggested a search. He gets excited by a group of boxes with old FBI documents misfiled in them, then he gets dead. Suddenly all kinds of people are interested in the girl who may have killed him and are willing to put some serious money into finding her.

What really worried him was the name that kept popping up. Beamon had met with David Hallorin about the Vericomm tapes two weeks ago. It was Hallorin's declassification program that Newberry was working on. There was a message on Beamon's machine from someone that worked for Hallorin. Hallorin had been a young prosecutor in D.C. during the seventies and would have undoubtedly had a thorough knowledge of Hoover's FBI. And . . .

Beamon leaned forward and started going through the pockets of the coat he'd thrown on the floor. He finally turned up the crumpled notes from his trip to Conrad, Maryland. Shuffling through them, he confirmed what he already knew. The house he'd broken into was owned by a wealthy businessman from Maine—Hallorin's home state.

The senator was a big fan of unorthodox and streamlined methods for getting things done. Was he applying that philosophy to his campaign? Perhaps Beamon had finally discovered the identity of his employer . . .

No.

It was just a coincidence, he told himself. It had to be. This was just a lover's quarrel.

But what if it wasn't? If Hallorin was interested in an old FBI surveillance program, it stood to reason that it pertained to Robert Taylor—the man creaming him in the election. And if that was the case, the question Beamon needed to answer was: What could he possibly hope to gain by putting himself between Senator Robert Taylor, the insanely powerful former director of the CIA and next president of the United States, and David Hallorin, a man whose entire life revolved around ruthless efficiency? Not a hell of a lot, was the answer.

So what were his choices at this point? Find the girl—if he could—turn her over, collect the better part of a quarter of a million dollars, and hope that he survived to blow it on attorneys. On the other hand, he could just make damn sure that he didn't find the girl and see how far he could stretch the hundred and fifty grand he'd already collected. Or, finally, he could try to find the girl and the truth—whatever it may be.

Not a good choice in the lot.

Beamon pulled out his address book and dialed a phone number from a business card paper-clipped into it.

"Hello?" The voice was still familiar after all these years, though a bit groggy.

"Steve? Mark Beamon."

Stephen Rose had retired five years ago as the assistant director in charge of the FBI's New York office and set himself up in a boutique investigation and consulting firm handling strictly high-class corporate stuff in the New England area. Since that time, they had made every effort not to speak.

"Mark Beamon? Why the hell are you calling me? Jesus Christ—it's almost midnight."

"Yeah, sorry about the time, Steve. How've you been?"

"Stephen. Fine. What the hell do you want?"

The cop in Maryland had told him that an out-of-state trooper had been sniffing around for Darby just after Tristan had been killed.

Interestingly, state cops were the people tapped to protect presidential candidates before they were assigned a Secret Service detail. And often even after the Secret Service signed on, they were kept around for odd jobs. This job, of course, being odder than most.

"Thought I'd throw some business your way, Steve—Stephen. How are your contacts with the Maine Troopers?"

"Good."

No surprise. Rose was one weird son of a bitch and not an ounce of fun, but he was as competent as the day was long. "I'm trying to find a young trooper. I don't have a name, just a description. Hell, I'm not even dead sure he's from Maine. Just a hunch."

There was silence over the line for a moment. "I can do it. I charge two hundred an hour, minimum of fifteen hundred for the job—could be more. A lot more if I have trouble getting back to sleep. Fax me the description and I'll send you the names."

"Actually, I need photographs, too. And I want them faxed to the police in Conrad, Maryland."

"Pictures? Your minimum just went to twenty-five hundred."

"Bill me, you asshole."

"I'll tell you what, Mark. I have a special deal for potential employees. One-fifty an hour."

"Excuse me?"

"I understand you're pretty much screwed at the Bureau. We've been looking for another hand here. Haven't been able to find anyone we're completely happy with."

Beamon didn't say anything for a moment.

"Uh, Steve. You don't like me. In fact, didn't you take a swing at me last time I saw you?"

"And I still can't believe I missed that fat, ugly head of yours. Look Mark, I had absolutely no incentive to put up with your shit when I was at the Bureau. But this is the private sector. I make money when my clients' problems get solved quickly and quietly. A lot of money. I guess what I'm saying is that business is business and personal is personal."

This whole month was starting to get downright surreal. "How long on those photos?"

"Get me the information tomorrow morning and I'll have it in a couple of days." Pause. "Mark. I'm serious about the job—we'll put together a compensation package I guarantee you'll be happy with. Think about it."

32

The Washington, D.C., weather had taken a turn for the worse and the wind was driving the cold between the gaps in Mark Beamon's topcoat. He adjusted his tie to be a more efficient wind block and stopped at the beginning of a brick walkway that split off toward a large brownstone set off from the road.

It was more ornate than the one Tom Sherman called home, but was somehow less impressive. Perhaps it was the overly efficient use of landscaping to make the tiny front yard look larger than it really was. Or maybe it was just his mood. The far-fetched suspicions that he'd formed the night before hadn't faded as he'd hoped. If anything, they'd gained force.

He still didn't know why he'd been summoned by Hallorin's man, having had only a brief logistical conversation with Roland Peck's secretary. Whatever it was, though, he was fairly sure it would further complicate his life.

Beamon walked slowly up the walk and rapped on the heavy leaded glass that made up most of the front entrance. A moment later the door was pulled open and Beamon found himself face to face with the tallest Asian woman he had ever seen.

"Mr. Beamon?" the woman said in thickly accented English that sounded strangely formal. "I am Mrs. Peck. Please come in."

Beamon stepped through the doorway, getting close enough to her to use his own height for perspective. She couldn't have been any shorter than six one, with a haircut that looked like it had been done with a ruler, and makeup that favored shades of dark gray. The long, black dress she wore was buttoned high around her neck, but hung in a way that accentuated the obviously surgically enhanced breasts jutting from her chest.

All in all, the impression was not that of your average corporate wife. She looked more like the product of an unholy union between a Russian power lifter and a Chinese witch.

"Nice to meet you, Mrs. Peck," Beamon said as she pushed the heavy door closed behind them. "Call me Mark."

She didn't smile and didn't reciprocate his offer to put their relationship on a first name basis, instead she gave a short nod of acknowledgment and turned to walk down the entry. Something in her gait suggested that Beamon should follow. He did so at a safe distance.

"My husband told me to offer his apologies for the last-minute change in plans. It seems that he was delayed at a meeting in Virginia and would have been inexcusably tardy if he had tried to make it back to the office for your meeting." Beamon got the impression that she was less speaking than exactly imitating her husband's words.

"Not a problem, ma'am. In fact, your house is actually easier to get to from where I'm staying."

He looked around him as they weaved through the old house, trying to get a feel for the Pecks as human beings, but not finding much he could hold onto. Furnishings were clearly the work of a professional decorator, obvious from the way the artwork matched the color scheme and was exactly the right size for the space it occupied. There were no personal photographs in evidence, nor were there any objects out of place. Everything seemed to have been purchased in the spirit of old, brown, and too heavy for one person to lift.

"Perhaps you would like to wait in Mr. Peck's office," the woman said, stopping in front of an open door. Apparently she wasn't on a first name basis with her husband either. Beamon let her have it with his warmest smile and walked past her into the deceptively large room.

"Mr. Peck called only moments before you arrived and is on his way. Can I get you anything while you wait?" she said, already turning and walking back toward the center of the house. The question had clearly been rhetorical.

The office was more expressive than the house that surrounded it. The generally unavoidable massive desk, leather chair, and expensive rugs were nowhere to be found. In fact there was no desk at all—only three round tables, each about four feet in diameter, placed in separate corners of the room. Each was piled high with papers, as was the floor around the edge of the room, and each was surrounded by three simple chairs. The fireplace cut into the far wall looked like it hadn't been used in a hundred years and now housed too many hardback books to count. As near as Beamon could tell, there wasn't a single drawer or file cabinet anywhere.

As would be expected, one wall *was* covered with framed photographs, but they seemed to be kind of a shrine to David Hallorin. It took a couple of minutes, but Beamon finally found the other similarity between them—almost all of them also included a thin, red-haired man that Beamon assumed must be Roland Peck. The pictures seemed to be in chronological order, going back some twenty years based on Hallorin's appearance and dress. In the early ones, Peck looked to be no more than a teenager. Beamon moved slowly along the wall, examining the pictures until he was within about a foot of one of the three tables scattered around the office.

He stood where he was for about a minute, pretending to concentrate on a photo of Peck and Hallorin at a picnic, and listening for anything that would suggest someone outside in the hall. The only noise in the house sounded like kitchen utensils clanging together and was well distant.

Satisfied that he wasn't being watched, Beamon leaned over the table next to him and began casually flipping through the stacks of papers on it.

Vinyl-bound financial reports, mostly. All from companies and partnerships he'd never heard of but that undoubtedly made up a portion of David Hallorin's empire.

He moved on to the next table, which seemed to contain only items relating to Hallorin's campaign. Despite the fact that there was no apparent order to the scraps of papers and articles lying there, Beamon was careful not to move anything out of its place—something told him that Peck knew precisely where every paper clip in this office was nestled.

Highlighted articles about Hallorin and his running mate dominated, with bound transcripts of his opponents' speeches running a close second. Beamon shuffled around the table a few feet and found a teetering stack of legal pads, the first of which was covered with elegant handwriting in red ink.

Its content was marginally more interesting than the rest of the stuff he'd rifled so far, but still contained nothing that could tell him why he was there or implicated Hallorin in anything unethical. For the most part, the short sentences and paragraphs contained the clever, seemingly off-the-cuff, retorts that Hallorin was quickly becoming renowned for.

"I didn't think it would be my responsibility to defend the African-American community tonight, but I feel obligated to point out that there are more whites on welfare than blacks." That one had been replayed a thousand times on TV—Hallorin had used it to zing Phillippe Mohamed on *Oprah.*

Beamon lifted the edge of the top pad with the end of a pencil and peeked at the one under it, still mindful of the open door. This one consisted of quotes relating to Hallorin's more radical ideas attributed to his dead wife. Beamon had never heard any of these specifically, but he had recognized the strategy they represented during the media's coverage of the campaign. Whenever Hallorin got backed too far into a corner, he would nail his opponent with a quote from beyond the grave. No politician alive would attack the memory of a man's wife. What a scumbag.

How did people live like this? Beamon wondered as he revealed the next pad with the end of his pencil. Not only did politicians have to carefully consider every word that came out of their mouths, most of it was prewritten for them.

The third pad seemed to be full of dumb-ass economic and political metaphors. *"Just because I'm stupid enough to run into a burning building when everyone else has the sense to run out, doesn't necessarily mean I'd make a good president."*

Beamon skipped over that one and was starting in on the next when he heard the unmistakable sound of a door opening somewhere in the house. He stepped away from the table and looked behind him at the one he hadn't made it to. Murphy's Law. It probably had a photo of Hallorin killing Jimmy Hoffa or making a deal with space aliens right on top.

Beamon crossed the office and was quietly browsing the Hallorin shrine wall again when the flesh-and-blood version of the red-haired man in the photographs jerked through the door.

"Mr. Peck, I presume," Beamon said, striding across the room and offering his hand. "It's nice to meet you."

Peck looked him in the eye a little too hard. He was no doubt dying to look around and see what Beamon had been pawing through in his absence, but wouldn't allow himself the luxury. Beamon suspected that Broomhilda was going to get a serious tongue-lashing for letting him wait in the office. If she was lucky.

"I'm so sorry I'm late, Mr. Beamon. All I can say is that it couldn't be helped. Absolutely couldn't be helped." He clipped off each word as though he was trying to win an award for pronunciation.

"Call me Mark."

"Roland," Peck said, and offered Beamon one of the chairs surrounding the table next to them. He looked vaguely nervous and moved in quick, birdlike motions.

"I appreciate you making time for me on such short notice, Mark."

"My pleasure," Beamon lied. "I have to say, though, I was surprised to get your message."

Peck dragged his chair away from the table and sat down with a good five feet between them. It was a strange configuration for a meeting: two men seated in what looked like kitchen chairs, facing each other with nothing between them.

"David was very impressed with you. Very impressed," Peck said, as though that was an explanation.

"The feeling was mutual," Beamon lied again.

"I know you're a busy man, so I'll get to the point."

Beamon was thankful for that. Not only was he dead curious, but there was something about this little man that made him uncomfortable.

"We have a position open—"

"In the campaign?"

Peck smiled—even that was a jerky motion—and shook his head. "No, no. I have very little to do with the senator's political life. I work on his corporate side—the opening is in our security division."

Beamon had to fight to keep from laughing. Could it be? Yet another job offer? Getting himself fired, disgraced, and indicted was turning out to be one of the best career moves he'd ever made. Any day now that kid he used to beat up in grade school was going to call and offer him a quarter of a mil to sit around and get fanned by beautiful women.

"You understand," Peck said, his sharp features suddenly reconfiguring themselves into a severe expression, "that everything we talk about tonight is completely confidential?"

Beamon's nod seemed to satisfy him.

"Should David not win the election this year . . . " To his credit, Peck's tone carried an uncertainty to it that actually didn't sound practiced. ". . . he does not intend to stay in politics. He feels that he's accomplished everything he can as a senator, and I've been urging him to come back and take an active roll in the management of his companies. I'm not confident that Robert Taylor has the faintest idea how to turn the economy or the country around, and if this recession is going to continue, we need David Hallorin back at the helm."

Peck let that sink in for a moment and then continued. "Obviously, the senator had been very open about his, um, innovative views and had been equally vocal in his criticism of the Middle East. Frankly, he's made enemies. Some we know about, some we don't."

Beamon nodded his agreement. Hallorin's proposed foreign policy toward the Middle East had been summed up by the press as "send 'em back to the Stone Age." In his mind, if America could lead the world away from fossil fuels, the Arabs wouldn't have the money to buy the nuclear toys and delivery systems that they so coveted. A practical idea to be sure, but less than popular with your more Allah-loving fundamentalist wackos.

"In any event," Peck said, "we are going to need much more sophisticated security capabilities than we have now. Much more. As opposed to having separately run security organizations for our different companies as we do now, we intend to create a central control point that all the separate offices would report to. As I envision it, we would have a consistent policy for all the different corporate arms and fairly sophisticated intelligence capabilities."

"Makes sense," Beamon said in the silence that ensued. He still wasn't sure what to make of all this. Another coincidence?

"The senator was very impressed with you. Very impressed. He wanted me to ask you if you would be interested in setting up and running our new security system."

Beamon felt his eyebrows rise uncontrollably. "Excuse me?"

"The position would pay four hundred and fifty thousand dollars per year with stock options that will probably amount to another two hundred thousand dollars or so. You'd be given a generous budget for setting up the program and acquiring staff of your choice."

Beamon made sure that his expression returned to something a little more passive as he tried to get his mind around what he was being offered. A highly prestigious job paying nearly three-quarters of a million a year in a time when unemployment was at record levels and he had just been fired. He hadn't known exactly what he was going to hear tonight, but this hadn't been one of his top guesses.

"I don't know what to say, Roland. I'm not sure I'm in the market for a job right now. I've got some legal problems that could—"

"I don't know the details of your troubles, Mark, but the senator does.

Obviously, it would be rather inconvenient if you were . . . incarcerated, while you were working for us. The senator intends to use his influence and our legal people to make sure that doesn't happen."

"And if it does?"

"*In the unlikely event* that it does, your deputy will take over until you are rel—until you return."

Beamon crossed his legs and laced his hands across his knees. "And if Senator Hallorin becomes president? Would I be out of a job?" It was a stupid question, but would at least give him a minute to think about just what the hell was going on here.

"On the contrary," Peck said. "On the contrary. If that were to happen, we would increase your salary to six hundred thousand dollars and significantly increase your personnel budget. We would expect that you would want to bring in some fairly expensive talent from the CIA and FBI to assist you at that point."

Beamon didn't respond, silently considering his position instead. This could be it, the end to all his troubles. The FBI's case against him was based almost completely on his financial inability to defend himself— they would likely run far and fast if Hallorin became involved. So in one fell swoop, his legal and financial problems were solved. He could go out tomorrow, buy a mansion and a smoking jacket, get Carrie back, and golf only the really good courses. All in all, it sounded pretty good.

The only drawback? Darby Moore. This job offer was far too perfect and far too timely to be accidental. Peck had made a mistake by tipping his hand and had counted too much on Beamon's desperation and hopelessly underdeveloped survival instinct. He was now seventy percent sure that he was already working for Hallorin and that the senator had started getting nervous when he'd begun digging into Tristan Newberry's life. It seemed likely now that this was nothing more than an attempt to sidetrack his investigation. A really, really good attempt.

"That's quite an offer, Roland."

"As I said, the senator was very taken with you."

"And as I said, the feeling is mutual. I'll tell you, though, I'm pretty partial to Flagstaff," Beamon said, deciding to have a little fun. He suspected that there was only one request Peck wouldn't give in to.

"We have companies all over. You can set up your office anywhere you want. Preferably in the mainland U.S., though."

"And I would have a written guarantee of unlimited legal support?"

"That's our intention."

"And that guarantee would be in effect indefinitely, no matter what happens?"

Peck had to think about that one for a moment. "Fine."

"Oh, one more thing. I'm working a little side job right now. If I do sign on with you, I'd like to finish it before I start."

As he'd expected, Peck suddenly looked uncertain. "We've already waited too long on this, Mark, and frankly, it's my fault. We want to be as flexible as possible here, but the one critical point is time. If you've already taken payment for the job and would have to return it to extricate yourself, I'm sure we could work something out."

"We're only talking a week or two," Beamon said, already knowing what Peck's reaction would be.

"I just don't know if we can wait that long, Mark. You're our first choice . . . " He let the unspoken "but we have other candidates" hang in the air between them.

33

"IRRELEVANT," the crowd roared. A hundred arms and half as many red, white, and blue signs pumped the air, causing eddies and waves in the human sea below him.

David Hallorin held his hands up, his watch flashing in the powerful lights trained on him. He felt himself starting to look at it, but immediately turned his eyes back to his audience. For a moment, the image of the watch was superimposed over them, the second hand moving in slow jerks that cinched down the muscles around his stomach a little more with each movement.

The energy of the crowd ebbed as he leaned in close to the microphones set into the lectern before him. "How many times we can blow up the earth and how many tanks and planes we have rusting away on our military bases doesn't matter anymore. The strength of a country today is based almost totally on economic power. Ask the Russians about that."

Cheers and bobbing signs again.

"Despite a hopelessly bogged down government, American business— you people—kept this country afloat. And you managed to do it a lot longer than I thought possible. Now, though, it's time for a change. It's time to create a government that's a partner to the private sector and not just an insatiable monster that sucks out money and throws up roadblocks."

The cheers were louder this time and echoed eerily though the cavernous manufacturing plant. He stepped back and looked around him at

223

the gleaming cranes and state-of-the-art equipment efficiently integrated into the walls of the building. The facility had been completed three years ago and was still one of the most technologically advanced in the world—the crown jewel of Hallorin Manufacturing.

"I'm proud of what we've accomplished here," he said, scanning the back of the building and making eye contact with each of the television cameras covering the event. "Not a single person has been laid off from this company during the recession."

The shouts were deafening this time.

The audience was made up almost completely of employees of this facility—his employees. It was Sunday, but nearly every one of them had shown up, and most, as had been encouraged, brought their children. Mixed randomly into the crowd at the feet of their parents, they would significantly increase the emotional impact of this event.

Hallorin nodded toward a fifty-foot-tall open door to his left and the picnic tables set up in the parking lot outside them. The sun had come out warm and bright and glinted off the balloons and flags tied to every available pole, car, and bench. "Don't worry," he said into the micro-phone with a sly grin. "I love to make speeches, but I won't talk so long the chicken gets cold."

The blue-collar crowd tittered self-consciously. The subject had obvi-ously been on their collective mind. Typical American stock, all of them. The sturdy, corn-fed inhabitants of America's Heartland. His own parents had had the same dull eyes and blank expressions. They, too, had been people who couldn't see any further than the end of their street and seemed proud of the inability. People who counted on men like him to create jobs for them so they had a reason to wake up in the morning. People who liked nothing more than to deride the "fat cats" in Washington, but who never hesitated to put their hands out when the subsidy checks came in.

In the end, though, his own parents' lack of ambition and intelligence had turned out to be a windfall. With Roland Peck's tutelage, he had learned to use their memory to extract tears from all but the most hard-ened political crowd.

Hallorin braced his hands against the lectern again and focused on the camera from CNN—they'd give him the most replays. "The world is look-ing for us to lead it out of this—"

The explosion was louder than he had ever imagined—it was impossi-ble to tell where the sound stopped and the vibration in his chest started.

The lectern took the brunt of the blast of hot air that slammed into him, but he was still staggered by its heat and pressure.

He glanced behind him when he regained his balance and saw the four Secret Service men who had been assigned to the podium lying on the wooden platform, dazed but apparently unhurt. The building's sprinkler system kicked in and Hallorin turned his face upward, feeling the cool water fade the sting in his cheeks and forehead.

The scene below him was chaos. Flame had engulfed the back wall of the plant and a white, mechanical-smelling smoke was starting to flow through the building. The crowd's cohesiveness was gone now. Some people were running full speed toward the open bay at the end of the building, seeming to follow the flow of the smoke as it was sucked out into the open air. Others moved more slowly with no direction, their minds still trying to shake off the impact of the explosion and process what had happened. Some, closer to what had been the source of the blast, didn't move at all.

All but one of the cameras seemed to be intact, protected by their raised positions along the back wall. He could see movement behind them as the smoke ebbed and flowed—they were still rolling.

Hallorin felt someone grab him from behind and begin dragging him back toward the door behind the podium. He allowed the Secret Service man to pull him a couple of feet, and then used his superior strength and bulk to break free. His other three protectors were on their feet now, too, and moving quickly in his direction as he grabbed the agent in front of him by the shoulders.

"NO!" Hallorin shouted over the sound of the sprinklers and the screams of the people behind him. He released the man and pointed down into the crowd. "Help them!" The other agents stopped a few feet from him, momentarily confused.

"Help them!" Hallorin yelled again as he jumped off the podium and ran to a woman who was trying to lift her husband to his feet. The Secret Service men still looked like they were unsure of what to do, but after a few seconds of indecision, all four jumped to the floor and ran to him.

"You! Get him out of here!" Hallorin said, pulling the man lying on the concrete to his feet and passing him to the nearest Secret Service agent. "You three—help the others get out!"

They did as they were told, weaving their way into what had been Hallorin's audience, lifting people off the ground and shouting orders at anyone who looked able to move under their own power.

Hallorin started toward the now diminishing wall of flame at the back, knowing that there would be no second explosion. The smoke became thicker as he continued, but the heat had diminished enough that it couldn't penetrate his soaked-through suit and the stream of water still falling from the ceiling. He pulled out a wet handkerchief and held it over his mouth and nose as he moved through the billowing clouds and nearly tripped over a man lying facedown on the floor. He continued on, knowing that he was completely obscured from the cameras now, finally coming upon what looked like a family lying motionless on the floor in a quickly deepening puddle. He ignored the adults and went for the two young girls lying next to them. One appeared to still be alive and one already dead. Both were black. He hesitated for a moment, calculating the media impact, then scooped up the dead girl and began stumbling blindly toward the exit.

The girl was small, no more than sixty pounds, and he was able to cradle her in one arm as he ran. When he had cleared the densest area of smoke and came into camera view again, he used his free hand to grab hold of a confused-looking woman and pull her through the open bay into the bright sun and clean air.

Once clear of the building, he dropped to his knees near a balloon-covered picnic table and laid the girl's body gently on the warm asphalt. He bent over her and looked down at her burned skin and blistered lips, finally opening her mouth and trying to resuscitate her, though he knew it was hopeless.

The chaos around him grew as he continued to make a show of performing CPR on the girl. Finally, when there would have been no doubt in anyone's mind that she was beyond saving, he fell back into an exhausted sitting position and pulled her body to his.

She would have never done anything significant. Had her parents managed to save enough to send her to college, she would have toiled in a mid-level position, retired, and died. If not, she would have worked for six dollars an hour and had five children the government would have had to support. But now she would influence the future of the entire world. She would live forever.

Hallorin dropped a hand behind him for support, finally looking up as though he was just becoming aware of the flashing cameras going off around him.

He was going to be the president of the United States.

34

Mark Beamon squinted as the early morning light reflecting off the small lake in front of him slipped in around his sunglasses. Most of the leaves on the trees had turned to intense reds and golds, creating an enormous quilt that covered the mountains around him.

The old A-frame cottage at the end of the dirt driveway looked like an overgrown birdhouse—a simple structure constructed of weathered cedar and broken wood shingles. Beamon paused in the middle of the driveway and took one more look at the lake and the small dock jutting out into it. It fit the vague description he'd been given, but he suspected that just about every house out here would. Street signs and house numbers seemed to be more a luxury than a necessity in this remote section of Maine.

Steve Rose had come through with typical efficiency. The day after Beamon had contacted him, the Conrad, Maryland, police station had been faxed pictures of eight Maine State Troopers who fit the rather general description Beamon had provided. There was no doubt that Terry McMillan was the man who had been in Conrad asking questions about Darby Moore.

The biographical data Rose forwarded to Beamon included an unfortunate paragraph putting McMillan in David Hallorin's protection detail until only about a week ago, supporting Beamon's fear that this case was going nowhere good.

He knocked on the front door, the sharp sound disturbing the stillness that surrounded him. When there was no response, he cupped his hands around one of the glass panes and peered inside. Most of the room was in shadow, illuminated only by the sun glare coming through the small windows at the back. Beamon tried the doorknob and, finding it locked, reached for one of the mittens in his pocket. He looked around him to make sure he was alone, but then rethought his plan of punching through the glass and instead ran his hand over the top of the doorframe. Nothing.

Jumping off the small front porch, he lifted a planter with a dead bush in it. Nothing there either. It took a few more minutes, but the key finally turned up under a canoe leaned against the house. The improvement in his breaking and entering skills was slow but reasonably steady.

The smell hit him the moment he entered and was powerful enough to force him back outside again. He slammed the door shut and pulled his cell phone from his pocket, dialing a nine and a one, and then letting his thumb hover over the last digit. He wasn't an FBI agent anymore. There was no more calling in cops and experts and ordering them around. No more people to do the dirty work and provide him with a nice clean sheet of paper containing their findings. In this instance, he knew that it would be much better for him if no one ever knew he'd been there.

Beamon put his hand back on the doorknob. *One . . . two . . .*

He twisted it on *three* and charged forward into a small living room with an open kitchen on the right. He covered his mouth and nose with his handkerchief and looked up at a ladder that led to a small loft.

Reluctantly, he closed the door behind him and made his way across the cheaply furnished room to the base of the ladder. Leaning his head against one of the rungs, he kept his breathing shallow, getting enough air to keep him from getting light-headed, but not enough to feel like he was taking the overpowering stench of the place fully into his lungs. The two hundred and forty-five grand that he had coming as of today was starting to look more and more like a slave's wage.

He started slowly up the ladder, stopping when his head cleared the floor of the loft. He couldn't see much of the man—only the back of his head and his arms were visible around the Barcolounger type chair. He seemed to be gazing out the window, but judging by the smell, his days of admiring the lake were probably over.

Beamon made his breathing even more shallow as he continued into the loft and walked up behind the chair, concentrating on the view that the dead man had been so interested in. It took a few seconds, but he finally managed to coax himself into looking down at the body.

It was probably McMillan, but that was based only on the short, thick hair graying at the temples. His features had been rendered unrecognizable, alternately bloated and cratered by the bacteria at work decomposing his body. Black splotches covered most of the visible skin on his face and hands, and his nose seemed to have partially sunk into his skull beneath mercifully closed eyes. Flies walked drunkenly across the body and littered the floor—going after one last feast before fall brought an end to their life span.

Blood had soaked through the orange velour of the chair and dried, turning it and the floor around it a dull reddish black. Beamon held the handkerchief a little tighter to his face and looked down at McMillan's right wrist. What had probably been a narrow slit when inflicted had swelled and now gaped open like a dead flower. There seemed to be no marks that could have been caused by a rope, though at this level of decomposition, Beamon probably wouldn't know them if he saw them. In any event, the design of the chair would make it tricky to secure someone to it. That left the obvious answer: suicide. Convenient and certainly possible. Maybe even probable.

Beamon looked down at the small table in front of what had, until recently, been Terry McMillan. The young man's badge was lying open on it next to his gun. Beamon leaned down to examine the picture on McMillan's ID, but the motion made his stomach roll over violently. He walked quickly across the ten feet of floor and down the ladder, bursting through the front door, taking a tentative gulp of fresh air. He increased the depth of his breathing carefully, not wanting to do anything violent enough to disturb the delicate balance that was holding down yet another wonderful first-class airline lunch.

The Maine air settled his stomach fairly quickly, and after about five minutes, he was able to go back into the house. He made a quick turn around the kitchen and living room, poking into cabinets and closets, and taking a quick peek into the bathroom.

Nothing particularly suspicious—beyond the body in the loft. No sign anything had been searched or of any struggle. There was food in the fridge, some of it still good.

Beamon grabbed a couple of oven mitts off the stove and went back into the loft. After a cursory search of the confined space, he stepped up to McMillan's body and poked at it with a mitted hand. It felt kind of like a half-full water balloon.

He held one of the mitts to his face and took in a quick filtered breath, then reached down to grab hold of the body, saying a silent prayer that no major parts would fall off it during this operation.

For once, his luck held. McMillan's body flopped over like a broken doll and exposed the back of his jeans. It took some doing, but Beamon managed to relieve him of his wallet without taking the mitts off, then retreated outside again.

He walked down to the lake, taking deep breaths and clearing his head. The power of the sun's rays burnt through his jacket and pants as he lay down at the edge of the dock and let his lower legs dangle over the edge.

McMillan's wallet didn't contain anything unusual: photos, plastic, roughly thirty dollars in cash, et cetera, et cetera. Beamon found himself staring at a picture of an older woman standing on the very dock he was now lying on. "What happened to your son, Mrs. McMillan?" he said aloud.

Had he been involved in Tristan Newberry's death—sucked into David Hallorin's personality cult and convinced that it was for "the good of the people"? Then, overcome by guilt, killed himself? Or had he found out what was going on and refused to play along? Any number of virtually untraceable drugs could have been used to keep him docile while his wrists were cut and his life was soaked up by that Barcolounger.

Beamon raised his arm and momentarily blocked out the sun as he looked at the calendar on his watch. He was supposed to be using his time to decide whether or not he was going to spend the next six months in a minimum-security prison playing poker with a bunch of embezzlers, bond traders, and former congressmen—not chasing trouble around New England.

And then there was Roland Peck. His deadline was tomorrow. If Beamon said no to the job offer, Hallorin would have to find another way to solve the problem of this particular former FBI agent poking around things that were better left alone.

Beamon didn't notice the quiet sloshing of water until it was only a few feet away. He raised his head and had to squint to focus on a man in his early thirties rowing a dented aluminum canoe toward the dock.

"Hi there," the man said. "Is Terry around?"

"Not home."

"Know when he's going to be back?"

Beamon propped himself up on his elbows and shrugged as best he could from that position. "How's the fishing?"

"Hasn't been that good," the man said, dipping his paddle in the water to avoid colliding with the dock. "But hell, look at this day."

Beamon nodded thoughtfully as he examined the man's face. There was no worry, stress, or pain there. Probably worked at a gas station or something—made just enough to keep his dinky little place on the lake stocked with fishing line.

"Hey, if you catch up with Terry, tell him Sean stopped by," the man said, executing a lazy paddle stroke that propelled him back toward the center of the lake.

"No problem," Beamon said as he laid his head back on the dock and started wondering what he'd done with his life. What had he actually accomplished that would matter ten minutes after he was dead? Would as many people remember him as they would Terry McMillan, or would his memory be contained only in a bunch of useless old FBI reports?

He shook off the thought, forcing it back to wherever it had come from. It was too late to ask questions like that, too late for regrets. Lately though, when he saw people like the young man in the canoe, he couldn't help wondering if they were the ones who had life nailed.

He remembered an article he'd read in *Rock and Ice* magazine that followed a young climber's various adventures over a six-month period. Every spectacular photograph shown in the article had been accompanied by a small handwritten account of how much money the young man had spent during the week. At the end of the six months, the subject of the article hadn't worked a single hour and had spent something like thirty-five hundred dollars. The really amazing thing was that included two trips abroad—he'd figured out how to fly as a courier for next to nothing. . . .

Mark Beamon glared at the woman standing a few feet from him as he dialed the pay phone for a fourth time. The frustrated expression on her face melted into one of intimidation, then uncertainty, and she finally started down the sidewalk in search of another phone.

Beamon turned his attention to a cop car cruising slowly through the parking lot as the ringing started on the other end of the line. His rental car was about ten feet away, with one wheel up on the sidewalk that ran the length of the Barnes and Noble store he was standing in front of. The cruiser didn't seem interested in his creative parking job, though, and disappeared around the back of the strip mall.

Beamon looked down again at the book in his hands—*The Worldwide*

Guide to Cheap Airfares—and crossed out the name of the last company he'd talked to.

"Eco-Courier, how can I help you?"

"Hi," Beamon said in a friendly tone. "My girlfriend is flying for you guys and she hasn't received her tickets yet. She's working and she asked me to call and make sure that they're going to be waiting for her at the counter."

"Sure. Could I have her name and date of travel?"

"Lori Jaspers," Beamon said, using Darby's friend's name. "I'm sorry, I don't remember when she told me she was leaving."

"No problem, let me put you on hold and take a look."

Courier companies often bought tickets in their own name and then switched them to the name of the person flying at the last minute, and that meant that there would be no record of the reservation that Beamon's friend at the FAA could get his hands on.

There was a click on the line and the woman's voice again. "Yup, they'll be waiting for her there. Thai flight 775 leaving L.A. at eight P.M."

Beamon threw the book across the sidewalk and missed the garbage can at the edge of the road by a good four feet. "And what's the date on that?"

"Uh, it's tonight—"

Of course. When else? Beamon hung up the phone and dialed Lori Jaspers' number from his address book.

"Hello?"

"Hey Lori? You gonna be around tomorrow?"

"Yeah . . . Who is this?"

He slammed the phone down and ran for his car.

35

The imaginary knife in Mark Beamon's side started to twist as he took the stairs to the LAX departure terminal three at a time. The clock above him read 7:55.

He sprinted through the glass doors and began pushing roughly through the crowd, scanning the long counters on either side of him for Thai Airways. When he reached the back wall, he was forced to stop for a moment and bent forward at the waist to catch his breath.

The Thai counter, in strict adherence to Murphy's Law, was on the other side of a barrier wall near where he'd come in. He ignored the protests of the people in line as he shoved his way close enough to see the departure board. Darby's flight was leaving on time. He looked at his watch: three minutes. Goddamn Asian efficiency.

Despite his body's vigorous protests, he started to run toward the crowded entrance to the departure gates and sprinted past a rather large man in a generic blue uniform.

"Sir, your ticket!"

Beamon ignored him and continued to duck and weave through the crowd, but was hit from behind when he tried to get around the metal detector. He managed to stay upright by bouncing off a wall and let his momentum carry him further down the concourse. "FBI—"

The hit that put him on the ground was, embarrassingly enough, from a sturdy-looking Hispanic woman. He went face-first on the floor and almost immediately felt a nightstick being forced into the back of his neck. The sound of running coming from behind him was quickly followed by the unmistakable jab of a gun barrel in his back. He couldn't move his head up, but he could see enough to discern that he was now completely surrounded by the poorly polished shoes of LAX security.

Without thinking, he opened his mouth to identify himself as an FBI agent again, but then closed it as his arms were forced behind his back and the familiar sound of ratcheting handcuffs assaulted his ears for the second time this week. He really just *had* to get his fucking job back one of these days.

He jumped as they pulled him to his feet, startling the five men and one women surrounding him, and probably almost getting himself shot. They slammed him back down to the ground, this time on his back, as he tried to find Darby Moore in the mental snapshot he'd taken of the people crowding the concourse.

His concentration was broken when one of the guards started feeling around in his jacket, finally making his way to the pistol he had convinced a sympathetic Maine cop to let him on the plane with.

"Gun!" he heard the man exclaim excitedly as he pulled it out of its holster and held it up like a prize.

"But sir," the young airport security guard said. "I *recognize* him. This *is* Mark Beamon. The FBI agent who—"

"I don't give a shit, son." The man sitting on the edge of the desk in front of Beamon spoke in a deep voice that didn't sound entirely natural. He was apparently in charge and seemed to take his job, and himself, fairly seriously.

"Nobody runs through one of my security checkpoints with a gun." He punctuated his words by glancing down at the .357 lying next to him on the desk and within easy reach of Beamon's recently freed hands.

"You understand that now, don't you, Beamon?"

When he didn't answer, the man resumed pawing through Beamon's wallet. "What the hell did you think you were doing?"

Everyone had come to a consensus as to Beamon's identity within three minutes of his arriving in the security office—it hadn't been a particularly difficult piece of detective work since Beamon had told them his name and handed them his wallet. Following that revelation, the two younger security guards reacted in the only reasonable manner—they had become visibly nervous. They, like Beamon himself, were anxious for him to be gone and to never think about the incident again.

Their boss, Buckaroo Bob, though, had seen things differently.

Beamon had expected him to do the sensible thing and simply turn him loose. When that started to look unlikely, he had assumed that he would call the local FBI office—which, as luck would have it, was run by a decade-long drinking buddy of Beamon's.

What he hadn't expected was for this moron to take it upon himself to carry out some kind of half-assed interrogation. Based on the clock above Ol' Tex's head, he'd already been droning for nearly twenty minutes, never moving from his physically elevated position on the desk and never once wavering from the John Wayne slur that must have been meant to be intimidating.

Beamon blocked out the meaningless words drooling from the man's mouth and started sorting out where he stood.

Not coming up with the courier angle faster had been a major screwup. If he actually still *had* a jurisdiction, Darby Moore was on her way out of it at about five hundred miles per hour right now. And that was a problem. While he had enough contacts and know-how to find just about anyone in the United States, in Asia he doubted he could find his ass with both hands. About all he would be able to do over there was walk around in a pair of Bermuda shorts and look for Caucasian faces. Hell, he'd be lucky not to get shot in a food riot or the endless abortive civil wars that constantly started and fizzled out all over that region.

Darby, on the other hand, had spent years over there, probably had fifty friends spread out over ten countries Beamon couldn't even pronounce, and most likely spoke the fucking language.

"... *in a lot of trouble.*"

Beamon looked up at the man hovering above him and screwed up his face. "Are you still talking?" He stood and casually picked up his pistol from the desk, surprising the security guard enough to actually get him to shut his mouth for moment. Beamon flipped open the wheel of the revolver and checked to see that it was still loaded. No one else in the room seemed to be breathing.

"Sorry to cut this short," Beamon said, punctuating his words by slamming the wheel back closed. "But I've really got to run. If you have any concerns about what happened here tonight, contact the local SAC. Use my name and he'll take your call." Beamon holstered the pistol and snatched his wallet off the desk. "If there's anything else, I should be home in a few days. Have the office here patch you through to me—they have the number." He could see the relief on the faces of the two younger guards as he passed by them. Roy Rogers's face was blank.

*   *   *

"Tommy? It's Mark," Beamon said, cupping his hand over the receiver of his cell phone in an effort to drown out some of the airport noise.

"Mark? Where are you?"

"L.A. Hey, you still keep in touch with that guy who runs the police over in Thailand?"

"Somporn Taskin? He's retired now, but yeah, I still hear from him now and then."

"Does he still have juice over there?"

"I don't know, things are pretty unstable politically, but if anybody does, it's him."

"There's a girl flying into Bangkok on Thai flight 775 in about fifteen hours that I'd like to have somebody keep an eye on. Someone good—it's important."

"So you found her?"

"Maybe."

"I'll give Somporn a call. He owes me. I'll see what he can do."

36

Mark Beamon flipped open the small cardboard box in his lap and exposed a steaming, Frisbee-sized pizza. He was about to tear off a slice when the background noise that seemed so constant in the L.A. airport faltered and then went completely dead. He looked at the people around him through the thick haze hanging in the lounge that kept the airport's smokers separate from the decent folk. The faces were all turned up toward the television bolted to the wall and all wore an intense expression of concentration.

Beamon abandoned the pizza for the moment and followed their gaze to a report just starting on CNN. He'd already seen the meat of it at least five times—everyone had. But that hadn't reduced its impact. Each time it was aired, the version was slightly modified with additional footage or a minor clarification in chronology as the splicing of the various source tapes was improved.

It started quietly with David Hallorin speaking to a group of workers at one of his factories. Then the powerful blast muffled by the microphones' limited capabilities. The picture shook violently, making Hallorin's image dart around the screen for a few moments, and then stabilized as the cameramen regained their equilibrium.

Hallorin's image was enhanced now, encircled by a patch of artificial light that set him apart from the rest of the action and made him stand out against the billowing smoke. Despite himself, Beamon felt a faint tickle in the back of his throat as Hallorin pushed his Secret Service men away and jumped into the crowd shouting orders. It grew to almost a lump when the unnatural ball of light followed Hallorin toward the fire and finally disappeared into the smoke. A moment later Hallorin reappeared with the little girl everyone now knew hadn't survived.

It seemed that Roland Peck had been right about being a little behind on stepping up Hallorin's corporate security capabilities.

Beamon turned and scanned the faces of the people around him again. They were all wondering the same thing he was—would they have reacted that way? Would they have jumped off that podium and run into the fire, or would they have let the Secret Service drag them out the back, stuff them into a limo, and spirit them away?

Beamon turned back just in time to see the photograph that was by now branded into the minds of probably half the earth's population. David Hallorin was on his knees in the parking lot. The dead girl's head was still in his lap and the smoke was still curling from his manufacturing plant's open bay door.

But those dramatic elements weren't what drew you into the photograph. It was Hallorin's face—the dazed expression had been captured with precisely the right mix of powerlessness, confusion, and pain. It was a Pulitzer Prize–winning image—a combination of the one that portrayed Nixon leaning against his desk and the one of the naked Vietnamese girl running from her napalmed village.

When the screen flickered to a room of press people lined up on folding chairs in front of an empty podium, the silence in the airport lounge deepened.

It seemed that Beamon's far-fetched theories of campaign conspiracies had been proven wrong. Hallorin had risked his life—*his life*—to save a single young girl who probably came from one of the families that he was supposed to so disdain. The incident hadn't changed Beamon's general impression of the man—Hallorin was an elitist who saw others as failed copies of himself: too lazy, unmotivated, or morally bankrupt to do what he had done in life. But that was just an overinflated ego—something Beamon had been accused of having more than a few times. The question was, would the man on the television above him kill to improve his chances at the presidency? Beamon was no profiler, but his gut said no. The declassification program, the Maine trooper, the impeccably timed job offer had all just been one of those strings of coincidences that sometimes popped up and threw a wrench into things.

Beamon felt around for the Coke balanced on the arm of his chair, unwilling to take his eyes from the screen as David Hallorin appeared at its edge. He watched the man's face as he strode confidently toward the lectern, trying to find in it what he had misjudged so badly.

He was still certain that Tristan Newberry wasn't killed by a poorly timed flash of PMS and a handy ice axe. In fact, he still tagged the political angle with a fifty percent probability. If the missing FBI file did exist, could the guilty party be someone who had been immortalized in it? Someone who wanted it suppressed? Someone who had known of its existence and been afraid of what Hallorin's declassification program might turn up?

Beamon found his Coke just as Hallorin positioned himself behind the microphones on the lectern.

"Thank you all for coming," he said, shuffling the papers in front of him. "I'm not here to make a speech, because there is really nothing I can possibly say that will make any difference to those who were injured and to the families of those who were killed in this incident. All I can do is tell you that they will be in my prayers and, I'm sure, the prayers of the American people."

Beamon missed his mouth with the straw as Hallorin did a little more paper shuffling.

"A very preliminary report by a group of independent experts that I hired at my own expense suggests that this was an accident involving the buildup of natural gas in a malfunctioning mechanical system—"

The press on the screen exploded, as did the people around Beamon in the airport. Hallorin held his hands up, quieting everyone involved. "You're going to ask me if I'm sure. I'm not. Obviously many of the policies I support would significantly damage the ability of Middle Eastern countries to purchase weapons systems and wage terrorism. If there *is* a connection to any terrorist organization, it will be found . . . "

The hands of the press shot up at Hallorin's pause.

"I know you have a lot of questions and I'll answer a few. I'd ask that you not question me about the cause of the explosion, because I just don't know any more." He pointed to a woman in the front.

"Senator Hallorin. How did you feel when you discovered that you couldn't save the young girl you pulled from the fire?"

Hallorin looked down at the floor for a few seconds. When he raised his head, he simply pointed to another reporter—this time in the middle of the throng.

There was a disgusted rumbling around Beamon aimed at the woman who had posed the question. Beamon turned and looked at the people behind him, sucking Coke through his straw. It was the first time since the crash of the economy and the leaking of the Vericomm tapes that he'd heard even a hint of public reaction moving against the press and in favor of a politician.

"Senator Hallorin," the second reporter started. "With only ten days left until the election, this morning's polls show your numbers skyrocketing. Do you have a comment?"

Hallorin sighed quietly into the microphones in front of him. "This is the kind of image-based decision making that I've been trying to get people away from. Look at what I believe, look at how I intend to run this country, and cast your vote based on that."

He pointed to a woman at the back.

"The stock market and the dollar have risen sharply since the incident—"

Hallorin held his hands up. "Hold it. This is turning into politics, which is exactly what I didn't want to happen. Whatever the cause, this has been a horrible tragedy—but one that is completely irrelevant to the election. Just because I'm stupid enough to run into a burning building when everyone else is running out, doesn't mean I'll make a good president."

Beamon drew in a breath fast enough to suck some of his drink into his windpipe and start a violent coughing fit. He got to his feet and walked out of the smoker's lounge, struggling to breathe in the relatively clean air outside. A couple more violent coughs more or less cleared his throat and left him standing, dazed, in the middle of the concourse.

The quote was exact. Precisely the one *he*'d read from that notepad in Roland Peck's office before their meeting, a full day before the explosion. The one he'd taken for an economic metaphor.`

Beamon felt the sweat start to break across his forehead. Hallorin had blown up his own manufacturing plant as a publicity stunt. He'd run into the chaos, knowing that the fire wouldn't spread, that the smoke wasn't noxious, that the building was still structurally sound. He'd killed those people—that little girl—for nothing more than a fucking photo opportunity. And like all things political, his reaction had been carefully considered and written out for him beforehand.

Beamon pulled out his cell phone and dialed Roland Peck's home number. It rang a couple of times before Peck's irritating voice came on the line.

"Hello?"

"Roland. Mark Beamon. I've decided not to take your job offer."

"Mark, let's ta—"

Beamon pressed the Off button on the phone and stuffed it back in his jacket.

37

"**C**'mon Darby," Sam said, still trying to mask the worried expression he'd had since she arrived. He took a few more steps away from the trees and out onto the white sand. "Hello!" he yelled at the top of his lungs. "Can anybody hear me?"

There was no answer, just the soft breeze and the quiet slosh of the waves as they gently folded over one another behind him. Darby adjusted her position slightly so that she could see through a hole in the dense foliage, mindful of the deadly snakes that liked to snooze in the leaves that she was standing on. As her friend had promised, the beach was deserted.

The last time she'd been there—two or so years ago—it had been packed with young Europeans and Americans sunbathing on the soft sand, drinking cheap beer in open air bars, and climbing the limestone monoliths that littered this part of southern Thailand.

Darby sidestepped again, putting herself in a narrow band of sunlight that burned into her. It was only seven in the morning, but the heat was already nearly unbearable, with humidity levels that kept everything just slightly damp all the time.

Sam motioned dramatically up the beach in the direction of a particularly impressive orange-brown cliff face that jutted some six hundred feet into the blue sky. "I'm telling you, Darby, I haven't seen a single square inch of Caucasian skin in two months. Shit, even the Thais don't come here anymore. No tourists means no money, and no money means you can't get here."

Darby kept her eyes moving along the shoreline but knew he was right. The normal clutter of long-tailed boats and their loud, pushy captains was completely gone. If Sam hadn't come to get her in his own boat, it would have taken her nine hours of bushwhacking through snake-infested jungles and over sheer cliffs to get there. It was a remote corner of the world made livable only by high-tech communications and transportation—two things that had completely broken down along with everything else in Asia. Railei Beach had, once again, become the middle of nowhere and a perfect place to hide.

"It's anarchy, Darb. There's no one in control." Sam pointed behind her in the direction of a small enclave of houses set up on stilts. "If anyone was, they'd have probably nationalized my house by now. Come on, let's go. You can tell me what the hell's going on on the way."

The plan that had seemed so right sitting in Wyoming wasn't as perfect now that she was in Thailand. The relief she'd expected to feel when she arrived at the nearly empty Phuket Thailand airport hadn't materialized. The normally friendly Thais seemed dangerous now, their eyes lingering on her longer than they should, wondering who she was and what she was doing in a country that had been all but abandoned—and in their minds destroyed—by the West. It really was chaos. Buses didn't run anymore, traffic drove over sidewalks and median strips unchallenged. Groups of unemployed men stood on street corners looking for opportunities. Any opportunities.

The customs agent who cleared her and her gear had lingered for almost a minute over her passport, the suspicion obvious on his face. After only about twenty seconds she'd wanted to break and run. But to where? Back to the safety of the States? It had turned out that all he'd wanted was ten American dollars. She'd parted with it grudgingly because she had no other option. Her funds were dwindling quickly.

She'd hoped that getting out of the immediate path of the men who were so efficiently tracking her would clear her mind, give her time to work things out. But it hadn't. She still felt like everything was out of control. Her normally unshakable calm had completely failed her in the face of the unfamiliarity of it all. She'd come to terms with the mountains trying to kill her long ago. It was just the balance of things; there was no malice involved. But this was something completely different. She felt herself getting paranoid.

She looked down the beach again, searching for any sign of life in the boarded-up bars and restaurants, but there was none. She looked up at her friend, and suddenly realized how ridiculous she must look, cowering in a bush. A stupid bush.

Darby stepped out on the beach and started toward a rocky path uncovered by the low tide. "Let's go."

He followed a few feet behind, silent until they left the sand and began scrambling over the jagged boulders to gain the beach to the north.

"So, what happened, Darby? What happened to Tristan?" Sam's voice was hesitant.

The cool water splashed up on her as the waves collided with the rocks, mingling with the sweat that had already drenched her. She tried to concentrate on that feeling and let everything else go. "Do you think I killed him?"

"No. Hell, no." Sam forced a smile. "I mean, I only met the guy once, but he just didn't seem that irritating."

"He wasn't. He wasn't irritating at all." She bent over to start down the other side of the boulder they were on, but stopped when she felt Sam's hand on her shoulder.

"Look, Darby. Have you thought this through? If you didn't do it, and I know you didn't, is running to Southeast Asia the right thing to do? It makes you look guilty. Have you thought about maybe going back and turning yourself in? Telling your side of the story? My dad knows some pretty heavy-hitting lawyers, maybe I could—"

Darby put her hand on his, silencing him. "Thanks, Sam, but it's more complicated than that. I'm just going to have to work this out myself, okay?"

He didn't immediately follow her down to the sand.

"I'm leaving next week, Darb," he said finally, jumping off the tall boulder and landing next to her. "This is as much my home as anywhere, but it's getting too creepy, even for me."

Darby nodded and started up the beach without saying anything. They continued in silence for another ten minutes and then cut right onto a steep, narrow trail rising into the jungle.

"You can stay at my place as long as you want," Sam said.

Darby stopped and looked back down the trail at him, wiping the sweat from her forehead with an equally wet forearm. "Sam, I appreciate you letting me stop here, but I don't want to—"

"Doesn't matter," he said. "Look around you—Railei is a ghost town. It's either you or a family of macaques. And you know how I feel about monkeys. Just promise me one thing."

"What?"

"You'll think about what I said."

"I'll think about it," she said truthfully. That's what she'd come here for—to think. So far, though, every strategy she dreamed up was a losing one. And worse, she was finding it impossible to let go of Tristan's memory, to separate her growing anger from her logic. As much as she wanted all this to go away—to make a deal, or to just keep running—she also wanted the men who had killed Tristan to pay for what they'd done.

"That's it. Right there," she heard Sam say from behind her. She picked up her pace a bit, hopping from rock to rock until she came to the base of the cliff. She craned her neck upwards, following the line of shiny bolts with her eyes, mapping each hole, divot and ledge in the rock face, calculating the optimal body position for each move. Normally, her mind worked through these kinds of sequences automatically, but now she had to concentrate. To try to block everything else out.

"I don't know, Sam. Maybe this wasn't such a good idea. I'm not really in the mood—"

"Come on, Darby. This is exactly what you need." Sam dropped his pack and began pulling a rope and a pair of shoes from the top. "It'll take your mind off your problems for a few hours. Clear your head."

When she didn't move, he let his shoes fall to the ground and crossed his arms in front of his chest self-consciously. "Okay, the truth is, I've got fifty-two tries on this route and I'm within two feet of doing it. If I don't get it before I leave, I'm afraid my elbows will be too old when it's finally safe to come back."

It was the least she could do for all the help he was giving her, for never questioning her innocence. In the grand scheme of things, another two hours weren't going to make a whole lot of difference.

"You first," Sam said as she slid her pack off and dumped the contents on the ground.

"What?"

He held a handful of quickdraws out toward her. "I don't want to tire myself out putting these up. You don't mind, do you?"

She shook her head and clipped the 'draws to her harness before sliding it on and tying into the rope.

"Great. Thanks. You're on belay, Darb. Whenever you're ready."

She laid her hands against the cliff and closed her eyes, trying to fill her mind with the texture of the rock. Trying to tell herself that she was safe now, back on the fringes of the real world where she belonged. She took a deep breath and reached up for a doorjamb-sized edge, pulling herself up onto it and bringing her feet up onto two similar ledges beneath her.

She felt out of balance. As she continued up, moves that should have flowed effortlessly turned into wild throws for the tiny holds that dotted the route. Each time she latched onto one, gravity grabbed hold of her and her body sagged dangerously toward the ground.

She barely made it to the first bolt, clipped a quickdraw into it, and snapped the rope through the other end. Her arms and shoulders already felt like they were on fire and there was a stream of blood running from the edge of one of her nails down the sweat-soaked back of her hand.

This was usually the best part—the burning of lactic acid in her muscles, the unavoidable cuts opened by the jagged rock. It had always felt like life to her. Now it just felt like pain.

"I'm going to hang," she called down. Sam took the slack out of the rope and she sat back in her harness, gently swinging in the damp breeze. There was no joy in it anymore. The harder she tried to fall into the unconscious alignment of mind and body that had always been such a high for her, the further it seemed to slip away.

"Are you all right, Darby?" Sam called up. "Hey, if you don't want to finish it, come down. I'll do it."

She slammed a hand into the rock face, setting her to swinging violently. "NO! I'm going to finish it."

She shoved two fingers into a small pocket so hard that she felt another cut open up. Ignoring it, she abandoned any attempt at technique or grace, just grabbing holds as fast and powerfully as she could.

She made it another thirty feet and latched onto a hold big enough to fit both of her hands. Breathing hard, she could feel the sweat running down her back so thick that it was actually trapping the heat to her body.

"What do you want?"

It was Sam's voice, but it didn't seem to be directed at her.

She managed to find a foothold just large enough to allow her to twist her body around and look down to the ground.

Sam was trying to back away, letting rope out to compensate for his increasing distance from the cliff. He had to stop after ten feet, though, when he reached the edge of a forty-foot drop-off. Five uniformed Thai men had more or less surrounded him and began speaking in rapid-fire Thai as they examined the rope he was holding.

"What do you want?" Sam repeated in Thai, fear edging into his voice.

"What you want?" one of the men mimicked. His companions laughed as he stepped forward and grabbed the rope that Darby was tied into, giving it a firm tug. She felt the sudden downward pull in her harness and her feet skittered off the rock, leaving her hanging from the cliff by her sweat-soaked hands.

"Get the fuck off that!" she heard Sam yell as he pushed the man away.

Darby brought her feet up again quickly, trying to take some of the weight off her exhausted arms. She looked down again, spotting the last bolt she had clipped about fifteen feet below her, then staring down at the ground forty feet below that.

Sam played out a few more feet of slack as the Thais started inching toward him again, then hit the ground hard when one of them drove a foot into his side. The additional rope that he'd let out kept him from pulling her off when he fell, but based on the position of her last bolt and the amount of slack, she was no longer certain that she wouldn't hit the ground if she came off.

Darby looked above her as the shouts below started to increase in volume and anger. The next bolt was only about five feet away, but the wall turned almost blank above her. She could already feel her grip weakening and what little focus she'd had slipping away. She'd never make it.

"She come down!" The words were barely decipherable around the thick Thai accent. Darby looked down again just in time to see her friend absorb another firm kick to the ribs and one of the Thais hang his weight on the rope. She tried to brace herself, but her feet slipped out from under her again.

The tension on the line and laughter below increased as the man lifted his feet off the ground and left her supporting his entire body weight as well as her own. They were ignoring Sam now, and in a desperate glance in his direction she could see that he had taken up what slack he could and braced himself. When he looked up at her and gave a terrified nod, she let go.

The way the wind felt as it blew through her newly cut hair seemed strange when mixed with the familiar sensation of falling. She let her body go completely limp, knowing that there was nothing she could do now but hope that it would be the rope, and not the ground, that broke her fall.

She came to an abrupt halt to the sound of a shrill scream from the man who had been trying to pull her off. She opened her eyes in time to see him stagger back a couple of feet, staring down at the deep wound the rope had cut into his palm. Judging by the volume of his friends' laughter, they thought that was pretty funny, too.

She had stopped about fifteen feet from the ground, close enough to see the rage on the injured man's face when he turned it up to her and pulled a knife from his pocket.

Darby tried to swing back to the rock but it was too far away. She searched hopelessly for a safe landing in the jagged boulders that littered the ground as the man went for the rope. He was within inches of it when Sam jumped to his feet and ran to his left, leaping off the ledge he had been standing on.

She felt herself pulled up about a foot as his body weight hit the rope, then she was in a free fall to the ground. Just before she impacted, the rope went tight for a moment—slowing her down enough to leave her lying among the scattered boulders dazed, instead of dead.

The Thai who had been injured was on her the moment her back hit the ground, knife cocked back in hand. She tried to grab a rock to defend herself but didn't have any strength.

"Stop!"

The Thai froze, knife hand still cocked by his ear and face still full of fury. Darby turned toward the voice and saw the blond head of Vili Marcek appear through the trees.

The Thai man on top of her adjusted himself so that his knee was planted painfully in her chest, effectively pinning her to the ground. The blood from his hand had spattered onto his face and combined with the rage etched there made him look like a deranged killer from a slasher film.

"My, this was close, was it not?" the Slovenian said, smiling as he approached.

"Vili? What . . . why—" Darby looked into his bright blue eyes, but the wind had been knocked out of her too badly to get a full sentence out.

Marcek placed a hand on the shoulder of the man pinning her to the ground. The Thai stood and let Marcek lead him past his companions to the edge of the drop that Sam had jumped from. Darby struggled to her feet and limped up behind them.

"He's the one who did that to you," Marcek said to the Thai, pointing to her friend's semiconscious form. He patted the man on the back and then turned back to Darby, who was trying desperately to unbuckle the harness at her waist and escape the rope tied to it. She looked up just as the Thai started climbing down the rock toward Sam.

"Stop! Vili—stop him!"

Marcek jumped in front of her and kept her from going to her friend's aid.

A moment later, she heard a loud grunt and the unmistakable sound of the impact of flesh on flesh. Marcek let her go just in time for her to see the Thai stand, leaving his knife buried to the hilt in her friend's chest.

She stepped backward and tripped over the harness that had fallen around her ankles, landing on her back among the boulders. For the first time in her life, she felt herself give up. Her muscles went slack and her brain seemed to short-circuit. She was only vaguely aware of Vili Marcek standing over her and the four Thai men scooping her off the ground. None of it mattered. Maybe they'd kill her. Then it would be over.

38

Darby Moore squinted into the blackness as the rotting wooden door opened, and was staggered by the stench that washed over her. The four Thai policemen holding her seemed to be temporarily confused. The ones who had already staked out the more interesting parts of her anatomy seemed unwilling to let go long enough to get through the door, afraid that on the other side they might end up with a less titillating selection.

The argument that ensued between the men was loud but brief. When a post-threshold hierarchy had been tentatively sketched out, she felt herself being shoved through the doorway and dragged to one of four empty cells along the right side of the narrow passageway. But it didn't really feel like it was happening to her. She felt completely disconnected—as if she was already half dead.

A de facto leader had obviously been chosen during the negotiations, and he was the one who accompanied her into the cell. Once inside, he jerked her around to face him and ran a hand slowly down her cheek. "You pretty." She looked at the handkerchief covering the deep cut her rope had left in his hand and wondered if all the blood on it was his or if some of it had come from Sam. The image of her friend's dead body lying below the cliffs that he'd loved so much melded with the one of Tristan's blood-spattered foot hanging from the door of her van, and her disconnection turned to fury too quickly for her to control.

In one smooth motion, she grabbed the man's injured hand and squeezed with everything she had. He opened his mouth to cry out, but then realized that his comrades were watching from just outside the cell. His teeth clenched tight, stifling any sound, and he forced himself to do nothing for long enough to prove that he couldn't be hurt by a mere woman. Then he swung his good fist at her head.

Darby released him at the last possible moment and ducked, letting the blow glance off the top of her skull. He connected solidly on his second try, and though the blow wasn't really powerful enough to hurt her, she dropped to her knees hoping he would be satisfied.

She wasn't that lucky. The next shot caught her in the back of the neck and had the Thai's full weight behind it. Stunned, she fell to her side in the wet, foul-smelling grime puddled on the floor. She brought her arms up to protect her face, noticing for the first time that Vili Marcek was standing just inside the door they'd brought her through. He was enjoying this.

"Enough!"

The Thai standing over her had been about to let loose with a vicious kick but froze at the sound of the man's voice. Darby lowered her arms a few inches and looked in the direction it had come from.

At first, all she could see was a sweat-stained, white dress shirt hovering in the gray gloom of the jail. When she concentrated a little harder she was able to make out a pair of dark slacks that blended almost perfectly into the stone wall behind them.

Darby redirected her gaze up a bit as the Thai retreated a few feet. Whoever the man was, he was white, but with dark, almost black, hair combed over in a way that suggested it was hiding a bald spot. The lower part of his face was padded with heavy jowls surrounding what once must have been a strong jawline.

"Get out," he said authoritatively.

The Thai man who had been beating her said something as he backed away. She hadn't been quick enough to translate it, but the lecherous titters from his companions made the meaning fairly clear.

She laid there in the filth until the Thai locked her cell, then pushed herself to her knees and stood, scraping the sludge from her side and staring directly at the man standing against the wall. She was sure now that she had never seen him before. She'd expected the man who had turned up at Lori's ranch, but it definitely wasn't him.

He turned to Marcek. "You, too."

The Slovenian looked like he was going to say something, but ended up just shuffling out with an expression of deep disappointment on his face.

"Tell me, Darby. Do you regret saving him?" the man said as Marcek pulled the door at the end of the corridor closed.

"What?"

"It's a simple question. Do you regret risking your life to save Vili? He obviously wants to see you dead for doing it."

"I never really thought about it."

The man nodded and leaned his considerable weight against the wall behind him. "It doesn't have anything to do with you rescuing him, you know. I've been unlucky enough to have had to spend a lot of time with him over the past two weeks and it's pretty obvious that he has some kind of infatuation for you. A man scorned . . . " His voice trailed off.

Darby had known about that. She'd let him down as easily as she could, but he'd gone nuts, showing up at places she was climbing, calling her whenever she was staying somewhere with a phone. The story had quickly made its rounds through the eternally gossipy climbing community and then the whole thing had ended with the rescue on Ama Dablam. The humiliation had just been too much for him.

"As big a fuckup as I've ever met," the man continued. "You'll be happy to know that he'll never get the money he's been promised. When I'm done with him, I'll put a bullet in the back of his head. I'll enjoy doing it, too."

Darby just stared at him, still trying to process what had happened to her and what, if anything, she could do about it. "Do you want me to thank you?"

"No, I guess not," he said, punctuating his words with a slow shake of the head. "Honey, I don't know what you stole—and I don't want to—but whatever it is, it was a big mistake."

"I didn't steal anything."

He didn't seem to hear her. "There's a gentleman on his way here now who's very interested in talking with you. I don't think you're going to enjoy the conversation much, though."

"I didn't ask for any of this," she said quietly. "It doesn't have anything to do with me. I'll tell them what they want to know. I don't really have a choice now, do I?"

The man took a deep breath of the foul-smelling air and coughed loudly as it lodged in this chest. "Doesn't really matter now. The Thais were asking an outrageous amount of money to help me find you. Comes out of my pocket, you know, so I had to do a little negotiating. I'm afraid I promised them whatever's left of you after your, uh, conversation."

She looked around her at the seeping walls and the hole in the floor of the cell that passed as a toilet, sucking her lower lip between her teeth and trying not to let her mind project the meaning of the man's words. "Why are you telling me this? You just want to be sure I know who's responsible for killing me?"

"No," he said seriously. "I guess I wanted to offer an apology. I've read and heard a lot about you in the past few weeks. A person like you shouldn't have to die like you're going to."

Darby stepped forward and wrapped her hands around the rusting bars, getting as close to the man as she could. "I appreciate the sentiment, but in the end, I don't think it's going to do me much good. Why don't you help me get out of here? It'll be good for your soul."

He laughed. "I feel bad, honey, but I don't feel that bad. I worked hard all my life and didn't get shit for it. This job is paying enough to get me a new house and a hell of a nice sports car, with some cash left over for gas." He turned and started for the door.

"You'd do this to me for money?" Darby called after him. "For money?"

"What other reason is there?" He stopped for a moment, but didn't look back at her. "I'm sorry, I've really got to get out of here. The smell is starting to get to me."

39

As morbid as it was, she'd played the game for years.

Blizzard, rockfall, avalanche, unidentifiable intestinal parasites and tropical disease. No matter how grim her situation, it seemed that she could always think of a time she'd been worse off. It would always be something like, "Sure it's a hundred and twenty-five below zero, but remember that time the rock we were anchored to started sliding toward the edge of a cliff and we couldn't get untied from it?" Unfortunately, that little mental trick wasn't working this time. Instead, she'd been forced to accept that the situation was hopeless and start to think about exactly what that meant.

The cell was almost completely desolate. The only sound came from the occasional drip of water as the humidity accumulated on the stone ceiling and finally fell to one of the puddles in the floor. She didn't have a watch, but from the position of the sunlight struggling through the tiny hole cut high in the wall, she assumed that she'd been there about twenty-four hours. She hadn't so much as heard another human voice since her brief conversation with the semiremorseful American who was responsible for imprisoning her here.

She couldn't decide whether her solitude was good news or not. The next people she saw would undoubtedly be very interested in what she'd done with their precious file. And that was another game she couldn't win. If she told them, she would be turned over to the Thais for disposal; something that would be extremely unpleasant and probably fairly time-consuming. If she resisted, they'd force her to talk *and then* turn her over to the Thais.

Darby's sense of smell had long since shut down, but she could still feel the heaviness of the air as she knelt down next to the rusted metal bed frame that was the cell's only piece of furniture. The night before, in the pitch dark, she'd managed to dislodge a good-sized stone from the wall and had spent the night working quietly with it on the edge of the bed. She wasn't sure how long it had taken, but now one of the wires that made up the empty mattress platform stuck straight up, the end ground to a shiny, razor-sharp edge. It gleamed in the weak sunlight like the escape it was. Her only way out of there.

She held her wrist over it, closing her eyes and trying to slow down her breathing. Her friend Sam, a gifted philosopher in a bizarre kind of way, had always been a staunch believer in the evils of karma. He'd decided long ago that if a person had too much good luck in life, it was just the gods setting him or her up for a fall. It looked like he'd been right. For both of them.

She pressed her wrist down on the sharp point, but not hard enough to puncture the soft skin there. A vertical slit in each would make her impossible to save, particularly in a country where the medical system had broken down along with everything else.

What would it be like? Would there be nothing—like before she was born? Would her soul go to a holding pen for reassignment to some infant still in the womb? Or were the Christians right? She certainly hoped not—their God wasn't much of a fan of suicide. He might decide to confine her to this cell for the rest of eternity, as effective a hell as anyone could ever dream up.

Time got lost as she knelt there. It was so much harder than she had imagined. She generally thought of herself as reasonably courageous but maybe it was just that she'd always been too preoccupied trying to cheat death to really think about it. The end of her life had never been more than a tiny spark in the back of her mind.

The sound of voices suddenly penetrated the sturdy wood door that led to the outside world, floating to her on the foul air. The words were Thai—too muffled and too angry for her to understand. As the shouting grew louder, she pressed her wrist a little harder onto the sharp edge of the wire. A tiny drop of blood was briefly illuminated and began winding its way down to the bed frame.

The shouting stopped as abruptly as it had started. The sound of a key rattling in the door echoed eerily around her, filling the sudden silence. This was it.

Come on, Darby. Do it.

She had a few more seconds. They still had to walk through the door and into the narrow corridor—giving her plenty of time before they could unlock her cell.

She watched, unmoving, as the door opened and three men came toward her through the gloom. Two were short, thin, and dark; obviously Thai, though one walked with a regal gait that she'd never seen in this part of the world. The other man was much taller and broader, most likely an American, and death to her.

Mark Beamon felt as though he'd been almost physically pushed back when the door opened. The smell was indescribable—different from the house with the rotting state trooper—but in its way, just as bad. The Thai "cop" with the keys walked through the door first, splashing through the oily puddles that had formed on the ground and becoming a little bit out of focus as he moved through the steamy haze inside. The elation Beamon had initially felt at having potentially found the elusive Darby Moore suddenly disappeared. There had to be some mistake. They couldn't have put that little girl in here.

"After you, Mark," Somporn Taskin said in an upper-crust British accent that seemed as if it should belong to a member of the House of Lords and not the retired head of the Thai police.

Beamon had been interested in a more clandestine entry into the jail where Darby Moore was allegedly being held, but Sherman's friend had opted to just stroll in the front door. The reaction to their arrival had been fascinating. No less than five cops had surrounded them, speaking to Taskin in rapid-fire Thai that was a little too loud, like frightened children talking to themselves. The unarmed Taskin had been completely calm, speaking in quiet tones that seemed to be physically wringing the sweat from the grimy policemen surrounding him. There was no mistaking that they were nearly paralyzed by their fear of this little Oxford-educated man.

In Beamon's experience, the power to intimidate was inherited with many jobs—and head of the Thai police was certainly one of them. But you couldn't inherit the ability to terrify. No, you had to earn that.

"No. Please. After you," Beamon said, a little embarrassed but making an effort not to show it. He didn't know if it was the reaction of the Thai cops or something that he sensed on his own, but he was uncomfortable with the thought of this impeccably dressed, painfully polite man getting behind him.

Somporn Taskin smiled graciously and strolled through the door, apparently unaffected by the condition of his surroundings. While Beamon had never even imagined anything like this half-abandoned jailhouse, Taskin seemed to be completely at home.

The already unbearable heat seemed to double as Beamon stepped reluctantly through the doorway. He covered his mouth with his hand and coughed quietly as he followed his host.

The scene was almost surreal. Darby Moore, wearing bright purple shorts and a red tank top, was kneeling by the frame of a bed, apparently praying. It looked like one of those old movies that had been hand painted frame by frame, like she existed in color and her surroundings existed only in black and white.

"It looks like you've gotten yourself into a hell of a mess, young lady," Beamon said, lighting a harsh Thai cigarette and hoping that it would help deaden his senses.

"Guess so." Her voice was almost too quiet to make out.

Taskin said something in Thai to the cop, who immediately started toward the cell door with a ring of keys.

"Stop," Beamon said before he made it to the bars. The Thai cop halted and looked back at Taskin, who did nothing.

Beamon's eyes had finally adjusted to the semidarkness, clarifying Darby and the cell around her. She wasn't praying. Her wrist was pressed against a jagged wire protruding from the bed. On her face was an expression of calm resignation. Shit.

"Somporn," Beamon said. "Would it be okay if I spoke with Darby alone for a moment?"

"Of course." Taskin motioned to the cop, who followed subserviently. "I'll prepare for our departure, Mark. Meet me out front whenever you're ready."

Beamon kept his eyes on Darby as the cop hung his keys on the wall and followed Taskin out. "I guess things are looking pretty grim."

Darby's head turned slowly toward him. "You're the man I saw in Wyoming."

Beamon smiled and wagged a finger at her. "You outsmarted me on that one. I was really pissed."

She looked around her. "Well, it seems like you won in the end. So, you'll excuse me if I cut our relationship short."

"No. No, I won't," Beamon said as she turned her attention back to the wire beneath her wrist. "You'd be the second young suicide I've seen in a week. I'm starting to get depressed."

When she turned her head to look at him again, her eyes were a little more lucid, a little more probing.

"Look, Darby. We really don't have much time here, so let me lay it out. I don't think I'm the person you were expecting. I know there's a man chasing you, I know that he's hired a Slovenian climber that you have a history with. Let me assure you that I'm not connected with them in any way—"

"Then who are you connected with?"

"Good question. I haven't actually worked that out yet. My name is Mark Beamon. I used to work for the FBI. Maybe you've heard of me?"

"No."

Beamon remembered that the girl's profile didn't exactly suggest a fanatical interest in current events. "All I can tell you is that I'm here to help you. I'm honestly not sure that I actually can, but I'm willing to try."

She laughed bitterly. "Like you helped Sam and Tristan? No, you want me safe and sound so that you can find out what I know. Nice try, Mr. Beamon, but any naïveté that I might have once suffered is gone now."

He flinched as she pressed her wrist down a little harder on the wire.

No one should have to go through what she had over the last couple of weeks and sure as hell no one deserved to end up in this place. The problem was, psychobabble just wasn't his forte. Especially when it came to this particular girl, whose motivations and lifestyle still baffled him. One thing he didn't question, though, was her ability to do what she was threatening.

"What if I am here to hurt you?" Beamon said, abandoning the sympathetic route that didn't suit him and moving back to logic, which had always treated him well. His words got her attention. While she certainly had the willpower, self-termination just wasn't in this girl's nature.

"If you've got that wire nice and sharp, you'll probably get a good vertical cut in one wrist and a marginal one in the other before I make it through that cell door. I'll yell for help and get a couple of those creepy little bastards outside to hold you down while I put tourniquets above your biceps. My ex-girlfriend's a doctor—forced me to learn first aid backwards and forwards. I imagine that would keep you alive long enough for me to make you tell me what I want to know." He paused to light another cigarette. "Don't you?"

His words had the desired effect—her wrist moved back a half an inch or so and she focused on him again. "Why would you want to help me?"

Beamon shrugged. Another good question. Utter stupidity and a self-destructive nature was the answer. But that probably wouldn't play that well under the circumstances. He opted to paint a more rosy picture.

"One, I've been paid a lot of money to, and two, because I have a thing for underdogs. That's why I got into the FBI in the first place. Hell," he said, letting his voice trail off in volume a bit. "I've got a goddamn Yale education. It's not like I couldn't have gotten a decent job."

She stared at him for a long time, obviously struggling with what to do.

"Seems to me like you've got nothing to lose," Beamon said finally. "Look, I don't mean to rush you, but I don't know where the guy who put you in here is and I'd rather not stay in one place for too long. If I'm lying, you're screwed whether you try to do yourself in or not. If I'm not, we have a chance, albeit a small one, to get out of this godforsaken country alive."

"You think you can just walk in here and make me trust you?" she said, looking back down at the shiny piece of metal beneath her wrist. Beamon's breath caught in his chest and he wondered what the hell he'd do if she cut herself. He could keep her alive for a short time, but the chances of finding a doctor anywhere within a hundred miles was about zero.

She suddenly stood. "I don't want to die like this."

Beamon let his breath out slowly and walked over to get the keys to the cell. "Good choice," he said, opening the door as she moved cautiously toward him. He held out his hand. "Mark Beamon."

"Darby Moore." She took his hand in a grip that seemed too powerful to belong to her.

"Nice to finally meet you, Darby. Now why don't we get the hell out of here before somebody decides to shoot us."

They walked quickly through the door at the end of the holding pen and out into the relative cool of the police station. There were four men in the front office, all cluttered around a single table pushed up against the wall. Beamon didn't make eye contact as he and Darby moved past them and out the door into the sunlight.

There were another five uniformed cops standing in the lightly traveled street that ran along the front of the police station, forcing the cars driving the road to slow and steer around them. The feeling of minor triumph Beamon had felt when they cleared the building faded under the weight of their stares.

"Do you have a car?" Darby said as the four cops from inside followed them out the door and took up a position behind them.

"Not exactly, but we do have a ride," Beamon said, scanning the street for any sign of Somporn Taskin. The brightly colored shops that lined the sidewalk across the street were mostly boarded up now, but still contributed to the visual distortion he was getting from the foreign surroundings. It took him a few moments to realize that Taskin and his car were gone.

"Shit."

Darby grabbed his upper arm and leaned in close to his ear. "I still have problems, don't I, Mr. Beamon?"

The whispers of the cops surrounding them grew to a more conversational tone as they quickly gained confidence. Beamon leaned forward and looked up the street again as the Thais continued to use Somporn Taskin's unfortunate absence to pump themselves up. "Call me, Mark, hon. After all, I think we're going to be sharing the same shallow grave tomorrow."

"Maybe we should get out of here, then," she suggested.

"Seems sensible." Beamon put a hand in the small of her back and they started down the sidewalk. The cops were yelling now, but it didn't sound like they were following. Beamon and Darby had covered about fifty yards when they heard the sound of squealing tires as a car came skidding to a stop in front of the police station.

"What the fuck is going on!" screamed an American voice that he didn't recognize.

Beamon looked over his shoulder and saw the head and torso of a heavyset Caucasian man in his fifties poking from the sunroof of a black Mercedes. "You recognize that guy?"

"Uh huh."

"Let's run." Beamon sprinted forward, dragging Darby along behind him. He heard the screech of tires again, and when he looked back, the car—and worse, the Thais—were coming up behind them fast.

"Down the alley," Beamon yelled. Their positions had reversed within a few seconds of their attempt at a getaway and Darby was now dragging him. He could already feel the blood pounding in his head, protesting the sudden exertion, stifling heat, and deadly Thai cigarettes.

"Come *on*, Mark!" Darby shouted as they ran through a narrow alley and into a crowded outdoor market. "If we cut through here, there's a big department store we can go through and get out the back!"

Beamon was unable to speak at this point, but followed along, already starting to stumble over colorful baskets of vegetables and slow-moving short people. He tried to stayed low, knowing that his brown head would poke up a good six inches above the Thai national basketball team's.

When he looked behind him, he could see the obvious disturbance in the crowd as the Thai cops chased after them on foot. He and Darby ducked around a corner and stopped for a moment, giving Beamon a chance to bend forward at the waist and try not to throw up.

"Are you having a good time?" Darby said in an exasperated tone with only a hint of breathlessness.

Beamon looked up at her, confused for a moment, but then the slight smile that he was wearing registered in his mind. "Sorry," he struggled to get out as he wiped the sweat from his stinging eyes. "My life's . . . been kind of complicated lately. There's a simplicity to this situation that's sort of appealing."

He peeked around the corner and saw that the single, large, disturbance in the crowd had broken into five smaller disturbances as the Thais spread out and tried to pick up their trail. When he turned back to Darby, she had a thoughtful expression on her face that seemed as out of place as his smile.

"I kind of know what you mean," she said, then grabbed him by the front of his shirt and surprised him by pretty much pulling his full weight off the wall he was leaning against and dragging him into a run.

"That's it," Darby said as they came around a corner and ran toward a large white building. When they ducked under its discolored awning, though, they found the doors boarded up. Another victim of Asia's economic collapse.

"No!" Darby yelled, and pounded on the cracked plywood.

"We're okay, Darby. Plan B. Gotta keep moving," Beamon gasped, wondering exactly what plan B was as he ran up the street, confident that Darby would be able to catch up without much effort. He'd barely made it fifty feet when the black Mercedes came skidding around the corner.

"Darby! Here!" he yelled, turning down a narrow side road.

She caught him a moment later and they sprinted along it, only to find that it dead-ended into the back of a dilapidated apartment building after a couple of hundred yards. Sparks flew from under the Mercedes as it turned up the road and barreled toward them.

"Up here!" Darby yelled, sprinting straight at the doorless building behind them. She jumped at the last minute and seemed to run up the wall for about five feet and then grabbed the bottom of a rusted pipe running along the wall. One hard pull on the pipe and she had her fingers clamped onto the bottom grate of a fire escape.

"Come on!" she shouted, dangling effortlessly from one arm as she watched the Mercedes coming at them with four Thai cops not far behind.

Beamon looked up at her and shook his head. "You've got to be fucking kid—"

A loud crack was followed by the better portion of the fire escape separating from the wall and crashing down to the street along with its one occupant. Beamon ran over to her and pulled her out from under a support beam just as the Mercedes skidded to a halt behind them.

Miraculously, Darby was able to stand under her own power and appeared to be completely unhurt. Beamon looked around him as the American emerged from the sunroof again and the Thai cops aimed a variety of automatic pistols in their direction. Nowhere left to run.

"*Now* you have problems," Beamon said to Darby as she shook her head violently, still trying to clear what was left of the effects of her fall.

"An interesting chase, Mr. Beamon," the man sticking out of the sunroof said. "Pointless, but interesting."

Beamon's mind was desperately trying to work through his options, but it seemed that there were none. He was almost completely exhausted, unarmed, and in a country where he knew one person, and that person had fucked him.

Darby's eyes were completely clear now and she obviously understood the seriousness of their situation. "Sorry, kid," Beamon said to her. "I think you might have made it without me."

She shook her head as the Thais slowly moved in on them. "Where would I have gone?" There was a deep sadness in her voice that for some reason made Beamon think of Carrie and Emory. He'd immersed himself in this case, wanting to escape making the hard decisions about his life, and it seemed he'd succeeded beautifully. It suddenly struck him that he would never see them again.

Beamon didn't notice the subcompact car turning up the narrow street until its driver started honking the tinny little horn. The sound prompted everyone involved to turn and watch the miniscule Honda coast to a stop behind the Mercedes.

"You'll have to accept my apologies, Mark," Somporn Taskin said as he stepped from the car. "I was unavoidably detained. Are you ready to go?"

The scene suddenly turned from terrifying to comical. The four armed

Thais had, once again, become uniformly docile and speechless at the sight of the unarmed man. The American hanging from the sunroof of the Mercedes didn't seem to know what to do as Beamon pulled Darby past him and toward Taskin's car.

"What the fuck is going on here?" he yelled as Darby ducked into the backseat of the Honda and Beamon opened the passenger door.

"What the fuck is wrong with you? Stop them!"

The Thais ignored him as they holstered their guns and began hurrying back down the street. Beamon could see that the man recognized the balance of power had shifted but couldn't figure out why.

Taskin paused in the open door of his car, looking up at the American over its roof. "Sir, your chances of surviving your stay in my country are diminishing very quickly." As always, Taskin's tone was utterly polite. This time, though, there was a subtle undertone that seemed to indicate that he was becoming irritated, and that anyone who irritated him ended up cut into tiny pieces next to the pieces of what used to be their families.

The American's expression suggested that he'd heard the same undertone as Beamon and had surmised that Taskin was absolutely capable of carrying out his threat if he should decide to bother.

40

Roland Peck pressed his back against the wall as David Hallorin grabbed hold of a heavy iron floor lamp and swung it into a bookcase like it weighed nothing. Sparks rained from the shelf's built-in lighting system, reflecting off the shattering glass and giving Hallorin a brief, supernatural glow.

"You've done nothing for me, Roland!"

"But I . . . " Peck started, finding it almost impossible to speak through his fear-constricted throat. The panic had struck suddenly and he knew he was losing control of it.

"Nothing!" Hallorin screamed again. "Why Roland? Why would you do this to me? I've treated you like a son. Was that not good enough? Is that why you decided to spit in my face? Mark Beamon, the girl, the file. They don't mean anything to you, do they? It's not your life on the line."

The words cut through him. *Like a son.* Hallorin had never spoken them out loud. Peck often fantasized that he was Hallorin's son, like he was the son of the greatest man alive. But now it was all coming down around him. This was his fault. His fault. He didn't deserve the things that David Hallorin had given him.

"I . . . I . . . spoke with Beamon, David. I spoke with him, offered him everything—"

"You didn't offer him everything! And what you did offer him wasn't enough. Was it?"

"He's not rational, David! I offered . . . I offered . . . " Peck hung his head and stared blankly at the floor. The rage had drained from Hallorin's eyes and the disappointment that remained tore into Peck. "No. It wasn't enough."

He heard Hallorin stop pacing but was afraid to look up.

"Beamon and the girl can never come back from Thailand, Roland. If they disappear in Asia, there won't ever be any questions—people will assume that they were just casualties of the violence over there. You have a rare thing here, Roland. Life doesn't usually give second chances. Use it."

"They won't ever come back, David. We have people over there; they'll never make it back."

Peck tried to convince himself that was the truth, but he couldn't overcome his sense of dread. The situation had degenerated into a ludicrous mess. Mark Beamon's lifelong friends and acquaintances had been willing—almost anxious—to abandon him to his current situation. But in Thailand, a place Beamon had never before been, he had been befriended by a man whom Peck had never heard of but who seemed to hold an almost unshakable position of authority there. Through Hallorin, Peck controlled almost unlimited money, but was finding it impossible to hire anyone willing to move against Somporn Taskin.

Peck closed his eyes tightly when Hallorin put his powerful hand on top of his head and gently pushed it back.

"Look at me, Roland."

Peck's face tightened.

"Look at me."

He opened his eyes to find Hallorin's face only a few inches from his.

"I've got nothing, Roland. Nothing."

"But you've moved up so far," Peck said anxiously. "So far. You're running second now behind Taylor . . . "

"A distant second." Hallorin turned and walked back across the office. "In one week the people will vote. History doesn't remember who came in second."

Peck had known this would happen. The polls had moved exactly as he'd predicted. Based on the press's perfect coverage of the explosion, the disproportionate number of undecideds had resolved their inner conflicts in Hallorin's favor and had been joined by a small but significant group of Taylor's supporters. It had brought Hallorin to within two points of the lead.

But then the unavoidable backlash had begun. The Democratic candidate's numbers, initially unchanged by Hallorin's heroics, suddenly plummeted as liberals, fearful of a mandated President David Hallorin, ran to Robert Taylor—the lesser of the evils. When the dust settled, David Hallorin was left seven points behind.

As he watched Hallorin move slowly across the room, Peck decided that he couldn't tell him about the problem that Somporn Taskin posed. The file was on the verge of being retrieved and that would be enough. Right now, only that mattered. Mark Beamon and the even less significant Darby Moore could be dealt with later.

"No one would have done what I did, Roland," Hallorin said, falling into his chair. "They would have run from the fire. The country—the people—need someone with courage to lead them. You have to make them understand that, Roland. You're the only person who can."

Peck dared to look directly into Hallorin's gray eyes and tried to control the trembling in his stomach. He could still see the pictures: Hallorin shouting orders, disappearing into the smoke, carrying out the little girl. Peck had already let fade the memory of the planning that went into it—setting up the mechanics and timing of the explosion, making sure there would be no chance of injury to Hallorin, the hours that the two of them had spent practicing his reaction. Now he saw the same heroic man as the rest of the world saw. And that man had chosen him as a son.

41

"**N**ow that's an improvement." Beamon took an exaggerated sniff of the air. "And you smell better, too."

Darby Moore, still damp from a recent shower, was wearing a blue golf shirt with "Phuket Country Club" tastefully embroidered on it and a pair of pleated khaki shorts. Unfortunately, the black rubber sandals that seemed only slightly less a part of her than her skin were still strapped to her feet. Despite his exhaustive efforts, she had refused the pair of fabulously expensive golf shoes he'd had his eye on for her. He'd bought two pairs in her size anyway, on Reynolds, Trent, and Layman—or more likely, David Hallorin. The moral here was never give a company credit card to the person you're setting up.

"What are we doing here, Mark?" she said, fidgeting with the waistband of her new shorts. "They know we're here. We could probably make it to Cambodia or—"

Beamon looked up from the rented set of clubs he had been picking through and frowned dramatically. "Cambodia? *Cambodia?* Cambodia has no golf courses."

Her nervousness seemed to tick up a notch. She still didn't trust him, despite his repeated attempts to put her at ease. He'd been completely unsuccessful in getting her to open up about what had happened to her and why—information that was becoming increasingly critical to their survival.

"Look, Mark. I appreciate what you did for me, but I really need to get out of here. I've got to keep moving."

Beamon hefted the hot pink golf bag containing a set of ladies clubs and handed it to her. "Yeah, you've done so well thus far."

He instantly regretted his words as the pain registered on Darby's face. Two of her friends were dead and she was undoubtedly blaming herself. "I'm sorry, Darby. I didn't mean it that way."

He slung his own bag over his shoulder and started for the first tee with her reluctantly following. "Look around us," he said as they walked.

She did as he instructed, letting her eyes wander to the armed men following behind them and the ones that had already taken up strategic positions near the dense line of trees that bordered the fairway.

"There are two more in the parking lot and another few in the clubhouse." He waved around them at the empty course. "Have you noticed that there's no one else around? The course is closed to the public as long as we're playing."

Beamon stopped and looked out over the first hole, spotting two more men standing near the green. Whatever Somporn Taskin's debt to Tom Sherman was, he obviously took it seriously.

"I don't know, Darby. Looks like we have one of the most powerful, and more importantly, sadistically violent men in the country extremely interested in our well being. Back home . . . Well, I don't know. Until I figure out what's going on, we're staying put."

Beamon pulled his driver and three-wood from the bag and began swinging them around, trying to appear more relaxed than he was. Hopefully, he'd been successful in making it look like "come within half an inch of getting your head blown off ten thousand miles from home" had been written in the "things to do" section of his day planner.

"But how long will it last?" Darby said. "How long can your one friend protect us?"

She was nothing like he'd imagined. He guessed it was the van, the lack of a job, the itinerant lifestyle—he'd expected a twenty-first century version of a hippie. In retrospect, it had been a stupid assumption—just the mind's tendency to file things and people into familiar categories. Hippies didn't spend their time testing their physical and mental limits in places where every decision could be the difference between life and death.

"How long? If I'm right about who's after you—and now me—I figure we'll be dead inside of three days," Beamon said, continuing to swing the clubs.

"What? Three days! We've got to get out of here!"

Beamon shoved a tee into the soft ground and tried to balance a ball on it. "To where? To sneak around the jungles of Southeast Asia waiting for another group like those Thai cops to catch up with us? That doesn't sound very attractive."

Darby clearly wanted to make a break for the jungle, but looked around her again at the guards and instead started chewing her thumbnail relentlessly. She was calculating something. Most likely, her chances on her own versus her chances with an out-of-work, soon to be incarcerated or dead, former FBI agent. Neither option probably looked all that rosy.

"What am I to you, Mark?"

Beamon was having trouble getting the ball to stay on the tee due to a slight tremor in his hand. A leftover either from the physical exertion of his unplanned sprint through the town of Krabi, or the psychological baggage of his near-death experience. He wasn't sure.

"Two hundred and thirty-five thousand dollars is what you are to me," he said, finally getting the ball into a stable perch. The quiet chatter from the Thai guards behind them faded to silence as he lined his driver up behind the ball and swung. The ball left the tee with a satisfying hiss and soared toward the sun that was slowly dipping into the sea ahead of them. Then it curved hard and disappeared into the dense jungle that the course had been cut from.

"Should have hit a few at the range," he said, bending over and snatching his tee from the pockmarked grass beneath him. "You do play golf, don't you, Darby?"

"Sometimes. On rest days."

"The ladies tees are up there."

"I'll hit from here."

Beamon shrugged as casually as he could. If he was right and the missing FBI file existed, then it almost certainly had something to do with Hallorin's bid for the presidency. There was only a week left to the election and he was fucking around on a golf course in the middle of nowhere. What was the alternative, though? Clearly intimidation wasn't going to work on the girl. He had to make her trust him.

Darby put her ball on a tee, straightened up, and leaned against her club. "What do you mean when you say two hundred and thirty-five thousand dollars?"

"I mean that I have been hired by an anonymous client to find and deliver you. I got paid one hundred and fifty thousand to take the job and I get the rest when I deliver."

"That's a lot of money. Would you buy a house and a sports car?"

Beamon crinkled up his eyebrows at the strangeness of the question. "You have to vacuum houses, and let's face it, I'm not the sports car type." He decided that his need for expensive lawyers to keep him out of jail probably was better left unsaid at this point—it made him look desperate and probably wouldn't instill a lot of confidence in the girl. "Look, Darby, I'm not prepared to sell my soul for eighty-five grand—it's worth probably double that. No surprises, okay?"

Darby lined up her club and slammed the ball with the force of all the anger, sadness, and frustration that had built up in her over the last few weeks. Her swing was flawless and the ball landed in the middle of the fairway some two hundred and fifty yards away.

"That wasn't luck, was it?" Beamon said as he picked up his bag. She shook her head and followed him up the fairway.

"Okay, Darby. I'm sorry, but it's time to make a decision. Are you going to tell me what I've gotten myself into, or are we just going to keep playing till the snipers show up?" He stopped and looked into her face, unable to tell whether the clear droplet running down her cheek was sweat or a tear.

"I'm completely lost, Mark," she said. "I always know what to do. But now . . . "

"You're making this too hard, kid. If I'm working for the other side, you're screwed. I've got you." Beamon reached into his bag for a club and was about to start poking around in the thick bushes for his ball, but then thought better of it. There were probably ten things in there that could kill a man in three seconds or less.

"I guess you do have me," Darby said. "But if you're not who you say you are, and you're just smarter than the guy in the Mercedes, don't play games with me, okay? When you get what you want, just kill me and be done with it."

Empathy had never been one of Beamon's strong suits, but he couldn't shake the sense of the enormity of the crime that had been committed against this girl. It wasn't the physical act of murdering her friends, or the frame-up, or the physical abuse. It was the way those things had changed her view of the world. They'd taken a girl who had built her life around freedom and joy, and over the course of a few weeks, dragged her into a world of fear, greed, and thoughtless violence. His world. The real one.

"Quick and painless," Beamon promised, motioning to the men following along behind them to hold their ground for a moment. He put an arm around her shoulder and pulled her out of earshot. "I'm going to make a few statements and you just say right or wrong, okay?" She nodded.

"You didn't kill Tristan Newberry."

"Right," she answered quietly.

"Tristan saw something important where he worked, probably in an old FBI file, and he told you about it."

She nodded.

"You were attacked at the New River Gorge."

Another nod.

"Now, were you taken to an old farmhouse in Maryland?"

"Uh huh."

Beamon smiled. "I'm particularly proud of myself for that one. But tell me—how the hell did you get away?"

"There were two men in the room. I grabbed one of them and pushed him over. He fell into a window and cut his neck. I . . . I think he probably died. . . . "

Beamon remembered the uncanny strength she had displayed during their sprint through the streets of Krabi. Bet that son of a bitch had been even more surprised than he had been—he'd obviously bled enough to make a new coat of paint necessary.

"You said there were two men in the room. How did you get away from the second?"

"I didn't. He let us go. He didn't want to be there the whole time, you could tell. He didn't want to hurt us."

Beamon ran his tongue over his front teeth. "Young guy? Twenty-nine or so, but with gray hair at his temples?"

She cocked her head slightly to the right. "Yeah. How did you know?"

"Not important."

"We ran," she continued. "Jumped out the window and ran. I didn't think there was any way they could catch us." Her voice started to sound kind of far away as she dragged herself back into the past.

"The butte," Beamon said. "You would have run straight up that butte. These guys were like me, right? They wouldn't be able to keep up."

She nodded. "But Tristan didn't have any shoes. By the time we made it to the top, his feet were all cut up."

He remembered the pictures of Tristan's body and the local sheriff's comment about how Darby had even attacked his feet with the ice ax. Beamon hadn't registered the wounds as unusual, assuming that he had been kicking at his attacker, trying to defend himself.

"Tristan said we had to split up," Darby said. "That he could keep ahead of the people chasing him, even with his feet torn up like that." She looked directly into Beamon's eyes. "I think I knew he couldn't. No, I'm sure I did. But I'd never been in a situation like that before—I was so scared . . . That's not much of an excuse, is it? For leaving him?"

"What could you have done, Darby? Stayed with him until they caught up? Then you'd both be dead. It wasn't your fault." Beamon calculated a respectful pause, then continued. "Now this is really important—life or death, okay? Did Tristan tell you what was in the file?"

Suspicion crossed her face for a moment. She didn't say anything, calculating again. If he was lying to her, the next words out of her mouth might kill her. She took a deep breath—as though she thought it might be one of her last. "No, he didn't. He just told me that the information in it could hurt some very powerful people."

Beamon sighed quietly. That wasn't what he'd wanted to hear. "Did you tell anybody else anything about this?"

The suspicion again, and then resignation. "No."

Beamon stepped back and leaned against his golf bag, staring at the ground.

"What are you thinking?" Darby said after a few moments.

He shook his head, not sure how much to say. Normally, he'd sugarcoat their situation, but this girl deserved better than that; she deserved to know what was coming. "I don't know, Darby. These people probably think Tristan told you what was in the file. You—and I—are a loose end to them now, and they're going to keep coming until they've tied it up. I'd hoped you'd have something we could use—something that could at least force a truce."

A confused expression crossed her face. "What about the file? Isn't there a way we could use that?"

He looked up. "Excuse me?"

"Tristan took the file . . . Oh, you didn't know that, did you? He told me where it was before we split up."

"What?" Beamon had been working under the assumption that Tristan was just in the wrong place at the wrong time. "He took it?"

She nodded. "He wanted to sell it to the papers."

Beamon stood up straight for a moment, but then sagged back against his golf bag. "But I'm sure he told the men who killed him where he stashed it."

"He did. They almost got to it before I did."

It took a moment for that to compute. "What did you say?"

"Yeah. I barely made the descent down this cliff in Utah. And Vili Marcek shot at me on the way back up."

"Are you telling me you *have* the file?" Beamon said, his mouth suddenly feeling a little dry. "The file's here?"

She shook her head. "It's back in the States. I didn't want it this close to me."

Beamon dropped his clubs on the grass and signaled the Thais guarding them to move further back. "Okay, Darby," Beamon said, speaking slowly. What is in the file? Taylor? Hallorin?"

"The presidential candidates? I don't know. I never looked at it."

"What the hell do you mean you never looked at it?" he said, suddenly aware that he was speaking too loudly. He lowered his voice. "What do you mean you never looked at it?"

She shrugged, suddenly looking a little intimidated. "Like you said, if I knew what was in that file, I'd never have a chance at getting my life back."

The logic was sound, but made Beamon want to pull out what was left of his hair.

"All I know," Darby continued, "is that the word 'Prodigy' is written across the outside of it."

Beamon leaned forward and put his face in his hands, trying to concentrate. It looked like he was right about the contents of the file. In the time before randomly generated operational names, it was often possible to glean information from what a project was called. Prodigy. Tracking young talents before they gained power.

"Okay, Darby," he said, voice muffled slightly by the hands still in front of his mouth. "Where's the file now?"

She hesitated for a moment and then decided that it was too late to turn back. "In an old forest service lookout tower about twenty miles from that house in Wyoming where you came looking for me."

"Lori Jaspers's house?" Beamon thought about that for a moment, then ran at the two surprised-looking Thai guards standing fifty yards away. "Give me a phone!"

They looked at each other in confusion.

"A phone! A goddamn phone!" he shouted, as though speaking the words louder would help them understand. He was about to grab one of them and start going through his pockets when Darby jogged up next to him. "Toh-rah-sahp!" she said. "Is there something wrong, Mark?"

Beamon ignored her, snatching the cell phone produced by one of the guards. "Lori's phone number in Wyoming—what is it?"

"Mark! Is there something wrong?"

He looked directly into her worried face, not really wanting to tell her. "Darby . . . If you were them and you didn't turn up the file at your friend Sam's house, where would you go next? You're traveling on Lori's passport."

42

Mark Beamon jerked awake for what must have been the tenth time and felt a fog instantly descend into his mind. He fumbled around in the dark next to him, finding the expensive transistor radio he'd purchased and clicked it off. The hiss of static that had been NPR when he'd first fallen asleep faded out of the earphones, replaced by the sickly hum of Darby Moore's pickup truck.

It was cold.

He wriggled toward the truck's tailgate on the foam pad beneath him and pulled the sleeping bag up around his neck. The night outside was dead black. He leaned up on one elbow and peered though the small window between the makeshift bed in the back of the pickup and the cab. All he could see was the shadow of Darby Moore's head and the dizzying swirl of snow as it rushed the windshield. He let out a breath that shimmered for a moment in the reflected light and sunk back under the sleeping bag.

Darby had slept through all but the eating and layover portions of their trip back from Thailand. A trick unique to climbers, he supposed. When the stress was too much and there was nothing to be done, it was best to just shut down, rest, and wait for your chance.

Unfortunately, he didn't have the same ability. The wheels in his mind had spent the last twenty-four hours grinding themselves to pieces. And what had he figured out in all that time? Not much that would be useful. Mostly dazzlingly useless conjecture.

According to NPR, David Hallorin had closed to within seven points of Taylor. A hell of an improvement, but still not exactly what anyone would call striking distance. And that had to be where Prodigy came in.

Beamon had considered the problem as carefully as his sleep-deprived brain could and concluded that there was nothing on Hallorin in the file. When Hallorin had decided that finger-pointing would be the cornerstone of his political career, his life had come under intense scrutiny by those he targeted. With any kind of skeleton in his closet, it was unlikely that his career could have survived.

And that brought Beamon around to Robert Taylor and Hallorin's classy and honorable unwillingness to go negative on the man in his campaign. There seemed to be a three-part strategy at work: first you set yourself up as squeaky clean and can-do—if somewhat self-righteous and unsympathetic. Second, you shatter the negative part of that image with an act of unparalleled bravery and compassion. Third, you get the guy beating you to drop out of the race and throw his support to you. Hallorin had already forced enough of an illusion of grudging respect between him and Taylor to make it all palatable to the voters.

Beamon kicked the window between him and the cab and waited for Darby to look back at him. He pantomimed steering a car, but she just shook her head and turned her attention back to the snowy road. Her face was drawn and paper-white in the reflected headlight, further robbing her of the healthy glow that had been so obvious in the pictures he'd seen of her. The interesting contradictions in her face—the slightly crooked nose perched in the middle of the perfect cheekbones and mouth, the sun-enhanced crow's-feet at the edges of her clear, youthful eyes—had seemed so unique and beautiful before. Now they combined to make her look a decade older than she was. As though her youth had been stolen by the recent sacrifice of her friends on the altar of David Hallorin's presidential aspirations.

He'd called Lori Jaspers' house no less than twenty times since they'd returned to the States and at least five times from Thailand. The machine had picked up each time. He'd called the local police, but even with a shameful amount of name-dropping, had been unable to get them interested enough to go out to her house. The cops seemed to think of Lori Jaspers and her friends as itinerants who for all intents and purposes existed outside their jurisdiction.

Beamon rolled over on his stomach and buried himself deeper in the thick sleeping bag, trying to let the darkness and gentle rocking of the truck lull him back to sleep. He tried to let his mind go blank—to force out thoughts of Hallorin, Lori Jaspers, himself. There was no point to it now, he was caught up in the current and the best he could hope to do was keep his and Darby's heads above water.

"Wake up, Mark!" Darby said in a loud whisper. "We're here."

The sound of the truck's back gate dropping was followed very quickly by a less than gentle gust of frozen air. Beamon opened his eyes to a dirty white sky and the cold of snowflakes dropping onto his skin, melting, and then running down his cheeks.

"Jesus," Beamon said, not moving. "You drove straight through?"

She reached into the truck and pulled the sleeping bag off him. The air instantly penetrated the light clothes he'd traveled in. Luggage hadn't been an option.

Beamon struggled out of the truck with Darby's help, breaking through the crusty snow on the ground when he slid from the tailgate. "Where the hell are we?"

"We're here."

When he looked up, he saw that they were parked directly in front of Lori Jaspers' barn.

"Shit!" he said under his breath, diving into the back of the truck and retrieving the .357 he'd managed to con a Nevada gun dealer into selling him. He dragged Darby behind the truck and aimed the pistol over the hood in the general direction of the buildings.

"Jesus Christ, Darby! I told you to wake me up before we got to town. Maybe I wasn't completely clear on the concept of a stealthy approach."

She slid down the side of the truck and into the snow. "I'm sorry I . . . I thought . . . "

He knew exactly what she thought. She thought that her friend was in danger and that he would have been overly cautious in his approach. She was terrified that something had happened to Lori and that it would be her fault.

Beamon looked around him uselessly. The house and barn were closed up and there were no cars in sight—but that didn't prove anything. There could be fifty men in either structure and another five hundred secreted in the empty, snow-covered tundra that surrounded them.

"Well," Beamon said, standing up from behind the truck, "if there's anybody waiting for us, we might as well go meet them. At least it'll be warmer in the house."

That's what Darby had been waiting to hear. She jumped to her feet and started to run around the truck, but Beamon caught her by the back of her sweatshirt before she got out of range. "No point in being complete idiots, though. Nice and easy."

The tension in Beamon's stomach increased to an almost unbearable point as they walked past the barn. The platoon of Navy SEALS he half-expected to come charging out of it didn't materialize, though, and so far he hadn't noticed any suspicious red dots of light on any vital parts of their bodies.

The front door of Lori Jaspers' house was locked, so Beamon struggled through a deep snowdrift next to the porch and peeked in a window. There were no lights on inside, but he could see well enough to note that it was much neater than last time he'd been there. The mattress on the floor was made up with blankets, and the dirty dishes and climbing gear that had been so evident a week before were all gone.

"Looks like nobody's home. Like maybe they went out of town." He turned to Darby, who was looking more and more panicked. She moved through the deep snow at a seemingly impossible speed, forcing him to chase her around to the back door. When he finally arrived, she was desperately yanking on the locked doorknob.

"Looks like they tidied up and hit the road, Darby." He wrapped his arms around himself against the cold. "Maybe they headed south?"

Darby gave the doorknob another violent tug and then kicked the door in frustration. "Lori doesn't have a key."

"What do you mean?"

"The farmer she bought the house from lost them years ago." Darby swept her arm around at the nothingness surrounding them. "It's not exactly a high-crime area."

"Let's see if we can change that," Beamon said, gently pushing her aside and slamming his shoulder into the door. The old wood cracked loudly and gave way on his second try. He let his .357 lead as he stepped slowly inside.

"This is all wrong," Darby said after they'd made a quick turn through the house. "It's never been this neat in here."

Beamon made another circuit through the house, looking for anything that might tell him its owner's whereabouts. Why would they take her? She made sense as a hostage only if her kidnappers left some kind of calling card or had a way to communicate with Darby. Neither was the case.

Beamon rejoined Darby in the small living room where she seemed to be wandering around lost. "Let's try the barn," he suggested.

It was similarly empty. They climbed up into the hayloft and found Darby's stash of clothes and equipment strewn out across it.

"No," Darby said in a barely audible whisper as she picked up a ski boot half buried in the hay. She stood there looking at it for a moment and then threw it powerfully against the wall. "I killed her! I killed her too, didn't I?"

"Take it easy, Darby. We don't know what happened." He kicked around her things for a moment, finding nothing, as he knew he would. "Help me out here, Darby. Why? Why would anyone be interested in Lori? You said you didn't tell her anything about the file or what had happened to you." He decided not to think about the possibility that they tortured her to death trying to confirm that she didn't know anything and then dumped the body. It was possible, but too goddamn depressing.

"I don't know." Darby dropped into the hay and buried her head in her knees. "Why would they kill Tristan? Why kill Sam? Because we don't mean anything to them. We don't have money or power or important jobs." She looked up at him with eyes that just couldn't understand what they'd seen over the last few weeks. "A man in Texas once stopped by a place I was camping to tell me that I was a waste of skin. That's what we are to these people. A waste of skin."

"Come on, Darby, you're taking this too personally. These men don't care about *anything* but their own power and influence. I was an FBI agent for more than twenty years and they'll be perfectly happy to do away with me too. Look, we need to stay on track here. We need to get our hands on that file before they do. It's our only way out of this."

She raised her head a few inches. "The file. The file. I don't care about the file. I want to find Lori."

"One will most likely lead to the other."

Darby considered that for a moment, then suddenly jerked her head in his direction. "Wait a minute. What if she did know?"

"Know what?"

Darby stood and began looking around the barn, fixating randomly on things that didn't seem to have any meaning. "I was stuffing it in a pack when she came up the ladder. I told her there was something I had to do." She looked over at the skis leaning against the wall. "I grabbed my skis and left. I came back about six hours later. I mean, she's the one . . . the one who showed me where that old lookout station was. We used to stop there to warm up when we were skiing in the backcountry."

Beamon hoped that wasn't the case. If it was, the file was gone and her friend was dead, leaving them pretty much screwed. "You think she might have figured it out?"

"Maybe. If they told her roughly what they were looking for, she might have put two and two together—"

"And told them where to find it."

"No way. She'd have to show them."

Suddenly, Darby was in motion. She tore into the clothes strewn out in the hay, stacking some behind her and flinging the others across the loft.

"What are you doing?" Beamon said.

"She could still be up there! If it's Vili and that man that came after us in Thailand, they couldn't have beaten us back here by that much. I've got to go after her."

She stripped off her jeans and sweatshirt and began pulling on a pair of long underwear as Beamon considered the possibility. It was remote, but at least it was something. "How do we get up there?"

"We? We don't. I'm going to have to ski."

"What about a snowmobile?"

She shook her head and continued throwing on layers of clothing. "Cliff bands. No way to get up there without going all the way around the back of the mountain."

Beamon looked down at the open door of the barn. The snow was whipping through it in waves that looked like small tornadoes.

"Hold on now, Darby," he said as her head reappeared through the top of a turtleneck. "I don't think going out there right now is a great idea. The weather isn't looking that good. Maybe we should wait it out and take snowmobiles up the long way. I don't think it's very likely that your friend's up there."

Darby stopped with one leg in a pair of ski pants. "But are you sure?"

He hesitated for a moment and then shook his head.

"I'll be back before morning, then," Darby said. "If I'm not . . . well, don't worry about it."

Beamon sighed quietly as she dug around for a glove to match the one in her hand.

"As much as I deeply, sincerely, want to, you know I can't let you go up there alone."

She stopped what she was doing for a brief moment and flashed him a sad smile. "Thanks, Mark. But you probably don't even know how to ski. You'd never make it."

"And you probably don't even know how to shoot a gun," he said in response. "If you do find them, what are you going to do—throw snowballs? How are you going to save your friend?"

That slowed her down a little. She stuck her nose in a small backpack and extracted the glove she'd been looking for, then turned and let her eyes move from his feet to his head.

"George's stuff is downstairs," she said finally, tossing her skis and a pair of boots from the loft onto a pile of hay below. "Let's see what we can find you."

The brightly colored Gore-Tex and polypropylene stretched uncomfortably over his midsection, but all in all the fit wasn't that bad. In fact, the boots were perfect.

"So you can ski?" Darby said, obviously a little skeptical.

"I'm not in danger of making the Olympic team," he said as she walked around him making last-minute adjustments to his gear. "In fact, I hate it with a passion on nice days. I just did it 'cause my old girlfriend liked to."

"Whatever it takes," Darby said, pulling something that looked like a tiny yellow walkie-talkie from her pocket. She flipped the power switch and zipped it into a pocket on his jacket that seemed to have been made for it.

"What's that?"

"It transmits a signal. I've got one just like it. I can use it to find you."

"Can I use it to find you?"

She shook her head. "It's kind of complicated. Best you just keep me in sight."

43

Mark Beamon continued to search his brain to confirm that this was, indeed, the worst day of his life. He could almost feel the cigarette tar freezing into little black icicles in his lungs as he desperately sucked in the frigid air and tried to keep up with Darby. Despite the fact that she was breaking trail through at least a foot of loose snow and wearing a backpack that must have weighed fifty pounds, he hadn't been any closer than twenty-five feet from her since they started.

The wind kept gaining force as they continued up the shallow canyon, blowing snow straight up, sideways, in circles. Without the familiar sensation of gravity pulling him to the earth, Beamon doubted he would have been able to discern up from down. Even with it, the visual tricks of the snow were giving him a mild case of motion sickness.

Beamon stopped for a moment, leaning against his poles and pulling his ice-encrusted scarf up over his mouth and nose in an attempt to warm the air a little before he breathed it in. Ten feet behind him, their ski tracks had already disappeared, victims of wind and drifting snow. And that pretty much sealed it. He was completely reliant on a goddamn twenty-seven-year-old girl for his survival. Without her, there was no chance he'd find his way out of the aptly named Wind River Mountains. A couple of lost hikers would find him in the spring with a string of obscenities still frozen in his throat.

The unlikely amount of sweat running down his back was cooling rapidly and forced him to start moving again before he'd fully caught his breath. He struggled forward, feeling the burning in his legs and shoulders and the desperate pumping of his heart start again almost instantly. Fortunately, Darby had stopped about fifty yards ahead.

"If the weather was a little better, you'd be able to see it over there," she said over the howl of the wind, pointing a gloved hand into the swirling snow and fog. Beamon let himself fall over into a drift, which instantly formed itself to his body and created a dangerously comfortable place to lie down.

Darby nodded toward a shallow depression in the snow that had survived near a dense stand of evergreens. It was about a foot wide and three feet long and looked suspiciously like ski tracks. "You see those?"

"They could have been made by anyone," Beamon managed to get out. His face was so cold his speech was noticeably slurred.

Darby spread her arms wide, poles hanging from her wrists by leather straps. "Who would be out here on a day like today?"

Beamon shook his head. "How much further?"

"Not far. Are you okay to go on?"

He nodded and looked around him. He didn't know shit about ski tracks, but even he could see that the ones in front of them weren't very old. Those sons of bitches could be standing behind a tree ten feet away and he'd never know it with visibility what it was.

Another half an hour of hard skiing seemed to take them nowhere. The snow was slowing down and visibility had improved somewhat, but everything still looked the same: white snow, green trees, gray rocks.

Because of the improved conditions, and despite Beamon's repeated warnings, Darby had pulled ahead another twenty-five yards or so. He kept struggling forward, trying to close the gap, but there was no way. Finally, he just stopped and pulled off his fogged-up goggles, letting the cold air dry the sweat on his face.

When he looked up, he saw that Darby had stopped, too. She seemed to be staring down a steep slope that started at the bottom of the fifteen-foot cliff she was standing at the edge of. Something in her posture worried him. He slid his goggles back on and started toward her as fast as he could, considering his legs felt like silly putty and his heart was on the verge of a permanent breakdown. He'd closed to within twenty feet when she suddenly stripped off her pack and jumped off the cliff.

Beamon watched, horrified, as she fell through the air and disappeared into an explosion of snow when she hit the ground. An instant later, she burst out of it, still upright, and began making fast, graceful turns down the steep slope.

Having no idea what was going on, he dug out his pistol and sighted along it, anticipating Darby's path. About seventy-five yards in front of her, he saw what she was moving toward. A broken patch of red and black, half-covered with snow. He lowered his gun and concentrated on the odd burst of color as Darby skidded to a stop in front of it. As she brushed away the accumulated snow, it took on human form.

Darby hovered over the motionless figure for a moment and then fell on her back in the snow. She lay there long enough for Beamon to fight his way to the lip of the cliff she'd jumped from. It was too steep for him to climb down and there was no way he was just going to throw himself off like she had. He couldn't even yell down to her for fear that he might be heard. All in all, he was completely useless.

Probably ten minutes went by—he couldn't be sure because his watch was trapped below God knew how many layers of clothing—before Darby lifted herself into a sitting position. Another five and she had removed her skis and was hiking back up the steep slope with them, violently kicking into the snow with every step. When she got close enough, Beamon laid down on his stomach and reached over the cliff. She climbed up a bit and silently passed her skis and poles to him before skillfully negotiating the rock face in her boots and gloves.

When she came over the top, she didn't say anything—just pulled on her pack, stepped back into her bindings, and started up the canyon again.

"Was it Lori?" Beamon said, before she got too far away.

She nodded without looking back.

"I'm so sorry, Darby."

"No time now, Mark. I'll think about it later." The pain in her voice was barely under control.

He should have stopped this. He should have found her faster. None of this should have ever happened.

Darby moved slower now, making it possible for him to stay within ten feet. The snow and wind had continued to taper off and there was actually a patch of blue sky in the distant west. On the negative side, the sun was pretty close to it. It was going to start getting dark soon.

The skiing got easier as the weather improved. But with the better visibility came the increased chance that they would be spotted. Beamon tried to stay alert, but exhaustion and the unfamiliar surroundings made it impossible. If someone had decided to set up an ambush, he and Darby were dead.

They had skied for another nearly unbearable fifteen minutes when Darby stopped at the edge of the densely wooded area that they had been moving through. Ahead of them was a windswept ridge that rose steeply and finally seemed to disappear into the sky as earth and snow suddenly dropped away. Just before that, though, was a small square building on stilts, perched in a position that would give it a one-hundred-and-eighty-degree view of the mountains and valleys below.

"Unzip the top of my pack and get the binoculars out, Mark."

Beamon had to take his gloves off, but finally worked the frozen zipper loose and pulled out a pair of binoculars. "I don't see anyone," he said, using them to scan the clearing in front of them. "But that doesn't mean a whole hell of a lot."

The lookout building was obviously abandoned—a collection of broken boards and shingles, with a rusted stovepipe protruding from what was left of the roof. There seemed to be no tracks around it—not that he'd have expected any with the wind gusts that they had suffered through earlier that day. He kept moving the binoculars back and forth, examining every square foot of the clearing, but there wasn't anything to see.

"I don't know, Darby . . . "

"What?"

"Maybe they got what they were looking for and took off." He handed her the binoculars and she used them to go over the same terrain. "Or maybe not. The New York Philharmonic could be sitting out there if they were in white tuxes."

He didn't belong out here; this is what S.W.A.T. was for. They'd have been so excited—cute new winter camo, white guns, skis. . . .

"So what do we do, Mark?" Her words were clipped and monotone, undoubtedly the by-product of trying to shut down her emotions and forget her friend Lori's frozen body at the base of that ridge.

"Well, we went through all the trouble of coming up here. You say you left the file in that lookout tower?"

She nodded. "Under the floorboards."

In the end, the file was the only thing that mattered. It was probably a trap, but their lives weren't worth much without it. "I guess we should go take a look, then."

She put her eyes to the binoculars again and moved them slowly across the empty snow in front of them. "They could be in the lookout tower. There's no way to tell."

"What's in there?" Beamon asked. "Is there more than one way in and out?"

"No. Only one door—it's on the other side. There used to be windows, but they broke a long time ago, and me and some friends boarded them up. Other than that, there's nothing in there. Maybe some Powerbars or something left over from last year."

"So it's not in use anymore."

She shook her head and moved to a slightly better vantage point. "See that steep slope behind it? The Forest Service decided that it could slide, so they ended up building a new lookout in a better location a few miles from here."

"Slide. You mean avalanche?" Beamon looked up at the steep slope dwarfing the tiny building. "That's all we fucking need."

"Relax, Mark. Snow conditions are pretty stable today. Besides, I've never seen that slope slide. I mean, the building's still there, right? More than likely, the Forest Service had some money they didn't know what to do with."

The certainty in her voice made him feel a little better, but he was still stuck in a completely unfamiliar situation and was dead sure that someone, somewhere out here, was waiting for him with a really, really big gun. The colorful Popsicle that had been Darby's friend Lori pretty much guaranteed that.

"Do you think they might be inside, Mark?"

"No. There's no way to see out. Sort of evens out the element of surprise if they can't see us coming and just have to wait for the door to open. If it were me, I'd be under it. Looks like there's a pretty deep indention under those stilts."

Beamon motioned to Darby and she followed him back down the way they'd come. After putting about a hundred yards between them and the clearing, Beamon turned to the west. He continued forward through the deep snow until he broke out of the densely packed trees and found himself at the edge of what seemed like an almost vertical snow slope.

"What about down there?" he said, looking along the edge of the drop-off to confirm that they were out of sight of the lookout tower.

"Down there what?"

"Could we go down there a ways and traverse to where we're right beneath the tower? If anybody's up there, they're expecting us to come up the canyon."

She looked doubtful. "Well, I could, but . . . "

"Come on, Darby. I've done pretty well so far, haven't I?" Beamon popped off his skis and walked closer toward the edge in his boots.

"Not too close, Mark."

The large evergreens at the bottom of the slope looked to be about a half an inch tall. He felt himself getting a little dizzy from the height and stepped back.

"Yeah, you've skied okay, Mark. You have." She closed her eyes and took a deep breath, seeming to gather her will. "Look, Lori's dead. So are Sam and Tristan. Getting you killed isn't going to do anything to change that."

"I don't see this as an either-or situation, Darby. If we lose control of the file, we've got nothing—no leverage to use against anyone. Do you think in that situation the men who have killed your friends are just going to leave us alone and hope that we won't do something desperate like try to get our story printed in the papers? Believe me when I say that I don't want to hang my ass out a thousand feet off the ground, but we've got a chance here. If not now, when?"

She looked down the slope for a moment and then dropped her pack into the snow. She dug out a stuff sack with a sleeping bag and tossed it to him, then went back to searching around in the pack, finally coming up with a rope and a shovel.

"Take the sleeping bag out of there and fill the sack with snow. As much as you can pack into it," she said, starting to dig a hole about ten feet back from the edge of the precipice.

He did as he was told, feeling the exhaustion in his arms as he shoved snow into the sack with his gloved hands.

"Okay," he said when he'd finished and rolled it toward her. She climbed out of the hole she had dug and started clearing a narrow trench of the same depth to the edge of the slope. He still had no idea what she was doing, but she seemed to, so he wrapped his arms around himself and tried to stay warm as she secured one end of the rope around the middle of the snow-filled stuff sack, dropped the sack into the hole she'd dug, then threw the other end of the rope off the edge of the slope.

Five minutes later, she had completely buried the stuff sack and was jumping up and down, packing the snow on top of it. She looked up at him and shrugged, then unstrapped the two ice axes from the outside of her pack and handed one to Beamon. He looked at the sharp edges and remembered what an axe just like it had done to Tristan Newberry.

"We'll climb down about fifty meters," Darby said, turning to face the slope and starting down it backward. "We're going to go down really slow, like this. Kick your boots in hard, balance yourself, and get the point of your axe in. Then one more step. If you start to slide, don't try to dig your toes in—it'll flip you over. Lay all your weight on the back of your axe."

"And the rope?" Beamon said as she continued down, illustrating the proper technique.

"If you get into really big trouble, try grabbing it." She shrugged again, or at least he thought she did; it was hard to tell under all the layers of clothing. "It might hold. If you're lucky."

"Great," he said, easing himself over the edge and starting down like she'd showed him. He paused just before his head ducked below the flat section they'd been standing on and looked down at Darby. Beyond her, the snow was completely unbroken for about five hundred feet. At that point, it was bisected by a narrow rock band that dropped off into space.

"How high is that cliff down there?"

"Doesn't matter," Darby said, stopping and digging her feet and axe in. "Okay, come on down."

"Doesn't matter?" Beamon said.

That fatalistic shrug again. "A thirty-foot fall will kill you, Mark."

Not exactly encouraging. Beamon continued down, his heart rate notching a little higher with every step away from flat land.

More and more the cliff below him consumed his mind. After about twenty feet, he was finding it hard to concentrate. It seemed that every move he made put him in a less stable position than the last, bringing him within a hairbreadth from skidding out of control like the fallen ski racers he'd seen on television.

Finally, he had to stop to try to get control of his breathing and fear. Not grabbing the apparently unreliable rope running along the snow to his right was one of the hardest things he'd ever done.

"You're doing great, Mark. Not much further."

He leaned his head forward about six inches until it touched the snow in front of him. "Sorry, Darby. I don't know why, but I've got to know. How high is that cliff?"

He heard her start moving again in a slow, steady rhythm. "Okay, okay. I'm not sure. Somewhere between six and eight hundred feet. Does that make you feel better?"

For some reason, it did. At least it was now a known quantity. "How long would you be in the air, you figure? You, know, before you hit the ground?"

The rhythm of Darby's descent suddenly stopped. "I kind of try not to think about stuff like that."

Sensible. Beamon continued down, adjusting his position so that he was placing one foot on either side of the rope. It might not hold, but he liked having it there in front of him. A few more minutes and he was even with Darby again. She had traversed a few feet to the right and was waiting for him.

"How are you doing?" she said, grabbing hold of his shoulder with her free hand, steadying him psychologically more than physically.

"So you do this for fun?" The clouds were breaking up above them and the sun was coming directly from behind, reflecting powerfully off the blank white that they were clinging to.

"No mistakes here, okay, Mark? This is where we leave the rope behind."

Murphy's Law reigned, as it always seemed to. Sideways proved to be trickier than down. He mimicked Darby's every move, silently thankful that she never strayed more than a few feet from him. He doubted that she could arrest his fall if it happened, but the companionship somehow helped.

"It's beautiful out here, isn't it," Darby said in an exaggerated whisper.

Beamon took her words as an opportunity to stop—his legs were feeling a little rubbery again. He looked around him, turning his head slowly so as not to disrupt his balance.

He actually hadn't noticed. When he'd looked below him before, all he'd seen was an unsurvivable fall. He hadn't taken in the sun glowing red off the rocky peaks or the pinkish-white glow of the aspen trees woven in to the forest below them. It seemed like you could see forever and that civilization and everything that went with it didn't really exist.

"I guess it is."

"Lori loved it up here," Darby said, turning her body dangerously and balancing on one boot as she looked out over the mountains. "Said she would never leave here."

She brought herself back to face the snow a moment later, once again trying to shake off the memory of her friend. "Are you ready? It's not much further."

"Lead the way."

She started again slowly, letting him keep up step for step, movement for movement.

After about another five minutes of constant motion, she stopped and dug in. "This is it. The tower should be above us."

Beamon looked up. All he could see was snow and sky, but she hadn't given him any reason to doubt her yet.

"And some good news," Darby added quietly. "Up's easiest."

They started in unison, eyes trained on the ridge above them. When the roof of the lookout tower appeared, it was directly above, just as she had promised. They both stopped and Beamon started to carefully reach for his pocket.

"What do you need?" Darby said.

"My gun."

"You concentrate on your balance; I'll get it."

It was kind of humiliating to have some little girl dig around in his pocket for his pistol and then help him take his right glove off. But the memory of the cliff below and the fact that no one was watching—hopefully—made the embarrassment bearable.

"Stay!" he ordered, starting to move up, carefully using his left arm to drive the ice axe into the snow as he moved.

She ignored his order, staying right alongside, ready to lend a hand should he need it. He looked over at her and saw an expression of infinite stubbornness. Darby Moore had clearly decided that no one else was going to die on her watch.

Beamon stopped again just before the stilts that supported the lookout tower came into view. He leaned against the wall of snow in front of him and drew in deep breaths of the cold air, trying to relax. Gunplay was a game for the young.

He unlooped his wrist from the strap on his axe and reached up, digging it in as high above him as he could. Taking one more deep breath, he pulled himself up on it.

Another impressive piece of deduction on his part—the shot that hissed past his ear unarguably came from the underside of the lookout, just as he had predicted. So much for the element of surprise.

"Jesus!" Darby yelled as she flattened herself against the slope. Beamon let go of his ice axe and balanced precariously on the toes of his boots, aiming at the shadow moving behind the snowbank built up beneath the stilts of the tiny building.

"Shit!" Darby squealed as a bullet impacted five feet in front of them and showered her with ice crystals. "Stop it, stop it, stop it!"

Beamon felt a deep calm come over him as another bullet hissed past him, this time almost close enough to feel. "Not good enough, asshole," he said quietly, and slowly applied pressure to the trigger. He felt the buck of the gun and saw the shadow he'd aimed at jerk backward. The moment of satisfaction and relief was short lived, though. The kick of the pistol had been enough to start him tipping backward. He dropped his gun and heard it skittering across the icy slope as he shot a hand out and just missed the ice axe still stuck in the snow in front of him. It felt like slow motion as he tilted back farther and farther. His hands clawed repeatedly at the snow, but there was nothing to grab hold of.

He'd just about resigned himself to the thousand or so foot ride when he felt the collar of his jacket tighten powerfully around his neck. Darby had managed to get hold of his coat and yank him forward, but the sudden motion cut his boots free and he felt himself start to slide.

He dropped about a foot or so before he jerked to a stop and was flipped around so that his back was against the snow. He felt himself choke on something, snow or fear probably, and started coughing violently as he stared down into the abyss.

"Mark! Mark! Are you listening? Don't get scared and make any sudden moves, but I'm starting to lose my grip."

Darby's voice snapped him back into reality and he craned his neck around to look up at her. She had one hand wrapped around her axe and the other around the collar of his jacket. That tiny little gloved hand was all that was between him and . . .

He moved as calmly as he could, grabbing hold of her arm and flipping himself over to face the slope again. A moment later, he had his boots dug in and had climbed up far enough to get ahold of his ice axe.

"Oh, shit," he coughed, gripping the axe so hard it was sending shooting pains up his forearm. "Oh, shit."

Darby let go of the front of his jacket and moved her hand to the back of it, helping him to maintain his balance. "I guess that's why climbers don't carry guns," she said as Beamon's choking slowly subsided. "Are you okay?"

He nodded, still unable to speak. Fuck private industry. Fuck the FBI. That warm, safe jail cell was looking better and better.

"You're sure? You're okay?"

"Yeah. Fine. I'm fine."

"Did you . . . "

Beamon turned his head with comic slowness and looked below him at the visible marks in the snow that his gun had made. "God, I hope so." He also hoped that the man was alone.

They started up together, eyes once again locked on the snow beneath the lookout tower. When they reached the top of the slope, Beamon waved at her to stay where she was and slid forward on his stomach. He was out in the open now, the proverbial sitting duck. He didn't care, though. At least the goddamn ground was flat.

Miraculously, he made it across the open snow and pressed his back against the bank guarding the underside of the lookout. He glanced back at Darby and gave her a tentative thumbs-up, then threw himself over the berm, holding his ice axe in front of him as a weapon.

There was no one there.

He looked around the deeply shadowed space, finding nothing but snow—some of which was tinted pink with blood. He crawled to the far side and looked out into the clearing. The steep slope rising into the sky two hundred yards to the east provided a flawless white backdrop, making the man struggling toward the treeline stand out perfectly.

Beamon burst out into the flat sunlight and started running after the man as best he could through the intermittently deep and wind-packed snow. He could hear Darby coming up quickly behind him and waved her off without looking back. He was about fifteen yards behind when the man turned, holding a pistol out in front of him. Beamon dove to the ground at the same time the man fell backward into the snow. The gun went off, but the bullet sped harmlessly into the darkening sky.

Beamon covered the rest of the distance in a crouch and ended up in a badly controlled slide and a brief struggle to relieve the man of his weapon.

"Fuck you," he said weakly as Beamon stood and aimed the gun down at him.

"Are you all right?" Darby yelled, running up behind him, but stopping short when she saw the blood spreading out beneath the man lying in the snow. Her eyes moved up his face and she instantly recognized him as the man who had imprisoned her in that horrible Thai jail cell. She took an involuntary step backward.

"Where is it?" Beamon said, not looking at the man, but scanning the trees at the edge of the clearing, searching for movement.

"Long gone," he replied in a faded, but still smug, voice.

Darby shuffled back and forth for a few moments, then pushed past Beamon and crouched down next to the man.

"I sent it on ahead while I waited here for you," he said, ignoring Darby as she opened up his jacket and cut through his sweater and shirt with a pocketknife.

Beamon looked around the clearing again while Darby wadded up a piece of nylon clothing and pressed it against the man's wound. This asshole didn't look any better equipped to get out of here by himself than he did. There was just no way he was alone.

"Where's the Slovenian?" Beamon said.

He saw Darby twitch at his words and then go back to working on the man's wound, finally taking his bare right hand and pressing it against the makeshift bandage she'd fashioned. That done, she stood and started walking silently back toward the lookout tower.

"Like I said. He and your file are long gone."

"Then, tell me about David Hallorin."

The man laughed and Beamon could see that his teeth were the same pink as the snow beneath him. "Oh, I could tell you some things about him. And I will when you get me to a hospital."

Beamon was suddenly aware of the absurdity of carrying on an interrogation of a wounded man on a frozen mountain in Wyoming. "Okay. Fine. We'll get you all fixed up. But how about you ante up a little information to motivate me? Who are you?"

The man coughed out another laugh. The crimson of his teeth had deepened a bit. "I think you're plenty motivated already, Beamon. You want Hallorin and I'm the only man who can give him to you." He looked past Beamon for a moment. "What's she doing?"

Darby had reappeared about twenty feet behind them and was digging in the snow with her ice axe for no apparent reason.

"I have no idea," Beamon said absently, trying to get the facts in his head into some kind of coherent order. What now? Dangle the son of a bitch over a cliff by his ankles? There was no point—this guy had him by the balls and he was smart enough to know it. Threats would just sound silly. His only option was to save this prick and hope to get the story later.

The sound of the ice axe repeatedly hitting the snow behind him intruded into his thoughts and eventually forced him to turn around. "Darby, what the hell are you doing? I can't hear myself think here."

She ignored him—a skill she seemed to be developing at an alarming rate—and smoothed out something that looked like a chair cut out of the snow. He watched passively as she stood and walked over to the man lying at his feet. Still perplexed, he didn't interfere when she grabbed the man's lapels and dragged him toward her construction as he howled and swore in pain.

It *was* a chair. She dropped him into it and stood directly in front of him.

"You're going to die," she said matter-of-factly. The man looked up at her like she was speaking Swahili. Darby pointed to the west, where the sun had turned the snow-covered mountains a deep purple. It was a spectacular effect, making it impossible to tell where the mountains ended and the sky began.

"It's one of the most beautiful places in the world," Darby continued. "A lot better than what you had planned for me. A lot better than you deserve, you son of a bitch."

She picked up her ice axe and started walking smoothly through the snow toward the mouth of the canyon where they had stashed their skis and other equipment.

"What the fuck are you talking about?" the man slurred at her back. "Get the fuck back here, you bitch!"

Beamon grabbed her by the arm as she passed. "Darby, we need him."

"This isn't New York," she said. He was a little shocked by the anger in her voice—it didn't seem to fit her. "What do you want to do? Call an ambulance?"

"No, I don't want to call an ambulance. I want to make a litter or something and drag him to a hospital."

"He's dead. Look at him."

Beamon did. Blood had soaked through a good half of his clothing and was actually dripping off him as he tried to stand. She was right.

"Last chance to unburden your conscience," Beamon said, taking a few steps toward the man.

"Fuck you! We had a deal. You get me out of here. You get me out of here and I'll tell you everything."

Beamon turned up his gloved hands in a gesture of helplessness. "I'll be lucky to get myself out of here."

"You can go to hell!" the man yelled as Beamon turned and started to follow Darby out. Surprisingly, though, he was finding it almost impossible to walk away. He'd been unfortunate enough to have killed men before, but he'd never left one of them to die. There had always been helicopters, doctors, hospitals . . .

"Wait, Darby," Beamon said, trying to increase his speed to a jog in the deep snow. For once she listened to him and stopped dead in her tracks. As he came alongside her, though, she didn't seem to be aware that he was there.

He looked behind him at the man who had now fallen from his makeshift chair and was attempting to crawl in their direction. "Jesus, Darby. I don't care if it's pointless, we can't just leave him—"

"Did you hear that, Mark?"

He had heard something. The wind? They looked up at the steep slope hanging over them and both saw a distant figure standing at the top of it.

"What the hell is that?" Beamon said.

Whoever it was, he was shouting down to them, but the distance and the wind made it impossible to decipher his words.

"It's Vili," Darby said as the quiet shouting stopped and the figure huddled to himself for a moment. When he straightened out, Beamon could see a plume of smoke rising from his hand.

"Oh, shit," Darby said quietly. She grabbed him by the jacket and started running, pulling him along behind. "Go for the trees, Mark! We've got to make it to the trees!"

She let go of him and sprinted ahead, seeming to float over the snow that he was becoming more and more mired down in. When he looked behind him, the smoke plume had left Vili Marcek's hand and was arcing gracefully through the air.

There was a muffled *whup* and a plume of white snow, followed by a loud cracking sound. Darby was far ahead by the time Beamon felt the low rumble come up through the ground into his feet and legs. She was nearly to the trees. She was going to make it. But he wasn't.

Beamon slowed and then stopped, turning back toward the slope just before he was engulfed in a billowing cloud of snow and ice. He felt it washing over him, gaining weight and force, filling his mouth and every gap in his clothing. The world flashed the white of snow, the red of the sunset, and the deep blue of the sky, more times than he could process as he was turned over and over by the irresistible force of the slide. He didn't bother to fight, instead closing his eyes and relaxing, waiting for all the colors to permanently turn black.

He didn't know how long it took—it could have been seconds or hours, but it finally stopped. Despite the darkness, silence, and lack of gravity, it wasn't exactly what he expected. If this was death, it was going to be a cold and boring afterlife.

He experimented with moving, but was held completely immobile by the pressure all around him. The flair of pain he felt in his right shoulder suggested that he was still alive, but he couldn't decide whether or not that was a good thing.

He suddenly realized that he wasn't breathing and tried to take in a tentative breath, but didn't get any air. Thinking that the snow was packed in around his face, he jerked his head forward to try to clear an air pocket, but found that nature had already created one. He forced back the panic that was starting to overtake him, finally realizing that he had snow packed into his mouth and nose. He forced what little air he had out of his lungs, clearing a passageway and starting to breathe again.

To what end he wasn't sure. There couldn't be more than a few minutes of oxygen in there with him.

He thought of Carrie and Emory, then about Darby, who was probably futilely searching for him in the thousands of tons of snow that had come down the slope. She wouldn't survive on her own. He was sorry about that.

The quality of the air didn't support deep thought for long. As he started breathing in less oxygen and more carbon dioxide, he could see the sparkling lights on the insides of his eyelids grow in intensity.

He was only vaguely aware of a sudden, sharp pain in his back and assumed it was a disk exploding or his spine giving way. Nothing to worry too much about at this point.

"Mark!"

The voice was muffled. It didn't sound real.

Another pain—less severe and in the back of his head. He couldn't ignore it this time, because of the cold rush of air that accompanied it.

"Mark!"

His head cleared a little and he could hear the loud crunch of snow reverberating in his ears. He abandoned the shallow breaths he'd been taking and sucked in a lungful of clean air.

"Mark! Can you hear me?"

He felt a hand clearing the snow away from his face and wiping it roughly from his nose.

"I . . . uh. Yeah," he said, opening his eyes to see the sky spinning sickeningly above him. He focused on Darby as she drove a bright yellow shovel into the snow above him. "Just relax, Mark. I'll have you out in a second. Can you move? Where are you hurt?"

"Everywhere . . . " He tried to move his arms. One remained immobile and felt like there was a knife in it, but other than that and the milder pain in his left ankle, everything seemed to more or less work. "I . . . I think I'm okay. How . . . how did you find me?"

She reached over and picked up something that looked like a bright yellow transistor radio. "Remember this?"

He reached up to his chest and felt the outline of the matching transmitter in the pocket of his jacket, then leaned his head back into the snow and closed his eyes.

"Do you have any idea how lucky you are, Mark?"

"How lucky?" Beamon said, looking up at the first stars appearing in the black and blue sky.

"Look behind you."

He twisted around, sending another charge of pain through his shoulder. The world fell away no more than three feet from where he'd come to a stop.

"What the hell happened?" Beamon said, laying his head back in the snow again. Darby slid down into his hole with him and began running her hands up his legs, squeezing intermittently and looking at his expression to gauge the level of pain. "It was, uh, kind of a bomb, I guess you could say."

"A bomb? A fucking bomb? Where the hell would he—"

Her hand suddenly clamped down around his ankle and the pain was enough to cut him off.

"It's a charge used to set off avalanches. You know, like ski patrollers use."

"Jesus."

He let the rest of her examination pass in silence. When she was through, she leaned back against the opposite wall of the bathtub-sized pit she'd dug around him. "The gods were smiling on you, Mark. The only thing I can find that's worth mentioning is an ankle sprain. I mean, you'll be black-and-blue for a couple of weeks, but after that ride . . . "

He wasn't impressed by her medical expertise. "You didn't even look at my shoulder and it hurts worse than everything else combined."

"Don't have to, I *know* what's wrong with that. Look at it, it's dislocated."

He decided against looking—the mental image the word *dislocated* conjured up was bad enough.

"If you're ready, I'll fix it for you," Darby said.

"That's going to hurt, isn't it?"

She gently grabbed hold of his right hand and elbow, and put a foot in his rib cage. "I'd put it somewhere between childbirth and accidentally setting your foot on fire," she said, and then yanked furiously.

The analogy seemed fair.

"You'll be fine here, Mark. No problem," Darby said, peeking into the small opening in the four-foot-by-four-foot snow cave she'd dug for him. "You're not claustrophobic, are you?

Beamon turned his head and let his headlamp shine on the white walls surrounding him. "No." In truth, he normally was, but relative to his recent premature burial, the accommodations seemed spacious.

"You're clear on how to light that stove, right? And the shoulder's not too bad?"

"I'm fine," he said glumly. The last thing he wanted was to be stranded alone in this frozen nowhere, but the combination of not being able to put weight on his ankle and not being able to hold a ski pole made it impossible for him to travel.

"Well, bundle up in that sleeping bag; it's going to get cold tonight."

"It's already cold."

His headlamp flashed off her teeth as she shot him an ironic smile. "No, it's not. Not for a couple more hours."

"Great."

Her head disappeared back through the small portal and Beamon heard the click of ski bindings. "I'll be back with a snowmobile as soon as I can. Probably mid-morning. Hopefully, anyway. Good luck."

44

"**N**o, David. No," Roland Peck said, pacing back in forth in front of Hallorin's desk. "We're okay. There's still time."

"We're not okay, Roland," Hallorin said, struggling to keep his voice even. "You let this get out of control. You have no idea who he is or what he has . . . "

"We can still turn him away, David. He said if we didn't accept his offer, he would destroy it and leave the country."

"And you believe him?"

Peck didn't. He didn't know what to think. When he'd hired Frank Sorvino to find Darby Moore and the file, he had initially refused to let Sorvino bring in the Slovenian. Too much of a risk. In the end, though, he had acquiesced. There had been no time for conservatism. The file and the girl had to be found.

But now it had degenerated into chaos. Where was Sorvino? And how had Vili Marcek come to call the campaign headquarters of David Hallorin? Thank God the receptionist had been confused enough to ring Marcek through to Peck's office and not discount him as just another crank.

Peck's heart jumped when the door to Hallorin's office reverberated with the sound of a short knock. A moment later, it opened and Hallorin's secretary poked her head in. Peck nodded slowly. There was no going back now. David Hallorin *would* be the president of the United States. The situation was still controllable. It had to be.

The Slovenian entered the office tentatively, tensing visibly at the sound of the door closing behind him.

Peck studied the young man for a moment, starting at the long blond hair framing his vaguely Asian features, then to the bulky down jacket covering his torso, and finally to the stick-thin legs sticking out below it.

He was beautiful. Strong, athletic, exotic. When Peck finally raised his head far enough to look Marcek in the eye, he could see that the young man's attention was focused on a point behind him. A point that he knew was David Hallorin.

Peck continued to watch Marcek's face as Hallorin rose from his chair and walked to the private side door to the office. He imagined that he could see Hallorin's reflection in the Slovenian's perfect blue eyes as he heard the door open and Hallorin leave the room.

"Can I offer you a chair?" Peck said, moving behind Hallorin's expansive desk and sitting down.

Marcek didn't say anything for a moment, but looked around the room at the wood paneling, antiques, and art. "Where did he—Senator Hallorin—go?" The accent was thick, but understandable. On the phone, Marcek had insisted he would only talk to Hallorin. Not surprising under the circumstance but, of course, impossible. A man like Hallorin couldn't be exposed to a situation like this. He had to be protected at all costs.

"The senator is quite busy, as you can imagine. Quite busy. I'm afraid he had another engagement." Peck was certain that Hallorin's brief presence would be plenty for the Slovenian, who would undoubtedly rationalize his absence in any way necessary to get whatever it was he wanted. And more importantly, it provided Hallorin plausible deniability in the unlikely event that there was a problem.

"You mentioned Frank Sorvino," Peck said. "That's the only reason we're meeting. Frank has done some work for us in the past . . . though that was some time ago."

Marcek looked confused for a moment. Uncertain.

"Can I ask what this is about?" Peck said, smiling with a condescending warmth. "While I'm not as busy as David, I do have an appointment that I can't miss."

The Slovenian's feet remained planted on the thick carpet, but his eyes darted nervously toward the door Hallorin had disappeared through as he tried to decide whether or not to shelve his demand that the senator be present.

"I don't have much time," Peck prompted again, smoothing his mustache with his forefinger and wiping away a few small droplets of sweat that had accumulated there. Had this beautiful boy brought him the prize?

A few moments later, Marcek seemed to come to a decision—the only one Peck had left him. The Slovenian reached into his down jacket and produced a single piece of paper. Peck watched him closely as he advanced, dropped it on the desk, and then retreated to his former position.

"What's this?" Peck sighed, reaching with exaggerated slowness for his reading glasses. He felt his serene façade crack a bit as he looked down at the sheet of paper.

The text was insignificant—a portion of a memo with no real context. The date and the slightly yellowed FBI letterhead, though, were all important. Peck pushed the memo back to the center of the desk and faked a violent coughing fit to excuse the tears that were beginning to blur his vision. All the planning, the risk, the work. It would have ended in nothing without this piece of paper and the others that had been generated with it. He realized now that he had never really been sure that the Prodigy file existed. That it wasn't just part of some kind of bizarre legend.

"A thirty-year-old FBI memo?" Peck said. "I don't understand. Does Frank have something to do with this?"

"He's dead," Marcek said. "And the FBI man."

Peck affected a sad expression while his mind recalculated his position based on the confirmation of what he'd already suspected. "I'm sorry to hear that. How did it happen?"

"Avalanche."

Peck leaned forward, thinking he hadn't interpreted the man's poor English correctly. "I'm sorry. Did you say an avalanche?"

The Slovenian nodded. "They were crushed."

"And the young woman?"

"No. She still lives."

Peck let that sink in for a moment. Mark Beamon had turned into a major problem, as Peck had always known he would. His death solved a number of issues and left Darby Moore defenseless. Peck's excitement notched even higher at the thought that he might have an opportunity to see her again. They had unfinished business.

Marcek approached again and placed another, smaller, piece of paper on the desk. Peck read the nearly illegible handwriting scrawled across it—apparently the name and number of a bank in Eastern Europe. Below that was an amount: three hundred thousand U.S. dollars. He struggled not to laugh at its insignificance, and the time and effort the Slovenian must have put into coming up with it.

"I have the rest," Marcek prompted. "It says Prodigy on it."

Peck felt another tiny burst of adrenaline course through him at the Slovenian's mangling of the word *Prodigy*.

"Well, Vili. As a servant of the public, I know that the senator wouldn't want to see an obviously stolen FBI file circulated—" Peck cut himself off. Marcek's brow had crinkled deeply and he had turned his head slightly as if to try to hear better. It was quickly becoming obvious that his English wasn't good enough to decipher the nuances of plausible deniability. Anyway, there was no time.

"Do you have it?" Peck said, abandoning subtlety and enunciating carefully.

Marcek had obviously anticipated the question. He shook his head. "Money first. Then I call and tell you where."

Peck leaned back in his seat and folded his hands together in front of him. "That's a great deal of money. How can I trust you?"

"I don't understand the file, it means nothing to me. Senator Hallorin is a powerful man, your next president, yes? I just want money."

It wasn't an elaborate answer, but it seemed adequate under the circumstances.

"Honor is very important to the senator. If we make a deal, he would expect you to abide . . . to live up to your agreement."

Marcek seemed to understand what he was driving at. "No more money after this. The senator is a powerful man. No more."

Peck stared at the young man for a long time, but his mind was filled with the image of Darby Moore. She was still alive.

He remembered her thin, tight body, the narrow scars along her nose, the smell of her. He'd fantasized about the day she escaped a thousand times. In his mind, it went differently. She would be tied to the small bed, sweat running along the muscles of her stomach and glowing in the fading light coming through the windows. The only sound would have been her muffled screams and the struggling of Tristan Newberry as he was forced to watch the things Peck did to her.

"No one must ever know about this, Vili."

Marcek's face broke into a wide smile and he folded into a shallow bow.

"The money will be wired today. And I'll expect your call this afternoon."

"This afternoon," Marcek said. He turned and started toward the door.

"You say that Darby Moore is still alive," Peck said, stopping Marcek with his hand on the doorknob. "What if we make it an even half a million?"

The Slovenian looked back over his shoulder. From his expression, it was clear that he had understood what Peck was asking and was more than willing.

"But I want to speak to her first. I must see her. Do you understand?"

A cruel smile transformed the young Slovenian's face as Peck wiped a few more droplets of sweat from his mustache. Perhaps this beautiful boy would like to join him in his "interrogation" of the girl. Yes, that would be fine. Just fine.

45

Beamon checked his speed again and forced himself to ease off the gas and let Darby's old truck coast to just under the speed limit. He'd been driving nonstop since he'd sneaked without incident from the Middle-of-Nowhere, Wyoming, hospital Darby'd taken him to. What he didn't need was for some state trooper to pull them over and shine a flashlight in Darby's face. That story was getting too long to go into.

With his right arm in a sling, he had to steer with his knees in order to reach the half-full beer balanced on the dashboard. Swallowing was almost more trouble than it was worth due to the inexplicable lump swelling from the inside of his cheek. He wasn't sure how the washing machine action of the avalanche had left that particular injury, but it was becoming increasingly clear that no part of his body had been left unbattered. Miraculously, most of the damage looked like it would heal.

Darby had offered—insisted—that he climb into the makeshift bed in the back of the truck and let her drive, but he'd declined. Driving always calmed him down and helped him think.

It had been an unusual couple of days, to say the least. His night in the Wyoming mountains had been an experience he hoped never to repeat. Bitter cold, dizzying darkness, the wind's constant scream as it blew across the entrance to the tiny cave Darby had dug out for him.

He had tried to sleep, but found it impossible. In the end, his exhaustion might have actually been able to overcome his body's busy little pain receptors, but it had refused to overcome the drop in temperature. All he could do was lay there, huddled in the sleeping bag, adjusting his position at least once every five seconds to ease his shivering and keep his circulation going.

He'd spent the first few hours of sleeplessness creating elaborate scenarios that would prevent Darby from coming back for him: another slide, her freezing to death, the interference of Vili Marcek, alien abduction. It hadn't taken long for that to get depressing, though, so he'd forced himself to focus on what he was going to do now that the Prodigy file was undoubtedly making its way into David Hallorin's capable hands. As it turned out, dwelling on the fact that he'd allowed himself to be stripped of the one thing that could keep him and Darby alive was even more depressing.

When the black cold surrounding him started to glow yellow with the coming dawn, he'd crawled outside the snow cave, leaned his back against a rock outcropping, and let the light of the rising sun soak into his chest. He could still feel the sunburn he'd suffered through the bruises and swelling on his face.

When the sound of a snowmobile engine had started to reflect off the silent mountains around him, he still hadn't the faintest idea what they were going to do. And despite the fact that he'd been hurtling toward Washington, D.C., at just under the speed limit for nine hours now, he still didn't.

Beamon looked over at Darby and saw that she had slumped down in the passenger seat and wrapped herself in her sleeping bag. He reached over and gently slid the empty beer bottle from her hand and propped it next to the small cooler at her feet. She stirred and then settled even deeper into the bag.

He was getting kind of worried about her. The dark circles under her eyes were taking on a noticeably green hue against the tan of her skin, and she'd been through at least a six-pack in the last two hours. She seemed to have learned to cope with Tristan's death, but the memory of her friends Lori and Sam was much fresher. Guilt was tearing her apart.

One problem at a time, Beamon reminded himself.

Steering with his knees again, he dialed the number of Gerald Reys's office into his cell phone for the tenth time that night. And for the tenth time, he turned the phone off before it started ringing.

His deadline to take Reys's deal and do some jail time in return for his pension had expired the day before. Reys was undoubtedly delighted, and Beamon doubted there was anything he could do or say to stop a full criminal prosecution at this point. The best he'd been able to come up with was a half-assed bluff that involved subtly mentioning Tom Sherman's offer of unlimited legal defense funds. The problems with that were twofold: first, he'd never take a dime from a friend—though Reys didn't know that. And second, it felt too much like begging. Maybe being trapped in a snow cave and then in a hospital was the gods' way of telling him not to take the deal.

"Karma," he said quietly to himself, and then shook his head. Five days with Darby Moore and he was already using words like "karma."

"What?" Darby's groggy voice. "Did you say something?" She adjusted herself to a position that allowed her to see the side of his face, but didn't fully emerge from the sleeping bag.

"Nothing. Go back to sleep."

"How do you feel, Mark?" she said, immediately reaching into the cooler at her feet and pulling out a fresh beer. "Are you okay?"

"I'll live."

She dug a bottle of ibuprofen out of the glove box and poured four into her hand. "Climber's candy. Open up." He did, and she dropped them in his mouth, then held her beer up so that he could wash them down without taking his good hand off the wheel.

"Have you figured out what we're going to do yet?"

"Still working on it."

She nodded silently and started in on her beer.

"Have you figured out what *they're* going to do?"

Beamon didn't look over at her, but continued to concentrate on the section of road cut from the darkness by the truck's headlights. "If I'm right about there being something on Taylor in that file, it isn't real hard to guess."

"You think David Hallorin's going to release it to the press?"

Beamon started to reach for his beer, but Darby beat him to it and held it for him while he took a gulp.

"Thanks. I doubt it. Notice how Hallorin's been so respectful to the Republicans during the campaign—and how that's forced them not to go heavily negative on him?"

Darby shrugged and shook her head.

"Take my word for it. No, I'm guessing that he'll get Taylor to drop out and endorse him. There are only four days till the election—the Republicans will still be fighting with each other about what to do when Hallorin's picking out a color scheme for the Oval Office."

"What about the other people in the file? Tristan said there were lots of them."

Beamon shrugged. "If there's anybody else worth blackmailing in it, I imagine Hallorin'll contact them as he needs them."

She thought about that while she finished her beer and reached for another. "Where does that leave us?"

"I don't know." That was a lie. It left them screwed. It left Darby a young woman whose corpse was necessary to end the investigation into Tristan Newberry's death and Beamon a man who, if left alive, might find a way to continue his recent success at toppling America's political elite.

Darby sat staring out the side window of the truck for a long time, concentrating on the darkness as if there was something to find there. "How could you kill for this?" she said finally.

Beamon took his eyes off the road for moment and looked over at her. "For what?"

"Power . . . money . . . "

He let out a short laugh that the swelling in his mouth turned into a snort. "If you were to throw in love, you've pretty much covered all the reasons people kill."

Beamon glanced over at her again and could see from her expression that she was giving his words more thought than they probably deserved.

"I guess I'll just never understand," she said. "If you're right about all this, three of my friends—three human beings—are gone because of David Hallorin. They were happy, they had families, they never hurt anybody. What could possibly make him think that he had the right to take away the rest of their lives? For nothing."

"I don't know if I'd call becoming the leader of the free world nothing, Darby."

"Really? What if he does win? In a few years, he'll just be one of the presidents between Washington and whoever's in office that kids can't remember on their history tests. When he dies, people will get up in the morning and have breakfast, and go to work, and watch their children play baseball—just like they did the day before. I mean, look at me. At the risk of sounding arrogant, I may be the best woman climber who ever lived. But someday, not very long from now, I'll just be a footnote in a few guidebooks—there'll be girls warming up on the hardest things I ever did. But that's good. Life moves on. That's the way it's supposed to be."

Beamon sighed quietly, wondering what Darby would think of the way he'd lived his own life. Probably better that he didn't know. "I understand what you're saying, but I think most people see it differently. There are a lot of people out there who would consider becoming the president of the United States a fair shot at immortality."

She took a thoughtful sip of her beer. "I know you're right. Do you ever watch TV when people trying to get elected make speeches?"

"Yeah. Sure."

"Have you ever noticed the people in the audience? How they cheer and wave their signs like this man or woman cares about them individually? Like their lives are going to be changed by this person?" She turned fully to face him, lifting her feet onto the seat and propping them against his leg. "I mean, come on. When's the last time the government actually did something that really made a difference in your life?"

"I might be a bad example, but I get your point."

"Everyone is responsible for their own happiness, Mark. No one can give it to you."

He watched her out of the corner of his eye as she dropped her empty beer bottle onto the floorboard and went for another one. Her voice was starting to lose the bitterness it had earlier in favor of a mellow monotone. Even though he knew it was purely alcohol induced, he decided that it suited her much better.

"You're not married, are you, Mark?" she said after a long silence.

"Married? No. Why do you ask?"

"Just curious."

"Actually, there's a woman back home that probably *would* marry me, though, if I was smart enough to ask her. Near as I can tell, it's her only character flaw."

"Is that a joke?"

"Nope. You probably think I'm here hiding out with you because of the ten guys with machine guns you've got waiting for me at my house. Not true. It's because I dumped my girlfriend and now I'm afraid of her."

"How long had you been together?"

"Long time."

She concentrated on the side of his face for a few moments. "You love her, don't you?"

He didn't answer immediately. "I guess I do."

"Then why did you dump her?"

He shrugged. "She just . . . didn't seem to fit into my life right now, you know what I mean?"

Darby nodded slowly. "I'm sorry to say that I do."

In his peripheral vision, Beamon could see a mellow smile spreading across her face—the first real one since he'd met her. "Would you like some advice?"

"Relationship advice from the only person I've ever met who's more career-obsessed than I am?"

She pursed her lips and affected an exaggerated frown. "A piece of timeless wisdom that I found carved into the wall of a forgotten monastery in southern Cambodia. I'm probably the only white person on the planet that has this knowledge, you know."

"What knowledge is that?"

She tilted her bottle up and drained the rest of it, looking more than a little unsteady when she tossed the empty on the floor. "A foolproof test to see if you've found your soul mate."

"Don't keep me hanging."

"People have spent their entire lives searching for this one fundamental truth."

"You're killing me, here."

"You need only answer one simple question to ensure that you've found the right person."

"Yeah?"

"If she were a guy, would you still hang out with her?"

Beamon looked over at her and rolled his eyes. "Southern Cambodia, huh."

"As far as you know."

46

Mark Beamon took a seat against the wall, as ordered, and studied the scene around him. The level of activity was more controlled than he'd expected, more dignified. Two days before the general election, the people staffing Senator Robert Taylor's campaign headquarters looked like they'd already won, blissfully unaware that David Hallorin still had one last trick up his sleeve.

Beamon still couldn't believe that this was the best plan his mind could concoct. He'd wasted too much time focusing on the all-important file—and more specifically how to get it back. That had been a dead end, though. After all the pain Hallorin had inflicted to get it, he wasn't going to leave it on his kitchen table next to a glass of warm milk and cookies. He was going to shove it in a concrete-and-steel safe and bury it fifty feet underground.

As lame and desperate as his current course of action was, Beamon was lucky to even get a shot at it. He felt more than a little guilty about getting Tom Sherman involved, but it had seemed rather obvious that a disgraced former FBI agent wasn't going to get a private audience with the man America expected to be its next president. Sherman was well connected at the CIA, where Taylor had spent five years as director. His former deputy had set up the meeting.

Beamon had been sitting alone against the wall for almost an hour when a woman in a blue business suit emerged from a set of double doors to his right. "Mr. Beamon. I apologize for the delay, but you understand that the senator is very busy. He's ready for you now."

Beamon laid down his fifth cup of coffee and smiled politely as he limped through the door she was holding open for him.

Senator Robert Taylor was sitting behind his desk, leaning back in his chair with his feet on what must have been an open drawer. It seemed impossible, but he looked even older in person than he did on TV. The craggy, but evenly colored, skin that had been plastered across every television screen in America was actually blotched with the red and the light purple of broken capillaries, and hung loose around his jowls and neck.

In the time-honored tradition of powerful men, Taylor ignored his entrance. Beamon approached to within ten feet of the desk and stopped, striking as respectful and submissive a pose as he could conjure up. He stood there for almost a minute, watching Taylor's pinkish-yellow eyes scan a document in his lap. Finally, the old man looked up, appraising him over the top of his reading glasses.

"Please have a seat, Mr. Beamon," he said, examining the bruises and swelling on Beamon's face, but not commenting. "My former assistant at the Agency called and told me it was very important that I see you. He didn't know why, but was adamant."

Taylor's calm boredom and mild irritation were wonderfully practiced, but the cracks in the façade were there. Even a politician—a professional liar—couldn't stay completely steady under this kind of pressure. Hallorin had already gotten to him.

"We seem to have a mutual problem, sir," Beamon stated. "I was hoping we could work together to solve it."

"And that is?"

"David Hallorin."

Taylor smiled with a perfect balance of condescension and confusion. "I'm not sure why David Hallorin is a problem for me, Mr. Beamon. I assume you've seen the polls."

Beamon didn't speak for a moment. What the hell was he doing here? Politics had always been something he ran from—a game Tom Sherman had always played for him.

"He has the Prodigy file, Senator. But you know that."

"The Prodigy file . . . " Taylor repeated, removing his glasses and letting his old eyes drill into Beamon.

Beamon shifted uncomfortably in his chair. A lot of this was still conjecture on his part. "Prodigy was an operation put together by the FBI under Hoover. It seems that the powerful men of that era were catching on to his tricks. He had to try something new—"

"I'm sure this is a fascinating story," Taylor broke in. "But I—"

"So he set up a program that identified young up-and-comers and had them watched before they became older and wiser. . . . " He stared Taylor fully in the face and let his voice trail off meaningfully.

"Why are you telling me this?"

"I believe he can use the file to his advantage in this election."

A shadow of anger crossed Taylor's face. "Is that accusation I hear in your voice, Mr. Beamon?"

Games. All these men did was play games. After all these years did Robert Taylor even know the truth when he saw it? Or had truth become indistinguishable from whatever shit his party was shoveling that particular day?

"At first, I thought Hallorin might use the information in the file to gain control of you, but it seems obvious that he isn't going to be satisfied with pulling strings from the background." Beamon paused for a moment. "He wants you to drop out, isn't that right, Senator?"

Taylor snorted quietly though his old nose. "I did some research on you, Mr. Beamon. You have no credibility. In fact, it's my understanding that you will almost undoubtedly be convicted of felony obstruction of justice and are going to spend some time in prison. I met with you out of respect for my former assistant, but I don't need—"

"Who do you think is watching, here?" Beamon said, temporarily losing control of his frustration. He spread his arms wide, motioning around the room. "There are no cameras to play to, Senator. You aren't going to make me forget what I know with a few smooth denials."

Taylor was speechless for a good five seconds. A week ago, he probably hadn't been spoken to like that in forty years. Between David Hallorin and Mark Beamon, this was shaping up to be a tough couple of days.

"Have you forgotten who I am?" he finally blurted out. Beamon rolled his eyes. He was starting to feel . . . Bulletproof wasn't the right word. Doomed was closer to the mark. The effect was the same, though. His tolerance for these tin gods had never been great, but now it was nonexistent.

"I have been a member of the U.S. Senate since you were in high school," Taylor continued, his voice coming up in volume. "I've chaired the Intelligence Committee, I have been both the majority and minority leader, I was the director of the CIA, and I single-handedly stopped Russia's slide back into communism. I have done more for this country than any other—"

"Spare me, Senator," Beamon said, cutting the man off before he started listing his Boy Scout merit badges. "What you've done, you've done for yourself. I should know, I have, too. This country's given you exactly what you need: power and prestige. And you'll forgive me if I don't think a policy of providing Russian Parliament members with enough houses, cars, and whores to keep them docile is one of the great moments in American foreign policy." Beamon struggled to his feet and walked to the edge of Taylor's desk. "People are already dead in this thing, Senator, and it's not over yet. You have the power to stop it. This is your moment. Pay the people back for everything they've given you over the years. One great patriotic sacrifice. Go public. Whatever you did, it was a long time ago. Save the country from David Hallorin and stake yourself out a couple of nice pages in the history books."

Beamon stepped back and forced himself to shut up, though his anger wasn't entirely spent. The years of dealing with men like this had festered inside him even more than he'd thought, and right now Robert Taylor personified all of them.

"This file," Taylor said in a voice that was eerily calm. "I take it you've never seen it."

Beamon didn't reply, but stood his ground in front of the desk as Taylor pushed a button on his phone. The woman who had ushered Beamon in appeared in the doorway a moment later.

"Marcy. Mr. Beamon will be leaving now."

47

Beamon pushed the portable computer to the edge of the table and gave himself a better view of the television. The mingled shouts of the press sounded like static as they came over the set's tiny speakers, drowning out Senator Taylor's amplified voice and forcing him to hold his hands up in a plea for quiet. Beamon pressed the volume button on the remote in his lap and notched the sound up a few decibels.

"My diagnosis is certainly not terminal," Taylor said above the fading din. "But it's made me question whether or not I have the energy to take on a responsibility like the presidency. America needs someone at the helm right now who is capable of one hundred and ten percent."

Beamon leaned forward until his forehead rested on the table in front of him. There it was. A mere six hours after their ill-fated meeting, and after forty years in public service, this was Robert Taylor's final act. Slinking away like a dog from a little embarrassment and leaving America, Mark Beamon, and Darby Moore in the hands of a murderous blackmailer.

"I've devoted my life to this country," Taylor continued, "so you can imagine how difficult this is for me." There was a dramatic pause, and Beamon started to feel a little queasy as he waited for the other shoe to drop. "The days of partisan politics are over. They have to be. America cannot afford to start the twenty-first century with an ineffective and bloated government. I've heard the people, and they're crying out for a system that works and that doesn't empty their pockets at tax time."

Now who was he starting to sound like?

Beamon rolled his head to the side and looked over at Darby. She was sitting ramrod straight on the other bed in the room, wearing a hotel-provided terry cloth robe. Below her still-damp hair, her face had frozen into a blank stare.

"And I believe that the people are right," Taylor went on. "Serious changes have to be made to bring this country—and the rest of the world—back on track. But be prepared—smaller, more efficient government makes demands of its citizens. Personal responsibility will be the theme that carries us forward."

The buzz from the off-camera reporters increased in volume again as the senator began speaking in Hallorinisms.

"I've had a number of meetings with David Hallorin since my diagnosis . . . " The buzz grew to a deafening level and Beamon felt an increasingly familiar sensation of helplessness overcoming him.

"I believe that he is the man to lead America forward."

"Fuck!" Beamon yelled, grabbing the portable computer next to him and throwing it in the general direction of the television. It bounced off the wall and landed on the floor with an unsatisfying thud.

"Please, please," Taylor said as Darby rose from the bed and walked unsteadily toward the bathroom. "If my party will allow it, I would like to continue in a leadership roll, and should Senator Hallorin's bid for the presidency be successful, act as a liaison between the GOP and his administration. We have a lot to get done, but I believe that if we work together, we can accomplish more in the next four years than we have in the last twenty. We—"

Beamon clicked the OFF button on the remote and leaned back, staring at the ceiling and letting himself sink into a state of deep relaxation. Practice for being dead.

He didn't know how long he stayed like that—no thoughts crossed his mind to mark time. What was there to think about? It couldn't be stopped. Not by him. Not by anyone.

When he finally pulled himself back into the present, he saw that the bathroom door was still closed. "Darby? You all right in there?"

No answer.

He pushed himself out of the chair and padded across the room in stocking feet, silently admonishing himself for losing control. She had been through enough without having to witness the guy who was supposed to be saving her throw a tantrum.

"Darby?" he said again, this time with his mouth almost touching the bathroom door. Nothing.

"You decent in there?" He put his hand on the knob and opened the door wide enough to allow him to peek cautiously around it.

She was sitting on the edge of the tub, leaning forward so that her head rested on her knees. A slight vibration in her shoulders was visible under the thick robe as she quietly sobbed.

She didn't seem to be aware of his presence, so Beamon just stood there, unsure what to do. It suddenly struck him how young she was. He wondered how an inexperienced, twenty-seven-year-old Mark Beamon would have handled being stuck in the middle of something like this.

Beamon ducked out and pulled two beers from the cooler they'd brought up from her truck. Taking a deep breath, he pushed back through the bathroom door and took a seat on the counter. "Here, it'll make you feel better," he said, holding the bottle out to her.

"I'm sorry," she said. "This is so embarrassing."

"What?"

"Sitting here crying like a baby. You may not believe this, but normally I'm pretty put together."

"I believe you. I'd be a Marlboro-flavored Popsicle if it weren't for you."

She let out a sad half-laugh and wiped the tears from her eyes with the sleeve of her robe.

"You must have been in worse spots than this." Beamon motioned toward her nose with the neck of his beer bottle. "What about those scars? You got them walking into a blizzard, didn't you?"

She nodded.

"Must have been pretty frightening."

"All I remember is that it was cold. The wind had kicked up and every-where you went it looked like you were walking through a crystal whirl-wind. Then the clouds came over the mountain and it got dark . . . " Her voice trailed off for a moment. "But that was different. In the mountains you know where it's coming from. It'll be the cold, or a fall, or a slide. I don't know where anything is coming from anymore. I don't understand what motivates these people, and I don't have the slightest idea of how to even *try* to stop them. I think about David Hallorin and Vili and the other men who are responsible for all this—for Tristan and Sam and Lori—and I want to kill them. I want to *kill* them, Mark. That's not me."

He wanted to say something wise, or soothing, or insightful, but he couldn't think of anything, so he remained silent.

"For the first time in my life, I don't know what to do," Darby contin-ued. "Other than to sit here and cry like a jerk while you baby-sit me."

"I wish I had something you could help me with, Darby. I know how frustrating it is to just sit around and wait in a situation like this, but to be completely honest, I'm not sure what *I'm* doing." He paused. "You probably didn't want to hear that, did you?"

She took a sip of her beer. "I appreciate you being honest with me, Mark. And I know you're doing everything you can. But where do we stand now? David Hallorin's going to win, isn't he? He's going to be the president."

Beamon nodded.

"I've been thinking, Mark. We don't have any proof that he has the file. We don't even know if it really exists—I just saw something wrapped in plastic. Maybe he realizes all that. I mean, we can't really hurt him— he's going to be the *president*."

Beamon stared at the empty white wall in front of him and tried to decide how much to say. He wanted to lie to her, to tell her they were going to be okay, to snap her out of the depression she seemed to be sinking into. But he couldn't. "Would you take that risk?" he said, sliding off the counter and starting into the other room.

She followed him out of the bathroom and watched silently as he lifted his portable computer off the floor. Miraculously, it was still working. The credit card Reynolds, Trent, and Layman had given him was, for some reason, still good, and he'd spared no expense at the computer store.

"Look, Darby. There's a trail of dead bodies connected to you. The cops are going to want to believe that you're responsible. Who are you to them? A homeless person with a death wish, right?" He paused. "I'm still not getting this tact thing, am I?"

She shook her head sadly. "You're right. That's exactly what they think about me."

Beamon sat back down at the small table by the wall and centered the computer in front of him. "I'm telling you this because I know you can handle it. And you said you wanted honesty, right?"

She nodded.

"It would be best for them, if you resurface, uh, not alive. Then you can't talk about what happened and the cops just close the book on your friend's death. I'm in just as bad a spot. Why would Hallorin risk letting me live—a man who has so many of the threads of their plan in his head? How do they know I won't—"

"Weave them into a tapestry."

"Well said."

She let the robe slide off her shoulders and pulled on a pair of jeans and a sweatshirt. "I'm going to go for a walk," she said, sitting down on the carpet to put her shoes on. "I need to get some fresh air and think."

Beamon frowned and tilted the computer's screen down so he could see her over it. "I don't know . . . "

"Come on, Mark. It's a safe part of town. And it's dark. Nobody knows we're here."

She was right, but the thought of her striking out on her own made him nervous. He was about to offer to come with her but knew she didn't want the company. He tossed her the cell phone lying on the table next to him. "If you see anything suspicious—anything at all. Call me. And be back in an hour."

"Okay, Dad."

Beamon stared at the door for a few minutes after she had gone, not sure if he made the right decision. She was looking more and more like a caged animal as the days wore on, and a little open space and solitude was undoubtedly what she needed.

The chances of one of Hallorin's henchmen driving by and recognizing her in the dark didn't seem very high. Hell, she was probably safer walking around at random than in the hotel with him.

He shook off his nervousness, going back to the computer screen and the endless pages of Freedom of Information Act documents relating to JFK's youthful indiscretions. After seeing the volume of the information, he understood Cindy Abrahm's reluctance to e-mail it to him. It must have taken a full day to scan this many pages.

In the end, though, it was looking like the whole thing had been a wasted effort. What exactly was he looking for? He was pretty comfortable that he'd already figured out more or less what the Prodigy file contained—so pouring over a thousand pages of moot information wasn't going to save his skin.

His only real hope was to figure out a way to cut a deal with Hallorin. The current circumstances, though, suggested that was unlikely. He had absolutely nothing the man wanted, no proof of any wrongdoing, and based on his meeting with Taylor, a less than persuasive demeanor when politicians were involved.

Beamon spent the better part of the next hour scrolling disinterestedly through the documents on the computer, mostly because he didn't have anything better to do. As he'd come to expect of classified government documents, they went on forever and said almost nothing. The bulk of it consisted of reports on Kennedy when he wasn't doing *anything*. There was a full ten pages on a birthday party for his six-year-old cousin.

Beamon took to a more liberal use of the PAGE DOWN button, finally turning up some of the documents relating to Kennedy's tryst with the alleged spy. Even that was mundane by current standards. It seemed that, like the press, the FBI at one time had a sense of decency. Thank God that hadn't lasted.

A few more pages flickered by and he stumbled upon a more detailed description of JFK's relationship with Inga Fejos. As was common with some of these old documents, along the margin something had been scrawled in pen. Initially, it wasn't legible, but after a few minutes he figured out how to make the computer focus in on the writing and magnify it.

When the door to the hotel finally opened, he barely noticed. Darby walked past the table he was sitting at and dropped onto her bed. "What if we just run, Mark?" she said. "I was stupid to go to Thailand, but there are other places. Places no one could find us. We wouldn't have to stay gone forever, just . . . Mark? Are you listening to me?" She slid to the floor and crawled up next to him, following his unblinking stare to the laptop's screen. "*Re-file*," she read. "*Not Prodigy. B.* You found something! Do you know who *B* is?"

Beamon reached out and shut the computer off. "That's not a B."

48

Tom Sherman turned off his headlights and navigated the car down the dirt road leading to his house half by moonlight and half by memory.

He'd originally purchased the three hundred acres and the small cabin at its center as an occasional retreat. Seven miles from Manassas, Virginia, it was only about an hour from downtown D.C. As time passed, though, it was becoming much more than an occasional escape. Workweeks seemed to end earlier and start later every month. It was only Sunday night and, despite the faxes that would be piling up in his DuPont Circle brownstone, he knew he wouldn't return there until at least Tuesday afternoon. It was all getting too confused. And he was getting too old.

Sherman pulled up to the small cedar home and turned off his car's motor, but didn't get out. Instead he held his right hand up in front of his face and examined it in the moonlight flooding through the windshield. It looked ghostly white and it shook. The drive through Virginia's countryside used to calm him. Now it all just followed him.

Sherman stepped out into the cold air and started immediately for the house, leaving the hanging bag containing his clothes in the backseat. He'd feel better in the morning, he told himself. He just needed to get into bed and sleep.

Halfway up the steps leading to the porch, he stopped. There was a dull, almost imperceptible glow coming from the window next to the front door. He moved a few feet to the right and examined it from a different angle, thinking it was his imagination or a trick of the moonlight. It wasn't. There were lights on somewhere in the back of the house. But he was certain he'd turned everything off when he'd left the week before.

He wasn't sure what to do for a moment. He couldn't call the police because he'd purposely left his cell phone in D.C. He could, of course, drive to the station a few miles away, but somehow, it didn't seem worth it. Instead, he walked quietly back to his car and pulled a .38 revolver from the glove box.

The front door was unlocked, confirming his suspicion that someone had been, or still was, in the house. He pushed it open slowly, holding the gun out at waist level as he moved through the entry and spotted the light bleeding from the crack under the closed door to the kitchen. He stopped and listened for a moment, trying to decipher the sounds coming from the other side. There was no getting around the fact that someone was there.

He should get the police, he knew. Or at least come at the kitchen from a less obvious direction, but in the end, he just couldn't bring himself to care enough about his own welfare to bother. He pushed the gun out a little further in front of him and simply walked through the swinging door.

The young woman standing at the island in the middle of the kitchen jerked back in surprise when she saw him, splattering a fair amount of balsamic vinegar on the floor beneath her. She took a step back from the plate of sliced tomatoes she'd been hovering over and raised her hands. "They were going bad. I swear."

"Darby Moore," Sherman muttered, lowering the gun. She put her hands down and started pulling paper towels off a roll on the counter.

"Where's Mark?"

"I think he's in your office."

Sherman nodded and started to turn away, but paused and looked down at her as she wiped the vinegar off the floor. "I want you to know that I'm sorry for everything that's happened to you."

She stopped working on the floor and looked straight at him, probing. "I believe you," she said finally. "Thanks."

"I've heard the stories," Beamon said as Sherman entered the small, neatly organized office. Beamon had taken a seat behind the desk in the back corner and was examining a framed photograph he'd taken off the wall. It depicted a very young Tom Sherman shaking hands with J. Edgar Hoover.

"You were one of his top aides before you were even thirty, weren't you, Tommy? He couldn't give you the title, but you had more of the old man's ear than anyone but Tolson."

Sherman stopped for a moment, examining Beamon's more glaring injuries, then crossed the office timidly and sat down in one of the chairs lined up in front of his desk. Beamon had to fight off the discomfort he was feeling at this bizarre role reversal. It had always been Sherman behind the desk and him in the hot seat for some screwup or another. And in a strange way, that's how he preferred it.

He put down the photograph and picked up a single page printed from his computer, looking one more time at the handwritten note in the margin.

Re-file. Not Prodigy. B.

"The initials are a little less confident," Beamon said, sliding the paper across the desk with his good hand. "But I'd say they're yours, wouldn't you?"

The symbol that Darby had mistaken for a "B" was actually the half-merged "TS" that Beamon had seen a thousand times before.

Sherman hesitated for a moment and then picked up the sheet of paper. His eyes ran across it for no more than a second before he wadded it up and threw it in a wastebasket by the wall. Without a word, he stood and walked across the small room to a sideboard topped with a collection of liquor bottles. "Drink?"

"I could use one," Beamon said.

Sherman looked a little unsteady as he returned to his chair and shook slightly as he pushed Beamon's drink across the desk.

"How stupid was I?" Beamon said, gulping down his first taste of bourbon in almost a year and feeling it attack the unhealed cuts in his mouth. "I thought I had the whole thing figured out. David Hallorin's got enough political juice to get my suspension turned into a felony rap, he'd know about old FBI files from his time as a prosecutor in D.C., and he's wealthy enough to throw three hundred thousand dollars my way to find a twenty-seven-year-old mountain climber. I'd have bet the farm I was working for him. But now it occurs to me that there's someone else who fits that description."

"Don't be so melodramatic."

"Melodramatic? You set me up!"

"I had nothing to do with your suspension turning into criminal charges—you did that all by yourself," Sherman said, forcing down some of the vodka in his glass with a distinctly pained look on his face. "I needed the best, and you suddenly became available. I hoped that you would find Darby before anybody else got hurt, that you'd turn her over to my attorney, and that you'd collect your fee and use it for your defense. She'd lead me to the file and it would be over. It would finally be over."

"And Tristan Newberry?"

"Darby killed one of theirs—one of Hallorin's men. Did she tell you that? We'd have had to call it even. Of course, I knew you wouldn't make it that easy on me."

Sherman picked up the photograph of himself and Hoover, turning it over carefully in his hands. "You'd think it would be hard to remember being this young. But I can. I can remember it all—what it was like to be starting life instead of winding it down, what it was like to have one of the most powerful men in the world think you walked on water. I would have done anything for him. And I did."

Beamon's discomfort was growing exponentially as the conversation continued. He'd planned exactly how this confrontation would play out. He would start with the upper hand, thanks to some explosive theatrics, self-pity, and the fact that he was on the moral high ground for once. Then Tom would explain the entire thing—how there was a bigger picture that he didn't see, how it had all been necessary. Then he'd let Beamon in on the master plan. With Sherman there was always a master plan. Complex, subtle, and infallible. But none of that was materializing. Beamon found himself completely unprepared for what he was seeing. Tom Sherman, hopelessly weakened by guilt and uncertainty.

"J. Edgar Hoover was a nut, Tommy."

Sherman shook his head. "No. People try to judge him based on the current context. You can't take a person out of their time. In many ways, he was a great man. In many ways, he wasn't. But I couldn't see his faults, I let myself get blinded."

"How old were you?" Beamon said, suddenly feeling an overwhelming urge to come to his friend's defense. "Twenty-eight? Twenty-nine?"

Sherman shrugged. "When the old man died, the Prodigy project landed in my lap. No one in senior management wanted anything to do with it. Times were changing. No one had the stomach for the political blackmail anymore. No one had Hoover's . . . conviction."

"Conviction?" Beamon said in a sarcastic tone.

"The people in it were Democrat and Republican, rich and poor, liberal and conservative. It had the potential to hurt everyone. I had to make a decision."

"Why didn't you just burn the fucking thing, Tommy? Or at least put it in a safe deposit box somewhere?"

He looked up from the photograph, finally meeting Beamon's eye. "I'm surprised you'd ask me that question. Aren't you about to be prosecuted on a trumped-up charge of destroying evidence?"

Beamon leaned back in his chair. "I see your point."

"No, as long as the file existed, no one was going to get divisive and try to come back at the FBI for assembling it. The stakes were too high for both sides. And if it ever came out that the file *did* exist, it could eventually be produced from a government archive—horribly misfiled, of course. And then I would simply say that the FBI had determined that the evidence in the file was obtained illegally and therefore decided not to pursue indictment."

"All the angles," Beamon said. "You had all the angles even back then."

"I thought I did."

"You hadn't anticipated a viable third-party candidate."

Sherman shook his head. "Why would I? It wasn't in the realm of possibility at the time. When Hallorin came out with his comprehensive declassification plan, I didn't think anything of it—too many years had passed. When I found out that he was using that piece of legislation as cover to search for Prodigy, he was already three steps ahead of me." Sherman put his glass on the desk and leaned forward, resting his elbows on his knees. "So now, during one of the most fragile times in American history, the political process has been completely subverted. And innocent people have died. All because of me."

Sherman walked over to the sideboard to refill his glass. He actually looked as if he'd shrunk, as if he was physically smaller than he had been last time they'd seen each other. It seemed impossible, but Tom Sherman, the man who had always been absolutely unshakable, looked like he was on the verge of collapse.

"Why didn't you just come to me, Tommy? Why would you send me into this blind?"

Sherman couldn't seem find it in himself to turn around and face him. "I told myself that it was because I didn't want you any more involved than necessary, that you wouldn't be able to handle knowing the file existed as delicately as it needed to be. I told myself all kinds of things.

The truth is simpler, though. I was ashamed. I just wanted it to all go away. I told myself that you'd find the girl, the way you always do, before anyone ever knew you were involved. You'd have the money to pay for your defense and I'd have . . . " His voice trailed off as he finished pouring the drink.

"What, Tommy? A clear conscience?"

Sherman turned and started out of the office. "It was already too late for that. I just wanted an end to it, Mark. I'm sorry."

49

"**T**ake this exit," Beamon said.

"This is nuts, Mark. The Dulles Airport exit is just ahead. That's the one we should be taking."

Beamon adjusted the sleeping bag, which was protecting his new suit from the truck's grimy seats. Three thousand dollars. It hadn't been easy to find a suit that expensive with the economy where it was, but he'd managed it. All neatly charged to Reynolds, Trent, and Layman, or more precisely, what was left of his best friend Tom Sherman.

"What are you trying to accomplish here?" Darby pressed, easing onto the ramp and aiming the truck through northern Virginia's light afternoon traffic. "This is a trap and you're walking right into it. You know you can't trust that son of a bitch."

Beamon had been more than a little surprised when he'd answered his cell phone the day before and heard David Hallorin's voice on the other end. The offer of a meeting and a truce was strained, but had sounded strangely sincere.

"But we *can* trust him, Darby. We can trust him to do what's in his self-interest. Right now, it might suit him to make a deal. And if that's true, we've got to take advantage of his mood."

"I'm not sure I want a deal anymore."

"Look, Darby, we've got nothing to work with, here. We aren't going to win this thing—the best we can hope for is not to lose. If he wants to talk, I'm ready to listen."

She shook her head. "This isn't going to work, we both know it. And we can't just let them—"

"Let them what? We can't bring your friends back. I'm sorry, but we can't. We talked about this. If we were on a mountain instead of the outskirts of D.C. you'd put them out of your head and try to save yourself. Right?"

Her knuckles had turned white around the steering wheel as her frustration became nearly unbearable. "I thought you said your friend was going to help us?"

Beamon hadn't told her about Sherman's involvement—she had enough to worry about without going there. "I honestly don't know if he can anymore."

Her face softened a little. "Is he okay? I mean, I don't know him, but he looks—"

"He'll be fine," Beamon said, though he didn't really believe it. He'd lain awake most of the night replaying his conversation with Sherman, trying to figure out what had happened to his friend.

Much of Sherman's meteoric rise through the ranks of the FBI could be traced back to Hoover's admiration of him as a young man. And much of that admiration, it now turned out, could probably be traced back to Sherman's handling of the Prodigy operation. That seemed to be more than his friend could bear. Right now, he was wallowing in the thought that his entire career—which, for him, pretty much translated into his entire life—was built on an illegal operation that he was ashamed of and now had blown up in his face. He'd be thinking that everything he was—his honor, morality, empathy, accomplishments—was a lie. That he, and not Hallorin, was responsible for the death of Tristan Newberry and the others. And all that self-flagellation had left him completely paralyzed.

Darby took her eyes from the road and looked over at Beamon—not a particularly dangerous act, since her truck couldn't break forty-five miles an hour anymore. "This smells like desperation, Mark. Take it from me, desperate acts get people killed. Let's just get out of here. See the world with that credit card of yours for a few years. They'll forget about us."

"They won't. And you know from experience, staying ahead of them is easier said than done. Besides, I'm not prepared to live the rest of my life looking over my shoulder. And neither are you."

"Let's make a damn stand, then," she said, turning her attention back toward the road. "I mean, if we're going to do something desperate and stupid, why not make it count?"

"I'm with you. What are you proposing?"

"I don't know. There's got to be something."

"This is it, Darby. Our best shot."

She sighed loudly and yanked repeatedly on the wheel, bouncing herself up and down in the seat. "Okay. But at least let me go in with you."

"And do what?"

"I don't know. What do you macho types say? Watch your back?"

Beamon laughed. "There are some pretty stringent rules in the macho-type club that you may not be aware of. One of the most heavily enforced is that you don't let a skirt watch your back. I'm afraid I can't make an exception, even for you."

"I could help."

"I know you could. But they want us both. As long as they don't know where you are, my chances of walking out of there are about ten times better."

"Better than what?"

"I wish I knew."

"It seems that our fortunes have changed since we last met, Mr. Beamon. Mine for the better and yours for the worse. I understand that you decided not to take the deal the FBI offered?"

Beamon stood in the middle of the office and stared at the wall behind David Hallorin. He could feel Roland Peck, the only other person in the room, studying him.

Hallorin's observation was, of course, accurate. Following Taylor's announcement that he was pulling out of the race, the Republican machine had blown itself apart. Half its leadership was hopelessly scrambling to find a precedent that would allow them to postpone the election, and the other half just seemed to be running in circles talking to themselves. The Democrats had taken a surprising amount of Taylor's support—skillfully nurturing the fears of those conservative voters who were smart enough to see David Hallorin for the scary son of a bitch he was. It hadn't been nearly enough, though. Hallorin's lead looked like it was going to settle in around the nine-point range, and tomorrow he was going to be voted the next president of the United States.

Hallorin didn't seem at all disconcerted by Beamon's silence and waved at one of the chairs in front of his desk. Beamon sat down in it without thinking and immediately regretted the act. He probably looked like an obedient sheepdog—not the way to gain standing over a man like Hallorin.

"I have to admit, for a while, we were under the impression you were dead," Hallorin said through a thin smile. The air of superiority the man wore was so thick it was almost opaque as he fed off his position of dominance over Beamon. It was like a drug to him.

"I think you must have me confused with the man you hired, Senator. I'm curious. Who was he?"

It was Hallorin's turn to fall silent.

"They'll find him when the snow thaws. I assume that he was a cop at some point in his life, so his prints will be on record."

It was Peck who spoke up. "His name was Frank Sorvino."

Beamon had heard it before. LAPD, retired. By all reports an investigator of exceptional ability and almost limitless moral flexibility.

"I'm a rather busy man, Mr. Beamon, so let me get to the point. I called you here to see if we can come to an understanding."

Beamon didn't answer right away, concentrating on staying perfectly calm. This was his and Darby's last chance. As slim as it was, he couldn't afford to blow it by letting this meeting degenerate like the one he'd had with Taylor. "About the Prodigy file?"

Hallorin's face remained an emotionless mask. "I assume that if you had any proof that this file actually exists or of wrongdoing by me, you'd be using it."

"I'm apolitical, Senator. I don't even vote. It's not my job to protect the American people from themselves. That's the beauty of a democracy. The people get exactly what they deserve." He silently admonished himself for tagging on that last piece of personal philosophy. Control. For once in his life, he had to maintain control.

"Your point, Mr. Beamon?"

"My point is that I don't want to spend the rest of my life waiting for the other shoe to drop."

Hallorin folded his arms across his chest and stared at the floor for what seemed like a long time but probably wasn't. "I guess I do owe you a debt of gratitude," he said finally.

"Excuse me?"

"You created the environment that made all this possible. The release of the Vericomm tapes that you timed so perfectly—the complete moral bankruptcy of the American government laid out in glorious digital audio. You made our job so much easier. In a sense, I'm going to ride the wave of voter resentment you created, right into the White House."

Beamon had repositioned himself slightly so that he could keep

Roland Peck in his peripheral vision. He could see that the angular, little man's nervous movements were becoming more and more urgent as his boss spoke. Perhaps David Hallorin had the same weakness as many of his peers—he needed to show off how smart he was.

"Do you remember, Mr. Beamon, when the American Dream was that you could work hard and achieve anything no matter where you started in life? Now people dream of tripping over a crack in the sidewalk and suing the city that laid it. Or of winning the lottery."

Beamon nodded to show that he was listening but had no idea where this was going.

"You see, the American people are like children. When things are going well, they demand their independence. But when there's trouble on the horizon, they run back to their mothers and expect everything to be made all better."

"And in this analogy, you're the mother?" Beamon said, and then cursed himself for opening his mouth. Fortunately, Hallorin's ego seemed to have grown so large that it had taken over the commonsense center of his brain. The sarcasm was lost on him.

"In a sense, I am. I'm willing to tell them what to do, how to solve their problems in a way that's simple enough for them to understand. They don't have to think for themselves at all. It's fortunate for America that the file did exist, don't you think? Robert Taylor has been this country's cross to bear for thirty years. I'm the only man that can lead us out of the hole he's dug."

Hallorin seemed to believe the legend he'd created for himself, to have convinced himself that it wasn't all a lie carefully manufactured for him by his staff.

"For the longest time I couldn't figure out why you weren't attacking Taylor in your campaign," Beamon said, looking directly into the eyes of the man who had engineered an explosion that had killed seven people. A man who was paving his way to the White House with the bodies of children.

"The file was the key, Mr. Beamon. Certainly there have always been people aware of its existence, but the concept—myth—of assured mutual annihilation kept it buried. It's truly amazing, when you think about it— that our government is manned with such cowards that no one used it before me."

More like dumb luck, it seemed to Beamon. And that was something that had been bothering him. If someone had found it before Hallorin, what would keep them from taking what they wanted and burning the rest?

"So how can we coexist, Mr. Beamon? I assume you've thought about this."

Beamon shrugged. "We just forget the whole thing. I don't pursue it, and you forget about Darby Moore and me."

Hallorin let out a short laugh. "That seems a bit one-sided to me. It's my understanding that you don't have anything to pursue."

That was true. There was the explosion that had put Hallorin back in the running, but how could he even come close to proving anything about that? The evidence he had was as unproducible as it was circumstantial.

"Who are you working for, Mr. Beamon?" Roland Peck cut in.

"For the longest time, I thought it was you," Beamon said honestly, then continued with a little white lie. "Now I don't know."

No one spoke for a long time, probably a good two minutes.

"You haven't asked for enough, Mark," Hallorin said finally, his tone taking on a pedantic air. "Do you know why the FBI's using you as a scapegoat?"

"Because they don't like me?"

Hallorin smiled. "Because they can. Politicians are schoolyard bullies—stupid and cowardly. Once you understand that, and the fact that they are solely out for personal gain, they're surprisingly easy to predict and manipulate."

"I'm not sure what you're driving at."

"How anxious do you think the FBI would be to put you through this if the president of the United States and the Senate majority leader were to write letters and express their displeasure at the action?"

Beamon thought about that for a moment. "Not very, I suppose."

"In fact, your job and your reputation would be returned to you very quickly, don't you think?"

"And how could I ever repay you for your kindness?"

"Much easier than you imagine, I think. I only ask three things. First, that when your name is cleared and you are reinstated to the FBI, you resign."

Beamon nodded. "What else."

"That you accept the job Roland offered you."

Beamon felt his eyebrows rise at the repeated offer of a million-dollar-a-year job. After a moment of consideration, though, he realized that taking a job at such an exorbitant salary would certainly give the impression of collusion, should he ever decide to make any of this public. It also kept him in a place that he could be watched. Hallorin once again proved that he was not a stupid man.

"We respect efficiency, Mark," Peck cut in. "You've proven your abilities and we like to hire the best."

Beamon bent forward in a hint of a bow, acknowledging the compliment. "You said three things. By my count, that's two."

"Darby Moore." Peck again.

"What about her?" Beamon asked, though he already knew. He turned to fully face Peck, suspecting that Hallorin wouldn't speak on this subject himself.

"Her motivations are too murky, Mark. Too unidentifiable. She's completely unpredictable, uncontrollable . . . "

Beamon nodded silently. It was true, she *was* all those things. But he'd kind of grown attached to her. It would take more than the promise of a seven-figure salary and a get-out-of-jail-free card to condemn her to death. He'd accept nothing less than a spot on the PGA tour.

"So what do you think of our offer?" Hallorin said.

He turned back to face the senator. "Can I think about it?"

Confusion flashed briefly across Hallorin's face, as Beamon knew it would. How could a man like him understand? In Hallorin's mind, he'd just offered everything that mattered: money, power, and reputation. How could he fathom that Beamon would throw all that away for a young woman who Hallorin undoubtedly couldn't differentiate from a bum staked out on a sewer grate? And with a little bit of misdirection, Beamon could use that confusion to buy a little more time. Not that he knew what he was going to do with it.

"Mr. Beamon," Peck said, obviously as perplexed as his boss. "We have the file. I believe that taking a high-powered, high-paid job is your best option. Particularly in light of the fact that you have no other options."

Beamon pretended that he didn't hear, keeping himself focused on Hallorin. "Don't get me wrong, Senator. I recognize the position I'm in and I'm inclined to take your offer. I just want to make sure that I make a deal that works for me."

Hallorin's smile was nearly imperceptible. They were back on ground that he'd traveled—David Hallorin understood negotiating. "You want to raise the price, Mark? You don't have anything to sell."

Hallorin was right. Beamon had been hopelessly outmaneuvered.

When he'd finally stepped back to take in the big picture, it had been too late.

How had any of this happened? How had Hallorin and Peck outsmarted Tom Sherman so easily? Not the shadow of the man that Beamon had left hiding in the wilds of Manassas, but the young Tom Sherman who had damn near taken over the Bureau before he was thirty-five.

The more he thought about it the more it nagged at him. Sherman said he'd never considered the possibility of a third-party candidate coming to power, but that didn't really make sense. Why was Hallorin the only man who could effectively use the information the file contained?

"Fine," Hallorin said. "Take a couple of days to consider your position. Speak to Roland when you've come to a decision."

50

Mark Beamon stalked up the steps to Tom Sherman's Manassas house and threw the front door open. None of the lights were on, but he knew Sherman was there. Hiding from his past. Where the hell else would he be?

Beamon moved purposefully through the semidarkness, but the house was empty. He slid open the glass door that led onto the back deck and found Sherman wrapped in a blanket, gazing out over his land. He didn't turn around when Beamon took a position behind him.

"Beautiful sunset," Sherman said simply.

"Lovely," Beamon said, moving forward to face his friend. "I talked to Hallorin."

"I knew you would."

Despite the red glow coming from the mountains, Sherman's face seemed pale and drawn.

"He didn't strike me as a stupid man, but I'm not sure he's actually the brains of that outfit. He's got this little leprechaun working for him—"

"Peck," Sherman said. "Roland Peck."

"That's right. Peck. I figure it was him."

"Him?"

"The one who's been running circles around you. Who found the file you worked so hard to hide and figured out a way to use it."

Sherman didn't respond.

"What was it, Tom, about ten years ago that we flew over to Saudi Arabia on that terrorism case? You remember that?"

Sherman nodded, but still seemed far away.

"You took a fucking umbrella," Beamon said, letting his voice grow to a dull shout. "You never, *never*, get caught short! You have a contingency plan for everything!"

"I was barely thirty when Hoover died," Sherman protested. "How could I anticipate the rise of a man like David Hallorin? Tell me. How?"

"Fuck David Hallorin! What if the Democrats had found the file? They'd have burned everything that had to do with their people and used it against the GOP. What would you have done then?"

"I hid the file so that couldn't happ—"

"But it *did* happen! And you'd have planned for that, wouldn't you?"

"Hoover was dead . . . " Sherman's voice was starting to shake a little. "I was all alone on this—senior management was running hard and fast. I had to make a decision quickly—"

"Come on, Tommy! The Democrats have the file! What do you do? *What do you do?*"

Sherman finally looked up at him. His eyes were dead without the reflection of the sunset. "Do you know what it's like, Mark? Of course you don't. You've *never* compromised, have you? You've been satisfied with your little personal victories on your little cases. You've never felt any responsibility— or even given a second thought—to anything beyond what's right in front of your face. I was responsible for the entire Bureau—the policies, the people, projecting where the next threat to America was coming from. I spent the last thirty years as one of the men who led this country. I believed in what I was doing. I believed in all of it."

He started walking toward the door that led into the house. "I have a lot more years behind me than I do ahead of me, Mark. And that's what I've done with them."

"You're full of shit, Tommy. Answer my goddamn question."

He didn't stop, so Beamon grabbed him by the arm. "The Democrats have the file. *What do you do?*"

Sherman didn't pull away, but he also didn't respond.

"It's something Hallorin said today," Beamon said. "He talked about the file and the assured mutual destruction of the people in it. The uneasy peace brought about by equal firepower. That's the way you set it up, isn't it, Tom?"

Sherman's face was still a blank.

"The explosion," Beamon said, trying to break through to him. "Hallorin tried to save that girl, right? Did you know he set the whole thing up? That's the man you're going to put in the White House."

Sherman reached out and opened the door in front of him, but didn't immediately step through. "David Hallorin's evil, isn't he, Mark? So much worse than all the rest of them. If he falls, America will be saved. Isn't that right?" He finally met Beamon's eye. "I've always envied your childlike view of the world, Mark. You must sleep well at night."

"What the hell happened to you, Tommy?"

Sherman started into the house, indicating that Beamon should follow. They ended up in the back bedroom, where Sherman pushed his bed across the wood floor and knelt. There was an audible click as he opened a hidden trapdoor, beneath which was a formidable-looking safe. Sherman worked the dial for a few moments and opened it.

"There were two originals made of everything. One went to the archive to keep us all on safe legal ground. The other has been with me all these years. But then, you'd already guessed that, hadn't you?" He dropped the file into Beamon's outstretched arms. "Here's your mutual assured destruction, Mark. The day before the election."

Beamon took a sip of his second bourbon and adjusted the heavy file into a more comfortable position on his lap. Much of it was useless. Suspected communist activity, a threat that history had seen fit to make laughable, made up a good half of it. Money, sex, and drugs made up the rest. The classics just never went out of style.

Beamon had tossed the marijuana-related files onto the commie hoard stack, deciding that it was another formerly heinous threat to U.S. security that looked a little silly in the current context. On the same pile, he tossed the files of men who had never lived up to Hoover's expectations and those who had already been exposed.

That left him with eight fabulously damaging and exhaustively documented stories on eight extremely powerful men. The most impressive and dangerous, of course, was the one containing the pictures of Robert Taylor, taken by none other than a young Tom Sherman. Beamon shuffled through the randomly ordered photos of the Republicans' family values candidate one more time—resisting the urge to organize them and see if he could make a movie by flipping through them really fast.

He extracted one of the more artistic compositions of young Taylor and his two naked companions and smoothed it out on top of the file. He stared down at it for a long time, looking for answers in the writhing bodies and the blank stare of that child's eyes. It was a bomb all right.

But how could he set it off without getting caught in the blast?

"She was twelve."

Startled, Beamon jerked his head in the direction of the voice. Tom Sherman was leaning—sagging—on the doorframe that led into the room.

"I did some background on her and the woman after I took those pictures. She was just a baby. I could have stopped it—my partner wanted to. But I didn't. I wouldn't."

Beamon looked down at the picture again, unsure what to say. "Where . . . where is she now?"

"She's dead. They both are."

"Is the silent treatment over then, Mark?" Darby said.

He hadn't much felt like talking after his less than successful meeting with David Hallorin, despite Darby's probing curiosity. After about an hour, she'd gotten angry and frustrated and they'd spent the rest of the drive to Manassas in silence.

"Yeah, it's over," Beamon said, crashing through the lower branches of a tree, swinging the six-pack in his hand like a machete. "But you may be sorry."

He took a seat in a folding chair across a low burning campfire from Darby. He'd tried to get her to stay in the house, but every time she'd politely declined—saying that she'd rather sleep in her own bed in the back of her truck.

He couldn't blame her, really. Between him sweating out their uncertain future and Tom sinking deeper and deeper into depression, the atmosphere was getting a little oppressive. The tiny clearing alongside the road that wound through Sherman's property was downright cheerful by comparison.

"So are you going to give me a beer and tell me what happened, then?"

"That's why I'm here." He tossed her a bottle from the six-pack and she deftly opened it on the edge of a rock.

"Well?"

Beamon tried to find the best way to paraphrase his meeting. Darby had finally gotten some sleep and had cut back on the beer a little, bringing some of the color back to her skin and erasing the dark circles that had painted themselves beneath her eyes. He didn't want to say anything that could cause a relapse.

"The meeting went well," he said. "Great, really. He offered to get the FBI to call off the dogs and wants to give me a job for about a mil a year."

Darby nodded, staring into the fire. "That does sound great. What's the catch?"

Beamon didn't answer.

"The offer doesn't extend to me, does it? I'm too weird and unpredictable. Besides, they still need somebody to take the blame for Tristan." She looked up at him and saw the surprise on his face. "I'm a quick study, Mark. Did you take the deal?"

"Hell yeah. I told them where you're camped and then went straight to the Ferrari dealer." He smiled easily. "I told him I had to think about it."

"So what's the future hold for Darby Moore, Mark? Anything?"

Beamon tapped his front teeth with his beer bottle for a few moments. "You have some options. I can get you a fake passport that looks better than a real one and help you build a new identity. You can run, try to lose yourself. It's what you wanted, right?"

She continued to stare into the fire.

"Here's the downside. They'll never stop coming—remember Thailand? And no more climbing—it's the first place they'll look for you. No associating with your old friends, no going anywhere you might be recognized. You'd have to completely reinvent yourself. Maybe get a job as a stockbroker or something—wear blue suits, drive a BMW. Be a person they won't be looking for."

"Where does that leave you? I assume that part of your deal is to give me up?"

"That's my problem. Don't worry about it."

"You said I had options, plural."

Beamon nodded. "I might have found some leverage we can use. Think of it as a bomb that'll most likely blow up in our faces."

"What is it?"

"That's not important."

"What if it doesn't blow up in our faces?"

"There's a slim chance that it could send David Hallorin down in flames."

Darby scooted back and leaned against the tire of her truck, suddenly looking very tired again. "So what should I do?"

"I don't know, Darby . . . I wish I could help you with the decision, but I don't think one option is really better than the other. The question is, what do you *want* to do?"

She stuck a foot out and kicked a small log onto the fire. Beamon could feel the warmth on his face and hands as the flames rose.

"Let me give you a scenario, Mark. There's a lightning storm coming in. You're a thousand feet up on an exposed rock face. The leader you're belaying takes a fall and is unconscious, but the rope isn't long enough for you to lower him down. What would you do?"

He understood the point she was trying to make. She was telling him that she was completely lost in her current situation—she wanted his help. But it wasn't his call to make.

"I guess I'd ask you to give me an honest appraisal of my options, and make the decision myself."

She finished her beer in silence and nodded toward the six-pack sitting in the dirt next to him. He tossed her another one.

"Did you see that BMW driving in front of us on the highway when we were coming back here from D.C.?"

Beamon shook his head.

"The guy had personalized plates that said 320I or something . . ." Her voice trailed off as she opened her beer against one of the rocks in the fire ring.

"I don't think I'm following you," Beamon said.

"The guy went though all the trouble and cost of getting personalized plates and in the end, all he could think to put on them was the model number of his fancy car. That's it. That's all he had to say about his world . . . I guess what I'm trying to tell you is that I like my life. I don't think I'd fit into the BMW crowd."

"I want you to go into this with your eyes wide open, Darby. I'm pretty good at finding people. But this ambiguous political crap isn't where my talents lie—this is more Tom's thing."

"You're worried about him, aren't you?"

"What?"

"I think he's a good man. He's just having a bad time right now."

"Darby, let's try to focus here. I'm telling you that I'll most likely get us both killed."

"It's up to you, Mark. It sounds like Hallorin's given you the opportunity to walk away from this."

"I'm not going to hang you out to dry, Darby. You know that."

"Well then, I think we should stick a knife in that man and twist it."

Beamon leaned back in as far as the makeshift camping chair would let him and took a deep breath. The air temperature was dropping fast as the angle of the sunlight became more severe. He held up his beer in a toast. "Better to die on your feet than live on your knees, right?"

She smiled sadly and returned his salute.

51

"**J**esus Christ," Beamon muttered to himself, and sunk further into the leather seat of his rental car. Despite the fact that they were now a good hundred yards away, the press still completely filled his rear-view mirror. An enormous semicircle of vans, satellite dishes, and well-coiffed slugs with microphones had put Robert Taylor's northern Virginia home under siege. Thanks to a combination of erratic driving, sunglasses, and his still slightly swollen face, Beamon had successfully maneuvered his car through them without being recognized. Maybe his luck was finally changing.

He eased the car to a stop in front of a barricade set up in front of Taylor's driveway. It looked like the local police had done a fair job of keeping the Godless Hordes at bay, but Beamon was still reluctant to roll the window down and give someone with a telephoto lens an unobstructed view. He watched a tired, angry-looking cop come around the barricade and walk toward his car. The man's annoyance seemed to grow exponentially as he leaned down toward Beamon's closed window and rapped hard on it. Satisfied that the cop's body would block his face from any prying eyes, Beamon rolled the window down halfway.

"Sir, unless you have an appointment, I'm going to give you precisely two seconds to—"

Beamon lifted his sunglasses and stuck his hand through the half-open window, cutting the man off before he could finish his threat. "Mark Beamon."

The man shook it, looking increasingly confused. "Sure, I recognize you. But what are you doing here?"

"I need to talk to the senator—it's kind of an emergency. He doesn't know I'm coming."

The cop looked more than a little uncertain and glanced back at the surrounding press. "Jesus, Mr. Beamon. It's Election Day. I don't know . . . "

"He'll agree to the meeting—I can guarantee it. It just wasn't anything I could go into over the phone. You understand."

Now, that wasn't entirely true. He had initially tried to call Taylor's campaign headquarters in D.C., but found that it had been dismantled with uncharacteristic efficiency. In fact, it almost seemed as if it had never existed—which was probably the point. After that, he had made repeated calls to Taylor's home and had been told each time that the senator's calendar was completely filled for the foreseeable future and warned not to call again. He'd never even gotten high up enough to talk to someone he could effectively threaten.

So, here he was at the man's front door, prepared to start flashing unfortunate photographs if it became necessary. He hoped it wouldn't.

"Look, Mr. Beamon," the cop said nervously. "All I can do is let you through here." He pointed to the next set of barricades about seventy-five feet in front of them. "Then you'll have to talk to the senator's people."

"I'd thought our business was finished, Mr. Beamon," Robert Taylor said, moving through the clutter that dominated the small office at the back of his home.

His mode of dress had changed radically now that his bid for the presidency was over. The jeans and peach polo shirt had undoubtedly been carefully calculated to give him a healthy, relaxed look as he scrambled to maintain his power base. The effect was less than successful, though. For some reason, the absence of the gray suit and red tie that had been his uniform for the last thirty years made him look artificial. Like a naked doll.

"I thought this would interest you." Beamon walked forward and put one of the more impressive Prodigy photographs on his desk. The old man glanced down at it for a moment and then swept it into a drawer.

"I suppose that you think I should be grateful to you for wrestling the file away from David Hallorin," he said, keeping an impressive poker face as his mind undoubtedly raced to calculate his options. "But you're too late. It's done."

Beamon thought he seemed kind of aloof for a man with such a small penis, but decided to keep the observation to himself. "You're right, Senator. David Hallorin is going to be elected—there's no stopping it. But he doesn't ever have to take office."

"I see. You think you're going to take his place as my blackmailer." Taylor stood and leaned across his desk, using his bony fists for support. "You aren't as clever as your reputation leads one to believe. Blackmail isn't very effective when you're demanding that your victim expose himself, is it?" Taylor's voice was confident and heavy with contempt. "I can guarantee you one thing, Mr. Beamon. If the information in that file is ever released, I will deny that David Hallorin had anything to do with it and will do everything I can to make sure this comes to rest on your narrow shoulders. The prison time you are already facing will seem like nothing when I'm through. And I believe that I will still have enough power to see you moved from minimum security to a place where former FBI agents are less appreciated."

Of course, Beamon had assumed Taylor would take this tact, try to intimidate him. But it was a little late for that—he'd pretty much had it with this whole situation.

"Senator, if I was facing a man who had a collection of eight-by-tens depicting me with a rubber glove up some Girl Scout like she was a Thanksgiving turkey, I think I'd keep the threats to a minimum," Beamon said, falling into a chair and stretching his legs out in front of him.

Taylor's mouth opened, but no sound came out. If this weren't a more or less life-or-death situation for he and Darby, Beamon might have actually had a good time. The political elite were surprisingly easy to shut up when you refused to kiss their proffered asses.

"Get the hell out of here!" Taylor finally shouted. Apparently, it was the most clever retort he could muster without the aid of a speechwriter.

Beamon heard the door behind him open almost immediately and knew that it was a Secret Service man peeking in to see if everything was all right. Beamon ignored him. "I don't think I was clear in explaining the situation, Senator. That picture isn't from Hallorin's file—he still has that. You know how the government is—everything in duplicate."

The anger on Taylor's face melted into one of guarded suspicion. He waved the Secret Service agent away.

"It doesn't matter," Taylor mumbled as the door creaked shut behind him. "It doesn't change anything."

"David Hallorin knows I have this," Beamon lied. "How much do you think my life is worth right now? Enough that I'd care if you branded me a blackmailer?"

Taylor started to tremble visibly. His eyes darted back and forth, and his jaw moved in a strange chewing motion.

Beamon maintained a façade of complete calm and confidence. He tried to picture the Tom Sherman of five years ago and how he would have handled this situation.

"You're a great man, Senator," he said finally. "You've done more for this country—given more to this country—than almost anyone in history. Bring in your best people right now and start your spin machine. Get on television and tell the American people the truth. That David Hallorin used information in his possession against you. That in deference to your family and colleagues, you didn't want this to go public. But now you know you were wrong not to have come forward. Show them what you're willing to sacrifice for this country. You don't need to go into any specifics—I give you my word that the file I have will never be released. And after you've accused him, Hallorin will have to be very cautious about releasing anything that could prove him a blackmailer. Then you just fade into the background. The press won't expend much energy digging for thirty-five-year-old dirt on a retired senator. They'll be much more interested in crucifying Hallorin."

"And if I don't?"

Beamon took a deep breath. "Senator, I doubt I'd survive a Hallorin presidency. I imagine I'd have to use the information in the file to try to make a case against him."

Taylor sunk back deeper in his chair and ran a hand through his still thick hair. He looked like he was having difficulty controlling his breathing, and Beamon leaned forward, thinking that he might be in the early stages of a heart attack. Before he could stand, though, Taylor looked up at him. His eyes were clearer than Beamon had ever seen them.

"Last time we met," Taylor started, "you said that I had done what I'd done with my life solely in pursuit of personal power. You were wrong, Mr. Beamon. When I started in politics as a young man, I had a vision. But then the process takes hold. Pretty soon it's hard to differentiate between furthering your own personal interests and furthering the interests of the country. And every year that goes by, blurs that line a little more. I'm guilty of letting that happen. I admit it. But I've done what I've done because I love this country."

Beamon nodded as respectfully as he could and hoped Taylor would refrain from humming the National Anthem.

"David Hallorin played me, Mr. Beamon. Made me forget why I do what I do; made me into a man like he is. I should have never let any of this happen. I made mistakes as a young man. But I won't let this country pay for them."

"It's all been torn down and now it's up to us to rebuild it!"

David Hallorin couldn't see to the very ends of the auditorium—the red-white-and-blue crowd faded to gray and then to black as he looked out into the distance. The sound, though ... the sound: thousands of people cheering and shouting—but that was nothing. Insignificant. Silent were the millions of people all over the country—all over the world—watching his speech on television. Waiting for him to speak. Waiting for him to tell them where he was going to lead.

"It's been a difficult race. A surprising race. My opponents are both fine men with many good ideas. I look forward to working closely with them during my presidency as we take the world out of this recession and create a new, even more powerful nation."

He let the crowd's energy and admiration wash over him as they erupted and drown him out. This acceptance speech had been too long in coming. Years of planning and positioning, waiting for the inevitable downturn of the world economy. The file, the manufacturing plant, the unexpected benefit of Mark Beamon's Vericomm tapes had all come together at the right moment in history. He was finally where he had always deserved to be.

Hallorin called his running mate onto the stage and watched him and his wife walk out, waving wildly to the crowd. Hallorin shook the man's hand and kissed his wife on the cheek, then stepped back and gave him the podium. He could feel the eyes of his audience follow as he moved back against the wall and shook hands with the men and women who had run the various details of his campaign—under the watchful and anonymous eye of Roland Peck, of course.

He turned his gaze, but not his attention, to his running mate as the man started into the speech Peck had written for him. As always, it was perfect, maximizing the man's youth and energy, but respectful of both Hallorin and Robert Taylor.

Taylor.

It remained to be seen how much real power the GOP would let him keep, but so far they were moving cautiously. Taylor was enormously popular—perhaps more so than when he was the leading candidate. The speech Peck had prepared for Taylor's announcement that he was dropping out of the race was one of the best he had ever written. It had magically transformed Taylor into a man who cared more for the good of the country than partisanship and his own personal power and glory.

The other Prodigy casualties hadn't yet been contacted. Right now, most of them were locked in meetings with their own parties, planning how they could sabotage Hallorin's presidency and ensure that there would be never again be a threat from an independent presidential candidate. But they would change their direction quickly when they found out that he had the instrument of their personal and political destruction.

Their and Robert Taylor's unwavering support, combined with the desperation and weakness of the American people, would make him the most powerful president of the last hundred and fifty years.

52

The speed, floating glide, and leather smell of the rented Cadillac was a welcome change to Darby's smoke- and oil-belching pickup. Beamon leaned back, taking his eyes from the empty road, and watched the unmoving stars through the skylight. He reached out without looking and turned off NPR's endless speculation about the Hallorin White House and tried to let the night sky's calming influence sink into him.

Beamon tried to remember from his history and poli-sci courses in college what would happen. Had a president-elect ever gone to prison? He didn't think so. As far as he could remember, none had ever even stepped down before the inauguration.

Was there even a constitutional provision for this? Would there be a new election? Would Hallorin's VP get the Oval Office? Would the Democrats take it by default? Speaker of the House? The guy that empties the Capitol's dumpsters?

It didn't really matter. What did matter was that Taylor had decided— been forced—to do the right thing. When this shit hit the papers, Hallorin was going to have much bigger problems to deal with than an itinerant mountain climber and an out-of-work FBI agent. Beamon was really going to enjoy seeing that son of a bitch go down.

The fact that, to get all of this done, Robert Taylor had to disgrace himself and his family was a shame, really. Beamon wondered if the American people didn't ask the impossible of their elected officials. They demanded men and women who were willing to tell them what they wanted to hear instead of the truth, and they left anyone who dared broach a difficult or controversial subject in the center of the loser's circle. They created an atmosphere in which only people willing to give up their dignity to scrape full-time for campaign funds would have enough advertising dollars to brand themselves in the minds of the electorate. And then they turned around and demanded unwavering honesty and morality.

Beamon shook his head and flipped the radio back on, searching for a station playing music. Why was he thinking about this crap? At this point, all that mattered was David Hallorin being too busy with indictments to come after them.

Beamon turned onto the dirt road that was actually Sherman's driveway and sped along it, allowing the Cadillac to absorb the deep ruts and potholes. He looked to his left as he rounded the last curve, slowing to a crawl and trying unsuccessfully to see through the trees to where Darby was camped. He wished he could convince her to stay at the house, but understood her refusal.

It didn't matter, really. He'd given her his cell phone in case there was trouble, but there wouldn't be any—David Hallorin was still waiting for Beamon's counteroffer to his proposition. There was no way that son of a bitch would ever believe that Beamon would sacrifice himself for Darby Moore. Besides, he was undoubtedly busy drinking in the euphoria of his election win.

53

It was a little big, but she could probably burn it in half.

Darby grabbed the log by one end and started dragging it through the fallen leaves and tightly packed trees. She'd pretty much depleted the deadfall in the area surrounding the tiny clearing she'd camped in, and tomorrow she would have to take the truck down the road a ways and fill it up. At least it would give her something to do. All this helpless waiting was starting to drain the life out of her.

She dropped the log next to the fire ring she'd built and hurried off to find a few more. The cold late-fall sun was only inches from colliding with the distant hills to the west. It wouldn't be long before the streaks of light burning through the branches above her would fade, making firewood hunting an unproductive and treacherous job.

Besides, it was in that half-hour of perfect twilight that Tom Sherman wandered down the road to sit with her by the fire. They'd talk for an hour or so about nothing in particular. She'd reminisce about things she'd done, people she'd met, and he'd tell her about his daughter, speaking like she was still alive, or about his work.

It seemed, though, that no matter how happy a memory he conjured, it was never enough to lift the deep melancholy that surrounded him. It was as if he had suddenly realized that he'd wasted his life on things that didn't matter and had dismissed as irrelevant the things that really did. Regret was one thing she hoped she never had to suffer through. The fear, guilt, and rage she was struggling with would someday fade. But regret fed off time and only grew stronger.

Darby picked up a few sticks small enough for kindling and jogged back to her campsite. It'd be enough—she'd turn in early tonight, try to force herself to sleep.

For the first time in her life, it seemed that everything was beyond her control. Resigning herself to the fact that her future was being determined by men whose lives and motivations were a complete mystery to her was proving to be more difficult than she could have imagined. She knew Mark was doing everything he could, and despite his manic personality and confused ego, she trusted him. He was the kind of guy you tied your rope into without giving it a second thought. The problem was that she was used to leading.

There was no point in agonizing now, she reminded herself. She'd made her decision not to run, and even though it was based on hate and thoughts of revenge, it had been the right one. No regrets.

Finished with her twig and dried grass construction, she pulled out her lighter and tried to clear her mind. It was easier not to face the things she had been feeling lately. Denial—a bad habit she must have picked up from Mark.

She was about to flick the lighter to life when the sound of an engine came floating up to her. She leaned forward and peered through the trees for a moment as a Federal Express truck struggled up the poorly maintained dirt road leading to Tom Sherman's house. She turned her attention back to her kindling, but glanced up again when she heard the engine slow.

The truck started picking up speed again almost immediately, and as it moved past, revealed a man standing at the far edge of the road. Darby leaned forward and squinted, thinking for a moment that it was just a trick of the deepening shadows and the trees partially blocking her view. But then the figure darted into the woods and disappeared.

54

Beamon leaned over the kitchen counter and looked out into the living room at Tom Sherman. He hadn't moved in over an hour except to take a few mindless pulls from the drink in his hand. He just sat there in front of the fire, staring.

Six months ago, when Beamon had first noticed the changes in his friend, he'd thought it was a little bizarre. Then, after some time had passed, he'd thought it was kind of sad. Now, though, it was starting to piss him off. The man had let himself become completely paralyzed just when Beamon needed his help most.

He wished he could bring himself to call Carrie. She'd be able to tell him how to snap Tom out of whatever it was that had a hold of him. Or better yet, send over a few magic pills that could wake him up for a few days. But he'd closed that door, and it was better to just leave it shut.

Beamon grabbed his beer off the counter and peered through the oven's window at the frozen pizza starting to bubble inside. He and Darby were on their own in this thing now. All he could hope for was that Taylor would do what he said he would and the whole thing wouldn't blow up in their faces.

The doorbell sounded just as Beamon was reaching for a pair of oven mitts. He looked behind him through the kitchen door as Tom Sherman slowly rose from his chair and started toward the front of the house. Had they locked Darby out? He didn't think so. Beamon leaned further over the counter, but Sherman was already down the hall and out of sight. He slid his hand over the back of his sweater and felt the hard outline of his pistol. Paranoid, he thought to himself as he started for the front of the house. He really was starting to get paranoid.

Beamon paused for a moment when the phone started to ring, but then continued around the corner as his friend pulled the door open.

There was no one there.

He tensed, reaching for his gun again, but then spotted the FedEx driver walking back toward the driveway. There was already one box on the porch, and by the time Beamon made it to the front door, the driver was digging around in his truck for another.

Beamon didn't follow his friend onto the porch, instead staying just inside the doorway as the driver struggled up the steps with the second box and laid it down on top of the other one. Sherman didn't seem concerned—he'd already looked at the labels and obviously recognized the return address.

The deliveryman smiled politely and bobbed his head as he held out an electronic clipboard.

"Thank you," Sherman said, taking and signing it. The man's response was another silent head bob.

When Sherman handed back the clipboard, the deliveryman took a step back, but didn't return to his truck. He still hadn't uttered a word.

Beamon chewed at his lip, concentrating on the man. There was something not right—he seemed to be making a conscious effort not to speak. "You. Say something."

"Mark! Look out!"

Beamon jumped out onto the porch at the sound of Darby's shout and grabbed for his gun. Unfortunately, he instinctively went for it with his right hand, which was attached to an arm that still wasn't in working condition. By the time he had his fingers around the pistol's grip, the deliveryman had a 9mm aimed at his chest and another man was crashing through the trees at the edge of the clearing with Darby firmly attached to his back.

Beamon had no choice but to go completely still as the man in front of him stepped back to give himself a wider view. "I'm still watching you, Mr. Beamon," he warned, shifting a little to allow him to better see his partner, who was struggling to unwrap Darby's arms and legs from around his torso. The accent was Russian, or if not, no more than a solid two iron from the Russian border.

Beamon suddenly realized he wasn't breathing, but couldn't seem to muster the concentration to start again. Ignoring the gun aimed at him, he turned and locked his eyes helplessly on Darby. Despite the much larger man's efforts, she had tightened her grip on him over the past few seconds, and now had her feet locked together over his stomach. Her left forearm had worked its way under the man's chin and she was using her right hand to sink it in deeper.

To Beamon, they seemed to be moving in slow motion as the man finally tired of trying to shake her loose and aimed his pistol back over his shoulder at the girl's head.

"Darby! Let go!" Beamon shouted, but she didn't seem to hear. His teeth clenched shut hard enough for him to hear them grind as Darby jerked away from the barrel of the pistol and arched her back wildly, pulling with everything she had on the man's neck. Even with the distance between them, Beamon could see the ropelike muscles and tendons suddenly coil across her bare forearms. What caused the dull popping sound, though, he wasn't sure of until the man's knees suddenly went slack and he crumpled to the ground on top of her. Darby laid there for a second or so, then suddenly scooted out from under the dead body like it was burning her.

The man with the gun trained on Beamon calmly muttered something in Russian. His face was devoid of emotion as he recalculated his plan in light of his partner's untimely death.

Beamon had been in a number of gunfights during his career—way too many, in fact. He'd lived through most of them more by luck and the stupidity of his opponent than anything else. Unfortunately, neither one of those things looked like it was going to work for him today. This guy was clearly a professional—probably one of the surviving dinosaurs of the KGB who had chucked their political philosophy and embraced capitalism a little too zealously.

"Come here," the Russian called to Darby.

Beamon glanced over at Tom Sherman as she approached. He looked completely brain-locked.

Darby stopped only a few feet from the Russian and stared him directly in the eye. The remorse and horror that Beamon had expected to see in her wasn't there. If she felt anything about killing that man, it didn't show.

"And who might you be?" the Russian said quietly, his eyes moving smoothly from one captive to another and then along the treeline.

She just stood there, glaring at him.

"Is there anyone else out there?"

She shook her head but still didn't speak.

When he nodded toward his dead partner lying on the grass, uncertainty was hanging at the edges of his eyes. "You get involved with very dangerous women, Mr. Beamon. Youstav was actually quite good at what he did." The Russian motioned Darby toward Beamon and the statuelike Tom Sherman with the barrel of his pistol. "If you wouldn't mind, young lady, I'd like you to very slowly bring me your friend's gun. Butt first, please."

Darby relieved him of his pistol as ordered and handed it grudgingly over to the Russian.

"Thank you," he said politely, turning to Tom Sherman as he stuffed Beamon's gun in his waistband. "I'm here for a file. I believe you know the one of which I speak?"

Sherman didn't seem to hear.

"It's inside," Beamon cut in when the Russian started to look a little put out.

"Good. Fine. We're going to go get it and then you're going to help me carry some valuables out of the house to my truck."

This wasn't good. Not at all.

"That's a union job," Beamon said, trying to buy a little time to think. "Last thing I need is trouble with the union."

The man smiled and tossed him a pair of handcuffs. "I wouldn't want to see you get in any trouble, Mr. Beamon. Why don't you handcuff yourself to the railing? I think Mr. Sherman and the young lady will be enough help."

Beamon started to feel a slight pain in his lower lip where he'd been chewing on it. He was screwed—and what made it really fucking intolerable was that he'd done it to himself. "This botched robbery thing is a bit over the top with three deaths, isn't it?" he said, attaching one side of the handcuffs to the railing and the other to his wrist with comic slowness. He was just stalling now and it was obvious.

"I'm a little embarrassed about that, Mr. Beamon, particularly with you here," the Russian said, starting to herd a seething Darby Moore and nearly comatose Tom Sherman back into the house. "Normally I wouldn't have taken this kind of last-minute job, but the money . . . " His voice trailed off for a moment, leaving his paycheck to Beamon's imagination. "All I can say in my defense is that this mimics the MO of a man who was recently released from prison, and whom I can guarantee doesn't have an alibi for this evening." With that explanation, they disappeared through the door and left him handcuffed to the depressingly sturdy railing.

When they reappeared ten minutes later, Beamon's mind was still a hopeless blank.

"In the box, please," the Russian said. Sherman tore open one of the boxes on the porch, placed the Prodigy file in it, and then covered the file with the pricey knick knacks Darby had brought out.

"Okay," the Russian said. "Just a few more of the bigger things—electronics and the like, and that will be all."

Beamon didn't like the sound of "that will be all." He yanked uselessly on the handcuffs as they disappeared into the house again, struggling to come up with something that would save their asses.

They reappeared with Sherman's television and part of his stereo system, just as the wind picked up and started to create a sad wail in the trees. Beamon watched helplessly as they crossed the dirt path to the FedEx truck and piled the stuff in the back. That was it, they'd had it.

As the Russian led Darby and Sherman back toward the house, Beamon noticed that the gusting wind had diminished, but the wail had grown louder. The Russian obviously made the same observation and froze at the bottom of the steps. It took only a few moments to become clear that it wasn't the wind. It was a siren. No, it was multiple sirens.

Sherman seemed to come fully awake for the first time in weeks when he saw the Russian's momentary distraction. He suddenly lunged at him, grabbing his gun hand and swinging wildly at his head.

"Tom! No!" Beamon shouted, throwing himself forward, only to be snapped back by the handcuffs.

There was no chance—there never had been. The Russian was far too fast and much too strong. He slipped the punch easily and paused for the briefest moment, seeing in Tom Sherman's eyes the same thing Beamon had—that he'd never expected to win.

Darby and Beamon both jumped at the sound of the pistol firing and watched Sherman topple back onto the stairs.

"Oh, my God, oh, my God," Darby cried as she dropped to her knees and pressed a hand against Sherman's wound, trying to stop the blood that was already flowing down his sides and through the cracks in the wood porch. "You . . . You son of a bitch! You shot him!"

Beamon focused on the Russian as he tried to get his mind back online. The sirens were getting louder and a hint of nervousness was becoming visible through the Russian's icy façade.

"Sound carries funny out here," Beamon managed to get out of his constricted throat. "Those sirens aren't far away—I'd say they've already turned up the only road in or out of here. You'll have to get out on foot."

He could tell that the Russian wasn't completely buying this—he was probably thinking that the cops were just chasing a local drunk. Fortunately, Darby was tracking on the conversation as she tried to stop Sherman's life from leaking all over the porch. She reached a bloody hand under her sweater and threw Beamon's cell phone down on the steps. "I called them, you bastard. Now maybe you'll get to find out what it's like to be shot."

The Russian looked up at the house for a moment, and then back at the treeline.

"They probably heard the gun," Beamon said, talking quickly. "And if they get here and find everyone dead, they'll be coming after you. You'll have a hundred rednecks who've been hunting this country for their entire lives all over these woods. And every one of them will have a rifle and a dog."

"Your proposal?" the Russian said. The sirens were getting loud now.

"I don't care about you—you're just a hired gun. And I'm sure as hell not going to send a bunch of local cops to their deaths chasing a pro. I don't want their blood on my hands."

The Russian looked at his fallen companion for a moment and then freed Beamon from the cuffs. They ran together toward the dead man and dragged him back to the base of the steps leading to Sherman's porch. The Russian dropped his gun next to the body and started backing away, covering Beamon with his own .357.

Once he'd disappeared into the trees, Beamon dropped down and pulled Darby's hand from Sherman's wound, replacing it with his own. "Get out of here, Darby! The cops can't find you here. Go back to your truck, and when they've all passed by, drive out. Call me on my cell phone later."

"No!" she said in a voice thick with emotion. "I can't! I can't just leave him—"

"There'll be an ambulance here in a five minutes. Go!"

Beamon pressed down a little harder on his friend's wound and felt the blood bubble up between his fingers as he watched Darby run for the trees. The cops were close now; the crunch of skidding tires was becoming audible beneath the scream of the sirens.

Sherman's eyes were half open and cleared a bit when he saw Beamon hovering over him. "I told you you were wasting your time," he choked out. "Hallorin wins."

Beamon shook his head slowly, feeling the rage building up inside of him. "Not Hallorin. He didn't know about the other file. And that son of a bitch was Russian."

Sherman's laugh was weak and humorless. "Robert Taylor. Your knight in shining armor."

He lost consciousness just as the first police car came skidding to a stop and two cops trained their guns on them.

"Fuck!" Beamon screamed suddenly. Robert Taylor. He was going to find that geriatric piece of shit and cut his heart out for this.

"I dislocated my shoulder a couple of weeks ago and I didn't think I had that much strength left," Beamon said, finding it hard to concentrate on the story he'd concocted.

The cop shrugged and leaned over the body to more closely examine the odd bend to its neck. "No big loss as I see it."

Fifty feet from them, two paramedics were hefting a stretcher containing Tom Sherman into the back of an ambulance. A few moments later, it was picking its way carefully but quickly down the dirt road toward the highway.

"So you say he heard the siren . . . " the cop prompted.

"Yeah. He'd made us help him carry out valuables and put them in the truck. What he didn't know was that I'd been on the phone . . . "

"The woman who called us. She didn't tell us her name."

"She's an old friend from college," Beamon lied. "I was talking to her when the doorbell rang. Told her to hold on and I put the phone down on the counter. She must have heard what was going on."

The sheriff scratched his head, seeing no compelling reason to dispute the rather unlikely story. "You're a lucky man, Mr. Beamon,"

Beamon nodded his agreement. Damn lucky. "Anyway, when he heard the sirens, he was distracted for a second. Tom was closest to him and . . . "

"The gun went off."

Beamon nodded. "I was too late. I knocked it out of his hand and got him around the neck. Like I said, looks like I got a little overzealous . . . "

"Matter of opinion," the man said. He apparently liked Tom Sherman and seemed to think that Beamon had been just zealous enough.

Beamon allowed his mind to wander for a few moments as the cop broke off from him and walked around, looking for nothing in particular.

There was no one to blame but himself for this. He'd underestimated Taylor, and now his best friend was lying in an ambulance, most likely dying. Sherman had been right. They were all the same—Hallorin, Taylor, whoever. After twenty some years in the cynical service of the government and now facing a trumped-up felony charge for the convenience of the Beltway elite, he had no excuse for not seeing this coming.

He couldn't seem to stop his anger and hatred from continuing to build, and he had to struggle to keep it off his face as the cop came full circle and leaned over the body again. "Trouble just seems to follow you around, doesn't it, Mr. Beamon?"

55

Through the back window of the tiny Japanese compact, Beamon could see two shadows moving through the parking garage. They were coming in his general direction so, for what seemed like the fiftieth time, he laid down in the cramped backseat and wedged himself between the doors. The pain in his shoulder was nearly unbearable as he tried to keep himself hidden, and that just fed his anger. It was 7:30. Where was that dumb bitch? Quitting time was two fucking hours ago.

He hadn't been to the D.C. hospital Tom Sherman had been transferred to—though he knew things looked bad. He'd told himself over and over that it wasn't his fault, that Sherman had fucked up bad and then fallen apart—a poor combination. Logic wasn't working for him any more than it had for Darby, though. The truth was that Tom Sherman had saved his ass more times than he could count and when, for the first time in their long friendship, Tom had needed help, he ended up shot.

There was nothing Beamon could do to change that now, though. All he could do was hit back.

Another half an hour went by with Beamon in an only slightly more comfortable position. It was fairly dark in this part of the parking garage—he'd made sure of that by strategically knocking out a few lights before he'd broken into the car. That, in combination with the fact that the car's rearview mirror was now in pieces on the floorboard, ought to be enough to suit his purpose.

When the echoing click of dress shoes became audible, he lifted his head slightly and peered out the rear window. At first, all he could see was a shadow moving in his direction. The figure slowly gained detail and color as it got closer, finally taking on the slightly pudgy female shape of his victim. It was about goddamn time.

He remained completely still as the woman approached and jabbed at the lock in the semidarkness. He could see her perfectly through the side window—attractive in a slightly disheveled, businesslike manner, with hair cut into a practical bob and large wire-frame glasses.

He followed her with his eyes as she ducked into the car, not noticing the missing rearview mirror until she had closed her door and was reaching up to adjust it. From the side, Beamon could see the confusion cross her face and then change to terror when he sat up and stuck the barrel of Tom Sherman's .38 in the back of her head.

"Oh, my God," she said in a panicked voice. "Please. Take what ever you want. I—"

"Shut the fuck up," Beamon said, his mood continuing to darken. She tried to turn her head, but he put a stop to that by moving the gun barrel to her cheek, which was billowing in and out with her short, desperate breaths.

He hadn't seen her in years. It seemed impossible, but she looked precisely the same. In fact, he was pretty sure she had been wearing the same oddly colored pantsuit the last time they'd run into each other.

Helen Block wasn't the sleaziest reporter he'd ever met, neither was she the most respectable. What he remembered about her was her drive and the fact that she was incredibly bright. Her star had continued to rise at the *Washington Post* as his at the Bureau had fallen. All in all, she had just the right combination of qualities to make this happen. A perfect instrument with which to inflict pain.

"You think you're about to have the worst night of your life," Beamon said, reaching onto the floorboard and grabbing hold of Tom Sherman's copy of the Prodigy file. He dropped it next to her on the passenger seat. "But you couldn't be more wrong."

He could see her straining with her eyes to see what he'd passed up to her, but she still couldn't move her head because of the gun. Even in the gloom Beamon could see her shaking. He started to feel a little guilt marring the perfection of his anger when a tear started to well up in her eye.

"Don't do that," he said, backing the gun off a little. He held out a small penlight to her. "Take it," he said. "Have a look."

She reached slowly for the light.

"I don't have all fucking night. Take it. Don't make me shoot you."

A moment later, she was clawing through the open file in her lap—more to please her captor than anything else. It wasn't long, though, before her fear started to fade and she began looking more carefully at the documents he had given her. A few more minutes and she seemed to have forgotten he was there entirely, the silence in the car only occasionally broken by the crackle of turning pages and the quiet grunts and squeals escaping her throat. Beamon leaned back and lit a cigarette in the clean-smelling car. Either because of the file or the gun, she didn't protest.

"Are these real?" she said finally. He could tell from her voice that she already knew the answer to his question.

"What do you think?"

"Where did you get them?" she asked, looking straight through the windshield at the concrete wall in front of the car.

"I used to be an FBI agent."

"I know you, don't I?" There was recognition in her tone, but he could tell that she hadn't figured it out yet. They hadn't known each other very well—it was one of the reasons he'd picked her.

"You don't want to know me."

She nodded her understanding. "Why are you showing me this?"

"I'm not showing it to you. I'm giving it to you. You go get yourself whatever experts you need to confirm that it's all legit. Then print it. All of it."

She looked down at the photos and memos that were now spilling over her lap onto the passenger seat and shook her head. "Jesus Christ, man. This is beautiful. Do you have any idea—"

Beamon pulled the handle on the back door, the sound cutting her off in mid-sentence.

"Wait!"

"You don't need me. It's all right there." He stepped out into the quiet parking garage, but didn't immediately shut the door. "How much you get for a Pulitzer these days?"

"Five grand," she said without thinking.

56

The nudity was blacked out, David Hallorin saw, but the face of young Robert Taylor was clearly visible. The photograph was a full eight-by-ten, reproduced in its original garish color on the first page of a special section of the *Washington Post*. According to the exhaustive text that made up the rest of the page, the photo, as well as the FBI memos and surveillance data that had accompanied it, had been reviewed by three independent experts from different corners of the country. All were in agreement as to authenticity.

It wasn't just Taylor, though—almost all of the file was there. Not the data on the few men who had already admitted to their crimes over the years, not the ones who had never risen from obscurity, but the rest. The rest were all there.

The gentle rocking of the van as it weaved through D.C.'s crowded streets usually had a calming effect on him, but today it was making him feel nauseated. Hallorin wadded up the paper in a single violent motion and threw it to the floorboards. He leaned against the side window and covered his eyes with his hand.

It had all been perfect. The meeting yesterday with the Republican leadership had gone even better than he'd hoped. Hallorin had made sure that everyone knew exactly who he was—the next president of the United States—and Robert Taylor had played the loyal lapdog.

It had been exquisite. The men who had spent their careers trying to tear him down, to discredit him, to strip him of the power that was right-fully his, had been completely off balance, fearing for their political lives.

They had treated him as the new leader of the country and a man who now had the ability to crush them under his heel if he should find it necessary.

Today he had risen at five-thirty to make final preparations for his meeting with the Democratic leadership and his former Democratic opponent. There, he was to play a different game—moderating his positions, deferring to their weak leadership. They were panicked, desperate for any crumb of control he saw fit to throw them, and he could have used that to his advantage.

But not anymore.

Hallorin let his hand slide from his face, looking past a terrified Roland Peck, into the flat light of early morning Washington. It had changed—he could already feel it. Something had altered in the city's tempo. The traffic was strangely light, as though the people who inhabited the city and kept the government limping along had decided to stay away. As if they had decided to lock themselves in the hallucinatory safety of their suburban homes and insulate themselves from the electricity of anticipation and dread that had jolted the country.

Hallorin picked up the cellular phone next to him and hit the RECALL button as the driver maneuvered the van smoothly through the downtown traffic as he did every day. As though nothing had happened.

And in a sense, nothing had. Yet. None of the men implicated by the file had come forward, despite the seriousness of the allegations against them. CNN was just picking up the story—no fancy graphics or historical musings yet—just paraphrasing the text they'd found in the *Post*. No foreign reaction at all.

"Have you gotten through to Taylor yet?" Hallorin said when his private secretary picked up the line.

"I left another message, sir, but no call back yet. I'll patch him through the minute—"

"Call him again."

"Sir, I just hung up the phone—"

"I said call him again, goddammit!"

"Yes, sir, I'll—"

He hung up before she could finish her sentence and tried to will his heart to slow down. Until now, the former Republican candidate had jumped at Hallorin's every word. Now he wouldn't return calls. What was he doing? What was he planning?

It was almost certain that Taylor would think that he was responsible for this, that he'd released the file after using it to force him from the race. To Taylor it would make sense: part of Hallorin's plan to tear down what was left of the government and improve his own standing. Was Taylor contacting the others? Would they put aside partisanship and combine forces against him?

Hallorin hadn't spoken since he entered the van, knowing how his silence affected Peck, using it to punish him. But now, he had to talk, to know what had happened, to create a contingency plan. He *would* be the fourty-fourth president of the United States. And he would do whatever had to be done to ensure that.

"How, Roland?"

Peck didn't answer immediately, apparently startled by Hallorin's sudden break from silence.

"How?" Hallorin repeated.

"Sherman. Tom Sherman," Peck said, finally.

"What?"

"Tom Sherman. He was one of Hoover's most trusted aides during the time the data for Prodigy was being collected. It's hard to tell how much power he had because he was too young at the time for Hoover to give him any kind of meaningful title. Far too young. But it is my understanding that even when he was only in his early thirties, his power at the FBI couldn't have been overestimated."

Hallorin remembered meeting Tom Sherman years ago when Sherman was the associate director of the FBI. He'd come away with the impression that the quiet, unassuming bureaucrat was probably one of the most dangerous men he'd ever shaken hands with—a seemingly impossible combination of Boy Scout and calculating son of a bitch. And to make him even more of a threat, Sherman had a personal fortune that rivaled his own. The man was untouchable. Hallorin had been ecstatic when Sherman retired.

"You think he had a duplicate file?" Hallorin shook his head. "Why Sherman? It could have been anyone from that era of the Bureau."

Peck held out a piece of paper. Hallorin wiped away the sweat oozing from his palms and reached for it.

"You're looking at a police report from Manassas, Virginia, where Tom Sherman owns a home. Three days ago he was shot in what looked like a burglary attempt."

Hallorin dropped the paper to the floor. "What does that have to do with the file? Who—"

"Mark Beamon was there," Peck cut in, speaking in his customarily clipped sentences. "He killed the man that attacked them. That man still hasn't been identified. It's too much to be a coincidence. Too much. Besides, anyone else who was close to Hoover is either dead or too old to orchestrate something like this. It makes sense—if any one party had gotten ahold of the file, he could have used the duplicate original to cancel out the effect."

Hallorin slammed a fist into the van's side window, creating a visible crack that ran all the way across. "How could you have missed all this, Roland? How?"

"I—"

"Shut up! Where is he now? Can we get to him?"

Peck shook his head, his lower lip quivering perceptibly. "There's no need to, David. Everything is going to be fine. I swear. I swear. My sources say he's in a coma. That he won't survive."

Hallorin fell silent, trying to sort out what had happened and where it was leading them. Over a fucking cliff.

"I've met Sherman," he said, when he was calm enough to speak again. "Based on what I know about him, I believe that he would have made the duplicate file. But why would he dump it to the press? He's too smart for that—he wouldn't give up his leverage that easily. What's he playing at?"

Peck's face curled into what, for him, passed as a smile. "According to the *Post* article, the press received the file from an anonymous informant the day *after* Sherman was shot."

Hallorin thought about that for a moment. "Mark Beamon."

"Friends for twenty years. I think that we have to assume Tom Sherman is the man we've been looking for—the man who hired Beamon." The smile on Peck's face widened, revealing his stunted teeth. "Sherman had just been shot—by whom and on whose orders I still don't know. Under those circumstances, what would a man like Mark Beamon do? Perhaps he would think that this is a fitting epitaph for his friend?"

"But he's left himself with nothing," Hallorin said.

"Exactly. He's all alone now. If we destroy our copy of the file, it's like it never existed. Anyone trying to trace the *Post*'s anonymous informant will end up at Mark Beamon's door. But don't worry, David. We'll get to him before that."

"Fuck Beamon!" Hallorin shouted suddenly, turning all his anger and frustration on Peck. "We have to get to Taylor or he'll bring all this down! I won't allow that, Roland. I won't allow this to fall apart now."

"You don't have anything to worry about from Taylor, Senator. Nothing. Your position is still strong. Taylor won't do anything overt. Succumbing to blackmail would make him look weak and unpatriotic. Revenge is too expensive for a man like him. You're holding the cards, Senator. You are. You have the power and influence to support Taylor now. There's still time to prove to him that you had nothing to do with this. Once Mark Beamon is taken care of, there will nothing in your way. You will be the next president. No one can stop you. No one."

57

"This is kind of surreal," Darby said, slowing her truck to a crawl in the struggling traffic.

Beamon looked through the dirty windows at the people who inhabited this upscale section of D.C. They seemed directionless, dazed. Small knots formed and dispersed with no apparent pattern or rhythm, and the usually respected boundary between the sidewalk and the road had become muddled. Washington, D.C., looked like it had become a parade route for the walking dead.

"Take your next left," Beamon said, closing his eyes to block out the scene around him and the intense sunlight that seemed to be reaching through his eyes and driving an ice pick into his head. "The hospital's only a couple more miles."

"I'm really sorry about your friend," Darby said for what must have been the tenth time. "He's such a nice man."

"Yeah. He is." Beamon intentionally crafted his tone to cut off the possibility of any further conversation. On the afternoon commemorating the biggest fuckup of his—or anybody else's—life, he was having a hard time conjuring up the energy for chitchat.

He had hoped the drive from Manassas to the D.C. trauma unit that now kept what was left of Tom Sherman alive would give him a chance to think. And it had—by the time they were halfway there, he'd already come to more conclusions than he'd wanted to. After more than a year of constant effort, he hadn't changed. He'd allowed himself to be blinded by rage; to consider only himself and his own passion for revenge. For a man who had based his career on futile gestures, this would undoubtedly be remembered as his crowning achievement.

When Beamon opened his eyes again, Darby was pulling into an out of the way space in the lot behind the Georgetown University Medical Center. She jumped out almost immediately—probably anxious to get away from her passenger. He hadn't exactly been a barrel of laughs over the last three hours.

"You coming, Mark?"

He didn't move. He'd spent the last four days avoiding this hospital, and wasn't sure what he was he doing there now. David Hallorin had probably surmised by now that Beamon wasn't seriously interested in the job as his security chief and would undoubtedly have people looking for them there.

"This isn't such a good idea, Darby. Maybe we should—"

"No way, Mark." Darby walked around the car and pulled his door open. "You've got to do this. I know it's hard, but he's your best friend. If anyone spots us here, you'll just have to figure something out."

She was right and he knew it. It wasn't the possibility of being picked up by his growing list of enemies that was bothering him. It was seeing the vegetable that used to be his mentor and friend. As much as he wanted to forget the image of the depressed and weakened Tom Sherman of the past few months, he didn't want to replace it with the image of a breathing corpse full of tubes and needles.

"He isn't going to know if I came or not," Beamon said.

"But you will. Five years from now what will you think of yourself if you didn't even bother to go see him before he . . . " She let her voice trail off.

"I'd think that I didn't want to remember that my stupidity killed my best friend."

Darby leaned in, unbuckled his seat belt, and pulled him from the truck. He didn't bother to resist. "Remember what you told me about Tristan, Mark? When I was wallowing in guilt for leaving him up there on that butte? You told me he was a big kid and knew what he was getting himself into. That it wasn't my fault. Maybe it's time you give yourself the same break."

Beamon leaned against the truck and looked down at her. She was wearing a blue baseball cap with *Access Fund* written across it and a pair of dark sunglasses. On the surface, it wasn't much of a disguise, but combined with the deeper changes that had taken place in her over the past month it was surprisingly effective. He couldn't pinpoint exactly what was different about her—maybe a subtle shift in the way she stood, or the way she held her head, or the curve of her mouth. Whatever it was, she had hardened. The slightly naïve and philosophical girl that he'd read about and who had still been hanging on in Thailand seemed to slip away more and more every day.

"Okay. You win, Darby. Lead on."

Tom Sherman's private room was at the end of a wide, depressing corridor. As they approached, it became apparent that their progress was being closely monitored by two men standing on either side of the door leading into Sherman's room.

"Hang back a little, Darby, and keep your eyes open," Beamon said, continuing cautiously up the hall.

"Can I help you?" one of the men said, stepping forward and blocking Beamon's path. His partner kept a calm but well-focused eye on Darby.

"I'm here to see Tom Sherman," Beamon said, sizing up the two men. Not cops and certainly not attached to the hospital. These guys had the look and feel of pros. He calculated about a sixty-five percent chance that both had spent some time in the Secret Service. "Who the hell are you?"

The man in front of him ignored his question and, despite the fact that Beamon was fairly certain he'd already been recognized, asked for ID. Beamon shrugged and pulled out his wallet, handing the man his driver's license. "Who hired you guys?" Once again, his question was ignored.

"Okay, Mr. Beamon," he said finally, handing back the ID. "Go ahead."

Beamon thumbed over his shoulder at Darby. "She's with me."

"Fine, sir."

Beamon walked the final few feet to the closed door and put his hand on the knob. He stopped there for a moment, taking slow, deep breaths and trying to visualize his friend lying motionless on a stark white bed wired to various monitors and bags of fluid, waiting for death. His hope was that the preview would lessen the impact of the real thing.

He must have looked like he wasn't going to continue on, because Darby reached around him, closed her hand on his, and turned the knob.

"Don't just stand there," Tom Sherman said. "Close the goddamn door."

He was sitting up in bed surrounded by open newspapers and looking much healthier than a man in an irreversible coma had a right to. Beamon opened his mouth to speak, but found it impossible to make a sound through the tangle of emotions surging through him. Confusion became relief, then shock, followed closely by something that may have been joy.

He was still trying to process what was going on when Darby kicked the door shut and ran to the bed. Sherman dropped the paper he had been reading and accepted a gentle hug from her. "Tom! They said you were dying!"

He adjusted his half-glasses on his nose as she pulled away and looked over them at her with a warm smile. "I'm sorry about that, Darby. It was a little exaggeration. Unfortunately necessary."

The change in the timbre of Sherman's voice was obvious the moment he had opened his mouth. There was no trace of the uncertainty and depression he'd sunk into. The controlled, authoritative tone and confident expression that had intimidated FBI agents and criminals for decades was back.

Sherman adjusted his gaze, still looking over the tops of his eyeglasses. "Mark Beamon," he said coldly. "I was wondering if you were ever going to come for a visit." He held up the newspaper he was holding for a moment and then set it aside. "An impressive piece of work. The Dow is off twenty-two. That's not points, that's *percent*, you moron."

Beamon looked at the floor and repositioned his feet uncomfortably. The silence spread out before him for almost a minute. Finally he couldn't take it anymore. "Tom, I didn't—"

"You didn't what, Mark?" Sherman said, cutting him off. "You didn't think? Foreign investment is flooding out of the country. The dollar took the worst one-day drop in history. You may remember that it wasn't strong to start with. The American people have spent the last three years being beaten down by the economy. Confidence in the government is at an all-time low and the front-runner in the presidential election dropped out at the last minute. The country was hanging on by a thread, Mark. Did it ever occur to you that maybe, just maybe, it wasn't the time to *pull out the scissors?*"

"They shot you, Tommy. What was I supposed to do? Let them walk? It wasn't even Hallorin, it was Taylor. They're all—"

"Taylor? *Of course* it was Taylor! Let me guess: you walked into his office, showed him the duplicate file and demanded that he expose himself and point a finger at Hallorin? Then what? He said he would, right?

Said that he'd been wrong to let his own personal problems get in the way of America's bridge to the goddamn future."

"Well, yeah. I figured he had no choice. . . . " Beamon stuttered, amazed at how truly stupid it sounded when his friend said it out loud.

"Well," Sherman continued. "That was a sublime piece of maneuvering, wasn't it? Do you want to know the real reason why I didn't come directly to you on this? Why you, with all that brainpower, never made it past middle management?"

The fact was, he really didn't. But the question seemed to be rhetorical.

"Because giving you any real power would be like giving a child matches. The real world is one big compromise, Mark. That's how you improve the big picture: compromise. Have you ever once stepped back to take a look at the big picture?"

God, he wanted a cigarette. "I thought you were dying, Tom. I—"

"Mark, you may have done more damage to America than any single person in history. Without the confidence of the rest of the world, this is just an oversized, English-speaking country."

Beamon finally held up his hands. "Okay, Tommy, enough. Your point is made. I screwed up. But I should have goddamn well never been put in this position—I'm not a fucking politician. I find people, remember? That's it—the big picture is your thing. But you fell apart, didn't you? You left me twisting in the wind."

As always, Sherman's face remained completely impassive, but when he spoke again, his voice had lost some of its angry resonance. "Touché."

"Maybe we can still bring him down," Beamon said. "I don't have much, but maybe we can find a way to use it against Hallorin. . . . "

Sherman shook his head as Darby came over and pushed some pillows up behind him. He grabbed her hand briefly in thanks before she retreated to her corner again.

"You're hopeless, Mark. You still haven't thought through the impact of what you've done, have you?" He slid his glasses fully onto his nose again and picked up his newspaper. "There's only one man who can save the country now."

58

It was the third time in a month that Beamon had found himself standing in David Hallorin's office—but this time was different. The uncertainty and vague sense of dread was still there, of course, but there was also relief. The sense of uneasy peace that came from knowing that this wasn't his show. He was just silent backup now.

Physically, Tom Sherman still looked like death. He followed Beamon in, walking with difficulty toward one of the high-backed chairs in front of Hallorin's desk, and sat with such painful slowness that Beamon had to force himself not to reach out and help.

The scene playing out in front of him would have been funny under different circumstances. Tom Sherman's pale, drawn face and weak body looked so small and pathetic when compared with Hallorin's carefully tanned skin and six and a half feet of solid mass. The senator's advantage was more apparent than real, though, and Beamon could see caution work its way into the mask he always wore. It seemed impossible, but the next president of the United States was afraid of the broken little man in front of him. And Tom Sherman knew it.

With his friend sagging safely in a chair, Beamon stepped back and tried to disappear into the wall like the loyal political aides he'd seen at the Vericomm hearings. He wasn't quite as smooth, but it seemed to work—Hallorin had already forgotten he was there.

Roland Peck, though, didn't have his boss's gift for dismissal. He'd managed to keep his seat, but his head was jerking from side to side, eyes flashing with an undecipherable flood of emotions. Every few seconds his gaze would dart in Beamon's direction and each time he looked strangely startled.

Beamon edged a little closer to Peck, unable to predict what the man would do in this situation. When he had closed the distance between them to a few feet, he stopped and returned his attention to Hallorin, who hadn't uttered a sound since they arrived. In fact, as near as Beamon could tell, he hadn't even moved. Hallorin was carefully appraising his opponent, taking in his obvious physical weakness. Beamon had thought that it was a mistake for Sherman not to try to hide his physical condition, but now he saw it—a clear message was being sent. Sherman's position was so strong he didn't need to bother.

"We have you, David," Sherman said, breaking the silence in the office.

Hallorin bristled, probably less at the content of the sentence than at the purposefully disrespectful use of his first name. "What do you have, *Tom*?" The condescension in his tone was well practiced, but didn't carry any real confidence. "All I see in front of me is a worn-out old man who doesn't realize his time is over. This isn't your America anymore. It's moved on and left you behind." Hallorin glanced for a moment in Beamon's direction and gave a short laugh. While Beamon looked healthier than his friend, he was still obviously a battered mass of half-healed injuries.

"And what's that supposed to be? A bargain basement piece of muscle?"

Beamon ignored the insult and concentrated on his peripheral vision. Peck had leaned forward in his chair in a single, quick motion, obviously wanting to be closer to his mentor but not courageous enough to stand. The desperate smile on his face looked like it was held in place by fishhooks.

Tom Sherman seemed completely immune to the charisma and forcefulness that had worked both for and against Hallorin during the campaign. His face was characteristically passive as he reached down and opened the briefcase on the floor next to him—a motion that must have been intensely painful for him. He laid the handful of papers he dug out on Hallorin's desk.

"What are they?"

Sherman didn't answer and the two men just stared at one another. Finally, Hallorin acquiesced and reached for them in as casual a motion as he could muster.

It had taken Beamon three days to collect the documents that Hallorin now had in front of him. Though time-consuming, the task had been surprisingly simple—as Sherman had told him it would be. It seemed that the philosophy Hallorin espoused at their last meeting had been right on: once you resigned yourself to the fact that powerful political figures were motivated solely by personal gain, it was a simple matter to predict their actions.

Beamon had visited Robert Taylor first. The man had shouted, cursed, insulted, and denied, but in the end it had been nothing but a meaningless and strangely pathetic display. Between the dead professional killer in Tom Sherman's yard and the fact that the only man he wanted to hurt more than Mark Beamon was David Hallorin, he no longer had many options. If Taylor signed the affidavit stating that David Hallorin had used Prodigy to coerce him into dropping from the race, the investigation into Sherman's shooting would stay with the Manassas police. If he refused, Beamon had assured him that it would become the target of an overzealous FBI/Interpol investigation.

Surprisingly, the others had been just as easy. Convincing the men who had been exposed by the Prodigy file to sign similar affidavits had, at first, seemed unlikely. As it turned out, though, truth in the political arena was inexorably intertwined with self-interest. In the end, they'd had nothing to lose and everything to gain. Beamon had not-so-subtly hinted that it was Hallorin who had released the file, and his plan was to use the power of the Oval Office to keep their pain alive and to use it to strengthen his position. If they did sign, Beamon had given assurances that Tom Sherman would do everything in his considerable power to see that David Hallorin was completely hamstrung. The White House would take on a conciliatory tone.

Hallorin's tan seemed to turn into a burn as his face brightened and the pace at which he leafed through the affidavits increased. Finally, he slammed them down on the table and jumped to his feet. "These are lies! You think you can discredit me, coerce me with this? The American people have made their decision. They have elected me!"

"They aren't *all* lies," Sherman said calmly. "But most are. Politics is about perception, not truth, David. I shouldn't have to tell you that—you based your entire campaign on the principle."

The sound of crumpling paper was surprisingly loud as Hallorin balled his fists on the desk, sucking the photocopied affidavits into his large hands. Beamon took a half a step forward, thinking that Sherman might be in physical danger, but his friend just smiled.

"Tiny little men," Hallorin said in a loud voice that sounded oddly hollow. The power and control that he always seemed to exude was falling away from him quicker than Beamon would have imagined possible. "They would do anything to save their insignificant positions. These are the liars and weaklings who destroyed this country! The American people chose me to lead them. Me! You have no right!"

Beamon suddenly saw the real danger of David Hallorin. It wasn't his lack of compassion or stripped-down utilitarian philosophy; it wasn't his all-encompassing ego. The truth was, he was a card-carrying nutcase—he really believed his own legend.

"I have no right?" Sherman said. "*You* involved me in this when you used Prodigy. Now, I'm going to do what I have to do to see that things are set right."

Hallorin stared down at the pale, huddled man in front of him. "I've . . . No. I worked my entire life for this . . . I will not let you—"

"Sit down and be quiet, David. "

"What? What did you say to me?"

Beamon could hear the anger creeping into his friend's voice, but knew that no one else would be able to. "I said sit down and shut up."

Hallorin remained frozen for a moment and then slowly sunk into his chair. That final shift in power was more than Roland Peck could take. He jumped out of his seat and lunged forward. "You son of a bitch! You can't—"

Beamon had been watching the little man's agitation level increase throughout the meeting and was ready for his little outburst. He shot his good hand out and caught Peck by the hair before he could cover more that a few feet. A sound somewhere between a squeal and a wail escaped Peck as his feet went out from under him and Beamon dragged him back to his chair.

Neither Hallorin nor Sherman seemed to notice the brief struggle. Hallorin exercised one last burst of energy and focused his concrete stare directly at Sherman. Beamon saw a trace of amusement cross his friend's face, and obviously Hallorin did too. He slumped back in his chair, looking suddenly exhausted. "Maybe I'll just take my chances."

"No, you won't," Sherman said. "You're no different than the others. You'll take whatever I give you."

Beamon got ready to physically intercede again, thinking that Sherman may have overplayed his hand. Hallorin remained motionless, though, and waited to hear what was to come next.

"As much as it pains me to do it, I'm offering you the presidency," Sherman said after a long silence. He looked down at the affidavits strewn across the floor. "Uncluttered by any of this. The country needs the illusion of a stable, responsible, hand at the helm—and you've been very effective at creating that illusion."

Hallorin's head rose a bit, but he didn't meet Sherman's eye.

"You'll name me chief of staff. You'll do nothing without my approval. Nothing. And you won't run for reelection at the end of your term."

"No!" Peck screamed. This time Beamon had to shove him to the floor and pin an arm behind his back to keep him under control. "David! No! We can fight this—I can fight this. You're a great man. You can't—"

"Shut up," Hallorin said.

Peck's words caught in his throat, and an expression of deep pain and betrayal crossed his face as Beamon hauled him to his feet and slammed him back in his chair again. Peck strained forward, searching futilely for a moment of eye contact with Hallorin. He looked so desperate that Beamon found himself almost feeling sorry for the man.

Sherman didn't wait for an answer to his proposal. He stood and started for the door, leaving the copies of the affidavits Beamon had collected strewn across Hallorin's office. "I'll expect to hear of my appointment on the news tonight," he said as Beamon fell into step behind him. His tone was dismissive.

59

Darby Moore bent her knees and used her entire body to throw the backpack into the bed of her pickup. It hit the back of the cab with such force that the entire vehicle rocked on its worn-out suspension.

"He's going to be *president?*" Her voice was nearly a shout, startling in the silent expanse that passed for Tom Sherman's front yard. She grabbed a water bottle off the ground and dumped it out into the fire ring at her feet. "That's the best you could do? Three of my best friends in the world are dead and he gets everything he *ever wanted?*"

"Not everything," Beamon said. "I told you. Tom will completely control him. I don't think you could ever understand how frustrating and humiliating that is for a man like David Hallorin. It's almost a fate worse than death."

She lifted a cooler off the ground and Beamon stepped forward to help her, but she jerked away. "*Almost* worse than death."

He shrugged but didn't say anything as she struggled under the weight of the cooler and shoved it violently into the truck. When she turned back around, she seemed to have gained control over some of her anger. "What do *you* think, Mark?"

The truth was, he didn't know what to think. What he *knew* was that he felt dirty. "I guess I think I would have liked to see him go down in flames. I would have liked to have had an opportunity to put a bullet in his head. I would have liked to pull his fingernails out with a pair of pliers . . . " He looked down at his feet and kicked a half-burned stick into the damp fire ring. "Look, I know it sounds lame, and I can't believe I'm about to say it, but there were bigger issues that had to be considered. I guess . . . I guess it's a fairly gray piece of justice."

Darby tossed the last of her gear into the back of the truck and slammed the gate shut. "I'd have died a horrible death without your help, Mark," she said without looking at him. "I guess I shouldn't be bitching. You saved me and now you're giving me my life back. I didn't think I'd ever be free again."

"Why don't we call it even, then," he said, sliding a small knapsack off his injured shoulder and holding it out to her.

"What's this?" She unbuckled the straps and peered into it. "Oh, my God!"

"There's a quarter of a million dollars in there," Beamon said, watching her paw through it. "You need to get lost for a little while. Hallorin's not after you anymore, but the cops are. Give me a couple of months to get that straightened out."

She buckled the straps again and shook her head. "I can't accept this."

"Take it, Darby. It's Tom's money. He wants you to have it, and believe me, he won't miss it."

She looked uncertain for a moment and then tossed it into the truck with the rest of her gear.

Beamon smiled. Most people would consider that much money worthy of riding up front. Maybe there was still hope for her yet. Maybe she would be able to forget the lessons she'd learned over the past two months and return to being the terminally optimistic young explorer that she was supposed to be.

"I don't know why, but I think I'm going to kind of miss you," she said, stepping forward and wrapping her arms around him.

"Not too tight, I'm still an injured man, you know."

She pulled back and smiled. "Make yourself happy, Mark," she said, and kissed him on the cheek. "I know you've got it in you."

He put a hand on her shoulder when she turned away, stopping her for a moment. "This is over now, Darby. Nothing else can be done. Put it behind you and make yourself happy, too, okay?"

60

It was the first snow that had fallen in D.C. all year.

Only about an inch of coverage so far, but the flakes were the size of a man's thumb and the lazy path they were taking to the earth seemed to be getting more and more direct. The cotton-filled air seemed to swallow sound, making the voice of the priest standing only a few feet away a soft, unintelligible drone.

Attendance could be generously described as spotty. Besides Beamon and the priest, only two people had decided to brave the weather to attend Roland Peck's funeral. One was his wife, who looked like she probably never missed an opportunity to wear black leather. The other was a slightly stooped old man with a shocking white beard whom Beamon didn't recognize. They all stood silently around the snow-dusted coffin, positioning themselves to maintain the maximum physical distance from their fellow mourners.

The priest raised the volume of his voice a bit, invoking God and humanity in a general way that made it obvious that he had never had the displeasure to meet the guest of honor. Beamon took a couple of steps backward until the eulogy once again faded into a quiet garble.

Beamon had been forced to talk to Roland Peck on a number of occasions after his boss had finally completely caved to Tom Sherman's demands. And every time he did, he noticed that the little man slipped a little closer to insanity. Peck hadn't been able to accept that anyone could control David Hallorin, a man who, depending on the day, he seemed to think was either his father, God, or the emperor of the galaxy.

Tom Sherman had used his considerable powers to try to keep the Leprechaun in control—underplaying his own involvement in Hallorin's impending administration, keeping Peck in the speech-writing and strategizing loop—but nothing worked. Peck seemed to blame himself for Hallorin's situation, and that failure was more than his tenuous grasp on reality could handle. Every day, he'd become more desperate and more unpredictable. The possibility that he would destroy the delicate balance that had been so carefully constructed started to become very real.

Apparently, Hallorin had found the situation unacceptable. The boy whom he had taken in at eighteen, who had masterminded his rise to the presidency, who had looked to him as a father, was found shot dead in front of his Georgetown home. A victim of random violence according to the police report, but more likely a victim of David Hallorin's all-encompassing ambition.

Beamon barely noticed when the priest fell silent and the coffin began to sink into the grave on quiet hydraulic rails. He watched with mild interest as the old man across the hole from him broke out of his motion-lessness and walked carefully over the slick ground to Peck's veiled wife, offering his hand. She turned her back on him without a word and started for her car as quickly as her spike heels would allow.

"You were a friend of Roland's?" the man said to Beamon as he worked his way around the open grave and came within earshot.

"I guess you could say that," Beamon answered, shaking the man's ice-cold hand.

"My name's Jeffery Tanin." He looked around him at the now empty graveyard. "I read Roland's obituary. It seems he did well—I'd hoped there would be more people."

"How did you know him?" Beamon said out of politeness more than a desire to prolong the conversation. He had a plane to catch and this graveyard seemed to have the effect of amplifying his uncertainty about the events he had involved himself in.

"I used to be a foster parent," Tanin said. "I had Roland for a few years when he was a teenager."

Beamon didn't respond. He hadn't known that Peck was an orphan. Now that he thought about it, he knew almost nothing of the man. What he *did* know, though, was that Peck was a murderer, pervert, and sociopath—all qualities he didn't much admire.

"Deep down, he was a good boy. . . . And so brilliant," the old man said—more to the grave than to Beamon. "But he was too far gone when he arrived

at my door. His mother died when he was four and his father was a nightmare. He had sexually abused Roland's sister for years, often in front of him.
No one did anything, though, until he finally killed her. She was ten, Roland
was twelve. I believe the man died in prison."

They stood there in the snow for a while longer. Tanin spoke, a little
incoherently, about Peck, and Beamon tried, unsuccessfully, to block out
his words.

He could admit that he had screwed up a lot in life. But it had always
been the result of doing what he knew was right. Until now.

Mark Beamon smiled imperceptibly, as he always did when he entered
the doors of the expansive Phoenix office of the FBI. He wandered
through it, taking in the sound and the smell, watching the young, ideal-
istic agents moving purposefully from desk to desk. This was the FBI. It
didn't have anything to do with politics or upper-level management or
compromise. This was what he couldn't force himself to leave behind. It
was just like an addiction—he knew it wasn't good for him, but he wasn't
strong enough to break the habit. Not yet anyway.

"Mark Beamon, back from the void!"

Beamon looked up from the floor at the sound of the familiar voice.
"D. Thank God." His indispensable secretary from Flagstaff had been initially resistant to the financial hardships that would accompany following her boss to his new post in Phoenix. Fortunately, with his newfound
political clout, Beamon had been able to make her an offer she couldn't
refuse.

"You all right, Mark? You sound a little down."

"Fine."

"Fine? Look around you! You're the head of one of the biggest offices
in the Bureau in one of the sunniest towns in the world!"

"Where would I be without you to put things in perspective for me?"

"Lost. Wandering helpless in the desert."

"Right. Exactly. D., really, I don't think I've said it out loud, but thanks
for coming down."

She smiled uncomfortably and shrugged her shoulders. "No problem."

"Okay, then. I'm going to go into my office and start to wade through
my mail. If any of the God-knows-how-many people that work for me
now want to talk to me, tell them I'm dead."

She nodded her understanding and went back to the box she was
emptying onto her desk.

All he'd wanted was to extricate himself from the legal problems that had been plaguing him and get back his little job running the Flagstaff office. The first part of that wish had been taken care of weeks ago. The Bureau had been quick to reevaluate his qualifications as a scapegoat when they'd received a letter from the attorney general stating that he had found the charges against Beamon to have no merit. The call from soon-to-be President Hallorin proclaiming his admiration for Beamon and his willingness to throw his full political and financial weight behind Beamon's defense hadn't hurt either.

The suddenness and force of the whole thing had so terrified the Bureau's senior management that they had not only personally apologized but promoted him to SAC of the fucking Phoenix office—a management nightmare that he still hadn't completely faced yet.

Beamon dropped into the expensive leather chair behind his ridiculously large desk and pulled a stack of mail onto his lap. He jabbed at the remote built into one of his drawers and heard the volume of the TV come up to an audible level, filling the room with David Hallorin's voice.

He'd heard the speech before, of course—a surprising little ditty in which Hallorin had suddenly taken on a pacifying tone. National Healing, Clean Slate, Meaningless Youthful Indiscretions, the Foundations of a Great Nation that will Rise Again—that kind of crap. With his new kinder, gentler approach, and his focus on bipartisan leadership, the press had started to jump on the David Hallorin bandwagon. The economy had taken a sharp upward turn, and people who hadn't voted for David Hallorin were starting to lie about it.

Of course, it was really all Tom Sherman. Hallorin didn't open his mouth unless Sherman had signed off on what was going to come out of it. The situation was killing Hallorin slowly, stripping him of his identity and the ego that had had been his entire existence for most of his life. It was more than the bastard deserved. And Tom Sherman was more than America deserved.

Beamon looked up from the mail when his favorite part came on. A reporter asked a rather pointed question about one of Hallorin's campaign promises and the old familiar anger started to creep into the new president's voice. A moment later, a demure-looking Tom Sherman stepped forward and whispered something in Hallorin's ear. With a pained smile, Hallorin announced that he had been told that he had time for only one more question and that pacifying tone magically returned. Beamon watched Hallorin walk from the podium and stared blankly at the television for a little over a minute as the press conference wrapped up, then went back to work.

He didn't open most of the mail, instead dumping it in a box that would go to D. for sorting and paraphrasing. He was about half an hour into clearing the desk when he came upon a letter with a colorful foreign stamp. There was no return address.

He stared at it for a few seconds, turning it over in his hands. He'd known for weeks now that Vili Marcek had been promised an additional two hundred thousand dollars for causing the death of Darby Moore. Beamon had been desperately trying to find either one of them, calling in damn near every favor he and Tom Sherman had, to no effect. Darby had obviously taken him seriously when he told her to disappear for a couple of months.

He took a deep breath and held it as he slit the top of the envelope and pulled out the single sheet of paper it contained. It looked like an old-style Teletype, written in English but with Chinese or some other Asian script across the top and bottom. The single paragraph in the middle of the page was a brief, no-frills report relating the death of Vili Marcek on a remote Himalayan peak. Beamon let out the air caught in his lungs in one long rush as he reread the report, lingering on a brief quote by Darby Moore, the only person to witness Marcek's two-thousand-foot fall.

Across the bottom of the Teletype, in bold capital letters, Darby had written a single line. He recognized it as a paraphrase of something he had said to her the last time they'd spoken.

A fairly black piece of justice.

Beamon stared at that sentence for a long time, remembering Darby in those brief moments—usually after she'd had a few beers—when she managed to forget her friends' deaths and their nearly hopeless situation. When she would spark with enthusiasm and innocence. He had hoped that she would be able to find that again, that David Hallorin hadn't taken it away from her forever . . .

"Mark. Mark? Are you okay?"

Beamon looked up at his secretary and balled up the Teletype. "Fine. Great."

"You don't look great," she said, heaping another pile of mail onto his desk and glancing down at the box that was overflowing at his feet. "I assume that's for me."

Beamon nodded. "Before you start on it, though, could you write up a press release for me?"

"Sure. What's it going to say?" She picked up a notepad off his desk.

"Something to the effect of 'At the request of the Fayette County Sheriff's Office and the West Virginia State Police, the FBI will be providing assistance on the Tristan Newberry murder case. According to an FBI spokesman, Darby Moore has been ruled out as a suspect based on new evidence.' I'll give you the list of people to send it to as soon as I find it on my desk."

She tore off the page she'd written on and dropped the pad back on the desk, causing an overly tall stack of paper to teeter dangerously. When she reached out to stop it, she spotted the small blue velvet box partially hidden behind a stapler. "What's that?"

"What?"

She reached across him and picked up the box.

"Don't—"

It was too late. She'd opened it and already her eyes had taken on that specific glassy look that women get when they see a diamond.

She pulled the gold chain from the box and examined the pendant attached to it with total concentration.

"Not gonna pull out your loupe?"

"God, Mark. This is beautiful. I thought you said you and Carrie weren't seeing each other anymore."

"I'm going to try to change that." Beamon held out his hand, but D. ignored him and continued her silent appraisal.

"Don't say anything about this, D. It'd be kind of embarrassing if she does the smart thing and throws that back in my face, you know?"